PARADISE

THE BOOK OF MIRIELLE

By

LOWELL NEKKO

This is a work of fiction in which all events and characters in this book are completely imaginary. Any resemblance to actual people is entirely coincidental.

No parts of this book may be copied, distributed, or published in any form without permission from the copyright holder.

This work and derivatives cannot be used to train machine learning models without the permission of the copyright holder.

Cover art by Lowell Nekko
Clouds graphic courtesy of Vecteezy.com

nekkobooks.com
New York

CONTENTS

IN THE PARK

Leo pictured Elise walking beside them, jointly holding their "miracle" child's hands, and smiling or biting her lips or furrowing her brow or making any of the other myriad faces she could install without a sliver of effort. His own visage was chiseled in granite compared to hers. He nudged his mouth into a smile, wondering if she could move her ears, that ancient forever girl.

The pain from the loss had dissolved in the river of time, leaving only a faint trace of agony in his mind. Leo was not a past dweller, and he had high hopes of crossing paths with her in yet another future life. After all, even in his wildest dreams and magic mushroom-induced hallucinations, he had never fantasized about seeing Elise again. It was not the same for Wasilla, regardless of how hard she tried to suppress the emotions. He could sense the flashes of grief each time her thoughts rubbed into the void in her heart. Was it because she had shared existence with Elise for far longer than he had? Or was it because his stint in the old world exceeded Wasilla's by several decades, letting him experience so much more?

"Steve is here!" Mirielle exclaimed, detaching herself before he could tighten his grip on her little hand, and ran in the direction of the tall hedges.

Leo knew the place. There was a gazebo nestled between the lush growth he used to frequent with the little one's mother. Steve was there. Hardly by himself! Leo chased after Mirielle. "Wait! Slow down! You may startle him!" he shouted unnecessarily loudly.

Steve pulled out, cursing. "Get dressed, quick!" he commanded Beatrice and reached hastily for his own clothes. By the time Mirielle emerged from underneath the branches with dirty palms and knees, he had barely managed to zip up. "Hey! Mirrie! You're a boy again?"

"Yeah! Ah, hi Bea!" The little one threw a greeting at the outline of a human lurking behind the leaves.

"Steve, throw me your shirt please!" the silhouette said.

Leo took the white tee-shirt from the bench and passed it to the naked woman. "You are larger than Elise, and the shirt isn't 4XL."

"Don't worry!" The young blonde girl stretched out her hand and took the garment.

"Ah, smart!" Leo laughed and looked away. "You have adapted well indeed!"

Beatrice crawled out of the bushes and returned to the gazebo, where she received an enthusiastic hug from the little boy. "Bea! Can I also play? Please, please, please! You two were playing hide-and-seek, right? Can I?"

Leo emitted a short huff, praising the Creator for making his child just a strong empath, then twisted his mouth, sucking on his cheek. He no longer knew if he had a daughter or a son. When Mirielle transformed for the first time, he literally poured hot coffee over himself. In the old world, that would have resulted in a serious injury, but here, after the initial scalding jolt, the blisters subsided and dissipated, leaving no trace. Only the echo of the expletives lingered. Being dead had its perks.

On that day, Mirielle had been playing in the living room with a ball. She stood still for a while, inspecting the round object in her hands as if wondering what else she could do with it besides lifting it up, then dropped it and giggled as it bounced a few times before coming to rest. Her hair became darker, and she aimed and clumsily kicked the ball. It traveled through the open terrace door, rolled underneath the railing, and proceeded to the street below. Mirielle turned to Leo, smiling, glaringly proud of her "achievement." She was two and a half and not yet conversant. Leo's gaze was immediately and irresistibly drawn to the little appendage between her legs. So much so that he moved the jug just enough to start pouring its contents over his wrist.

Wasilla had appeared at the door and glanced at the angry man, then the toddler, then back again. Leo caught her eye movement and hissed, "She transformed. Look closer."

Mirielle pivoted toward her. Wasilla's eyes widened and she took a deep breath, staring at the little boy with dark brown hair and blue eyes. "Oh! Er, but how? Ah, never mind. Shit!"

The child laughed and morphed back. Wasilla rushed, lifted the kid, and hugged her tightly. Mirielle began crying and trying to wriggle out.

Leo patiently waited for the blisters to dry out; the pain was less intense now. It wasn't the first time he had injured himself. He smirked—so much better than rushing to the doctor.

"That was new. She is Lizzy's clone according to Ruth and now—" Leo stopped mid-sentence. If the little girl was a copy of her mom, who was the boy? Elise's brother, Anton? Or . . . Leo tried to shake off the thought with force. These pictures from his early childhood, they were in the old world, and his recollection was unsteady, but the features seemed familiar. He closed his eyes and retrieved the mirror, trying to remember. And suddenly he shrank.

"Huh?" Wasilla loosened her grip on Mirielle and hushed her while peeking behind the counter. "You?" The little boy looked up and nodded. Then reverted.

"Looks like she mirrored me too."

"Are you sure?"

"As if we can make her transform again." Leo let out a grunt. "But he looked familiar. And when I tried to ascertain, I transformed too. I have no memories of myself at this age, but we had pictures. I tried to see these and, well, you witnessed what happened. But you, what do you think? You saw both. I mean me and the boy, didn't you?"

Wasilla didn't answer immediately. She put Mirielle on the floor, stood upright, and nodded slowly. "Yep, I think that it was you."

Leo reached for a cigarette. Wasilla went on the terrace, looked over the railing, then stepped back inside and invited Mirielle. "Come, sweetie, let's go fetch the ball. Come, baby, come!"

*
**

Leo closed the lid of his memory box and turned to Beatrice. "Where are your clothes?"

"I adapted," Beatrice answered in a high-pitched voice, commensurate with her current size.

"To what?"

"To this world, dummy!"

"You mean you walk around naked? Like her?"

Beatrice nodded.

"But people can see you. Mirielle can. And you died old!"

"I always transform."

"Well, good to know. But we have a kid amongst us now who is far more sensitive, can detect you from afar, and catch you not only naked but literally in the act."

"In a way, that makes it even more exciting!" The young girl in front of him giggled and winked. Leo squeezed his lips and looked past her. "Sorry." Beatrice blushed.

Silence took hold for a while between the two, making room for Mirielle's laughter and Steve's roar in the distance. Then Beatrice broke it. "He's good at entertaining children, isn't he?"

"I guess so."

"How does it come that she turns into a boy when she sees him?"

"Steve has two daughters, you know?"

Beatrice dipped her head.

"He always wanted a son. They, er, Mirrie, overheard him on a couple of occasions. Maybe that is it. I must ask," Leo said, then embarked on another trip down memory lane.

**

Steve and he had been sitting in the park, sipping beer, chatting, and observing Mirielle playing in the sandpit with Wasilla, the latter having transformed into the youngest possible version of herself. The child became frustrated by the failed attempts to erect a tower—the sand was too dry and unable to retain the shape after the bucket was lifted—and turned her attention to the blue rubber ball resting nearby.

Mirielle picked it up and threw it at Wasilla. "Catch, Wass!"

Unprepared, Wasilla let the ball bounce off her knee, roll, and come to a halt at Steve's feet.

"Steve, ball please!" Mirielle extended her arms, ready to catch.

Steve rose from the bench and directed the ball to the girl with a mild kick. Then he prepared to sit again, when the ball returned. Steve laughed, kicked it back, and sat with a sigh. "Man, I still wish I had a son. I tried to play soccer with the girls, but they were not interested. They didn't care about cars either . . . other than riding in them."

Leo had sealed his lips about Mirielle's transformation. He and Wasilla kept the first event to themselves. It had been several years since it happened, and Mirielle stayed a girl after that. Until today. Changing his mind, Leo said in passing, "Did I tell you that Mirielle can transform into a boy?"

Steve mumbled, "No, but I can see that now."

Leo followed his friend's stare. It was firmly parked on the young boy in a red and blue dress standing a few meters away and trying to aim his kick.

"It's you she's projecting, isn't it?" Steve asked. He intercepted the ball and remained still, his face elongated.

"Steve, give it back, let's play!" called out the boy.

Leo got up, dislodged the ball from underneath Steve's foot, and passed it to Mirielle. "It happened only once before, and she was much younger, couldn't yet talk. Looks like that, though. I transformed, too, back then, and Wass said that we looked alike." Then he had an idea! He stared intensely at Mirielle for a moment, then closed his eyes and shrank.

"Yay, Daddy, I didn't know you can do this!" Mirielle giggled.

Wasilla had reverted and had joined Steve on the bench.

"Why didn't you tell us? About the transformation?" Steve asked her.

"There wasn't much to tell. It was a blip; it occurred only once when she was two and a half."

"This is amazing! None of us can change sex. I wish I could." Steve chuckled. "So much more to experience, right?" He jumped up, laughing, converted into an older brother, stole the ball from Mirielle, and dribbled it away.

**

"Hey, where are you?" Beatrice said, shaking Leo's shoulder.

Leo nudged it upward, eyes still focused on a point in the distance, and said, "Back in time, when Steve saw it for the first time. We were here, on the other side, by the kids' playground." Leo proceeded to tell the story. "It is weird, it feels weird. When Lizzy's mom, Ruth, said that Mirielle was Elise reincarnated, it didn't make sense at all, for we here are hardly made of flesh; it could have been just a close resemblance. Remember how everybody saw you in Eric when he was—"

"Yeah!" Beatrice cut his sentence short.

Leo looked at her quizzically, seeking the source of her irritation. The young girl had clenched her fists between her legs, staring down. He tried to soothe her—his hand reached and caressed her golden locks. She was born a work of classical art. She leaned away. He retracted the limb and asked calmly, "Why did you start dyeing your hair? You look great as a blonde too. And why did you choose red?"

She gripped the bench with both hands. "How many jokes involving blondes do you know?"

"A lot." Leo laughed. "Why?"

"And how many jokes about redheads?"

Leo probed the depths of his memory. "None," he mumbled after a while. "Nah, don't tell me you were that smart at twenty!"

"I wasn't smart. I just got tired of hearing how dumb blonde girls were, and I didn't want to be blonde anymore."

"But you could have become a brunette."

"Redheads are the rarest. But it was impulse, really. I was pissed after hearing the latest asinine joke. I went to the nearest supermarket, and I just grabbed a box from the store shelf, the first one that wasn't blonde, and then made a mess in the bathroom at home. But Mom said that it looked good on me, and I continued . . ."

"It *did* look good on you. Bitch!" Leo smiled. "It helped you steal my heart and smash it into a thousand pieces. But I would have fallen for the blonde you too."

"You were shunning me at the beginning, remember?"

Leo sighed and stretched his mouth again. So long ago was that, yet so fresh in his mind. She was the popular girl in the office; everybody wanted to be her friend. But not him. He was attracted to her indeed; however, considering his chances practically nonexistent, he chose to ignore her and get on with his life and the girls he thought were within reach.

"Was that the reason you made the move?"

"Yeah. There's no point in denying it now. I was so unaccustomed to men not being hooked. But it was also refreshing. The experience, I mean, of not being put on a pedestal."

"I was under the impression that you expected precisely that and turned on me because I considered your appeal to be coincidental."

"That too." Beatrice accompanied the admission with a nod. "Emotions drive us. I was in denial that I wanted it, but that was untrue. But it didn't play a major part. And I am sorry for the hurt I caused you."

"All is forgiven; just enjoy the afterlife." Leo leaned backward, crossed his legs, and sent his thoughts somewhere else.

Beatrice looked at him from under the cover of her long eyelashes. She wanted to caress his hand but felt that the wall he put between them was still there. And she was projecting an eight-year-old girl now. Mirielle and Steve laughed in the distance as Beatrice and Leo were lost in another world, some six decades ago, each reliving in their minds their own version of the past.

Leo had just broken up with his girlfriend, and Beatrice saw an opening. She inserted herself into his daily routine, pretending not to see him in the elevator on their way up, but standing close enough so he could smell her perfume. She said a simple "Hi" and lingered in the office kitchen when they both went there for a cup of hot brew. She never tried to make small talk; she knew that he was not adept. She just wanted to discreetly signal her interest. When their gang went to the pub, she kept switching chairs until she finally sat right next to him. By this time, he had deciphered the coded messages and struck up a conversation. They found common themes: music, art, books.

She was not a hollow head despite her natural hair color and her sexy looks. Not all blondes are dumb, and not all brunettes are smart. How did this shit come to be? She wanted to be the first in her immediate family to earn a university degree. That never came to pass, unfortunately. Perhaps if Leo had stayed home, she might have succeeded. She was attending a preparatory course in the hope of achieving this goal.

She also modeled nude from time to time at the Academy of Fine Arts and lent a keen ear to the conversations there. She did not object to baring it all for the aspiring artists, for a fee of course, but was so tired of other men constantly undressing her with their eyes. There was more to her desire to conquer. She genuinely liked Leo, the young man who seemed to keep her clothes on when looking at her.

Leo was friendly and respectful and took it slowly. He walked her home after parties with coworkers, then they started going out regularly. They took strolls under the big trees or along the narrow streets of Old Town, going to the movies or spending time in cafés overlooking the city or nestled between old homes. Just the two of them. They held hands like shy teens in a Japanese anime; they kissed, then waved goodbye.

She found it romantic and calming but also challenging in a way—she felt desire, she was getting turned on by the touch, and she sensed his body twitching when they hugged and knew that he was eager too. She expected him to finally take her somewhere, his place, a friend's place, a hotel, even a back alley. Other men she dated grew angry and upset much earlier in the relationship when she declined intercourse. She lost her virginity at sixteen and enjoyed a long year of elation in the arms of her then-boyfriend, Moritz, but after two pregnancy scares and a matching number of boyfriends bailing out, she had a long pause, and Leo would be only her third. She was hungry and unwilling to wait anymore, perhaps precisely because he was not pushing for it. When he walked her home that night, she invited him inside. She had never done that before, still fearing her father, despite him not living there; she could not forget the beatings he'd given her after he saw her with a boy. But she'd been free of the brute for years now, so why fear a ghost? They sat on the couch, had some liquor, started hugging and kissing, but Leo still held back. Until she swiftly removed her blouse and let her breasts do the talking.

Leo understood. He helped her out of the rest of her clothes. "Is your mom here?" he whispered in her ear, then nibbled lightly on the lobe.

"Mmm," she grunted quietly.

"Let's go to your room then . . ." His palm touched her breast, his lips, her cheek.

"No . . ." She unbuttoned his shirt with one hand and wrapped the other around his neck. Leo kicked off his shoes and unzipped. He wriggled out of his jeans while kissing her. Her heart was pounding, and her desire became all-encompassing. This guy was different; he lacked the assertiveness of her prior partners. Was that good or bad? She reached and fondled his penis, while kissing, then straddled him and guided it into the welcoming cavity between her legs. The response of her body was to quiver in delight; sparks flew throughout her frame. They were quiet, rocking slowly with hands caressing each other, taking deep breaths and exhaling unhurriedly. The pleasure mounted; even the air touching the skin of her naked body became involved. It was sweet of him to ask her whether to pull out. She took a chance and said, "No." It paid off; his squirting triggered her too. She wanted to emit a loud moan, but her mom would hear, so she just shivered and huffed barely audibly, then leaned and kissed him.

She had wondered what he would be like. He was gentle, he cared, and he was not averse to oral sex. That was new to her. On that day she received cunnilingus for the first time in her life, even before she herself had fellated anybody. She was falling in love with this guy for sure. She wondered whom he had mastered his skills with.

"Leo!" She returned to the present.

He jerked. "What?"

"Who taught you how to make love?"

"Huh?"

"When we had sex for the first time, do you remember?" She continued without waiting for an answer. "You were good, very good, in fact. Who taught you?"

Leo squeezed his lips. "Dunno, no one in particular. Came naturally. Dulci gave me a blow job for the first time; I returned the favor the best way I could. She liked it, so I figured you would too."

"Dulci . . ." said Beatrice quietly, then burst into laughter. "Dulcinea! I remember her. The one with the curly brown hair. Dulcinea! Like in *Don Quixote*!"

"Ah, just shut up, everybody laughs. It is her parents' fault, not hers. She hated it."

"Is she around by any chance? Or any other ex?"

"Not that I know of. They were all younger, like you, and women also live longer. Besides, there aren't that many to speak of. Lizzy,

Olive, Dulcinea, you, and Beth. The rest were fleeting, inconsequential affairs and one-night stands. I had a few crushes too, but the only one that is around is . . ." He paused. "Erm, Wass."

"Wasilla? She's queer."

"Back then I had no idea. She was just a cute girl, and since when do hormones care whether our crushes are homosexual or not?"

"Yeah, you've got a point."

The silence lingered for a while, no longer meddled with by the distant voices of Steve and Mirielle. They must have descended to the river. Then Beatrice spoke again. "It's been like six years since Elise drifted away. How are you coping?"

"Mirielle keeps me occupied. And research; I am still trying to make sense of this world. And other stuff. You know, the plane? It is almost done."

She knew. Leo was now building a lightweight airplane in the warehouse. She was unsure if he lacked the imagination to dream one up or he didn't want to. He always liked making stuff. And she herself had not dreamt anything up yet, as it was challenging, very challenging. Perhaps she was not cut out for this or not desperate enough. But that was not what she wanted to know. "What about love? Sex? Do you go celibate?"

Leo laughed. "I masturbate," he answered simply. "I don't know if that counts."

"Oh!" The honest answer made her arch her eyebrows. She hesitantly extended her arm and laid a hand over his. "But why? Sorry if it comes out corny, but you have an ex-wife to fall back on."

Leo twitched when the young blonde girl touched his hand and whose green eyes pinned his. "Well, I still have some pride left. I didn't want to come begging for a fuck."

"But you wouldn't be begging; you knew that I desired you."

"You were with Steve; you looked settled, and at least at the beginning, I wasn't yet ready to let the memory of Lizzy go. I know that emotions and rationality are oft at odds, but this is what I wanted."

"Steve . . . he's been mourning Joseph. You do know that the fella drifted away, I suppose. Also, he seems to have grown bored with me. We no longer share space; we just give each other carnal pleasure now and then. Carnal, heh!" She chuckled. "I like him, but it is you I desire. Isn't it déjà vu? You are not chasing after me, you keep your distance, just like back then, and that makes me want you even more. Did I hurt you that much?" Her last words came out from a very tight throat.

Leo's face darkened. He was not blameless himself; it was unfair not to let her know. He wanted to reach out, hug the girl, and tell her what he realized a long time ago about their breakup, but then a call came: "Dad! We had a swim! In the river!"

Mirielle was still a boy. They had shed their clothes somewhere and were now trying to sprinkle water on Leo and Beatrice. Steve was approaching in the distance. He had kept his trousers on because they were dripping wet.

"Where did you leave your clothes?" Leo rose to his feet, ready to embark on a search. Mirielle must have inherited the trait from their mom. They kept undressing, no matter how many times they were told not to. "But why? It feels so good" was always the answer, and lectures about decency had so far produced no results. Maybe he and Wass made a mistake letting Mirielle run around au naturel when they were very young. Maybe that had stuck. Or he had truly naturalized after living in the United States for decades, as nobody else seemed to care.

"Over there, I guess." Mirielle's stretched arm pointed, and they transformed back into a girl.

Leo rolled his eyes. "Steve's here; can't you stay a boy?"

Mirielle looked up at him puzzled. "But Bea's here too."

Beatrice guffawed as Leo's argument collapsed.

He waved his hand dismissively, extended it for Mirielle to latch on to, and said, "OK, let's go."

A NEW BEGINNING

Beatrice sensed his approach, pushed the book aside, rose from the sun lounger, and put clothes on. Then she walked to the front door, opened it, and gasped. "What the fuck!" The old man in front of her did look familiar; she could see features she'd always known. He was still tall for his age, and slim, but she herself also lost mass in her late seventies, so that did not surprise her. Leo's sparse white hair was cut very short, and he had a beard. He kept the beard; rather, she had seen it before when he projected an age past their last encounter in the old world. He told her once that he had become a caveman for a while after the divorce—he had stopped shaving and had let his hair grow—then had chosen to keep most of the look. But he never went all the way to true before. Not in front of her. She stepped to the side and made room for him to enter. Then closed the door. "Take a seat somewhere. You must be tired at your age."

"Are you being sarcastic? You know that not to be the case here."

"Sorry, it slipped out. Old-world thinking."

"Strange coming from you. You adapted very well to this realm, better than most. It was your idea how to ensure that Mirielle was not the only kid around."

"I was sincere."

"You were, yes. And I didn't come to argue, but to confess."

Beatrice wrinkled her forehead. "Confess? Confess to what?"

"Will you go true please? Show me your true self."

"No!" Beatrice quivered at the request. "Please no!" She had kept her youthful visage at almost all times since she learned to transform, reverting probably only in her sleep, but then she was not sure, because she never slept with anyone who would bear witness. Not that there was a soul in this realm who could do so, yet she was apprehensive.

"But why not? There's nothing to be ashamed of. I am not a model citizen either." Leo tried a soft tone. "Elise wished that she had grown old—"

"That was her! I don't! I hate it!" The woman began trembling, her hands clutched at her chest.

Leo stepped closer and gently encircled her in his embrace. "OK, as you wish. Now is obviously not the time." He stroked her long red hair, buried his head in it, and drew a breath through his nostrils. She smelled fresh, maybe with a hint of perfume, but he was uncertain; perhaps it was just his memory of her adding the scent.

Beatrice said with a tense voice, "Sorry, yes, maybe some other time." Then she clenched her teeth, closed her eyes, and shape-shifted a bit.

The change, though, was still palpable. Leo stepped back to check it out, hands still on her shoulders. "Thank you," he said and smiled. "Let's be, what, fiftyish then?" He tried to match the age. Beatrice nodded approvingly, took his hand, and led him to the sofa, grabbing her pack of cigarettes on the way.

Leo sat and inspected the room. It was light and spacious, with big sliding doors opening toward a large terrace. The apartment was on the top floor of the building, in a late two-story addition to the original four levels. Leo wondered whose memory it came from. "Comfy pad. Your recollection?"

"No. I needed a change; I liked the building. I went to the top floor and checked the doors. One was unlocked."

She must have needed a change indeed. That was how this place worked. Most of the time, if you needed something, you got it. True communism. In life, Leo had received some brainwashing in the army and then did some research on the ideology at university as a side interest. Then he went to Hungary to check it for himself. What he saw was nothing of the sort. The original intentions may have been good, but the result had been shortages and tyranny. Mostly, as he also noticed some bright spots. It was somewhat easier to make acquaintances, and listening to the latest smuggled rock album was always an event. But it was Hungary he went to, not the USSR. However, that was in the past. He was here to apologize to his ex. Besides, neither country existed anymore.

"You keep saying that you are sorry for what you did to me, yes?" Leo said.

"I am. I made you suffer humiliation, and I destroyed your career. Everybody looked down on you in Japan. You came home with no job and a broken self-esteem, all because of me." She looked away, her face turning slightly red.

"Well, I am sorry too. I also screwed up. I put my professional ambitions over you. I forgot that you had your desires and goals too. I didn't work for the common good. I did only what I fancied, convincing myself that I was doing it for the three of us. We both made mistakes, but mine was worse."

"How?" Beatrice looked at him.

"I know what happened to you later, the abuse, the beatings . . . Eric told me."

She dropped her head and sighed.

"Because of me, you ended up like this. I thrust you into evil hands!" Leo continued, "So here I am, to let you know of all this. And after you came, I was too obsessed with Elise to be of any help. And, truth be told, it was she who made me realize my screw-up. Anyway, we can't go back in time and change our past ways, but as she used to say, we are given a second chance here, so better not waste it."

Beatrice nudged closer without saying a word and took his hand. Then as if on command, the two thrust toward each other, locked lips, and extended tongues. The feelings they harbored for each other, long suppressed, were finally set free.

If there were a clock, it would have gotten tired of ticking. Eventually, Leo peeled himself from his ex-wife and stood back. He wanted to see the aged Beatrice, to make sure that her eyes were still green. She took good care of herself. As the socialite she became after they divorced, she was expected to look good, and it showed. She had put on some weight, and the tiny wrinkles stretching out of her eyes and around her nose and mouth were clearly visible, but the eyes were still mostly the same. Somewhat sad, lacking the sparkle they had in the early years of their doomed relationship.

Beatrice took the opportunity to try reenacting their first intimate night. As she did back then, she pulled her shirt up and threw it onto the floor, then realized that she was not projecting twenty-two and froze instantly. Trying to cover her sagging breasts would seem odd and may turn him off, and she did want him. She had no doubt.

Leo looked at her, then slowly kneeled in front and helped her out of the sweatpants. He drove his palm along the inner side of her thigh, gently guided her legs apart, and touched her sweet spot with his thumb. Then he bent forward and introduced his tongue. Beatrice pushed his head down and moaned. The passion was reborn. The cunnilingus was just the start, she hoped. Steve . . . Steve never did that. And Rudy. What was it with them? Were they ashamed? But now it was good! So very stimulating! She let out a deep moan and tousled his hair. He never went bald, it seemed. But that was irrelevant; she'd found bald men attractive too. Maybe she should ask him to shave his head . . . Then she lost the thought. The muscles in her groin contracted briefly as Leo's playful tongue traveled along her labia. She wanted him inside her, but not immediately, no. Beatrice rubbed her breasts, sending feedback down, and quivered when the waves converged. Leo emerged from the depths and crawled slowly up, tracing a path with his tongue. He arrived at her lips and probed gently. Beatrice parted them, while blindly reaching for his dick. It was warm and firm in her hand. She eagerly accepted him, gasping noisily as the penis glided in and lit a flare. When the fiery sensation subsided, she checked his face through her half-closed eyes, then slowly traced her lips. Leo was looking at her, smiling while rocking leisurely, savoring the enchantment.

She smiled in return; the pleasure was hers too. After a fight, not so much. The moment of elation was brief and left a sour aftertaste; however, the ugly fights were many years in the past, and the two of them had met anew. Beatrice began panting and delivering short, high-pitched moans as Leo increased his speed. She closed her eyes completely and pushed all thoughts away. Then the ecstasy arrived and took possession of all her senses for a while.

This time, Leo didn't ask whether he should pull out. When he finally burst, he kept rocking, then kissed her lips and asked, "Did you finish too? I still can't always tell."

Beatrice nodded and patted the cushion. "Come here, I want to cuddle up."

Leo handed her a cigarette, then lit another for himself and sat next to her. She bent her legs on the couch and rested her head on his shoulder.

"You are wrong," she said and squeezed his hand.

"About what?"

"About thrusting me into evil hands. Yes, I needed you, but I never said so, did I? It was pride. The beauty could not bring herself to ask for the attention she craved because she was too accustomed to getting it automatically. I took it all for granted. Then I made bad choices. You didn't sell me to Christian; I married him on my own accord." She drew from her cigarette and tried to make rings but failed and quickly waved the unsightly clouds away. "Money is not a recipe for happiness."

"Money, yeah . . ." Leo puffed three perfect rings and smiled. "Irrelevant now, but in the old world having some didn't hurt."

"Having a lot got me—" Beatrice stopped abruptly.

"Got you what?"

The memory shook her, but she continued in a level voice. "Stuff, I guess. Mansions, jewelry, designer clothes, yachts, sports cars. Isn't that what people want?"

"Come on, you are smarter than that. You are deflecting."

"It didn't buy me happiness, that I admit. Security and certainty maybe." She didn't want to mention the real reason for her earthly demise. She wondered if their son, Eric, knew. Anyway, not all rich people were like her other exes, that was something she was certain of. Not all rich kids are spoiled. Her luck sucked perhaps. Also, violence comes from poor people too. Like her father. A school friend from her old working-class neighborhood ended up in jail for beating up two prostitutes and a gay man to a pulp. Weird, though, the guy was attending seminary, preparing to be a priest. Beatrice sighed.

"Listen, I can't tell what you are thinking, but as an empath, I know that it is sad. So, may I suggest another round? I think I'm up to it now."

Beatrice laughed heartily; he still had that ability to blurt out words to turn her mood around. She put out the cigarette and leaned forward.

"If you are still uncomfortable with your appearance, we can shape-shift."

"Uh, uh." She shook her head; her mouth was already full.

**

"Are you going to tell Wass about us?" Beatrice asked after they both had slowed their heartbeat down to normal levels.

"What is there to tell?"

"That we are . . ." Her heart sank. Maybe she read too much. Maybe he came just to say hi and a bunch of other stuff, and the encounter was a one-off and they had not really reunited!

"That we are back together? Sure!" Leo winked and smiled.

"Ah, bastard! You got me for a moment!" She slapped him on the wrist. "I'm gonna rip your tool off!"

"I promised her no secrets long ago. So, yes, I'm gonna tell her even if you disagree. And rip my dick off. Here, it will grow back anyway, so how's that even a threat?"

"Yeah, but it will hurt for a while."

"Are you that desperate?" Leo crossed sight with her. "But I don't know what after-living arrangements to make, if any. We are not just dating, are we?"

"So, you don't want me moving in?"

"Sorry, no. Not in the loft. It is not just the memory; there's also Mirielle. They might see you as a substitute for their moms in my life, and that may cause them pain. And I love the little sprite. I would go to lengths to avoid that. We are more than adults; we are better suited to deal with emotions."

"Moms?" Beatrice raised her eyebrows, stretching the "s."

"Yeah, moms. Elise and Wass. All they know is Wass, but they are aware that Wass is not the bio . . . er, the birth mom. They know about Elise."

"Why are you using the fluidity pronoun for her?"

"Isn't it obvious? Can one get more gender-fluid than that? Being able to shape-shift from a girl to a boy and back."

"I would stick to 'she' and 'her.' She is a girl most of the time. And switch to 'he' and 'him' when she turns into a boy. You are taking it literally and I don't think that what being gender-fluid is."

"Perhaps. Anyway, they don't seem to care what pronouns people use. Their maternal grandparents call them 'she' regardless; Mom and Dad are like you."

"Let's go on the terrace. I'll mix something to drink." Beatrice lifted her still shapely butt off the sofa and hauled it in the direction of the kitchen.

Leo lingered, then sprang up and followed her. "I will help." He put his arm around her waist, swung her, and found her lips. Beatrice gleamed. She had waited for this moment for something like eight years. One never knew exactly in this world, but it was a long time. She was surprised that her desire to reunite with Leo had not faded but remained rather buoyant and that she had the patience to wait without getting angry and frustrated. Was it because she had developed feelings for Elise too? She tried to act on these only once, on impulse at the very onset, but the other woman turned her down, and she never chanced a shot at it again. She wouldn't have minded being in Wasilla's shoes, though. Steve was a good man and entertaining too. And Rudy. Should she let Leo know? Probably.

"Hey, Leo."

"Yes?"

"Steve isn't the only person I have been seeing. There's also a guy from school. His name is—"

"Ouch! Shit!"

SOME LIKE IT HOT

Beatrice pulled a bottle and two glasses from the corner cabinet and began dispensing the booze. "Sorry, I forgot to warn you to watch your feet."

"I shall fix this threshold," Leo said, looking at the transition piece between the parquet and the tiled floor of the hallway. A nail had proudly raised its head and had pricked the defenseless sole of his right foot. "How did it come to be broken, though? Abnormal for this world."

"It was like that since I moved in. But I've never stepped on it, so . . . I don't really know," Beatrice said and pushed the ice tray into his hands. Leo knocked cubes out and into the glasses and grabbed the bowl of roasted peanuts from the countertop.

"Were these here?" he asked.

"No."

Leo smiled. He had fancied fresh roasted peanuts before they entered the kitchen. He bowed.

"Why did you show me your butt?"

"I didn't."

"You did! You just bowed for no reason, facing away from me. You didn't fart, did you?" She sniffed cautiously.

"Have you ever passed wind here?"

"No, but you have a propensity to do shit nobody else can."

"Like?"

"Like impregnating ghosts."

"Don't tell me you want another child from me. Here?!"

Beatrice sat on the lounger, sipped from her glass, and placed it on the table. "If I am completely honest . . ." She pursed her lips. "I . . . I am sometimes envious. But then I think of Jansen, and it all goes away. But then Mirielle is so sweet!"

"You are welcome to spend time with them. That will be helpful considering our plans."

"And what exactly are our plans?"

"Find another place to be together. An apartment or a house. You found this pad."

"Why don't we search this building! It is nice; there ought to be more unlocked doors!"

"Right now?"

"Let's finish the drinks first." Beatrice lifted her legs onto the lounger and closed her eyes.

Leo shouted, "Green!"

"What?" She sat up.

"That's it! Larger! Larger!"

"Ah, prick!" He'd pranked her. He was referring to her closing her eyes and that he liked them. This was his way of expressing his admiration. Seldom would he throw a regular compliment. It used to upset her until she figured it out. "Can't you just say that you like my eyes? You bitched endlessly about your father, but you are in a way the same—always indirect."

Leo drank and said, "You are right. Somebody helped me understand—"

"Yeah, I know who that was. Just say 'Elise.' I won't be offended in the slightest. We are, er, very mature people now." She glanced at him and winked.

"Well, yeah, it was her. So, what was more interesting to me was why I was doing it, why I was avoiding just throwing a straight compliment. Like that you looked good, which you did."

"Past tense?"

"It is different now. You can shape-shift, but overall, you still do look great. Satisfied?"

"Thanks, and?"

"I guess I consider it unfair to people who do not look good due to no fault of their own. Very few are gifted like you."

"You are considering only one side of the story. You don't have to be a model to be attractive. If people take care of themselves and pick the right clothes, anyone can look good."

Leo cringed. "I know, but . . . what about after they remove their clothes?"

"You are not a beauty either; how can you dare criticize?" Beatrice smiled.

"You see what I mean? The arrogance of the naturally gifted. What did you do to deserve adoration? Did you put any effort in? I don't remember you doing so."

"Oh, yeah? How would you know? You were petting the monkeys in South Africa and the geishas in Japan. I was dieting, exercising, and torturing myself to get rid of extra weight and stretch marks and keep in good shape—"

"You? Dieting?!"

"Shit, it shows how little you know about me, and we were together for ten frickin' years! But you spent them in the office and overseas!" Beatrice let her anger loose.

Leo cowered. "Calm down please," he said softly.

She saw him munching on his lips.

"Guilty as charged." He shook slowly his head. "I criticize self-absorbed people, but I am one too. I didn't even know that my girlfriend and wife for a decade was dieting and exercising to maintain her appearance. This is sad. I was not there. Not there even when I was home. You see, I had even more reasons to apologize to you. Sorry, Bea!"

"Apology accepted. Also, see what may happen to attractive people, especially women: We become overconfident, we think that we can control men's hearts, and we may end up in jails, tortured and abused. Mine was comfy and lined with gold, but how many pretty girls end up on the streets? Not being pretty offers protection to a girl. She is not sexually desired, not lusted after, and she gets a chance to have a normal life. In our part of the world, she can get an education, build a career. I wanted that . . ." Beatrice looked down into her glass. She blamed him for having to abandon these dreams—getting her pregnant, then taking his sorry ass overseas.

"Yeah," Leo said, "but physical beauty still gives advantages to those who are smart. It opens doors. Most pretty girls in Europe end up in brothels because they are dumb and greedy—remember all the Eastern beauties after the Iron Curtain fell? They rushed to the West in search of easy money, and they got literally screwed. And as far as you are concerned, you said that you made bad decisions. But let's change the subject now. We have no means of reaching the old world to try to disseminate advice, and even if we could, people never listen—"

"Some do. Some do, and this is why talking publicly is important. Any idea how we can participate?"

"Participate in what?" Leo's stare was blank.

"In the discourse. Sending messages back. Like, when somebody pops in here and then gets resuscitated. We talk to them."

"Nah, that is, unless someone close happens to be near death and we are in the right place at the right time, but the chances for this happening are practically nil. What's interesting, though, is that those claiming near-death experiences that I've heard of see a tunnel and bright light. Did you see a tunnel and bright light?"

"Not exactly. The glare was from the, er, the sun—the curtains were not drawn—but no tunnel. I woke up in my old bed in my old home."

"Same here. Anyway, back to my lousy habit. Introspection says that I feel guilty that I cannot be physically attracted to otherwise great ladies. And to conceal the guilt, I avoid direct compliments. I seldom complimented Lizzy either."

"Ah, the benchmark!"

"And you can't help being sarcastic when she's involved."

"Remember Some Like It Hot?"

"Yeah, 'nobody's perfect,' was that it?"

Beatrice nodded and both laughed.

Then Leo asked, "When was the last time we went to the movies together?"

"Before Eric was born."

"Seriously! Yeah, that makes sense. Wanna go now?"

"Where? To the movies? What movies are there here?"

"You don't know? Great, so I have a surprise for you!" Leo downed his glass, sprang from the lounger, and transformed.

Beatrice tried to guess the age, then gave herself a shape-shift. "Is that OK? Would we not be let in unless we are teens?"

Leo did not answer. He grabbed her by the waist and swung her around, his eyes sparkling. "This is a fantastic perk we have here, to be young again and again and again! No more good old times! Listen, why don't you dress up as in those days, going out on a date?"

His excitement was certainly contagious. She changed quickly, and in no time, they headed down to the street, hand in hand, laughing and spinning. Leo pulled her into a side alley, pinned her against the wall, ran his hands over her, kissed her, and led her deeper into the passageway. Then they turned left and soon found themselves on a quiet, leafy street.

"Here?"

"No, not yet."

They crossed and sank into a tunnel leading to a backyard. Then they entered a building, one of the old ones, went up to the first floor, then down the main staircase and back onto the street, or rather, the boulevard. Beatrice knew it: the wide two-lane sidewalks lined by two rows of old chestnut trees, then the granite pavers of the motor traffic lanes, then two more sidewalks and two more rows of trees. The place in the old world was vibrant, always brimming with life. Cars, bikes, and sightseeing buses screeched and rumbled on the rough pavers;

people were killing time in the cafés and pubs and mostly window-shopping due to the high prices of the goods in the many indie boutiques and the large Armani and Chanel stores. The two of them were also part of the crowd in those days.

Leo swung her around, then drew her close and kissed her again. He was like a teenager who had finally gathered the courage to confess his feelings and had found out that his love was keenly reciprocated. That was contagious as well. Beatrice shelved her true age, dropped the load of her long past, and was ready to be wild and carefree again. This time, she pulled him close and kissed him, her tongue drilling deep into his mouth. When she was young, she did this just to annoy the passersby; it didn't matter who she was kissing. Some people got it quite wrong. She also got beaten up badly by her father when he saw her once. But that was then.

"It's here!" Leo braked in front of an Art Nouveau building. The intricate typeface combined its letters in the words: THEATER ALAMINE, EST. 1927. The window was decorated with movie posters, featuring Marlene Dietrich, Charlie Chaplin, Jack Lemon, and one Norma Jeane Mortenson, also known as Marilyn Monroe.

Leo pulled open the door and let Beatrice in. The foyer was richly decorated and the air cool. On the walls hung framed vintage movie tickets.

"Wow! Now I remember this place, but I was never in here; I only passed by. Nah, really? *Some Like It Hot?*"

Leo nodded. "You can ask for any movie you like here, if it is at least a century old. Well, around that. Movies like *Flashdance* and *Star Wars* would not be shown. But there are theaters for more recent flicks. Did you not know?"

"I didn't think of going to a theater. I wished for a full-wall TV set, and I got an old model flat-screen, but it is good enough for me. The last time I went to a theater was with you in that shopping mall in Midrand. I've misplaced its name. Anyway, we saw *Independence Day.*"

"Aw! A long time ago indeed. Shall we?" Leo pointed at the door. "Maybe upstairs?"

"Lower level's fine."

The couple sat in the middle of the middle row, the lights went out, and the movie began. Leo had a different idea at the onset of the adventure; however, he changed his mind. Just being here with the attractive blonde girl with large green eyes made him happy. Her laughter, her slapping his thigh, her holding his hand in the dark, him knowing that they were friends again, it was priceless. He readily forwent the contemplated sex act.

When the flick was over and the lights were back on, Beatrice turned to him, leaned on the armrest, propped her chin on her hand, and smiled. "Shall we see another?"

"Are you up for it?"

"Obviously!" She stretched her neck for a kiss.

"OK. Care to pick?"

"Mmm. King Kong!"

"*King Kong*? OK, your call." Leo's smile mirrored hers.

She turned in her seat toward the screen and closed her eyes. The lights went out again. The projector hum was heard and then . . . color flashes. Then came the credits in Japanese. Leo frowned. What was Beatrice up to? "Bea, this is not *King Kong*, this is *Godzilla*."

"Yes, King Kong vs. Godzilla!"

"Are you doing it on purpose? What are you trying to say?"

"What? Ah, shit, no! Sorry! We can cancel, right?"

"It's OK." Leo took her hand. He played with her fingers for a while. Then he suddenly dialed up the volume of his voice. "Hey, this gives me an idea. What about moving again to Japan? The four of us. Change the scenery. Me and you—we fight our old demons, chase them away, even kill. With a katana sword!"

Beatrice rested her head on his shoulder and looked at the screen. "OK!"

"You started telling me something back at your place but seems you changed your mind. I noticed. No obligation to report, but I must admit that I am curious; therefore, who is he?"

Beatrice smiled. Ah, old Rudy Hollenmeyer. He was cute and a good man, albeit unsophisticated. She experimented with kinks with him, playing dominatrix, and he loved it. They were having so much fun. Would Leo object to her continuing to be Rudy's mistress from time to time? Perhaps not. He was in an open relationship for years. "The Holy Trinity" as he called it. Anyway, there was no urgency to find out.

"As I said, a classmate of mine. You don't know him. His name is . . ."

RUDOLPH

Beatrice opened the door and let Rudy in first. She didn't want to know how he really looked. She was perfectly content with the tall, skinny guy with pale blue eyes, blond eyebrows and straight blond, almost white, hair. How things change. In their teens, he had a crush on her for ages and a hard time hiding it; she didn't find him attractive but accepted his friendship, probably adding to his anguish. Well, maybe anguish was a strong word, but he was certainly hoping for more, like dating, intimacy. Eventually, he gave up and they never met again after leaving school. She missed his friendship, though, and she understood that it was difficult for a straight, unpopular dude to be just a friend to a girl like her.

When they met here, she found herself at crossroads. She was much wiser now and far less concerned about appearances other than her own. Other people, upon being unable to see their faces, simply stopped giving a damn, but not her. Not knowing how her face looked made her squirm and pick at her nails. Rudy, he was a man, and there weren't many around who she could be with. He was here; therefore, he was a decent man.

"Hi Rudy!" she greeted him without pomp.

"Bea!"

"It would be stupid to say, 'Long time no see,' but it would also be a statement of fact, wouldn't it?"

Rudy laughed. "You can still make me feel like a fly circling a light-bulb. How did I find you?"

"At least it is not like a fly circling a pointy poop. I appreciate it!"

Both guffawed. *Maybe touching me would have burned him as it burned Leo*, thought Beatrice, but instead she said, "Well, now that we have met again, I guess sharing stories would be the thing to do next. Shall we go someplace to sit and enjoy some local brew?"

Rudy looked uncertain, his eyes dancing, trying to find a spot to rest, but then he nodded in agreement and finally parked his gaze on her.

"So, how did you die?" Beatrice started.

"Die? Why die? I am not dead."

"Yes, you are!"

"No!"

"Yes!"

"Whatever . . ."

Beatrice took his arm and led the way to a nearby bistro.

"OK, dead or not, you are seeing me, right? So, assuming that you can choose and pick, what would you want to do with me? Be honest!"

"Wow, if I am indeed dead, this must be hell, and you the devil or one of his underlings!"

"Why?" Beatrice protruded her lower lip.

"Because you are tempting me. You know I was in love with you, and I wanted you so much back then, but you let me just close enough to pick a scent but not touch."

"Well, unreciprocated feelings are not uncommon. Sorry, I liked you as a person and I had a lot of respect, but no feelings indeed, not the kind you were after."

"This is what I meant when I said that you were tempting me. I fall for you again and the story repeats, and my punishment is one-sided affection. I had a fair share of these to be honest; I must be mad to want more."

Beatrice had no reason to disagree. All she could offer now as an extra was sex, something she denied him outright in those days. "I understand. Let's see, back then you were a respected friend of mine, someone I could confide in and seek and receive help from, someone I was willing to assist when needed and also listen to."

"Thanks," Rudy mumbled.

"I cannot give you love as is understood in the old world."

"What old world?"

"Are you listening!" Beatrice raised her voice.

"Evidently, or else I would not be asking questions, would I?"

"Right, fine, I cannot give you love, but I can offer physical intimacy if you want. Think about it. We will meet again!" Beatrice abruptly dropped his arm, turned around, and walked away.

"Hey, Bea!" Rudy called to no avail; she did not stop.

He did decide to take the offer as it stood. After all, what is love if not a desire to be intimate with a specific person, accompanied by acute lack of sound judgment related to that person. They did it in a back alley for the first time. He was clumsy and he finished quickly, then he blushed and started stuttering. Beatrice chose to give him a blow job to prevent his self-esteem from taking an unrecoverable dive, and that was the action for that day. Then they talked.

"So, you think that you are hallucinating?" she asked.

"Yep, I have colorectal cancer, and I get a lot of morphine injections. It is not the first time I've hallucinated after a dose."

"But?"

Rudy turned a blank face at her. "But? Butt? I don't get it. You are not making sense."

"I mean, this hallucination is nothing like the previous ones, right?"

"No, it is exactly like the previous ones, the last batch, to be precise, three or four. Just that it is lasting unusually long. I should be conscious by now. You know, the first time I had it, I met Granddad. Then him again and my great-grandparents. Now you. Truth be told, I don't mind lingering around. It is far better than being awake in the hospice."

He'd been here a couple of times before and then back! That was big! That was a way to communicate with the old world! She had to tell Leo and the others! But then she had to ascertain—was he dead or not? Would he not make the trip back any moment now? Would Leo be able to see him so he could interrogate? So many questions. She felt dizzy, her head spun, and she jumped.

⋆_⋆

"What happened? Are you hurt?"

Beatrice had slumped on the floor. Rudy was chained to the cross and was making awkward twists trying to free himself, his rigid pin bouncing left and right. She touched her forehead and looked up. "I'm OK, I just jumped . . ." She staggered to her feet and checked her balance, then the environment, then herself. Aha, they were in the playroom. She was clad in leather corset, fishnet thigh-highs, and polished high heel shoes. "Where were we?" she asked.

"Er, playing . . . are you sure that you are OK? Uncuff me, please!"

"Just yank harder, that oughta break the links. Don't ask me how I know." She nudged upward the corner of her mouth.

"Shit, ugh!" Rudy struggled some more before the restraints snapped, then peeled the leather mask from his face and offered his arm. "Come, let's sit."

"I jumped from the conversation we had when we did it for the first time. How long since then? It must have been a while, judging by what we are doing now; I wouldn't have been in a rush to take you here. Or maybe you took me first? I don't know right now. Have you ever jumped?"

"Hey, slow down. Yes, I have jumped, and it has been something like a year. I think that I am either in a coma or, as you said many times, dead indeed. But why the rush? You know that you will remember."

Beatrice shrugged. "Maybe because you said something important back then, something I wanted to act upon . . ."

"Ah, communicating with the old world. Yes, you told your ex-husband, and we've had several conversations with him since then."

"Conversations? With Leo? Could he see you?"

"No, you were relaying."

"Ah." Beatrice felt the sense of urgency subside; the rest would come back in good time. She looked at the butt plug in her hand. "Good to know. Do you want to continue?"

"Yes, but not here. Let's go for a swim." He started unstrapping her, his hands casually rubbing her nipples.

"I can't swim!" Beatrice giggled and tried to wriggle out of the costume.

"I will teach you!"

"Well, I will not drown even if I sink. We shall try it underwater! Like . . . fully submerged."

Rudy paused. "You mean banging in SCUBA gear?"

"No, just banging. The gear is unnecessary here. But breathing water must be learned. It is scary, very scary, until you pop out of it."

"Ah, magnificent! I am in! But I wouldn't mind a dry exercise first." He pushed her down and held her still, waiting for a go-ahead. She smiled and parted her legs. He was still clumsy, but also cute. Was he a virgin when he died? Did she ask? He had gained confidence, he was not entirely submissive, and he took the initiative.

When he pulled out and sprinkled her with his holy sauce, she still had a ways to go. Why did he do that? It seemed that doing so gave him a bit of extra kick, but it was selfish! She slammed her knees into one another, and her palms spread the sauce as she wondered whether to pass him a dildo or fan the ambers.

"Get up! On your feet! Don't move!" Beatrice commanded, rubbed his dick, then blew. The gamble paid off. Rudy was back in business fast, and they rolled on the mat. She straddled him, pushed his shoulders down, and guided his source of pleasure inside her. Then she started moving her rear at her own pace, near satisfaction yet short, for Rudy wasn't Leo. Beatrice tried to forget that for a moment, leaned closer, and kissed Rudy on the forehead, then rubbed his cheek with hers. Rudy reached for her breasts, and his touch precipitated a desired boost. She gasped, sat upright, and rocked her hips, the tension between her legs rising to a crescendo, then flaring in a bouquet of sparks. Beatrice continued swaying for a while, catching her breath, then came to a halt, let go of Rudy's hand, and wiped her face.

She rolled to the side and sat. Rudy was silent and still. Then he reached and tried to tug her down, but she resisted and instead grabbed his still-willing penis. Her hand began delivering long, leisurely strokes; her gaze moved until their eyes met and both smiled.

"I suppose that underwater, the movements will be by necessity slow and the stimulation lacking. What are we stimulating here? Nerve receptors as in the other world?"

"We will see when we try it. As to what we are stimulating, is there no research?"

"Not that I know of. And this world is low tech if you have noticed. But Leo found a microscope."

"Ah, and what?"

"Men are sterile. What comes out of you just resembles sperm. By the way, what did you do for a living in the old world?"

"I was a chauffeur."

"Is that why you are driving me insane?" Beatrice giggled.

"Oh . . . Am I? You come up with all the naughty stuff." Rudy's voice was shaking; he seemed to be on the verge of releasing.

Beatrice intensified the strokes; Rudy quivered and fired inside her cupped hand. She fanned her fingers. She knew now that she was the leader. "Well, no, you are not; it was just a figure of speech. I don't know if anyone can do it. I think that it requires overwhelming emotions, and I am barren when it comes to these. Sorry." She turned her head to check his face.

"I'm good, don't worry! This is the best time of my life, and I love you for that!" He propped himself on his elbows and looked her in the eyes. "As a friend, I mean . . . Well, whatever, what we are having is what I think I wanted all along—" Rudy stopped abruptly and dropped his head.

Beatrice detected his discomfort and changed the subject. "Did you tell me how you lived? Did we talk about ourselves?"

"Yeah." Rudy appeared relieved. "I told you I was unmarried. I had a fiancée, but we broke up. Then I took care of my nephew and niece when their parents died on that plane the Russians shot down over Ukraine."

"Ah, and what about your parents? Couldn't they take care of them? I think the memory is coming back, some of it. I asked you that before, right?"

"Yes."

"And?"

"You said your memory was coming back."

"Right, sorry." Must have been something bad; he was reluctant to repeat it.

"They abandoned us. We were raised by our own maternal grandparents, and by the time Sis died, the grandparents were already too old. It was nice to meet them here, though. Good people. I still don't understand how Mother ended up like that. The other pair was quite mean."

"Yeah . . . I suppose I told you how my life went, no?" she asked.

"You shared bits of it, yes. How your father treated you and your mom, how you married rich, and that was not great, and then you repeated, hoping for a different outcome."

Time to change the subject again, Beatrice thought. She did not remember if she told him how she died, but what if she did? She was not in the mood to be reminded of her sad demise right now. Or maybe Steve was still the only person to whom she had told the truth.

"Want some more naughty stuff?" Beatrice asked, dangling the butt plug.

"No thanks, let's call it a day." Rudy had become detached, lost in thoughts.

"Sure." Beatrice looked at the pieces of clothing and footwear strewn across the floor, stood up, and proceeded to collect them one by one. Then she surrendered Rudy's stuff and put her own garments on.

Rudy held the door open for her.

"Thanks!" She gave him a peck on the cheek. "See you soon!"

⁎⁎

"Hey, Bea!" Leo shook her shoulder when the lights shone.

She opened her eyes and sat upright. The movie was over. She produced a guilty smile. "I think I dozed off."

"I think you were fast asleep." The skinny boy next to her giggled. "But don't worry; I was bored too. I never liked the flick."

"Then why did you let me choose it?"

"Because I thought you liked it, as simple as that." Leo led the way out of the theater.

Next door was the Inner-City Mall. Beatrice wondered how the old movie theater had survived the competition, though she assumed probably because it became specialized in vintage flicks. Or maybe it did not; maybe it was just somebody's memory. The mall, though, was definitely one of hers. She used to frequent it with her friends. They rummaged through the floors, sometimes chased by security for being a nuisance. Some of her friends shoplifted; one even got caught. The gang was getting out through a narrow egress corridor, at the end of which was a fire exit, and someone amongst the escapees blocked the steel door with a garbage can. Poor Uwe spilled his loot, tried to pick it up, and the delay sealed his fate. He was apprehended by the guards and handed over to the police. But he was underage and got away with a warning and a few belt lashes courtesy of his dad.

"Ice cream?" Leo suggested.

They swerved and entered. She had not been in the mall for decades. A bout of nostalgia found its way to her heart. The décor reminded her of days long-gone. It was old and new at the same time. Outdated, from the eighties, with too much beige and gold, yet looking as if newly installed. Leo went to find the ice cream stall, and she continued walking down the hall, inspecting the merchandise. It was vintage too. Pastel colors, blazers with shoulder pads, vinyl records, and VHS tapes. She sighed. The times weren't bad. Her father was still around, but she was also very popular and full of hope for the future. She reached the lobby and pushed the button, remembering the rides. An elevator was on this floor, and it parted its doors. Beatrice stuck her head inside, then stepped in with memories still popping in her mind. The elevator cabins had golden mirrors in those days, now just flat beige panels with polished brass inlays.

She missed the doors closing shut behind her. Only the slight jolt and the acceleration made her aware that the elevator had moved. When the bell dinged and the doors retreated into their slots, she stepped outside and looked around. She had traveled, but where to? Köennendorf? Was it not that hotel the four of them paid a visit to several times before Elise drifted away?

"Ah, there you are!" a girl greeted her after emerging from the adjacent elevator.

Beatrice's jaw dropped. "Lizzy?" Had she also jumped back in time?

"Negative, it's Mirielle," the girl snapped. "We are at the bar, hurry up!"

REVELATION

They were there indeed. Wasilla, Leo, Steve and his on/off girlfriend Margot, and Elise, or was she Mirielle? Margot—she probably would have become the maid of honor had Steve and she not split. Beatrice and Margot got along quite well in those days, as Margot did not feel intimidated. She was like an older, confident, and generous sister. Beatrice missed her after she left. Had she remained around just for a tad longer, the two might have become besties. Beatrice was popular but had difficulty making true friends.

"Sorry, guys and gals, I just jumped. I've been bouncing around like a ping-pong ball. My memory is totally fucked right now," she said hurriedly.

Leo gave her a brief hug. "Shall I report then?"

"Are we in Köennendorf?"

"We are in Vegas, baby!" Steve thundered. "Now that you have arrived, let's go."

"This place . . . this hotel, it reminds me of the one in Köennendorf."

"Ah, they are similar. You know—hotels. Or our memories make them look alike. Or the designer of this world lacked imagination or did not get paid enough. There could be a thousand reasons, and as you know, we have no fucking idea how to test for the right one!" Leo shrugged and rolled his eyes.

Beatrice had flown to Las Vegas many times in the old world. Her other husbands, Leonardo and Christian, both had business interest in the hospitality and gambling industry, and old Otto simply liked to gamble. He was a high roller spending small fortunes, and she was his doll, always by his side in the casino, obligated to look great and socialize with his peers. She was tempted to do more than socialize, considering his bed habits or rather the lack thereof, but she was afraid. Otto never laid a threat; the other two did, but by the time she married him, the fear had already settled in.

"Why Vegas? Money is not a thing here. What does one gamble with?" Beatrice asked while scanning the scenery. It looked as she remembered it to be. Caesars Palace, Bellagio, The Venetian, Luxor. Bellagio was imploded in '37 and The Venetian in '44, but she remembered them, and they were here now. This realm had ways to create reality different from the old world, one of them being resurrecting dead resorts.

"Precisely for this reason. We wanted to see what Vegas would be like in this world."

"There were no slot machines in the foyer. It is not a promising start." Beatrice's gaze came across the girl's back. She whispered to Leo, "How old is she now? And how are we doing? Me and her?"

"Thirteen."

Beatrice gasped. Six years, even more, considering how long ago her liaison with Rudy was. She bit her lip and braced for a massive punch—the longer the jump, the harder the avalanche of memories would hit.

"What?" Leo looked at her.

"I've jumped across the galaxy! Six years give or take!"

"'Galaxy' is greatly exaggerated, but it is still a lot. Let me soften the blow a bit. You two are doing just fine. We all moved to Japan after I completed the airplane."

"With it?" Beatrice laughed. It was a lightweight, pilot-only contraption, but she could not help it.

"Thing is, Mirielle hates being reminded as a copy of their mom."

"You are still using that pronoun, eh?"

Leo ignored the question.

The group reached Bellagio. The water show was in full swing despite there being no large mob to derive enjoyment—only the six of them, and they had just arrived. But there were certainly others like them, ghosts, unattuned to each other's wavelengths. The weather was not particularly hot. It was on the pleasant side, yet the water droplets that landed on their skin when the wind gusts sent them their way were pleasant.

Mirielle removed her top and spread arms in the air above her head, exposing her chest to the mist, eyes closed. She slowly spun, letting the droplets land on all sides. Leo shook his head. Then he crossed gazes with Wasilla, but she just shrugged.

"Mi—" Beatrice tried to be helpful.

Leo waved a hand. "You will recall. It is useless."

"Then why are you still being fired up?"

"They are my daughter, er . . ." He seemed to have noticed the conflict with the pronoun.

"Just let her be." Beatrice smiled.

"Thanks, Bea!" Mirielle chirped with a grin.

"Listen Mirrie, are we really good? I feel like walking on eggshells right now, as if you despise me and—"

The girl crouched slightly, then leaped and ended up right in front of Beatrice. She hugged her and buried her head in Bea's cleavage. "We are good, Bea, don't worry. You are—hey, Dad, what was that thing?"

"Projecting."

"Yes, you are projecting. Probably. But that said, I also feel unsettled, I don't know why. I can't relax."

She is just like her mom, Beatrice thought. *Looking like her, acting like her.* It must have been hard on Leo and would probably get even harder as Mirielle aged, because she was aging. She was a baby, then a toddler, then a young girl, and now she was a teen.

"Well, if something bad comes our way, you will switch to a boy and help Steve and Dad fight it off." Beatrice tried to be funny.

"Maybe," was the answer.

She really seemed worried, walking with her gaze down, paying no attention to the things she'd never seen—the resorts, the billboards. What else? No buses or cars. But the resorts were impressive; they should strike a fancy.

"You don't seem interested in the view, do you?" Beatrice said.

Mirielle shook her head. "No, they are all fakes. Big, flashy, and dumb. I like the water features, though!" She swirled around as if the mist from the fountain was still reaching her. "And the pools!" Mirielle ran in the direction of the nearest one, shed the rest of her clothes, and splashed in the deep end.

"That is not a bad idea, heh?" Steven swerved off the path toward the pool.

"I don't have a swimsuit," Margot chimed in and shook her breasts.

Beatrice laughed at the sight. *Are her boobs what give Margot her confidence?* She made a mental note to ask.

"Who needs one here?" Wasilla asked and disrobed.

Steve followed suit and jumped into the pool. Leo sat at the nearby table and held his head with both hands for a while. Then he rose suddenly, cursed, and joined the group. Margot was next. Only Beatrice stood on the pool's edge. She talked bravely to Rudy about underwater intercourse, but she was still terrified. She never drew water in her lungs; she just relayed what Steve had told her.

Leo sent a splash in her direction. "Come in, on the shallow side, and I'll meet you there. It is time to learn how to float at least. Did anything happen to you in the old world? Like having to do with water? Usually, such aversion is due to some trauma."

Leo's last words unlocked the vault! Beatrice took a step back and sat on a lounger. Her hands rose as if for a Muslim prayer, palms up. Her skin turned pale, and her teeth began to chatter.

Leo climbed out and rushed to her, followed by Mirielle. The girl wrapped her arms around the older woman and gasped with force, crying, "I can feel it, Bea! I can feel it! What is it? It hurts! Please stop! Ugh . . ."

The party was over. Beatrice was shivering with her mouth ajar and an empty gaze. Leo kneeled and held her hands. He could feel it too, the pain Beatrice was broadcasting.

Wasilla leaped and began stroking Mirielle's hair. Steve looked around for a glass of something. On the other side of the pool, there was a bar; he dived and swam across. Margot had frozen, like a statue; only her eyes were flipping back and forth, water dripping and pooling at her feet.

Beatrice finally breathed. Staring at a point she ground her teeth, licked her lips, then grabbed the edge of the lounger and squeezed it until the tips of her fingers turned white.

"My . . . fuckin' . . . father . . . tried . . . to . . . drown . . . me . . . in . . . the . . . tub!" she said slowly, deliberately emphasizing each word. "FUCK!"

"Bea, Bea, no!" Mirielle continued to cry. "You are hurting me! You . . . you are hurting yourself! You will disappear! Please, stay here . . . stop!"

Leo understood what his child was talking about. Beatrice had lost opaqueness, just like Elise did before she drifted away. She was dissolving into the air, then solidifying, then becoming translucent again. They could see faint streaks of light as she pulsated, traveling throughout her body—mostly red. Suddenly she sprang up, shoved Leo aside, wriggled free from Mirielle's embrace, and walked away toward the exit, her body letting more light pass through at every step. Mirielle tripped over the lounger with arms still stretched out and cried, "Bea, don't leave! Bea! Mom!"

Beatrice slammed hard on the brakes. She turned slowly, with a distorted face. "What did you say?"

Mirielle sobbed. "I said 'Mom.'"

"I am not your mother!" Beatrice hissed.

"Not technically, no." The girl looked up and met her eyes. "But you also took care of me, not as much as Wass and Dad indeed, but still, it counts. You love me, I know, I can feel you all, and I love you too." Mirielle wiped her nose with the back of her hand. "I can feel your pain, it really hurts, but we love you. Wass, Dad, Steve, and I. Margot there was always your friend. We can help, please stay!"

"Or else you will drift away. And end up in a dark and lonely place," Leo added and helped his child up. Mirielle wrapped one arm around his neck and outstretched the other at Beatrice.

Beatrice's fury had clearly subsided somewhat as her body turned opaque again and her face began shedding the strong red hue. "If I stay, will you do what I ask of you?"

Mirielle looked up at her eyes again, snorted, and nodded.

"Then please get dressed!"

"OK." The girl rose and started walking backward toward her strewn clothes.

"And stay dressed!" Beatrice returned to the lounger, sat, buried her face in her palms, then looked up and around. She grabbed Leo's hand and shook her shoulders without a sound.

Leo crossed gazes with Wasilla, nodded, and smiled almost invisibly. If she could hear his thoughts, she would certainly agree, for he was thinking, *Just like their mom!*

*
**

Later in the evening, Beatrice shared the event that Leo's words unearthed from the deepest crevice of her mind. When she was around five, she was alone with her father and probably sought his attention as any five-year-old would do. Her memory was foggy on the details, but what she now remembered clearly was her crying even louder as her father hit her again and again in his attempts to silence her, then him cursing repeatedly, dragging her, and pushing her head under the water in the old cast-iron bathtub and the liquid gushing into her mouth and the pain when she inhaled it with her nose as she tried to breathe. Then her mom, Ulrica, screaming and pouncing on her father. Only Ulrica turning up from work at that very moment had probably saved Beatrice's life. The memory was short and well suppressed until today. She had no recollection of what had happened next, but it took many more years and beatings until her mother finally filed for divorce, not without Beatrice's urging and promises of support. He threatened to kill them both but ultimately left them alone and to her knowledge found another victim. Domestic violence was seen as an inescapable part of life in those days, and only the most egregious cases were taken seriously. And the bastard was attractive, too.

"Good riddance!" Beatrice announced at the end and raised her glass.

"Here! Specially made for you!" Mirielle, clad in a black-and-yellow sleeveless dress and silver shoes and with clean face and combed hair held up with a flower-shaped clip, pushed some brown, crumbling object on a plate in front of her.

"Thanks, sweetie, but why the showoff? Dresses are not your forte; you wear unisex stuff. When you are wearing something, that is!" Beatrice said cheekily and stroked Mirielle's hand.

"You see me as a girl, which I mostly am, I think, so I chose this outfit to make you happy." Then she added hastily, "For tonight, though, and other special occasions, not for every day."

"I don't regret staying, Mirrie. Thank you!" Beatrice pulled Mirielle closer and hugged the girl, her heart racing. "Thank you all!" She patiently crossed gazes with every other person in the room, also grateful that in this world she didn't wear eyeliner and other makeup. "Now," she turned to Mirielle, "will you tell me what this is?"

"Well, it was supposed to be a chocolate cake."

"Ah, to me it is! Let's eat!"

**

The hotel room was quiet, and the ceiling was animated by the multitude of colorful lights flashing through the partially closed blinds. Beatrice tossed and turned for a long time. Then she called, "Leo?"

"Mm," Leo grunted.

"Wass?"

"Yes?" Wasilla answered sleepily, turning on her back and stretching.

"There's one more thing I should tell you, now that Mirrie is not around. I must let it out, forgive me. And I think now's the best time."

Leo turned the light on and sat on the edge of the sofa he was relegated to for the night, shoulders slumped. Wasilla rested her head on her palm and looked at Beatrice.

Beatrice took a deep breath. "What you learned today wasn't the major shitty event in my life. I didn't die from a stroke; the truth is, eh, my son killed me."

"Eric?" Leo wheezed out and straightened his spine.

"No, moron! Jansen, the younger one, Christian's son. He hit me with a bronze statuette when I turned him down for more dough. He was a compulsive gambler. I don't remember if I died instantly or it dragged on. The next thing I knew was Mom and our old home."

"Phew! That's bad. You really had a miserable life!"

"Well, that was it. As of today, you know everything. We can get some sleep now." She pointed at the lamp Leo had just activated. The light went out, allowing the flashes from the billboards and awnings to return. Someone crawled into her bed. Beatrice, still trying to convince herself that revealing her secret was the right thing to do, made room for the visitor out of habit, not knowing if it was Leo or Wasilla. Then came the kiss. It was definitely from a woman.

"Thanks, Wass!"

"Ah, stop it, it is what we do to soothe each other, is it not?"

Beatrice wanted it to be Leo next to her too but settled for just Wasilla.

Leo assumed his previous position on the sofa and looked up at the dancing streaks of light. It was good that he stayed with them. There were plenty of beds, but in other rooms, and Beatrice would have perhaps postponed the confession and continued carrying the weight for who knew how much longer. He wanted to take some of her pain away, somehow. People envied her for her looks and popularity, perhaps even more so after she married into wealth, but she'd had it rough, very rough apparently. Even he might have been a bit skeptical if he had been told back then about her misfortune. He sat and reached for the cigarettes. He could hear the women kissing quietly. He didn't want to disturb them, so he sneaked out onto the terrace and lit the cigarette. His desire to know more about this world had also returned along with the frustration. He could hear the distant hum of ghost traffic. The freeway was in view, deserted, making the dissonance between sound and vision almost painful to bear. If there was only a way to set up a test.

What was the commonality between Elise and his ex-wife? Both became translucent at some point, but it was Elise's time. She was not angry and full of hatred and spite. Beatrice was furious; if she could, she probably would have torn her father to pieces on the spot. He had no idea where she wanted to go, but he was certain that the dark emotions caused her to change. Then there was the case with Peter. He faded completely in an instant when he attempted the rape.

Could malevolence be a test? Could it be proven that it caused the same effect, how could he name it, say, "expulsion"? But who would volunteer? That would mean bringing out the worst in oneself. Was he himself capable of hating so much as to trigger it?

Leo extinguished the cigarette and decided to check on Mirielle, who was sleeping in the other room of the suite. He carefully pushed the slider open and stepped inside. Mirielle was resting on their side facing away from the glass. Leo sat on the edge of the vacant bed. He could make out their features, the dancing streaks on the ceiling providing just enough illumination. Two out of his three kids were "accidents," but he loved them, nevertheless. They bore no guilt for their parents not being careful. He always got upset when friends called a kid of theirs a "mistake," even more so if the "mistakes" were in attendance and could overhear. Mirielle, unlike regular children, was unequivocally unexpected. Children did not exist prior to them in this realm, and they were also so different from everybody else. What were they indeed? Mirielle aged, and they could switch sex at will. What else could they do that he was still unaware of? A miracle indeed.

The man kneeled beside his child's bed, very gently pushed the dense locks of hair up, and kissed them on the temple. Mirielle opened their eyes. Seemingly recognizing him, they held his hand and murmured, "Leo ... Leo Hans ..." Then smiled sleepily and closed their eyes again.

He froze! He'd heard very clearly what they said. Mirielle never called him by his names! It was always "Dad"! Their mother, though ... she did that; she often used both of his names. He remembered the day Elise drifted away, and he, exhausted, drained, dozed off in the armchair only to be catapulted forward through time to face an older Mirielle, whom he mistook for their mom and addressed as "Lizzy?" "Leo Hans?" she said back then, then blinked once or twice and switched to "Daddy." They were like two completely different people for a moment. They—maybe Mirielle was "they" in more ways than one. He shivered at the thought. So unusual, and outright scary! He rolled on the empty bed and tried to calm himself down, inhaling and exhaling slowly and listening to his faux heartbeat.

VEGAS

Beatrice's eyes were still closed, but she was acutely aware that the day had arrived. Wasilla was still next to her, breathing, as if that was necessary, and delivering a faint flowery scent. Beatrice cackled silently, as the association the scent triggered was that of an automated bathroom air freshener set to spray at regular intervals. Then she frowned, disgusted with herself, popped one eye open, and scanned the room. They were still in the hotel. Leo was not on the sofa. She remembered him sneaking out on the terrace, but after that it was a blur. However, her other memories had returned, all six years, accompanied by—to her surprise—only a mild headache.

She examined the records, then squinted for a moment and exhaled quietly with a wide-open mouth. Mirielle had indeed accepted her gracefully. Wasilla and Leo had become her stars. She had never been more content with her existence. Had these memories been in place when the recall of her father's actions came, she would not have been that angry, not at all. She kissed Wasilla and slipped out of bed.

"Mornin'!" Wasilla drew her eyes open and smiled.

"Sorry, I didn't mean—"

"Nah, that's fine. We are not cats; we must spend some time awake." Wasilla turned around and surveyed the room. "Where's our man?"

Beatrice shrugged. "He's not far, perhaps next door with Mirielle."

"OK." Wasilla removed the sheet and set her feet on the carpet. "Let's find out."

Beatrice observed with interest how Wasilla's disheveled hair took shape and the red spots on her face disappeared. This world . . . she was no longer apprehensive about her appearance, but she nevertheless kept transforming. She gathered the courage to reveal her true self to them a long time ago, shortly after they moved together to the land of the rising sun. Shape-shifting ensured that her choice of clothes would be age appropriate. It was self-respect and respect for others. Wasilla and Leo started doing that too, but only on occasion. Wasilla died young at thirty-nine, and Leo wore the same regiment of age-neutral clothes. Men had it easier indeed, even in this world.

Only Mirielle needed the touch of the comb. And to wash her face, but as usual, there was no bathroom. But there was a jug of drinking water and a full kettle! Beatrice pushed Mirielle out onto the terrace and poured water in the girl's hands. Then she did her best with the comb, thinking that it was time for a haircut.

"Where did you get yesterday's dress from? Did you wish it?" she asked while trying to untangle the rebellious growth.

"No, there are boutiques in the foyer; some have clothes. Did you like it?"

"Yeah, it looked good on you. You looked good in it. I love it when you dress like a girl, but I am not going to interfere with your preferences. Wear whatever you like."

"Even if it is nothing at all?"

"You can't wear nothing." Beatrice refused to be dragged into an argument.

"Why? The king with no clothes did! But I get it, you don't want to talk. Anyway, do you wanna pick another one? I will wear it today."

"Tempting." Beatrice considered the offer for a moment. "OK!"

On their way to the boutique, Beatrice spotted a salon. At school she had studied to be a hairdresser. She still had most of the skill, and she had been in charge of Mirielle's upkeep since she had moved in.

"Er, Mirrie, what about a haircut too? Your hair has become entangled; I am sure that I am hurting you when I pull."

Mirielle shrugged and veered in the direction of the salon.

"You wear unisex clothes, so what about a unisex hairdo?"

Mirielle shrugged again. "I can't see it, so why should I have preferences? Those who can see my head may. So, do whatever you want."

Beatrice took the scissors from the antiseptic jar and cut aggressively to shoulder length. Then a bit more, so that it would look right on a boy too.

"Can you switch to your other self for a moment please?"

Mirielle complied. Did Leo really look like that at this age? Beatrice's mouth arched upward at the thought. Then she shaped the remaining hair and said, "I think we are done!"

Mirielle patted his head. "Thanks, much lighter, feels good."

At the boutique the boy spread his arms. "Here, pick one. The shoes are next door."

Beatrice looked around. Her eyes were drawn to a light purple-blue short silk skirt. She took the hanger from the rail and another one with a laced skirt, then headed in the direction of the blouses.

"Do you like these?" Mirielle had fetched a pair of striped canvas shoes.

"Mm, could you switch back please?" Beatrice felt awkward trying the garments on a boy. In her part of the old world, that had become normal—boys and girls shared clothes, particularly in the North—but she never caught up with the trend. "Come, try these on, and I will fetch a top."

"You know that they will fit."

"Yes, I want to see if they look good on you, and that is not guaranteed."

Mirielle huffed and slipped into the silk skirt first. Beatrice gave herself a mental pat; her eye was good. She pulled out a blouse that caught her fancy and handed it to Mirielle to try on. Then another one. And more.

"Hey, stop it! I'm not going to wear all that. The deal was for one set."

Beatrice didn't want to admit that she enjoyed looking at the young one as she tried different garments. It had never happened before. Mirielle wore whatever was on the hangers in the closet, which was what Leo and Wasilla wished for her. Beatrice sighed. "OK, take the purple skirt and the black blouse, this one, yeah . . . and you can keep your choice of shoes. And thank you!" Beatrice pulled the now girl to her and kissed her, then let go.

"Ah, here you are!" Wasilla entered the boutique and made her way between the rails to where they stood. When Mirielle came into full view, Wasilla froze. She blinked with her mouth ajar, then licked her lips and inhaled deeply. "Nice, very nice!"

"Really?" Mirielle asked hesitantly.

Beatrice squinted. The tone of Wasilla's voice was somewhat off.

"Yeah, sure, I am not used to seeing you like this!" This time, Wasilla sounded more sincere.

"I was wearing a dress last night, wasn't I?" Mirielle replied.

"Yes, unusual too," Wasilla said quickly.

"If you like me wearing dresses and skirts, why do you always put me in shorts and tees?"

"Because your grandparents are struggling to accept a boy in a skirt," Beatrice interjected.

"But Dad wears skirts, the Scottish ones, and sarongs! Geez, this dress code of yours is so confusing. And when I wear nothing, you still complain!" Mirielle angrily removed the garments, threw them on the floor, and headed for the exit.

"Mirrie, wait!" Beatrice raised her voice. "You promised something for today, no? We can still talk, though, I grant you it can be weird. Customs and shit!"

Mirielle stopped. "OK," she said, looking down, then returned and put the clothes back on. "Shall we leave now?" She pointed at the door.

"Fuck!" was on Leo's tongue when he sighted the kid. He swallowed the curse, then generated another one and swallowed it too. Then he ruffled Mirielle's hair and smiled. "You look upset. May I inquire about the cause?"

Mirielle shoved his hand aside and proceeded toward the exit. He waited for the approaching women to come close, then asked, "Bea, why did you do that?"

"Did I do what exactly? Pick some nice clothes? She extended the offer."

"Ah, I see . . . but what about the hairdo?"

"Bea, don't you realize it?" Wasilla hissed. "She is a copy of her mother, a perfect one. And now, with these clothes and the haircut, it is Lizzy herself!" She started crying. "I . . . I can't, I can't," she stuttered.

Leo pulled her into his embrace, where she continued to sob.

Beatrice looked down. "Sorry, I did not think of that. You are right. Sorry. I'll ask her to change! And the hair will grow!"

"Never mind, we know that it was not intended to hurt anyone," Leo said. Wasilla just switched embraces, perhaps in confirmation of the sentiment, then sobbed one more time and stopped.

"Well, here's where the pronoun comes in handy," Leo chimed in philosophically. "I never thought of Elise as 'they.'"

"Yeah, very helpful indeed! You thought of me as your twin sister, and it took you ages to change that and let me give you a hand job!" Wasilla answered.

Beatrice gasped and her green eyes grew larger. Then she burst into laughter. "What?"

"Hey, losers, aren't you coming? Steve and Margot are getting impatient," Mirielle called from the revolving door and rode its inertia back to the street.

Steve and Margot glanced at the girl in front of them from time to time. Mirielle sensed the attention and wondered what the big deal was with her new clothes. She let them pass and inspected the adults one by one. That world they all came from must be a weird place.

Steve leaned toward Leo. "One distraction on the tail of another. We came to check the local slots, but seems the world had something else in store."

"What do you mean?"

"When she greeted us earlier, we thought that Elise had returned somehow."

"Ah, Mirrie is a copy of their mom indeed. But keep it to your-selves; you know how upset they get."

"She is a beautiful girl you have here; why do you keep using this stupid pronoun?"

"But they are also a, hopefully, beautiful boy, and the pronoun is entirely apt," Leo responded with a wink.

"You can always switch to 'he' when she becomes a boy and back. This is what I do," Steve said.

"Just let me be, will ya!" Leo retorted and sank into the casino.

Margot pulled Steve aside and gave him the look. The man threw his hands in the air and followed his friend inside the house of sin.

The space was mostly empty. There were no jingling slots, no poker and craps tables, no roulette, no clouds of blue smoke, and no crinkled patrons pulling portable oxygen cylinders around. All they could see were rows of pinball machines and claw-crane boxes, stuffed with toys and treats.

"Ugh!" Steve wailed. "How disappointing! You can't hunt here, you can't fish here, and you can't gamble here!"

"What is it?" Margot asked upon entering. Then she inspected the space. "Ah, crap!"

"Why can't you fish here?" Leo asked. "I've seen stores se—" he corrected himself, "er, dispensing fishing rods and tackle."

"Because the fish never bite, that's why!" Steve scrunched his brows.

Mirielle glanced at the toys, then ran straight to a pinball machine. She launched a ball and began punching the buttons. Soon after, she transformed into a boy. When the last game ball evaded the flippers and sank into the belly of the box, he pulled the plunger for another round, then registered the shift in shape and looked hesitantly over his shoulder back at the adults.

Leo chuckled, then gestured an "OK."

Mirielle let go of the plunger. He had no idea why performing certain actions felt more comfortable in male shape. Would he turn back into a girl if he played with the claw cranes? Later, the pinballs were fun.

"What now?" Leo moved his gaze away from his child and turned to his friends.

"Try finding one fitted with the right equipment?" Beatrice proposed.

"OK, but what will we gamble with, assuming we come across such a place? We have no money, there is no money in this world, so what is a game of chance without the hope of winning and the risk of losing?" Steve then shook his head slowly. "Nothing indeed. Perhaps this is why there's nothing. But we can bet with chips!"

Leo thought that he could detect hope in his friend's voice and rushed to squash it. "Still, you gain and lose nothing, so the chips would also be worthless. In the old world, you exchange them for real money."

"Ugh, fuck!" Steve cursed loudly again. Then cowered, obviously remembering the presence of the youth. "Oops!"

"'Fuck, as in kissing and hugging and licking and moaning?'" Mirielle asked over his shoulder, then slammed the machine after losing the bonus ball, turned, and reverted to a girl.

The adults in the hall could not help the awkward silence. Then Leo took a deep breath and shook his head. "Mmm."

"I get it. Judging by your long faces, it is something I am not supposed to do. Yet! But can I at least know?" Mirielle asked.

Leo raised his hand when Beatrice opened her mouth. She was just the third in line, so to speak; he was the kiddo's dad. In the old world, sexplaining would hardly be necessary; Mirielle would have gotten all the info by now—the Internet, the school, the street. He beckoned Mirielle and put his arm around the girl's shoulders. "Phew! OK, I will crack the nut."

Mirielle turned to the others and said, "I saw a paintball-shooting parlor on our way here. Are you up for a fight?"

Steve looked around. "Let's hope that it won't be like this."

On the street Mirielle wrapped her arm around her father's. "Well, tell me what fucking's all about."

Leo blushed. "It is a dirty word . . . and, also when people, er, make love. Listen, can you be a boy while we talk?"

"But I am wearing girl's clothes right now."

"It shouldn't matter. It doesn't matter. You are fluid anyway."

"What's that?"

Leo freed his arm, put it around the child's shoulders, and shaped his lips into a tube. "We will get to that too. *Fucking* also means having sexual intercourse. We do it purely for pleasure here, but in the old world, it is how people procreate, that is, to make new humans—"

"So, you fucked Mom, and that made me. Then how's it purely for pleasure here?"

Leo heard Steve giggling, put some extra distance between them, and continued, "The way you put it is generally considered very rude and in poor taste." He was speaking slowly, carefully choosing his words, so engulfed that he didn't notice that Mirielle remained female.

Behind them Beatrice thought that if the little one was indeed a perfect copy, her old rival was a lovely creature. No wonder Leo fell for her when she was just a tad older. *What would an aged Elise be like?* she wondered. Had Elise married Leo, would their marriage have lasted? She herself was often angry, vengeful, desperate, and left life disillusioned and bitter. *What would an older Mirielle be like?* This world was gentle and safe, and that certainly was going to make a massive difference. Then her thoughts invoked the place they now called home. She hated it when she was alive; she felt that it robbed her of her dreams and her dignity. Her downfall started when she went without Leo to that damned resort. But now she was happy with life there. Was it because she was dead, and the place was not actually real?

JAPAN

Going back in time, over a year passed before they put the plan into action. Leo wanted to finish his airplane and have some fun with it before they moved. He worked as fast as he could, certainly trying not to run Beatrice out of patience. She started visiting the warehouse often, playing with little Mirielle and becoming the child's stylist. Mirielle finally got a proper haircut. While clipping the locks, Beatrice wondered what they were made of. What the child was made of. What everything here was made of. Still atoms? Or was there nothing at all but thoughts? Leo had managed to plant his doubts into her.

Everybody cheered when he flew for the first time in his toy. He could have just jumped from a tall roof. He was so enamored of the experience that he dared ask her to stay some more.

"OK," Beatrice agreed, "but why don't you fly it to Japan? This world will certainly be so kind as to bend as needed and take you to the right place even in the air. Just reach water where you are unable to see shores, and space will fold."

"I might give it a try; it makes sense. But first we go by the airport."

"By the airport?"

"No airliners in this realm, only airports. We go to one and fall asleep. The next morning, we may be where we want to be, or the transfer may be delayed. It is more entertaining than just waking up in the desired location. Have you never traveled here since you arrived?"

"Always by car."

"Ah, Mr. Gasfart!"

Beatrice giggled. Steve was a petrol head indeed.

"And they're riding on the highway to Honshu," Leo sang to the tune of "Stairway to Heaven."

"What was that?" Beatrice scoffed and pushed her hair off her face.

"A song about Steve farting gas."

"Yeah. But this is not a new song. These are just new lyrics, out of Weird Al's repertoire."

"You know about that guy?"

"Yeah, remember the parody of 'I'm Bad'?"

"'I'm Fat.'" Leo also laughed.

"Are you sure that we shall move to Toyota City? It may be too harsh."

"Dunno. Any proposals?"

"Takayama. Very picturesque."

"I would prefer something on the beach. With speedboats."

"And tsunamis?"

"And tsunamis. We're not going to get hurt, and it could be exciting—akin to a horror movie."

"Ew!"

"And I also want a house with an ocean view." He smiled disarmingly and she gave in.

Then came the day of the departure. To make the experience even more special for the already excited Mirielle, the adults packed some luggage, then the members of the flock were delivered one at a time to the airport by shuttle Steve.

"What now?" Wasilla inquired when Steve dropped her off and pulled out a picket sign reading: HAVE FUN!!!

"The flight is canceled. We will wait for it to be rescheduled." Leo smiled goofily. "No, seriously, we all must fall asleep. God willing, we will wake up in Nagoya."

"What is God, Daddy?"

"Er, why don't you ask Walid?"

Mirielle froze for a few seconds, then said, "An old, bearded man," and turned her attention to the vast space of the terminal. She looked at the pictures of airplanes, spread her arms, and ran, saying, "Zooooooom!" Then she started reading the information board. "International departures time destination flight remarks one one colon three zero New York kay tee zero nine seven one canceled . . . Mom, what is all that?"

"I'll explain," Leo said. "Shall we take a stroll?"

Mirielle readily grabbed his hand.

By the time the sun was out for the day, the travelers had all acquired long faces with the lips either straight and level or arching downward. Mirielle started grumbling, "I wanna go home!"

"Not to Japan?" Beatrice asked.

"What's in Japan? Why are we going?"

"You know why—to have fun. See?" She pointed at the sign Steve left behind.

Mirielle walked to a pair of empty chairs and stood still. Then climbed on the adjacent pair and snuggled up.

Beatrice rose and approached Wasilla. "Your people over there?"

"Yeah, good guess. Care for a drink? Ah, I am jaded." Wasilla set aside the crossword puzzles magazine she was entertaining herself with.

"Not my idea." Beatrice looked at Leo, who had stretched across four seats. Was this experience really needed, or could they have done without it? "Sure, I am, heh, heh, on the same flight."

Leo's back started hurting and he sat. He planned on them waiting in the business lounge, but it was locked. An older woman looked at him across the footpath. Leo rubbed his eyes. "Do I know you?"

"No. You must be Leo?" The woman spoke with a palpable accent.

"Ah, sorry, you must be Fatimah. But how? Am I doing it again? It has been a while. Nice finally meeting you! Er, where are the ladies?"

The woman smiled. "Slow down and breathe. Wassi's coming," she said and nodded at a point behind him.

"Huh?" He turned to look. Wasilla and Beatrice were approaching, tottering with smug expressions on their faces, accompanied by a young man.

Leo turned back; the old woman was gone. He pivoted to the ladies; the young man with curly hair had disappeared too. He faced the chairs again, and his gaze came across Mirielle. They quickly shut their eyes. He nudged the corners of his mouth up, thinking, *Kid,* then scratched his head, wondering what happened just now.

"Here!" Wasilla shoved an almost empty bottle of Cognac in his face. "Will help get to our destination faster."

He took the bottle. "I just saw your mom. And possibly Walid."

"Yeah, the jerk is here." Wasilla dropped in a chair. "Geez, I am, ugh, inebriated. Look after the kid, will you?"

Beatrice sat next to her, looked at him, winked, and dispatched an air kiss.

"Come, bitch." She pulled Wasilla closer, and the two leaned against each other and closed their eyes.

The lights in the terminal suddenly dimmed. Leo thanked management, stretched back across the four seats, and tried to fall asleep.

**

Leo sat, frowned, and rubbed his eyes. The day had come—rays of light were streaming in through the massive glass panes of the concourse.

"Daddy, what are these?"

Leo looked at the object in Mirielle's hand; a tourist brochure it seemed to be. Leo scanned the hall again. They were not at home; the airport trip had worked!

Leo took the brochure and checked it more thoroughly. "This is Japanese writing." He flipped the brochure. "Ad for a hotel."

"Ah, can you read it? You must teach me!"

"I can't read Japanese, but see, there is some English text. You can read English, right?"

"Japanese letters are interesting. And there are so many of them."

"These are not letters." Leo pointed to the kanji. "These here are like letters. But I forgot which was which." His finger glided over the word *hoteru*.

"Huh?" Mirielle's confusion was plastered on their face.

"We'll have plenty of time for these. Now, do you know where Bea and Wass went?"

"Yeah, to find water."

Leo looked at the empty bottle on the table and nodded. "Mm. And Fatimah and Walid?"

"Grandma's here." Mirielle pointed in the direction of an armchair. "Wass told her to keep an eye on me. So, when we want to travel far, we must come to one of these sleepover places—airports."

"Well, not necessarily," Leo admitted. "We can just go to bed at home. But isn't it more fun?"

Mirielle looked down with hands behind their back and said unconvincingly, "Yeah . . ." then dropped the pretense. "It is boring. But these airports are big!"

Flying would have indeed been more exciting. Leo sighed, stood up, and stretched and flexed his frame.

"Hey, Dad!" Mirielle pulled his shirt. "Who are these people? And why are their eyes stretched?"

Leo followed the vector demarcated by the little arm and gasped, "Shinji?! Mayumi?!" He grabbed the pointing arm and dragged Mirielle. They entwined their legs and fell. "Ah, shoot, sorry!" Leo slowed down and lifted Mirielle on his shoulders.

"Mr. Hackensack!" The Japanese man bowed. "Welcome to Nihon!"

"Call me Leo." Leo laughed wholeheartedly and awkwardly hugged his friend.

The man's eyes turned into slits, and his eyebrows furrowed. "So you can tease me for my accent?"

"I'm sorry, man, I promise not to do it. I was a dick." Then he turned to the woman. "Mayumi! I hope you died at one hundred years old!"

"Close." The woman also bowed. "I was ninety-two and Shinji was eighty-seven. And you, Leo-san?" Her accent was mild.

Leo was bubbling on the inside at seeing his old and only Japanese friends. He had been hoping to, in fact. In his excitement he bowed with Mirielle still riding on his shoulders, and they almost tumbled to the ground. Shinji threw his hands forward, arresting the unplanned descent.

"Oops, I am so absentminded and clumsy today," Leo apologized, then added with confidence, "and this on top is Mirielle, my kid!" Shinji reacted—reasoned Leo—therefore he was seeing them.

"Hi, Mirielle!" Mayumi waved. "I'm Nakagawa Mayumi. And this is Shinji, my husband. Really, really nice seeing you!" Her last words rang as genuine as they could, albeit she seemed a tad confused.

"I'm so sorry, Leo-san!" Shinji barked suddenly, doing his best to hit the "L," and bowed.

"Huh? For what?"

"That Mirielle-chan passed away so young!"

"Ah, no, no!" Leo took Mirielle off his shoulders and kissed them on the cheek, before carefully putting their feet on the floor. "They were born here! They are seven now."

The faces of his friends became long, the eyes blank.

"I will explain; it is an exciting story! Come, someone else you know is here." He turned sharply around and crashed right into Beatrice.

"Damn, I tried to sneak up on you!" She laughed and addressed the other pair. "Shinji, Mayumi! Ah, gosh, you bring memories." She hugged the woman.

Leo poked her. "This is Japan."

"No worries, Leo, this is a different Japan." Mayumi smiled and hugged Beatrice in return. "No one here, you see." She pointed around. "Same in Europe, I suppose?"

"Yeah, same. Now, Shinji, Mayumi, er, kun, we came to settle. There are three more people with us that you can't see. Hell, I can't see two of them myself. Anyway, so far so good, we arrived. Now we must move into a hotel and start searching for a place."

"'San' would be better, but don't worry about the honorifics." Mayumi laughed.

"I have—" Shinji started; however, Leo hushed him.

"OK then, let's find you a *hoteru* . . . ugh, a hotel. Follow us, please!" Shinji sighed, pivoted and walked in the direction of the escalators.

Leo handed Mirielle to Beatrice and turned around to look for Wasilla. She was politely waiting a few meters away with suitcases and bags already loaded on trolleys.

"Your family ready?"

"Affirmative. Some commotion and freeze-frames there. You saw someone, right?"

"Yeah." Leo pushed one of the trolleys. "Friends from our days here—Shinji and Mayumi Nakagawa. The only friends. We are going to find a hotel to check in to and then look around for a permanent place. I think Shinji had something in mind, but I don't want to spoil the experience for Mirrie. Sorry for the inconvenience."

"Stop apologizing. I'm with you and so is Bea and Walid and Mom. Don't add significance to last night. People get bored and drunk on trips, and we all have the right to be moody from time to time, right?"

"Rrright!" He tried to give Wasilla a brief hug, but the trolley veered away, and Leo quickly returned his hand on the handle.

Shinji led them to a train platform.

"No shortcuts here?" Leo mused aloud. "And . . . trains!" A commuter train pulled into the station. The driver's cab flashed quickly past him; then the train came to a stop.

"Get on!" Shinji waved, but Leo remained still, a wild grin plastered on his face.

"Hey, Daddy, move!" Mirielle pushed him from behind.

Leo came back to his senses and quickly rolled the trolley through the open door. "Train! A train! A train ride!" He guffawed then turned, hugged Beatrice, and pushed her down into a seat. The doors closed and the train pulled delicately from the station. Leo jumped and landed a few centimeters away from the starting point as the train accelerated.

"Why so thrilled?" Shinji asked.

"We have no trains! I haven't traveled in one for ages. Is there a train driver?"

"We have trains. On demand. I can't see a driver, so I don't know."

"But can you also teleport?"

"*Terepooto*? As in 'move instantly around'?"

"Yes."

"Er, I think so. You open a door, and it leads to another place."

"Yes! Wow! Trains!" Leo started swirling on the handrails like a child.

Mirielle shared in his excitement, jumping up and down, and transformed into a boy. "Trains! Trains! Hah-hah!"

The hosts' jaws dropped.

LIBERATION

Back on presumably the other side of the world, Ruth felt somewhat emboldened by the thought that her granddaughter was unlikely to barge in on her, retrieved the books from the top shelf of her wardrobe, placed them on the mirrorless dresser, and closed her eyes. When she opened them again, she would appear sixty years younger to anyone who saw her around the time she passed—Anton, his ex-wife, and his children. Not Simon, though, as he departed first. But he would notice a difference nevertheless, as at the time of his earthly demise, both were pretty wrinkled.

Ah, the damn faggot! He denied her so much! But she couldn't blame him; these were the times. These are still the times in many places in the old world. Just before she passed, the Moscow massacre was all over the news. The "removal of deviants" as the Russian authorities called the use of lethal force on protesters angered by the recriminalization of homosexuality. Amazing! There were still Russians brave enough or foolish enough to protest. She hoped that these people ended up here, in this world. It was far from perfect, but good people were free to be themselves.

Or were they? The programming was so hard to cast aside. She sat in front of the dresser, took out a book, and paged through it. The printed images sent butterflies fluttering in her groin. Why was it a sin—making love, touching oneself? This is what the pastor often kept droning about in her youth. She wasn't much of a believer. A traditionalist, yes, but somehow religion did not catch up with her. She attended church to avoid arguments with her parents. She yawned throughout the sermon and studied the other parishioners—the adults, the girls, the boys. Most people looked bored. The younger kids were fidgeting in the pews. The adolescents were exchanging glances. Some were passing notes. She couldn't wait for the service to be over. But other than that, she was an "exemplary" girl. She kept herself neat and clean, she did not fall for the fabulous four, and she never wore bright stockings and miniskirts. She learned to cook and take care of the home.

She was content. And very shy. Each time a boy kept his gaze on her for longer than a second, she blushed and looked down. And she had gotten attention, more so as she grew up and, as it was customary to say, "blossomed." But she'd felt awkward around people and had no friends. There were a few girls from the neighborhood she socialized with, until late puberty hit and these girls began talking dirty, baring their legs, smoking, drinking, and flirting. She felt out of place and withdrew.

Then one day, she came home and found Simon and his folks. Simon was not very tall but was well-built and with somewhat girlish facial features. She didn't fantasize about guys like him. She dreamed of tall blonds with chiseled cheeks and square chins. He was sitting perfectly still on the couch, hands clutched between his legs, obviously feeling uncomfortable, and his parents were sipping coffee alongside her own at the dining table.

"Rue, come join us," beckoned her father. "We want you to meet someone."

She was nineteen, fresh out of school, and working as a typist in a law firm. She fell into her waters in the law firm with its strict dress code. She hung her purse and coat, changed into slippers, and went inside.

"Rue, Simon, Simon, Ruth." The introduction was short, and the intentions became clear soon. Simon was twenty-four, studying engineering, and looking for a bride. Ruth was too shy to ask why. The guy looked all right, and the times of arranged marriages were behind, but the anxiety of having to find a husband on her own coerced her to agree.

Had she known the real reason, would she have accepted? Certainly not! Not back then with her old mindset. But was her life that much worse, being married to a gay man? She had no way of knowing. She knew of plenty of painful divorces and spousal abuse. Three of her old acquaintances went through such ordeals and came to her door to share and envy her for her stable, uneventful family life. Simon was a good husband and a friend, and she had no idea that their erratic intimate moments were not the norm. She was wrong to kick him out when he confessed. The man did his best. He took good care, he slept with her, he gave her two great kids, and he consoled her when Elise died. His heart was broken too, but he remained firm and helped her get through.

Ruth turned and tried to see her reflection on the polished surface of the wardrobe. The face was a dark smudge as usual, but she could make out the rest. Leo's mother told her that everybody in this world suffered from a form of face blindness. Was Annette serious? But she was good! She helped her find the reason to forgive and enjoy existence. She encouraged her to try the things she feared—seek the naked company of others, touch herself. Ah, what a fool she was! She had to die and get treatment from a deceased psychiatrist to finally experience life!

She unzipped her jeans and eased them down, then ran her palm up her thigh, following the movement in the reflection. Then she slowly unbuttoned her blouse and let it crumple at her feet. Would straight men find her attractive? Sadly, there was no one to ask; she wasted this chance with her shyness and rigid conduct. Straight men found her daughter attractive, though, and Elise inherited a lot from her. Did her daughter really practice the things in these books?

Ruth rolled her nipples and sighed as the butterflies flew to her brain and disturbed its peace. She licked her fingers and began tracing circles over her areolas. Tiny tentacles of pleasure swirled on the inside in response. She smiled . . . She would have been ashamed of her actions in the old world, but she was proud now. Proud of casting aside the fear and embarrassment. She removed her panties and again checked the wavy reflection on the varnished surface. Her hand moved between her legs, and her pinched fingers crawled inside. Her eyes did not close. She wanted to observe. She pushed on the walls, then rubbed the clitoris. The butterflies scattered; she shivered in response. Then she reached for the toy, inserted it, and gasped. Her mouth remained ajar as she drew the toy out, then pushed it back in. What would it be like to be bound?

She pushed it in. And pulled it out. She wanted to ride a man. Ah, what a fool she'd been! And be bound . . . She did want to try, but she couldn't do it all alone. "Aggg . . ." She moaned angrily and accelerated the pace. Who could she ask for help? Was her desire normal? Was it not too kinky? Was she not insane? In and out, faster! Her entire body was shivering, the smudged reflection in the varnish too. Simon! And Boris! They were weirdos! In and out! Her breath trembled. She no longer kept her moans constrained. Out and in! What was the elation waiting for? Here! Now! Great! She pressed her eyelids shut, then pulled out the dildo and dropped it on the floor, tears rolling down her cheeks. Ruth wiped them with her palms and fondled her breasts. Then she ran her hands down her abdomen, crossed them on her thighs and opened her ears to the sounds.

The apartment was quiet, and she could sense no approach. She bent down, lifted the toy from the floor, and placed it next to the open book. No surprises this time. She recalled how she was almost caught in the act a few months ago and chuckled. She was near the climax when the buzzer in her head went off. She scrambled into her clothes, gathered the books, threw them inside the wardrobe, slammed it shut, and blocked access to it with her frame a mere instant before Mirielle opened the bedroom door without knocking and stormed inside.

"Nana!" She hung on Ruth's neck as soon as Ruth bent down for a kiss.

Ruth gazed aside as she often did. She adored her grandchild; however, it was also impossible to look at her and not think of Elise.

Leo walked in next. "Hi, Rue!"

"Mirrie, let go please." Ruth assumed an upright pose after the child released her grip. "What's up? Are you two alone?"

"No." Wasilla closed the apartment door. "You look radiant. And smug!" She smiled.

"Nana, look at this!" Mirielle transformed into a boy and began jumping around like a baby gorilla and grunting, "Ugh! Ugh!"

Ruth gasped. Then caught the resemblance. "Leo, is that you?"

"Confirmed."

"Er, does she have a . . ." Ruth hesitantly pointed at the child's crotch.

Leo nodded, laughing.

"So . . . she mimics both of you . . . well, what can I say, weird world."

"Tell Simon so he doesn't get a shock. Do you like this place?"

"Yeah, I couldn't stay alone in the old one. Too many memories, and Lizzy's room . . . it is empty now, just the floor and walls. Everything disappeared after she drifted away." She didn't mention the dildo and the two richly illustrated books.

"My great-grandmother's room drifted away with her." Leo said.

"No," Wasilla disagreed. "You two shared a room; it simply stopped switching."

"You may be right," Ruth said. "Lizzy always had her own." Then she turned to the child. "Come here, sweetie." She crouched, and Mirielle ran to her. "What is your name now?"

"Mirrie!"

"But you are now a boy!"

The child looked at Ruth quizzically, then insisted, "I am Mirrie! Mirielle!" and promptly switched back.

"OK!" Ruth raised her hands, thinking of who she preferred, the girl or the boy. "Come back, Mirrie, show me again."

Mirielle transformed and pushed his shorts all the way down. "See, I have this thing now!" pointing at the little penis.

"You shouldn't do this, sweetie," the grandmother objected.

Leo chuckled in the background.

"Why? You see, now I don't." The child switched back to a girl.

"What do we do?" Leo shook his head "I have no idea. How do you tell a small child—"

"I see the problem," Ruth agreed. "Did you speak to your mom?"

"Yeah, and Mirrie pulled the same stunt. She seems very proud of her ability and the new appendage. Anyway, Mother was also at a loss."

"And mine too," Wasilla chimed in. "We are up for some fun, aren't we?"

Ruth's expression changed. "You are lucky, guys. Your existence has meaning: raise this child. And twists and turns along the way, different from what you've lived through before. I wish that Lizzy could also be around, but . . ." Her eyes became moist. She raised her head. "Well, be happy, OK?"

"Mirrie is not just ours. She is yours too. She is your granddaughter; don't you feel the same? A bit?" Leo pinched the air with his fingers in front of Ruth's face.

She pushed his hand away. "It is not the same. She reminds me of my daughter, and I don't know whether to cry or smile. When she's around, I go bipolar, ecstatic that my little Lizzy's back and heartbroken that it is not actually her. Then happy that Lizzy was a mom, even for a short while. Then I get very angry that it didn't last. Maybe I would feel better if she kept your visage."

"That's multipolar in my book—" Leo started. Wasilla smacked him on the neck and hugged Ruth. Leo switched to the version of himself with the lush long hair just in case.

AYUMU

In Japan, Mirielle, the boy, appeared frozen in front of the TV with the game controller in their hands.

"Who's with them?" Leo asked and sipped from his beer.

"Ayumu," Shinji said. "How come he, er, she, er, can see everybody?"

"That's why I use 'them.'" Leo chuckled, entertained by his friend's confusion. "Anyway, they can't see everybody, only the people we ourselves can see. You can see this Ayumu, and so can they. Who's Ayumu, by the way?"

"Mayumi's nephew. He's young. Relatively speaking, of course. He passed during the Noto earthquake; he was twenty-nine. He had the misfortune to be hit on the head by a loose storefront sign."

"Well, only a few are blessed with glorious deaths," Leo said sardonically and took another sip. "Sorry we cut ties, man. That was before Shitbook, and I had too much on my mind."

"Shitbook?"

"Facebook."

"Naah!" Shinji guffawed. "Quite apt!"

"By the way, this is me." Leo nodded at Mirielle, then shrank to the same size.

Shinji's eyes became round. "Oh, impressive!"

Leo reverted. "In their girl form, they are a copy of their mom."

"Her, er—" Shinji stuttered.

"Don't worry."

"The Japanese is very good!"

"I believe so; they learn very fast. Sometimes I can't help thinking that they already know. They learned to read and write eloquently in less than three months. Well, not Japanese." Leo laughed and clinked his friend's beer can. "*Kanpai!*"

"*Kanpai!* I never learned all kanji myself; they're doing very well."

"By the way, I must get a gift for Mayumi for tutoring us. What does she like?"

"Ah!" Shinji looked smug. "What she likes the most she wouldn't take from you!"

"How do you know? Would you let me try?"

"Only if you let me kiss Bea!"

"Typical men talk; you never stop." Beatrice frowned as she entered the room, accompanied by the hostess, drinks in hand. She sat next to Shinji and looked questioningly at Mayumi. Mayumi laughed and nodded. Beatrice leaned, wrapped her arm around Shinji's shoulders, and pushed her tongue inside his mouth.

His eyes grew even rounder. "Oooh! A kiss from the queen!" he rumbled when Beatrice withdrew.

"Hey!" Mayumi called out.

"Don't worry, honey, you are the empress! Bea—just queen."

Mirielle glanced at them with puffed up cheeks. Then shouted, "Ah, no!" He lost the game in the split second he moved his attention away from the screen.

Only Ayumu heard it. "Sorry, friend, my win again! Care for another round?"

Mirielle nodded.

"Ah, you are not giving up easily! I guess that's good." Ayumu started choosing another avatar. "So, you can be both a girl and a boy."

"Yes."

"But who are you, the girl or the boy?"

"I am me. Why do you keep asking?"

"Well, I know of no one else that can be both. It is interesting."

"It is just my shape, not me."

"Then why are you a boy now? You came as a girl."

"Dunno. When I play battle games it is more fun in this shape. Or when I kick a ball . . . or climb trees . . ."

"Ah, so you climb trees. Do you like climbing trees?"

"Yes! Dad built me a tree house. It is very nice. I must show it to you sometime. But it is back home. We must have a sleepover at the airport."

Ayumu raised his eyebrows. "Why would we have a sleepover at the airport?"

"Dad said that this is how we do long-range travel."

"I see . . ." Ayumu nodded slowly. Sleeping over at airports—what a ruse! "I know places to climb; are you interested?"

"Yes!" Mirielle became a girl and rested her head on the young man's shoulder. "Ah, Ayumu, you are such a good friend!"

Ayumu twitched uncomfortably. "Man up, please, game's about to start!"

Mirielle complied and added, "There. But it is not fair!"

"What?"

"I am ten and look at you; you are old!"

"Old indeed." Ayumu chuckled and transformed.

The two boys—one with blue eyes and wavy tresses dropping well past his shoulders, and the other featuring stretched almonds beneath his brows and straight black hair—reached the second platform of the tower and sat on the edge, breathing heavily. The view was fantastic even from here, but they had two more platforms to conquer to reach the top.

"Beautiful, heh?" the black-haired boy said.

"Yeah!"

"Wait until we reach the top. From there we can see all the way to Mt. Fuji!"

"Really?"

"Nah, I wish. But the view is great nevertheless."

"Maybe your wish will come true," the blue-eyed boy said. "We're in my world."

"If my wishes could come true, I would be surrounded by cool chicks."

"What do you mean?"

"Ah, never mind!"

"What? Tell me!"

The black-haired boy sighed. "I wish I was not so alone. You know, in this world. I wish I had more friends, girlfriends . . ."

"I can be your girlfriend!" The blue-eyed boy transformed.

"You are a friend, Mirrie. I was talking about grown-ups."

"I will grow up!"

"Do it and then we'll talk." Ayumu laughed. "Now, rest is over, let's go!"

Ayumu had loved climbing since he was a child. He started with trees and emergency ladders; his mother had nearly had a heart attack when she saw him balancing on the ridges of warehouse roofs. Then he moved to telecom towers and rock faces. He was a member of the climbers' club in high school and then at university and even won several rock-climbing competitions. He could have become a champion! The adrenaline rushing into his bloodstream at the thought of a fall, the feeling of conquest bubbling from inside him when he reached the top, and the nature of the emotion were hard to describe! His limbs were like the limbs of a gecko, sticky, and he never fell, not in the old world. And to think that he was killed by a stupid neon sign! What a shame.

He continued climbing after his death. That kept his mind focused on something else and made him feel alive. Until the day he lost his grip for the first time ever and discovered that he could not die again.

Not by falling. That dulled the adrenaline release, but he could still enjoy the view, and he carried on. And he learned that he could fly. Something lost, something gained.

He looked below him and slowed down. Mirielle was far behind, more mindful of the height. The wind was stronger here, and the light felt brighter.

"You still good?" Ayumu asked when Mirielle caught up.

"Yeah!"

"Are you sure? Your face is very white and your eyes, heh"—Ayumu chuckled—"way too European."

"Huh?"

"You look scared, dummy!"

Mirielle tried to reshape his expression. "No! Let's go!"

"OK. Another twenty-five meters."

At the top, Ayumu stood up, stretched, and looked around. Impressive! It was the same in the old world. From this vantage point he could see all the way to the waters of the bays—Mikawa on the left and Ise on the right. The Toyota factories were also down there. He could even hear traffic hum. The sound effect always puzzled him: Why was there a hum in a world with no traffic?

Mirielle crawled out of the hatch and tried to stand but quickly dropped on all fours.

Ayumu smiled. He had a rookie in his hands. He was going to toughen Mirielle up and have company. Climbing to the top of a seventy-five-meter tower was not at all easy for a novice, yet she made it. Or was it "he"? Ayumu squatted next to his friend. "Look around! Fantastic, eh?"

"Mmm," Mirielle confirmed without lifting his head. He was scared, no doubt. Ayumu raked through his hair. Yeah, he himself had felt his legs turning into rubber when he had set foot that high up on a small, unsecured platform.

"Shall we now go down?" Mirielle's voice was trembling.

"Sure, do you wanna fly?"

"How? Dad has a small airplane, but it is pilot only, so he never took me up. He promised, though, to figure out something and send me in the air."

"We don't need airplanes."

"Okay . . ."

"Then stand up and come here."

Mirielle rose, legs shaking. He made a step toward the edge and grabbed Ayumu's hand.

Ayumu helped him stand steady. "No need to be afraid. In this world nobody dies. When we jump, we will float in the air for a long time until we land. You can steer with your palms. But for now, just hold tight, OK?"

Mirielle nodded and clutched Ayumu's hand tighter.

"Ready? On three we jump. *Ichi, ni, san, hai!*"

The boys leaped into the void. Ayumu began the slow descent he was accustomed to, but Mirielle dropped like a stone. Both screamed. Mirielle grasped at him; however, he was already out of reach. Mirielle's eyes expanded as he helplessly swung his limbs, the air whooshing past his ears, then he reverted to a girl. Ayumu's heart sank. He tried to dive but all he could do was watch the distance between himself and Mirielle rapidly increase.

The urgency jolted Leo into action. He dropped the book on the floor, followed by the glass, catapulted himself from the armchair and over the table, ran into the foyer, pulled the front door open, accelerated down the footpath and onto the street, gathered all his strength into his legs and leaped in the air with open arms. Something dense collided with his chest and hit his nose. He grabbed it, twisted his body, curled up, and met the ground sideways. His elbow cracked and the rough asphalt filed off a large patch of skin. He rolled once and came to a stop. The excruciating pain paralyzed him. Mirielle continued to scream and kick.

"Mirrie!" he wheezed through his clenched teeth. "Mirrie! It's Dad!"

Wasilla jettisoned from the house and threw herself over the child. Beatrice followed, pushed her away, and tried to grab Mirielle and pull them from Leo's arms.

"Don't touch her!" Wasilla kneed Beatrice in the stomach; the other grunted and rolled on the ground. Wasilla took her place. "My baby! What happened? What?" Then she came to her senses. "Ah, fuck! Bea, sorry! Fuck! Mirrie, calm down, baby!" She grabbed the child's hands, immobilized them, and started kissing the little fists. "It's Mamas and Dada. Calm down, dear. Please, calm down."

The screaming died out, and Mirielle became catatonic—eyes wide open, unblinking, oozing fear. Then their body began to shiver violently, and they started crying. Leo clutched them tighter, but the pain from the broken bones stabbed his brain. He groaned and relaxed his grip. "Take care of them, oh, fuck!" He unfurled slowly on the ground moaning.

Wasilla lifted the child with some difficulty, found her balance, and carried them inside. Beatrice kneeled by Leo's side and caressed his forehead.

"Go." Leo nodded, the pain contorting his face. "I will wait here to heal. Find out what happened."

"Later. I'm staying here. Wass can handle it. Can you stand?"

"I suppose so, but what's the point?" He tried to move. "Ouch! I'd rather be still for a while. Light me a cigarette, will ya, please!"

"If you shrink, I will be able to carry you inside."

"Oh!" Leo grunted. "Seriously, Bea, what's the bloody point?"

IT IS DECIDED

Shinji removed his shoes, stepped in, and immediately bowed deeply. "I'm so sorry, Mirrie-chan! Very sorry!" He froze for a second, then resumed his apology. "We are so sorry, Mirrie-chan!"

Mirielle giggled.

"Mirrie!" Leo raised his voice.

"Shinji slapped Ayumu on the neck!" They pointed to Shinji's right.

"Mirielle!" Leo turned the volume up another notch.

"It is fine, Leo-san! The brat did not bow deep enough!"

"Apologies accepted, Shinji. Just get up, shit happens. He had no way of knowing. I was also unaware that they were incapable of flying. We assume so many things."

"Leo-san is so right, yet Ayumu should have not been so reckless." Shinji got up and joined Leo in the kitchen niche. Leo took three cans of beer from the fridge and another one with juice. "Ayumu is over eighteen, right?" he smiled, then pushed the juice and one beer across the countertop. "Mirrie, take care of Ayumu, will you?"

Mirielle grabbed the cans and ran away.

Leo popped his. "*Kanpai!*"

"Arigato! Kanpai!"

"I know that they are different from us, but this was, er, unexpected. Does that mean that they can die?" Leo looked at his friend as tears filled his eyes.

"You are crying, Leo," Shinji said.

"So what? I'm no samurai!"

"Sorry, I meant no offense, the faurt is all ours!"

"Yeah, you are farts." Leo couldn't resist the opportunity presented by Shinji's thick accent, then bit his lips. Shinji laughed, though. "Being serious now, let's stop seeking who to blame. They are OK, and we learned a valuable lesson. Just that this event drives me crazier. What is this place, what is Mirrie, what are we? Have you ever tried to find answers?"

"Sometimes, but frankly all I can think of is sex!"

Leo guffawed wildly. Such honesty from the usually reserved Japanese man. "Same here. Tell me more!"

"What is there to tell? Cultural shit aside, we are all the same. Or you want to hear the juicy parts?"

"That's immature, but why not? But wait, what about a 'tell-all' party? With the ladies?"

Shinji thought, then barked, "*Yossha!*"

Mirielle handed the beer to Ayumu and pulled the tab of her juice. She considered for a moment and outstretched her arm. "Do you want juice, Ayumu? And I will have the beer."

"Huh?"

"Do you want the juice?"

"No, why?"

"I want to try the beer. My folks keep saying that it is too early for me to drink alcohol. But when they do it, they laugh more and talk funny. I want to try it, see what it is like."

"No. I already did something very irresponsible; no same mistake twice. Kids shall not consume alcohol!"

"But why?"

Ayumu weighed his answer. "Because it changes you when you drink it. And it can change you in a very bad way."

"Like what?"

"Like turn you into a bad person. Somebody who's violent and vile."

"Like Jessica's dad." Mirielle looked down. How did she know, though? Her step-grandmother never mentioned anything. She gazed at the ocean. It was a high tide, and gentle waves were licking the sandy beach. "Hey, Ayumu, let's go for a swim!"

"I can't, I don't have a swimsuit."

"Who needs clothes in the water!" Mirielle tried to prove her point.

Ayumu instantly turned his back at her. "Don't do that!"

"Do what?" Then she recognized the blunder and transformed. "Is this better?"

Ayumu threw a quick glance over his shoulder and saw a young boy. "Yes, but you better get dressed. We're in Japan."

Mirielle patted his leggings and put them on, followed by the shirt. "I'm done!"

"Thanks!" Ayumu sighed.

"This is another one I don't understand, the clothes. I must always wear something, but Dad and Moms may not. I see them naked all the time. They don't know it. They hide, but I peek. And when they're naked, they are feeling good. I can sense it."

"Your moms?"

"Yeah, Wass and Bea. But they are not my true moms. They just raised me, mostly Wass. My birth mom, Elise was her name, drifted away shortly after I was born. Everybody says that I am her clone."

"How?" Ayumu wrinkled his forehead.

"I look exactly like her, and Grandma Rue says that I also sound like her when she was my age and that I behave the same."

"And who's the boy then?"

"Dad." The boy dropped a casual answer and became female.

"Aw!" Ayumu let his drink slip from his hand, cursed, and bent to pick it up. Mirielle wrapped her arm around his neck and pecked him on the cheek. Ayumu sprang upright, as if stung by a wasp.

"Listen, we shall climb again!" Mirielle looked up and their gazes crossed. "I was scared and still am, but it is also, er, climbing is also exciting."

Ayumu wondered, *Does she get the adrenaline rush I used to get and enjoy?* She injected a fat dose into him when she fell. He hadn't experienced the sensation in a very long time. But it was very different when somebody else was at risk. His utter helplessness at that moment made him cry. He didn't want that awful feeling, absolutely not!

"That may not be a good idea, not so soon anyway."

"Why not?"

"Because I'm afraid!" Ayumu exploded. "Afraid that you may die, cease to exist! Ah, damn it!" He looked at the white sand beneath his feet. "Let's go back, shall we?"

Mirielle grabbed Ayumu's arm and walked silently beside him. He tried to shake off the hand inconspicuously, but that only made Mirielle's grip tighter. Hes eyes couldn' t settle on a spot. Then he decided: no more Mirielle. He accelerated his pace, opened the door, pushed her inside, and shouted, "Uncle Shinji, we are back! I'm leaving now."

*
**

The two did not meet again until Mirielle turned sixteen. Shinji pushed, "C'mon, what's the big deal. You keep refusing. It is just a kid's birthday. Does she not deserve some normalcy in this crazy place?" The uncle couldn't fathom that, to Ayumu, Mirielle was not just a kid. He stayed the course, but the desire to see her grew stronger with each passing year and finally got the best of him. His resistance crumbled, and this time he went. When he saw her, his heart felt like bursting.

A BRIEF MANIFESTATION

Mirielle had sat on the steel fence, wearing ripped black stockings, a miniskirt revealing red panties, a dark purple blouse also torn, boots, chains, and a spiked collar on their neck. They were holding a beer can. A six-pack, already short of two containers, was perched on the redbrick fence post next to them.

They drank from the can, burped, and laughed. "Excuse me!"

"Fits the image. Why a lowly goth now?" Their father took a sip from his brew.

"Well, why not? I wanna try it."

"All by yourself would be hard, and my acting skills suck."

"No worries, Dad, you don't have to be everywhere for me." Mirielle jumped from the fence and hurled the can in the rubbish bin. Then took the remaining beers and the cigarettes, waved goodbye, and walked away.

Leo followed them . . . her . . . him with his gaze until they turned around the corner, then scratched his scalp and walked inside the house. Ah, that trait . . . No wonder so many people in the old world were so often outright hostile toward trans individuals. The confusion . . . nobody wanted that. The weirdness of the proposition, the cognitive dissonance . . .

And he himself—did he not go too far? Most people simply switched pronouns as Mirielle changed shape. Maybe—he inhaled deeply—maybe he was desperate to differentiate his child from their mom, and this was his way. Mirielle was Elise reincarnated. Right now only the outfits they chose set their female form apart from her. Was it deliberate, Leo wondered? If so, how did they know what their mother liked? Not the androgynous stuff, the girly clothes.

Perhaps he was overthinking it. Shall he just not sit and watch the sunset with a drink in hand? He raised his gaze. The sun had already moved behind the mountain range. He pushed the front door open, walked inside, slumped into the nearest armchair, and lifted his feet onto the table, arms crossed, resting on his chest. Then he unfolded them, scratched his head again, and exhaled noisily. Mirielle was not an ordinary adolescent, no prior experience to rely on. Were they happy with their life —life in a strange world and with no one else like them? Leo sensed tension and unease in them at times, but upon inquiring, the answer was along the lines of "Nobody is always in a good mood." True, he had no argument.

He detected motion behind him and twisted his neck. Wasilla immediately halted her advance. "Caught in the act." Leo stretched his mouth.

Wasilla smiled in return and sat on the armrest. "Are you day-dreaming?"

"No. Thinking of Mirielle and the life they have. We are in uncharted territory. That gives me lots of anxiety. I want them to be happy, but if I were them, with no peers, no friends . . . ugh!"

"I understand. I am worried at times too. But is there anything we can do? As you said, uncharted territory. No other choice but be reactive." Wasilla leaned and gave him a gentle kiss on the cheek. She then turned his face at her and looked him in the eyes. "Relax." She reached up and, barely touching, guided his eyelids down.

Ah, the lesbian in his life. The lesbians. Sometimes he forgot that Abigail was queer too and was thinking only of Wasilla. But Abigail was his daughter, and Wasilla, well, she was his "sister" for a while. Until one day, a year or so after Elise drifted away, she came into the living room, stood in front of him, and dropped her nightgown. He remembered looking up and raising his eyebrows. "Wass?"

"I can hear you yanking sometimes."

Leo blushed. "Er, so?"

"I also masturbate; maybe we can help each other."

"But . . ." Leo tried to find words. He was sure that his face was bright red. "You-you are my sister, and you are also queer."

"I am queer indeed, but not your sister, no."

"OK, true, but . . . I don't know. You are not attracted to men, so how can I help you?"

"We can try, who knows."

Perhaps. Simon and Ruth were managing somehow; in fact, he could not recall seeing Elise's mom so glowing and relaxed. Her happiness seemed to be overshadowed only by the drift of her daughter.

"I, er, I . . ." Leo admitted to himself that looking at her turned him on. The sister thing was not holding water very well. Wasilla kneeled, hesitantly extended her hand, and placed it in his crotch. Then she pressed lightly. Leo clenched his teeth. Incest was what he had programmed himself to think of when she was involved. He grabbed her hand, lifted it, and kissed the palm.

"I am not your sister," Wasilla repeated softly.

"I know. What would you have done if you were in my shoes? Something had to give. I had a crush on you, remember, but you are untouchable as far as I am concerned."

"Not anymore; you can touch. And I have mixed feelings about this too."

Leo again kissed the hand he was holding, then pulled the gown and covered Wasilla. "Let me think about it. Let *us* think about it. You wouldn't be offended, would you? I mean, it feels wrong to force you into something you are not cut out for."

"You are not forcing me into anything; I am here of my own volition. I . . . I love you, Leo. Not like Lizzy did, but you grew on me a helluva lot over the years as a person. Even your reluctance to let me give you pleasure; it makes me want to do it even more. No offense, but I no longer perceive you as a man. Do you know what I am struggling with right now?"

"Of course I don't."

"Your hair, your body hair. Ugh!" Wasilla wrinkled her nose. "But OK, let's rethink it." She smiled, then suddenly leaned forward and kissed his lips, stood up and walked away, nightgown in hand.

Leo chuckled quietly and pondered. That was unexpected. Perhaps he should shave his body to make it less repulsive, but he would be as hairy as before the very next time he woke up from his sleep. Still, it was worth a shot. He appreciated what Wasilla did, and he desired her intimacy, no doubt, but with sex it was never just about him; it was about them, regardless of who he was with at any given time.

⁂

A week later, when Ruth picked up her granddaughter for another sleepover, Wasilla took a prolonged gaze at him, then asked, "Well?"

Leo had no doubts; it was a reminder. He approached silently and laid his hands on her shoulders, then caressed her cheek, leaned, and buried his face in her hair. It smelled clean and fresh. She twitched, causing Leo to spring back. He bit his lips and shook his head, as if trying to dispose of some guilt.

Wasilla glided her index finger down his nose, pushed the tip, and smiled. "OK, take your time."

Had she reached down to his treasure or sought his lips, maybe he would cross the threshold, but hell, she was queer. How could she find intimacy with a man enjoyable? Would he be able to rise to the occasion?

Once planted, the offer Wasilla extended was difficult to uproot, though. Suddenly, his body awoke to its own desires, to wishing to again be touched by someone else. He didn't think of Beatrice; the memories of Elise acted as a brake. Instead, he found Simon and asked him for help.

"It will grow back soon," the other man said.

"I know, but I need to do it."

"May I ask why?"

"Well . . ."

"OK, fine, sorry, doesn't matter." Simon waved his hands. "We must find a barbershop; it would be far easier with pro tools."

As soon as the deed was done, Leo rushed back home and changed to a long-sleeved shirt, then casually peeked into Wasilla's room. She had kneeled on the floor in front of a large canvas, needle in hand. She liked needlework and was creating beautiful pieces, which then went to excite the eyes of anyone she could see. They also placed her works in shops in Old Town and saw them disappearing. Maybe other ghosts liked them too and took them home.

"Want me to put the canvas on an easel?" Leo asked, nodding.

"Yeah, that would be nice, thanks." Wasilla looked at him and squinted. Did she notice the change? Leo readily showed her his back; there was an easel in the storage room downstairs.

When he returned, she had undressed and was sitting quietly on the edge of the bed, holding a flower in her hand; there was a vase on her windowsill, now short of one of its occupants. Her tresses were let loose, and her cheeks were turning red. Leo leaned the unfolded easel against the wall and unbuttoned his shirt. "Is that OK?"

Wasilla rose and ran her palm down his chest. "Much better, thank you!" She looked up smiling. Leo dropped the shirt on the floor, caressed her cheek, and asked, "Well, what now? Forgive me for being non-assertive, but I, well, I don't know what would turn you on, give you butterflies."

"Let's get rid of the remainder of your clothes first." She unbuttoned his trousers and pulled the zipper down.

Leo did the rest himself, took her hand, and touched it with his lips. Wasilla kissed his own. Leo pressed his palm against her cheek and let it linger there for a while, then shyly touched her breasts. Wasilla closed her eyes and traced his flanks with her hands, then wrapped her arms around him and cuddled up, while rubbing her body slowly onto his own. His heartbeat accelerated; the touch felt amazing! At this moment he wished he had the Internet to find out what queer women liked, but all he could do now was let her take the lead and look for hints. His private part, though, didn't care. Leo could not control the uprising.

Wasilla wasn't helping either when it came to that. She pushed her palm against his dick and pressed it, drew his nipples into her mouth, and traced circles around them with her tongue, then nibbled lightly. She seemed to like rubbing into something, as she did it again, more vigorously this time. Yeah, he remembered! She and Elise did that a lot. He tugged her down as he sat on the edge and directed her to straddle his thigh. She cooperated, found his lips, and offered her tongue. Then she started rubbing her petals in the freshly shaved skin. Leo felt a mild jolt and took a deep breath.

"Ah, baby . . ." Wasilla moaned quietly, her eyes closed. Then she nudged them open, crossed gaze with his, and added, "Yes, I know it's you."

Leo smiled. She wrapped her arms around his neck and continued, speeding up, her breathing getting faster and more vocal. Leo's hands kept running over her. He was eager to go in but kept his teeth clenched instead. Wasilla was moaning loudly now, having clutched his hand with both of hers, glancing occasionally through the tears rolling down her face. Then she arched backward, shivered, and slid down on the floor. She grabbed his penis with both hands and pushed and pulled repeatedly, while biting her lips. It was Leo's turn to cast a moan. Suddenly, she drew his penis into her mouth and rocked her head. Leo squinted for a moment then laid hands on her shoulders. *Why did she do that?* Not something he would expect. But why stop her either? He could barely hold it anymore. "Wass!" he called as a warning. "Wass!"

She withdrew the buzzing appendage an instant in advance and rested her head on his thigh, observing the eruption. "One day I may try its taste," she said and looked up.

Leo shook his head. "Amazing! I, er, I didn't expect you to go this far. As if you exactly knew what to do. Thank you!"

"C'mon, man." Wasilla rose and straddled his thigh again. "We've watched each other many times, haven't we? You also knew what to do. Wanna do more?" She playfully shook her breasts.

"We must switch places."

"Why?" Wasilla stood up.

"You will see. Now, sit." Leo kneeled low, pushed her legs up, and put his tongue to work. She rocked her hips.

This is how it started all those years ago. They learned to enjoy each other in the flesh. They were careless at times; on several occasions, one or the other caught the puzzled gaze of Mirielle standing by the door, sucking on her thumb or with her stuffed bunny in her hand. But for some reason both dismissed it and carried on. A guilty pleasure that was, was it not?

"I am amazed that you made me enjoy intercourse with a man."

"You were a good teacher." Leo bit lightly on her earlobe.

"No, you were a good observer. And listener." She leaned backward and pinched his cheeks.

True, after that first time, he simply asked her what she liked. He let her straddle him, hold his legs spread, insert his arm in the gap between them, and rub her labia with his forearm. Wasilla rested her arms on his shoulders and slowly rocked her hips.

Then the guilty pleasure reared its head again. Mirielle appeared in the door frame, smiling, boots in hand. When they saw the scene, they froze, the smile faded, then they took a step back, threw the boots, ran upstairs, and slammed the door of their room.

Wasilla paid no attention, just a noise in the background. Leo squeezed her hand. "Wass, Mirielle . . ."

"Mirrie! I love her!"

"They're upset!" Leo brought his arm to a halt.

"Ah, how?"

"They saw us again."

"So?"

"They were upset," Leo repeated. "Did you not hear the door slam?"

"Hm, weird. She is aware that we are banging, she knows what it is, she masturbates for sure—I was doing it at her age . . . No, there must be something else. OK, let's try to find out." She abandoned Leo's lap and headed up.

Leo slipped into his clothes, zipped up, and followed.

Wasilla knocked on the door. No response. She glided her hand over the handle but did not push it down.

"Mirielle, did we upset you?" Leo raised his voice. Still no response. He leaned against the wall, hands behind his back. He saw no reason to apologize; a glimpse at one's parents enjoying themselves was no big deal.

The latch clicked and the door slowly went ajar. Mirielle looked at them with moist eyes. Wasilla reached for their hand; however,

Mirielle hurriedly hid it behind their back. Then stepped to the side to let them enter.

"You shouldn't be pissed, Mirrie." Leo switched walls.

"I am not. I've never been upset with your making love. I can only be envious because I am still a virgin and my chances at finding partners are slim, but that's all." They smiled wearily, fidgeting their hands. "It was her . . ."

"Her?" Wasilla spoke first.

"Yes, her . . ." Mirielle's voice was unsteady. "It was Mom."

"Wait, wait, wait . . ." Leo departed from the wall. "How could it be your mother? Yes, you two look practically the same, but she drifted away shortly after you were born!"

Mirielle slowly shook their head. "No."

Leo stepped closer and took his child's hands. "Please explain." He led them to the bed, and both balanced on the edge. Wasilla kneeled on the floor.

"Mom lives inside me . . . I am her."

"But how?" Leo let out.

They shrugged. "I started having flashbacks to times before my birth. I remembered you two, I was with you two . . . not as Mirielle . . . as Elise . . ." They looked at Leo, shivering. "I also know the things you know, Dad, but it is different. I have your memories as well, but I am never you."

Leo looked around, got up, pulled a blanket from the closet and wrapped Mirielle, stroked their hair, and sat back. He'd done embarrassing shit for sure, which they were allegedly aware of, but he pushed the thought aside; his concern now was for them alone.

"When you said that it was Elise and not you, what did you mean? What did you feel?"

Mirielle cowered.

"Wass, get Mirrie something to drink please."

Wasilla trotted downstairs and in a while she returned holding a glass of juice and was fully clothed. Mirielle held the glass, gulped, and proceeded. "It is me and Mom sharing this body. When she has control, I am dormant. I don't know what is going on until we swap, and then I remember her actions. It is the same for her. We share memories . . . whatever we do, whatever we feel, we both get to know."

"When did it start?"

"Mm, not sure, has been a while but not that long. But she is getting stronger; she took over on her own. Today."

"Can we talk to her?"

Mirielle sighed and closed their eyes. Then shook their head. "I can't make myself sink, and she's not helping. Ugh! It is so hard to describe! I can't reach her right now . . ."

Multiple personality disorder was in Leo's mind, but it also could be something else. This was a crazy, crazy world. He had to ask his mother for assistance.

"Mirrie, in the old world your Granny Ann was a doctor and had dealt with such cases—people sharing a body. Maybe she would have advice for us? I suppose your mom knows that we need to talk, yes?"

"Perhaps . . . she should have the memory of the conversation as I do. And I know you are referring to nutcases, and she was a cuckoo doc—"

"Mirielle!"

They cowered again. "Sorry!"

"Ugh, as much as it pisses me off when you blurt out something like that, I am also in a way relieved." He did not elaborate further. He stood up and strode toward the door, followed by Wasilla.

"Leo!" Mirielle suddenly cried out. "Wass!" followed by a thud.

The zombies braked and turned in sync. Mirielle had kneeled on the floor, hands clutched to the chest, eyes open wide, looking at them and panting. Their voice trembled when they spoke. "That was her . . . Mom."

Leo joined them on the mat, held Mirielle's head, and looked them in the eyes. "Lizzy? Elise, please come out!"

Mirielle slowly turned their head from side to side, dragging their father's hands. "She sank again. Sorry, Dad."

Leo embraced them tightly. "Not your fault. Not your fault. Wow! You *are* a 'they' after all!"

Wasilla slapped him hard.

"Ouch! What did you do this for?"

"You are so insensitive at times with your jokes."

"That wasn't a fuckin' joke! That's a fact!"

"Dumbass! Do you think that Mirrie is having fun? Leo, I can't believe it!" Wasilla threw her hands in the air. "You have a heart of gold, but sometimes you are such an inconsiderate jerk!"

"Mom!"

A pair of eyes quickly moved questioningly to the caller.

"Mom, er, Wass," Mirielle clarified, "it is OK. I know Dad; I'm fine."

"I guess that this is what makes me attractive," Leo murmured while massaging the spot. "Pure golden hearts are boring."

Wasilla awaited the moment he exposed his neck and slapped him again. Mirielle couldn't help but laugh.

WHAT IS LOVE?

Ayumu nibbled on his lip when Mirielle showed up at the school, wearing a uniform. He had volunteered to be her classmate for the upcoming "academic" year when they met again at the sweet sixteen birthday bash. Nobody knew what the season was. The cherry trees blossomed, then a few days later it was like late summer, then spring again, or a brief winter. But Mirielle's parents were trying hard to establish a semblance of normalcy and insisted on her attending school and going through the rites to the extent possible. But with no other kids, it was a lonely affair, which the parents tried to overcome by shape-shifting and pretending to be peers. He was moved when his Aunt Mayumi shared the story and revealed that she had volunteered too.

When the opening day was agreed upon, in the morning Ayumu found a uniform neatly stacked on his desk and donned it, then twisted his neck trying to catch a glimpse of himself. He was aware that the face was out of reach, but the rest of his physique was not taboo, and thinking of those days made him feel nostalgic. And alone. His friends were still alive and that was good, of course. Probably. So, when his eyes focused on the girl at the door, his heart rushed.

"C-c-come in," he stuttered.

Mirielle stepped inside, stood in the center, bowed down, and then said in Japanese, "Good morning! My name is Mirielle, and I am honored to be here with you today!"

"Just pick a desk," Ayumu answered, having managed to reclaim his composure.

"Ah, are you the local bully?" Mirielle smiled and sat at the desk next to him. "You are so rude."

Ayumu cracked a laugh. "I could be. It is up to you."

"How?"

"No idea. I will let you know when I figure it out."

"Arigato!"

"Attention everybody!" a male voice sounded.

Ayumu started laughing uncontrollably at the sight of his uncle pretending to be a teacher. Then grunted, "Ouch!" and held the burning spot on his neck.

"Show respect, you rascal!" Mirielle rubbed her hand.

"Seems you are the bully now."

"Silence!" Shinji barked, eliciting more laughs.

The first day was entertaining, and he recalled information he'd forgotten as his uncle went through the lessons for the day. He kept glancing to his right. The girl was sometimes absorbed by the story his uncle was telling and sometimes bored. Sometimes she laughed at Shinji's clumsy jokes and at others scoffed. She looked so human, so ordinary, yet so magical. He dragged his feet in the direction of his apartment, his sighs leaving a trail in the air behind him.

Ayumu forfeited the elevator and climbed the façade to his balcony, flexing his muscles and suppressing his thoughts. He was in love with Mirielle. He'd been in love with her for a while. She was older now; things would not be weird if he confessed. But he was ancient in comparison.

*
* *

Mirielle could detect the stream of affection emanating from the left. She knew that it was called "love"; Ayumu was in love with her. She liked Ayumu, but was it love too? She liked Walid as well. Her mom liked Steve, not her father. Mirielle wrinkled her nose. *Why not Dad?* What was the difference between liking and loving? Why was her mom in love with her father, but only liked Steve? She delved into memories; then Shinji's voice brought her back: "Mirielle-san, will you answer the question?"

"Er . . . I-I did not understand."

"Your Japanese is perfect; don't give me that!" Shinji furrowed his eyebrows.

Mirielle heard something like hiccups coming from the desk on the left; she glanced over. Ayumu had gagged himself with both hands, his face bright red. She looked up at his uncle. Shinji's eyes were flipping from her to Ayumu and back, his lips squeezed into a tiny slit. He then grunted and landed a blow on Ayumu's head with the book he held in his hands. Ayumu's laughter erupted unrestrained.

Shinji sighed and turned to her. "Seriously, Mirrie-chan."

"OK, I am sorry, I wasn't listening. What did you ask?"

When school was over, Mirielle declined the offer to be walked home and climbed the path to the old temple. Incense was burning as usual, delivering a pleasant, calming aroma. Would new sticks appear if she watched closely? The air next to her moved as if someone fanned it with their palm, and the agarwood fragrance tickled her nostrils. Mirielle stepped to the side. Was belief a thing here or were the dead performing the rituals because they induced tranquility and a sense of well-being?

The churches back in her original hometown—the smaller ones—were often under lock and key, and the pompous cathedral on the top of the hill felt like a museum. It was accessible, but there were no burning candles, no smell of frankincense, and everything felt untouched, sterile. The interior décor was also somewhat off. She had spotted unfinished woodwork, and the icons—the faces of the saints—were sometimes smudged as if the painter's hand had jerked. She had consulted her parents' memories and confirmed that that was not the case in the other world. But then she also did not find many memories of church interiors.

Mirielle liked coming to the temple, curling up under a tree, and sliding into a daydream. She sat in the soft grass, leaned against the trunk, and closed her eyes. Then she popped them open.

Elise ran her gaze around and stuck her thumb into her mouth. Yeah, why was she crazy about Leo? Why was she in love? She craved his presence and his embrace. With Steve—yes, it was comforting snuggling up into his large frame, but not strictly a necessity. She could easily shrug off his inattention, whereas when Leo was absorbed in his thoughts, she felt abandoned. Her heart didn't melt from Steve's touch. Depending on the location, it was arousing indeed. The location—yes, it had to be specific, her vulva, her thighs, her breasts. With Leo, anywhere his hands made contact, the emotion was that of attraction and desire—to be held, kissed, penetrated. Yes, "penetrated" perhaps sounded harsh, but it was a fact; she wanted him inside her. She missed him so much! Wasilla and Beatrice had him now. She withdrew her thumb, her eyelashes flickered, and her consciousness slipped away.

Mirielle wiped the saliva on her skirt, rose to her feet, went to the altar, pressed her palms together and bowed, then stepped back and headed home.

Ayumu wondered whether to tail her further but then decided that following her to the temple without her consent was bad enough. He waited for Mirielle to disappear and ran upstairs to the altar. He clasped his hands and bowed, praying for strength to confess. Then he rose abruptly, dismissed the prayer, and sat on a bench, his shoulders slumped. Prayers. They changed nothing. Perhaps added a bit of hope, but that was all.

"Mirrie-chan!" Ayumu called from the corner.

Mirielle lifted her gaze and parked it on the boy. He had shape-shifted down from his usual twenty-nine. She swallowed the rice ball bite and waved him over.

"Sorry, I shall not disturb you now." Ayumu was ready to reverse course, but Mirielle shook her head.

"No, it is OK. What's up, big brother?"

"Er . . ." Ayumu stuttered. Her words lashed him where it hurt. Big brother confessing in love! What was he supposed to do now? He blushed, as his eyes focused on a point behind her. "Er, I-I was wondering if you would want to see a movie outside home." There! He strung a full sentence together without stuttering too much!

"Sure! Can I also bring another friend?"

"Who?"

"Walid, my mom's little brother. He also comes to school with me, but you can't see him, and I still lack strength to change that."

"What d-do you mean?" The stutter returned. So, there was another!

Mirielle appeared detached for a moment, then said, "Nothing. I just wish it was not like that."

"Er, OK." Perhaps he had to make a move now! "He, that Walid, do you like him?"

"Yep!" Mirielle dangled her legs, then stopped, took the lunch box, and offered it to the confused teen. "Here, have some."

Ayumu shook his head. "No thanks." Food was not on the list of his desires right now. He frantically searched his past for guidance. What did he do when he was alive? What did he tell Keiko, his girlfriend? Where did all important memories go? His face twisted, then he felt a jolt when Mirielle laid her palm over his hand. He clutched the seat of the bench.

"I can tell that you are confused and, well, probably in love," Mirielle said softly. "You know that my sensors are more powerful than yours. Is that not so?"

Ayumu nodded briskly, his heart pounding. He turned and confirmed, "Yes, you are right. I am in love with you!" Then quickly looked away, his hand burning under her palm, yet unwilling to depart.

Mirielle let the silence linger for a while, then spoke. "I-I am not sure if my feelings toward you are this intense. I feel you close, a good friend, but I understand that being just a friend can be disappointing—"

"And?" Ayumu raised his head.

"And maybe . . ." Mirielle's eyes suddenly changed, and the rest of the sentence sounded hurried and cold. "We shall learn to live with that."

Ayumu reverted to true, got up, and bowed deeply. "Of course, Mirrie-chan!"

She said nothing, just kept staring at him. Ayumu hissed, pivoted, and walked away with wide strides. Tiny tentacles of hate tried latching onto his mind, but he clenched his teeth and beat them back into hiding. Love was often one-sided and he knew that. Keiko was the one in love with him, but he only liked her—albeit a lot. Now it seemed it was his turn to be liked.

WALID

Walid never dared show his true self to his sister's girlfriend. She tried a few times, then gave up and until her drift both saw each other as kids. He liked what he observed, he always did, but his sister, the scar, having to explain . . . it was too much, and he took refuge in age. He was ten when they last met and she was twelve.

He consoled his sister, though, when the relationship was on the brink. Wasilla cried a lot and called it quits when Elise went to live with a man she knew and met again, but was it the loneliness of this existence or something else? At the end, his sister resigned and invited Elise back into her life. And she'd been happy ever since. Well, with some exceptions, of course. Accepting Leo was a rational decision, not an emotional one, but then big sis grew to love the man. Odd. Then the time of the lingering drift became associated with a lot of anguish too. Yet, she had a life. He would have just existed if not for the sacrifice Wasilla made.

Then Mirielle was born. He could see her! He wanted to be in the room to observe, but Wasilla kicked him out with the excuse that it was too crowded. Then she came out with a baby in her hands. Cute little creature!

Walid was drawn to babies somehow. For a man, that seemed strange, he thought, but this wasn't his only peculiarity. He also wanted to play with dolls when he was a kid. He had those flashes of memories when he played with his sister's, then blanks. He was envious of Wasilla's dresses. This was how he got the scar. Once—he was eleven and a half—he slipped into a dress and danced in front of the mirror until their father saw him and yelled at him to get changed without delay. Walid ignored the order and continued dancing in the hallway.

Furious, his father, Tarek, came to him, pulled his hair, and took a forceful swipe with his hand. His commemorative ring tore the soft skin and bruised Walid's right eye. He screamed as the blood gushed out. Unperturbed, his father hit him again and ripped the dress, leaving him part naked. Then he didn't take him to the hospital. The order was to stay at home until the wound healed by itself and a total ban on mentioning the true cause of the injury. The official version stated that it was received while on a trip to Beirut; the Jews did it with their frequent bombing of the largely defenseless city. The wound healed and the damage to his eye was superficial and left no lasting effect, but the scar remained.

Walid was afraid of his father. Everybody in the household was. The man was very strict and forceful in his parenting. When a child disobeyed, the man did not hesitate to pull his belt. Disagreeing was not an option. Their mom had to always wear long sleeves and a scarf. When Wasilla trimmed short one of her skirts and was seen wearing it, Tarek yelled as usual, lifted the skirt, and belted her once, leaving red marks across her thighs. When she disobeyed and wore the skirt again, he belted her mercilessly and began drawing lines with a permanent marker or a ball point pen on her thighs. One thing Walid had to grant his father was his persistence; he kept doing it until she finished school and one day ran away.

On that day he was very sad. She confided in him of her plan, but he didn't take it seriously until she failed to show up in the evening, and their mother came out of Wasilla's room sobbing, holding a squashed envelope in her hand.

"You!" She pointed angrily at their father. "You made her do that!"

"Do what?"

She slammed the envelope on the table. "This!"

Tarek looked inside, pulled out a piece of paper, read it, and cursed, "*Haywan!*"

"Yes, you are an animal!"

For the first time, Walid saw his mother furious and brave. He knew what the message said; one waited for him, too, under his pillow.

Tarek hit Fatimah with the back of his hand, the same way he had delivered the smack to Walid that made the scar. Her head bounced off the wall, and she fell to the floor. Her nose was bleeding. Tarek then squashed the paper and threw it at her. "*Alkalbat alqadhiratu!* I gave her roof; I gave her food! And this is how she repays me!"

Walid stood frozen, silent. He wanted to defend Wasilla, he wanted to defend his mom, but he was unable to. He was a damn coward! Walid started crying. His father gave him a contemptuous glance and stormed out of the room.

Fatimah staggered slowly to her feet. "Your sister has left us. I wish I had her strength. Pray for her, Walid!"

From there, it was all downhill for him. He hated himself for not being able to stand up to his bullying father. He felt uncomfortable in his body; he found it to be too weak, neither woman nor a man. He had an unsightly scar and no facial hair to speak of despite his age. He wanted to wear tight leggings and makeup and dreamed of being a performing artist—a dancer or a mime. He even took secret lessons with Wasilla's help and joined an amateur troupe. They performed at festivals sometimes, but mostly basked. The heavy makeup ensured his anonymity and hid the scar, and those were relatively happy days. One of the girls in the troupe, Carla, seemed to like him—she was often around him, stealing glances. She even kissed him a few times after a good performance or for a holiday. "Merry Christmas, yay!"

Wasilla noticed and pushed him. "Man, go for her. I know attraction when I see it." But he was too insecure. When Wasilla left, he blamed himself—his cowardice and unmanliness. He took to drinking, but he was too weak for even that—the nasty hangovers made him go sober again. Somehow, though, he carried on.

Then somebody recognized him during a street performance, and the information reached his father. Tarek confronted him on the spot. "Did I not tell you to man up!" He rummaged through Walid's room and discovered the costumes and the gear. What followed was another mighty smack. "All this goes into the trash! And no more theater crap! I want a scientist! A man!" Walid cowered and sobbed. His father went ballistic. "*Kus!* You make me sick!"

Walid could take no more—no more of his father and no more of himself. He bought rope from the hardware store across the street, climbed the six floors to the attic, chose a truss, carefully prepared the noose, inserted his neck, and kicked the old chair. He did not die instantly; he kept struggling for several minutes until the lack of oxygen shut down his brain.

When he awoke, he screamed in horror. He was back in his room!

*
**

"You screamed." Mirielle shook him lightly. "Did you have a bad dream?"

"A dream?"

"Yes, you dozed off."

"Ah, sorry, Mirrie."

"No problem. So?"

"It was the nightmare—the day of the suicide." Walid looked to the side.

"You don't have to be ashamed. You cannot turn back time and change a damn thing. Existing with so much guilt, why do you have to do that? It solves no problem." Mirielle felt sorry for her friend. All he wanted was to be free to live his own life. She rolled closer and pecked him on the cheek. Walid reached and squeezed her hand.

Mirielle liked him too, like Ayumu, maybe more. She remembered Walid as always being there, and she had grown attached. He played with her when she was a small child. She rode on his shoulders and on his back. He would transform into his young self and take her on excursions in the neighborhood, through overgrown backyards and side alleys. She would become a boy, and both would chase a ball, climb trees, explore the buildings. He would dress as a girl, and they would play with dolls.

"I wish I was like you." Walid sighed.

"Yeah? In what sense?"

Walid smiled. "Turn myself into a girl at will. As you do."

"I am primarily a girl who can take the shape and characteristics of a boy. Dad calls me 'they' because of that . . . sex fluidity, you see?"

"I think I wanted to be a girl. I felt that my mind did not belong to this body."

"Even if I do this?" Mirielle turned and targeted his lips, but then her eyes twitched, and she hit the brakes.

Walid arched his brows. "Do what?"

Mirielle stuck her tongue out, thumbed her ears, and wiggled her fingers.

Walid chuckled. "Yeah, even when you do that."

"Good, I like impersonating monkeys."

"Have you ever seen one? I mean, a real one."

"No, and I stand no chance." Mirielle shook her head.

"Well, then we shall go to a zoo, maybe even to Africa."

"Are there any real people here?" He was not getting it; people around them were often forgetting that simple fact.

"Ah, this is what you meant. You are right; there are none. And yeah, I don't think that monkeys do what you just did, even the real ones. But keep going."

"Sure!" She inserted her index fingers in her nostrils and pulled up. "Gaaaa!"

Walid laughed. He wanted to draw her in his arms, but her body language kept him at bay. He always liked the bubbly, unashamed kid, but then, as she grew older, it became increasingly harder for him to ignore her femininity. He was drawn to her and very confused at the same time. He wanted to be a girl, yet he was attracted to one.

She paid no attention to his lack of facial hair or to his big, ugly scar, and they also formed a troupe and entertained the seers from time to time.

"Why are you dressing like that?" Walid asked. For a while now, she'd clothed herself in ripped stockings, military boots, and tutus, and wore chains or spiked leather collars, having abandoned her androgynous style.

"Mm, I like it. It is fun. I can't see my face, but I can catch a glimpse of the rest in panes of glass, and, well, I'm going through my ugly period."

Ugly indeed. Her outfits hurt his eyes, but he didn't dare criticize. She adopted the tutus from their shows, as wearing one for the dances made sense. Perhaps this was her way to be creative and express personality. And he had to admit that there was something provocative in her appearance, something that warmed his blood, something sensual. He pouted and squeezed the seat. Then he grabbed her and tried to find her lips with his, but Mirielle swiftly turned her head, and the kiss landed on her ear. Walid pulled his arms back and stuttered, "S-sorry!"

"Ouch!" she cried out and covered the lobe with her palm. "Ugh! That was bad."

"Sorry!" Walid blushed and cowered. As he always did! He was awful! Weak!

Mirielle looked at him and sighed. "I get it, but I am not yet ready, Walid. And please be more assertive; you are ninety-five!" She furrowed her eyebrows. "I mean, there's nothing wrong with having feelings, but you act as a teen."

Walid nodded slowly. "You are right," wondering when this about seventeen-year-old girl became so perceptive and wise. Then he heard a buzzing in his head; somebody was calling. Was it his mom? "Something's happening; I shall go." He stood up. "May I?" He bent forward.

"That's better!" Mirielle smiled and offered her cheek.

Walid pecked it and ran.

Mirielle followed him with her gaze until he swerved into a street, and she could follow no more. Then she turned her head around, surveying the surroundings, listened for a nearby presence, then unzipped her skirt, slid her hand inside the panties with pinched fingers, split the labia, and rubbed. Her mother's habits were undoubtedly alive.

MALERIELLE

Mirielle wrinkled her nose and buried her hands in her dense hair while looking out through the window of her room. The ocean was angry today. The waves were high, their crests foaming in the distance from the strong wind. Why was Elise so much against it? She wanted to experience it in person; she was old enough. What if she were male? As in Malerielle.

Mirielle looked down and touched his penis, then swallowed hard. He had paid no attention to the appendage before, when he shape-shifted. The penis was there, just hanging, small, never doing anything. He paid no attention to his vagina either, until he began to feel tickling, when he touched, and the area became lush. The penis tickled too. He held it again, lifted it, and rubbed it with his palm. The tingles flared anew, and the penis grew larger. Mirielle browsed the memories he held. Ah, yes, this is how it worked. He wrapped his hand around it and squeezed a few times, precipitating tension of the muscles in the groin. Suddenly, he felt a desire to insert the penis somewhere, preferably in a cavity slippery and warm. Like a vagina. His own? But that was impossible. What did his dad do with no pussies around? Ah, lie in bed naked and stimulate the nerves. Kind of what he was doing lately in his female form. Did his dad feel the same degree of pleasure as himself or his mom? Mirielle stretched into his bed. The cold linen caressed his body. Mirielle enjoyed the sensation, flaring at each rub and stroke. It was very similar to what he elicited from his other thing. He switched hands. The tiny sparks became more intense as he labored. Then he kneeled in bed and changed hands again, working faster. The sparks turned brighter still. Mirielle closed his eyes; his long hair fell over his face.

"Mirrie, you may be late for school," Beatrice said after opening the door. "Oh, sorry," she mumbled and quietly shut it.

Mirielle twisted his mouth as the charge in his groin kept going up. Then it spilled out in liquid form, and his entire body shook. He moaned, his heart racing, his hand tightly wrapped around his dick, wanting to squeeze every last drop of pleasure from it; however, in a while, the penis began shrinking. Mirielle took several deep breaths instead, and the pounding inside his chest wound down. He looked at the remains of masculine pride in his hand and pouted. So, this was what it was like to be male.

Shit! Didn't Beatrice say that he was going to be late? Mirielle jumped from the bed and pulled the closet door open. Next to his tartan skirt and white blouse hung a navy-blue *gakuran*. Mirielle smiled—the ancestral spirits had spoken. He was going to be a boy today.

Walid jerked backward in his chair at the sight of the boy standing at the door of the classroom. Where did he come from? He had not seen a new face for ages. Then he emitted a loud sigh—Mirielle! She'd decided to be a boy today. She hadn't flipped to her male persona in his presence in years; he had almost forgotten that it existed.

"Good morning, everybody! My name is Mirielle, and I am honored to be here today!" The boy bowed.

Walid did not catch all the words. His Japanese was lagging despite him being a faithful classmate. He was unable to see Mayumi, their Japanese teacher, and had to learn the language aided by Mirielle. But as she grew older, she became more of a distraction than help.

"Hi! What are you up to now?" He greeted him when the boy sat at the desk.

"Speak Japanese!"

"Why?"

"Because! To get better at it, of course."

"Why?" Walid repeated stubbornly. He felt dread engulfing him. He hadn't considered the drift for quite a while. Mirielle's insistence on improving a skill that might soon be completely useless reminded him that he was overdue. Who would remember the cowardly scarface from eons ago? His mother was dead, his sister was dead, his father was dead. Only his brother was not on the list; however, Jaques was six years his senior and, being rough and condescending as Tarek himself, certainly didn't make it here rather than be still alive. No way.

"What's wrong? Your face is white; you look afraid," Mirielle whispered as if Mayumi could hear.

Walid glanced at the boy and huffed, "I am a coward, didn't you know? Not in the mood today."

"Stop that nonsense! Can I improve said mood somehow?"

Walid checked the boy conversing with him head to toe. The male uniform fit well. Everything looked good on her, even the zebra stockings, the ripped orange tutus, and the chains. But why did his heart skip a beat at the sight of the tall boy with blue eyes and long dark hair shaped into a ponytail? Was he attracted to her male form too? Walid blushed; he could not deny his arousal!

Mirielle moved closer with the Japanese textbook in her hands. "Here, let's do it together."

"Is Ayumu here?"

"No. Just the two of us and Mayumi-sensei."

"Aaa . . ." Walid bleated, unable to make a comprehensible word.

"Ugh, you are horrible today!" Mirielle frowned angrily, then sought his eyes. When the two gazes crossed, Mirielle said softly, "Hey. How can I help? You are really down, it seems. What about improvising something after school? With me as a boy. It will be fun; we've never done it before. Mom liked body paint, and miming lends itself to it, but she never mimed. Perhaps she'd enjoy it."

Walid threw Mirielle a curious glance. What was that about her mother enjoying miming? She drifted away, what, sixteen years ago. Ah, perhaps Mirielle misspoke. Walid quivered—she had the same demeanor, even as a boy. It was somewhat disturbing, a completely different appearance, yet the same sunny girl.

Seventeen years! Or were they? What if time here ran at a different speed than on Earth? That would explain him still being around. Perhaps Jaques was not yet over a century old. They, the ghosts, always clung to old-world habits and conventions and, respectively, always tried to measure the passage of time in familiar units. An hour, a day, a month, a year.

He himself gave up on that, well, what felt like a long time ago. There were no moon cycles to frame a rough month, no seasons to partition the year. There was no year! The moon could go from new to full in the span of a few hours. It was a hot summer day today, but tomorrow the trees may be leafless and the ground covered in snow. Many ghosts had notebooks, keeping track of days. Those with computers should have had digital clocks, but there were none.

He remembered that shortly after relocating here, they tried to visit a Seiko factory; however, the realm refused. Before that, Wasilla blabbered about some experiments Leo and his father tried to conduct, like monitoring the sun or something, but then she went silent. Probably the tests had failed. Songs like Pink Floyd's "Time" had no meaning here. "Ticking away the moments that make up a dull day . . ." Or not quite—the days could still be dull, if not for her, er, him, er . . . Walid could not figure the right pronoun now. He glanced to his left, then looked at the blackboard, which was filled with kanji. Or was it kana? Whatever. Walid glanced again. The boy next to him was diligently writing them down in the squares of his notebook.

"Do you wanna learn Arabic too?" Walid asked.

"Hush! I'm busy!"

Walid shrugged. Working on the shows was good enough.

*_{**}

Mirielle wiped the makeup from Walid's face and sat, waving the towel, waiting for him to return the favor. Walid lingered.

"I feel like starting from scratch," Mirielle said. "Different body, different costume . . . it needs getting used to it."

"You were clumsy indeed."

"I know. But I will get it right. I am more flexible when I am a girl. And smaller. Dad—he was clumsy too. Especially when dancing!" Mirielle burst into laughter, pushed and balanced the chair on two legs. "But Mom loved it, loved him; she didn't want a pro dancer."

"How do you know so much about your parents?"

Mirielle sighed. "They shared."

Walid looked quizzically at the boy.

Mirielle caught the sentiment and added, "Ask your sis. She's heard it all."

"Ah, OK. I was puzzled for a moment. Your mom . . . do you remember anything?"

Mirielle sank in thought. Should he tell the truth or stay mute? Then he remembered that the makeup was still on and tossed the towel. "Here, wipe my face."

Walid approached, pulled out a chair, straddled it, and started removing the paint. He had done that many times before, so why was his hand unsteady now?

"You know, I wanked this morning," the boy said casually.

Walid's hand stopped. "Ah, how?"

"Are there more ways than one?"

"N-no. I guess . . ." Walid blushed.

"Why are you ashamed? My detectors scream that you are; don't try to deny. You also do it, don't you? But you are embarrassed. Why? What's so wrong with it?"

"Because we are not supposed to do it, that's why. But we can't help it." Walid threw the towel on the dresser. "Gonna take a shower now." He went to his locker, wrapped his large red towel around his hips, slipped out of his undies, tossed them on the shelf, and slammed the steel door. Then he headed to the gent's bath.

Mirielle raised his eyebrows. Don't masturbate in public—this he understood with ease. Pleasuring oneself was a private deed. But being ashamed of doing it in solitude and out of sight was a completely different matter. Why not? It felt good and there often were no partners around for a full fare. Walid—who was his partner? And Mirielle's own parents—they shared the fun and were not ashamed. Mirielle removed his clothes, untied his hair, and followed Walid into the gent's shower room.

Walid did not notice Mirielle until it was too late. The boy stood in front of his enclosure, observing silently. Walid let go of his engorged penis and turned to face the wall, blood rising to his face. "What are you doing here?" he shouted. "This is the men's room!"

There was no response. Walid feared to look. He just stood there, under the running hot water and shrouded in steam. An arm crawled around his waist, and a hand wrapped around his dick. Mirielle! He froze. Was she still a boy? Walid nudged his gaze downward, trying to catch a glimpse, but Mirielle was out of sight, only the hands. But that was enough to tell that she was still male. The hand moved slowly at first. He, though, did not. The hand was determined; it had no shame. It squeezed the glans and twisted as it moved along the shaft. It knew how to induce pleasure! Who taught it or was it how Mirielle was born? Now Walid did not want her to stop; he wanted her to take him to the end! Her, him, he liked both! He threw his head backward, squirted, and rolled his hands into tight fists. The hand's movements gradually came to a stop, as his manhood shrank.

Walid's mind went blank. He turned, looked straight into the blue eyes, then kneeled and drew the boy's penis into his mouth.

SWEET AND SOUR

Beatrice ripped the last strip, eliciting a loud "Ouch!" from the vocal cords of her victim. Then she ran her hand down the thigh. The skin was a bit bumpy and inflamed, but there were no hairs that she could detect. It would be smooth and silky soon.

"Why do we have to do it this way?" Mirielle asked and rubbed the now itchy patch.

"You can use a razor if you want, for everything, but this lasts longer. I couldn't find depilating cream, only wax strips. If it hurts too much, you can keep the hair. I doubt that anybody would care about it. All *you* can do here is wank."

"Hm . . ."

Beatrice lifted her gaze. What was the meaning of this sound? She saw Mirielle wanking in her male form; she certainly did it as a girl and that was OK. Who could she have intercourse with? Her dad? Beatrice shivered then said, "You know, I am very hairy. Wanna see?"

Mirielle nodded.

Beatrice shape-shifted and lifted her leg on the chair. "How's that?"

Mirielle giggled. "Hah, you have natural pantyhose."

"More like fuzzy socks." Beatrice chuckled.

"You are about my age now, right?"

"Sixteen," the blonde girl said. "I started grooming myself at sixteen. Or seventeen, it is all foggy, too many years have passed."

"Why did you change hair color?"

"Don't you already know? You have your dad's memories."

"This detail is missing. Maybe he forgot it, or you told him after I was born."

Beatrice checked her storage banks. Yes, she did tell Leo the story when they reconciled. Mirielle was six back then.

"Well, because . . ." Beatrice repeated the narration for his daughter.

"Seriously? People in your world are that petty?"

"Could be far worse. I was lucky in a way. Men found me attractive and when I was young, my maintenance cost was very low. I didn't have to diet. Grooming, a few exercises. Then flash cleavage or a leg and men were hooked. Only your dad resisted."

"Yeah, I know."

"You sure do. But do you know why? Well, never mind, he told me."

"He believed he was out of your league."

Beatrice nodded. "Yeah, right! But he wasn't! I still don't understand that in him. He's a good-looking man, kind, intelligent, quite attractive. Hey, will you please transform?" Beatrice felt a sudden urge to see young Leo, and he was at home. Then she guffawed.

"What?" The young man squeezed the armrests.

"Your . . ." Beatrice laughed again and pointed. "Your pussy-do . . . It looks funny with a dick!"

"Ah! You styled it, didn't you? You should have gone light on it. Then shave it all." Mirielle reverted.

"As you wish." Beatrice reached for the razor and the shaving cream. With a few strokes she removed the rest of Mirielle's pubic hair.

Mirielle ran their palm over the mound, then transformed. "How's that? Still funny?"

Beatrice's gaze was blank. Then her eyes flickered and focused on the area between Mirielle's legs. "Leo? When did you shave? Ah, crap." She had jumped.

"When were you?" Mirielle asked.

"Dunno . . . I was having sex with Leo in a salon." Beatrice looked around. "This one. Anyway, why are we here, sweetie?"

"To make me presentable, as you put it. My birthday bash is today."

*
**

"So, she showed you her weenie?" Ruth asked while swirling her glass.

"Yep, and she was so proud!" Annette said, drew from the cigarette, and exhaled exactly a couple of rings in two short puffs.

"Hah, hah, she did the same to me . . ." She burped. "Oops! Pardon me!" The wine was running circles in Ruth's head. She spilled half her drink over her tunic. "Damn!"

Annette topped up Ruth's glass, giggling, then added to her own. "Cheers!"

"Sheers!" Ruth fluffed, clumsily clinked her glass, and took a gulp. "I think I got a bit drunk," she said mostly to herself, staring down. She then reached out, grabbed Annette's hand, and gave it a long smooch. Then laughed. "You are great!"

Annette looked at her smiling yet with her eyes sharp. She had never seen Ruth drunk before. Ruth evolved her wardrobe some time into the treatment and had now become quite loose—she flaunted her legs in minidresses, sometimes her breasts. They went to the Mediterranean, the two of them, as part of the treatment, and she dared to undress in full on the beach, finally overcoming her irrational fear of being seen as born. Oddly, her daughter had screamed to be seen for twenty-odd years and could be diagnosed as an exhibitionist. Which, of course, in this realm did not matter. So different were the two.

"I was a fool!" Ruth confessed.

Annette didn't want drunk confessions and looked around for an exit, but Ruth held her hand. "Why did we not meet earlier, in the other life? You changed so much for me; you . . . you made me feel good about myself. Thanks, Ann!"

They had met before in prior life, but not as a doctor and a patient, just for brief moments crossing paths at the school. Annette had a hard time digesting that the shy woman with outdated clothes was her son's girlfriend's mother. Elise was bubbly and a rebel, and Ruth was the ultimate conformist.

Annette's eyes moved and stopped on Simon. Yeah, Elise was more reminiscent of him than she resembled her mom. His soft features and his dense, wavy hair—she had them both. But her mom was the source of the large, round eyes. Elise's copy sat a few meters away; it was so easy to compare.

"I was a fool!" Ruth repeated. "And now I have no friends. I mean that type of friend, like Lizzy had Leo . . ."

Annette was familiar with the grievance, more than she wanted to be. She felt the urge to change seats, but who knew who the empty chairs belonged to. Invisibles. That's why Ruth couldn't make new friends here; nobody could.

Wait! Who was the woman with giant breasts sitting next to Steve? Had she seen her ever before? Annette started digging deeper and deeper into her memory. Ah, yes, Steve Haaspert's girlfriend, one of them—now she remembered her. They met a few times in the hallway when Leo threw parties at home. Yeah, difficult to forget entirely a girl so "gifted." There was also that other girl with the small face and round black eyes, looking a bit like a mouse, she'd seen Steve with, Annette recalled. But she was not around. Was she still alive? She was cute, though. And this one perhaps cursed her "gift" for giving her backaches. Did she get breast reduction surgery later in life? Would have been a sensible thing to do. Annette shifted her gaze to Simon. Leo made them see each other, probably in his newly found anguish after Elise's departure. But the man next to him?

"Hey, Rue, is that Boris?" She pointed. "Over there, next to your hubby."

Ruth was chewing on a piece of cheese. "Mmm."

"Can you see people that you don't recognize?"

Ruth lingered, her eyes trying to focus on each person's face as her gaze traveled around the room. The significance of Annette's question seemed to finally reach her brain, for she straightened her spine and exclaimed, "Wait! You can see Boris? But how? Leo, again?"

"Leo's hardly madly in love with him. I don't think that he can even see him. So, no. What about those two over there?" She pointed at Steve and his companion.

Ruth's eyes grew wide.

"Hey, don't stare, it is rude." Annette elbowed her patient, but it was too late. Steve caught the stare and looked at them. His eyes moved from Ruth to Annette, then back.

"Stay here." Annette got up, patted Ruth's shoulder, and tried to locate Leo. He wasn't in his chair. Beatrice's seat was also vacant. Damn, they were a hundred years old; did they have to behave like teens? Then she shook her head—why not, indeed.

Next to Wasilla was a woman and a young man, neither of whom Annette had ever seen. She caught the similarities—they must be Wasilla's mom and her brother. Next were her ex, Richard, and his widow, Jessica. She knew these two.

Annette went outside and tried to sense the presence of her son. The ocean was delivering lazy waves in the darkness. The sky was clear, but the moon was new; only a tiny sliver was reflecting sunbeams back to whatever this place was. She heard the faint noise of lips kissing. She walked quickly and turned the corner. Leo and Beatrice were all over each other. When they saw her, they let go and began hastily adjusting their clothes.

"Sorry to interrupt, but there's something—"

"No problem, go ahead," Leo said.

"I think that I can see more than I should. There's a man with Simon and a woman—"

"Boris! What woman? One with big boobs?"

"This one I remember. Not her name, though, but, eh . . ." Annette waved her hand and pressed her lips together.

"Yeah, her boobs . . . she's Margot Stein. Who else?" Leo said fast.

"I think Wasilla's mother and brother."

"That's a lot!" Leo took a deep breath. "OK, let's try not to startle anyone. You go back and we will come in a minute."

"Weird, isn't it? What do you think is happening?" Beatrice asked after Leo's mother left.

"Must be Mirrie. Or some worldwide event." He kissed her quickly. "OK, let's go!"

Mirielle had curled up in the large armchair in the far corner of the hall, alone, head in her hands. Leo noted the new faces, cursed himself, and headed straight to Mirielle.

"I fucked up. Sorry!" He made a puppy face. Mirielle looked at him. Their eyes were reddish and wet. Leo felt the teeth of guilt sinking into his heart, and his face twisted even more.

Mirielle could no longer hold the laugh. "Leo, did you just soil yourself?"

"Huh?"

"Your face. Pity you can't see it."

Leo tried the blind man approach, which compelled additional laughter. "Ah, you are sweet."

"Whatever! Sorry again. It was your day today, and we, the old self-absorbed farts, forgot you."

"You did." Mirielle pouted.

"Are you? I mean, are you making people see?"

Mirielle nodded. "Yep."

Leo had no idea what to say next. He scratched his head.

"Ah, you also have fleas."

He looked at them. "You lost me."

"Your expression is that of a guilty puppy. You scratched your head just now; what conclusion can a logical thinker draw?" Mirielle dropped their feet on the floor.

Leo chuckled uncomfortably. They were right.

"Come, let's go to the table. Bea, say something. You look like a fish out of the water."

Leo did not move. "Tell me more about the trick. I don't even want to turn back for fear that they will all start to scream."

"When I push a bit harder, I can broadcast what I see. Your interactions when you are unable to see each other are weird; they make my head spin. I am more resilient to it now, but it is still dizzying."

"What is dizzying?"

"What I see. People passing through each other, objects replicating, then merging back . . . that is why I sometimes hold my head. I am not always crying."

Leo remembered how he saw the coffee cup duplicating when he visited his father with Elise and she was still not visible to his dad. Multiply that by ten! It could be tough.

"But you are sometimes crying, correct?" Beatrice said.

"Are you not? You are with Leo now, but what about before? What about your life?"

Leo twitched when something inside his brain clicked. He ran his palms down his face. "Unbelievable! I need some fresh air. Care to join?"

"Mmm." Mirielle ignored the shoes lying on the floor and proceeded barefoot. Beatrice was about to join them, but Leo touched her arm and shook his head.

Outside, Mirielle leaned against the wall and glanced at him shyly.

He pulled out a cigarette, lit it up, drew slowly, then exhaled and let the silence linger on.

"I want to talk to Mirielle," he said as calmly as he could when he finally delivered a sound. His heart was racing, and his hands were shaking.

Mirielle did not respond, just hesitantly moved their arm in his direction but stopped short of touch.

"Please!"

"No."

"Lizzy! Please!" He held gently the arm.

"No!" Mirielle shook his hand off and repeated, "No!" Then shoved Leo out of the way and ran toward the beach.

"Lizzy!" He rolled his ankle and fell, then sprang quickly and followed them with a limp, cursing.

Mirielle leaped over the pony wall, reached the foreshore, kneeled and started pounding with their little fists, splashing water and wet sand around. Their eyes red, tears rolling down their cheeks, falling and mixing with the tears of the sea. "No! No!"

Leo wrapped his arms around their body and clutched them. Mirielle tried to wriggle out, frantically twisting and scratching, but he held firmly. "Breathe! Breathe deeply!" He couldn't hold his own tears. "And cry," he added quietly.

Mirielle's body shook violently with each sob. Then the convulsions subsided, and Leo felt the being he held in his arms relax. He loosened his grip. Mirielle had sensed the opportunity and tried to pull free and run, but Leo reacted fast.

"Where are you trying to escape to?"

The being cowered and started crying again. Leo kissed the wet locks. "Talk—damn, my love! Damn it, Lizzy, talk! Why not? I know they're in there. I wanted to apologize."

The being shook their head slowly and wheezed, "If I let her out, I won't be able to return."

"What do you mean? I fuckin' love you so much!" Leo wanted to merge with the other one forever.

"We can no longer share the body; one of us must go. OK, it's going to be me!" The being wailed. "It's gonna be me."

"Wait!" Leo shouted. "Wait!" He squeezed tightly the body he held as if that would prevent the surrender which was about to occur. He was torn, as was the thing inside him passing for a heart, desperately trying to splice himself back and set foot on stable ground. "Don't Lizzy go!" He recalled the play of words from the day on their way to the library. His voice softened. "Don't."

"It must happen. One of us must disappear. Or we will both go insane. I was selfish. I am her mother; it is I who must leave. But I don't want to." The being sobbed again. "I want to stay with you! And her! And Wass! And I am scared, Leo!"

Leo rose and slowly helped the girl up. He was hurting, both his stupid leg and his emotions. But he would trade the leg for his Elise and his daughter at any time, if he could. And for some clarity. He didn't know how to think of the silhouette next to him: "she," "they," "Mirrie," or "Elise." He limped to the pony wall, holding the being's hand, and they both sat.

"How did you know that it was me?" the being asked.

"Ah . . ." Leo sighed. "Bits and pieces really. Mirrie never calls me by name; it is always 'Dad.' They—"

"'She,' call her 'she.' I will explain. Now go on."

"Er, she doesn't like going barefoot, unlike you. And Bea never shared her sad past with her."

"I see. You are mostly right. Except for Bea. We—me and Mirrie—share memories. What you knew, I know. You didn't want to be with me for life when we were alive. What I know, she knows. What I feel, she feels. We are one, yet—"

"Wait, why me? What I . . . ah, you had my memories too, OK. But why not my consciousness?"

"That I don't know. Perhaps because you were not due to drift away. I think that this is where it went all wrong."

"In what sense? How? Were you always here?"

The being nodded and stretched their legs. "Mirrie is a girl. She can take the shape of a boy, your shape, and . . . ah, I'd rather her explain later. When she was born, she was just a shell; then her mind began shaping up. I was inside her when you were losing me in those days. I was her and she, me. I think that I did not drift away but started dwelling inside her instead. I was unconscious for a long time, waking up occasionally, having glimpses of you or Wass, then sliding back. Her personality developed in the meantime, and when I was awake, we had a hard time . . . it is not easy to describe. Our language lacks words for these sensations. How shall I put it? Like, both of us wanted to control the body. When she was younger, I could easily overtake her, but those presences were brief for some reason. I would slip away after a short while. Then the periods of being conscious grew longer; however, she was also stronger, so she held me back. Leo, call Wass, please. I will wait."

Leo wiped his nose, snorted, took a ragged breath, and headed inside. The new faces were gone. The chairs appeared empty. The old faces turned to him. "Mirrie is not feeling well; they need to rest for a while. You carry on. Wass?"

Wasilla rose and approached, her long silk gown making rustling noises. "Why are your clothes wet? Have you been crying?" She sounded alarmed.

"Yes, I have. Come with me."

"Mirrie, what's wrong, baby?" Wasilla touched the seated girl's cheeks and tried to wipe off the traces of tears.

"This is not Mirielle . . ." Leo said.

"Liz! Oh, my God, Lizzy!" Wasilla pounced and seized the slim frame, tears splashing all over her face.

"You don't believe in gods, cutie."

"I do now! Ah, my God, you are back!" She leaned rearward and inspected her dear friend head to toe to the extent possible in the scarce light, as if hoping to see more than just the disheveled mien of her adopted daughter, then thrust forward again and enveloped the other in her arms. "I am so glad!" She locked lips with the being, then abruptly pulled back. "But wait! Where's Mirrie?"

"Inside me; I am her too. I want to say goodbye. That's why I asked Leo to call you."

"Not another one! No!"

"I can't stay, baby. Only one of us may remain or our brain, our consciousnesses, rather, will turn into mush. We will both dissolve; only the body will remain. Hell, it, too, may dissipate. It *will* dissipate.

It is consciousness that maintains the form here. Exactly the opposite of the old world. I am her mother. I must let my child be! And I was supposed to drift away eighteen years ago, wasn't I? I got a hefty extension of stay."

"B-but . . ." Wasilla stuttered and then her shoulders slumped. "What about a few more days?"

The being—the sad teenage girl, the mature woman, the ancient soul—looked down and shook their head. "Negative, I'm afraid. A few more hours, yes, but Mirrie is getting weaker, I am growing stronger, and neither one of us has control. It seems that we have begun feeding on each other; whoever is awake gets to devour the sleeper. If I don't surrender soon and let her take over, she will be gone."

"Then let's stay together for as long as you deem fit, just the three of us, er, the four, right? Let's send the others home!" Wasilla pleaded.

"OK, let's do that." The being smiled wearily and caressed Wasilla's hand.

GROSS

The guests went home in a flash. The trio sat silently on the pony wall, rubbing shoulders. The moon was suddenly full, painting an undulating path on the swaying surface of the ocean.

"Guys . . ." Elise sighed. "May I ask for one last—"

"Yes?" Wasilla raised her head.

"One last time we . . . make love." Elise blushed and cowered.

Leo stiffened. As much as he wanted to indulge, the being was also his child. "No!"

"Why not?" Wasilla demanded. "She is Lizzy, not Mirielle."

"She is both. Mirielle will know. Is that not so? Sorry." Leo sent his gaze walking along the moon path.

"Mirrie has seen and felt everything we have done before. She has recollection of it, the emotions, what it was like kissing, rubbing, touching, having you inside me. The ecstasy, the fear, the joy, the loneliness, the warmth, the pain, how it felt to give birth. She birthed herself in a way. Yeah, wacky, I know, but it is the same for her as it is for me. But I understand your concern. Apologies, I was inconsiderate and selfish again." The being touched his hand, sending a burning jolt to his head.

Leo bit his lip. It was different here. They were not human; they were . . . ghosts! Could ghosts commit incest? Was it still wrong? Damn, it would be so easy if he were a redneck. Hell, why just a redneck? That guy Fritzl—Leo screamed inside. Why was he thinking of such bad things? What was next, cannibalism? He wanted her, damn! He wanted her dearly, but he was so afraid that he would hurt the other one with a massive presence in his heart, the being native to this world.

"Leo!" Wasilla's voice reached him from afar, then he felt her hand on his shoulder. "I know that it is very hard, but try unchaining your mind from the old word. I-I . . ." She stepped over the pony wall and sat next to him.

"Mirrie is not your biological kid. That I guess makes it easier for you," Leo said, glancing at her.

"No, but neither you are her biological father. Probably not father at all. This is a role you assumed. Everything is an illusion here; you know you are sterile, and we don't bleed. But Walid is! He is my biological brother!"

"Wass!" Elise sobbed.

"What do you mean? How's that related?" Leo mumbled, his confusion almost driving him to eat sand.

"I sleep with Walid from time to time." Wasilla's voice was firm, unapologetic.

"Well, it's none of my business. I'm not going to judge."

"Don't you want to know why?" Wasilla asked angrily.

"Well, sis, go ahead." Leo sighed. "Share."

"Walid died at nineteen and existed on his own for ages in this world. He had no life back there, no afterlife either. Father never loved him, and Mother was too weak to compensate. And I abandoned him! He craved intimacy, love, as all of us do, but here . . . you know how it is! You are freakin' lucky, Leo! Unbelievably so! You exist in paradise! To other people, this place is hell!"

Wasilla pounded on her knees. He could sense how hard it was for her to speak and laid his hand over her fist.

"You don't know what it is to be alone, with no one to care for and caress, with no one to love, with no one to love you in return! And no hope of ever meeting such a soul! I-I overcame my nature, all of it, and I made him smile and experience a loving touch. You certainly wondered why the lesbian did so well with a man, did you not?"

Leo slowly moved his head back and forth.

"Well, there it is!" Wasilla sprang up, sat next to Elise, and kissed her, then bared her breasts and helped the other out of the blouse.

Leo detected a change and looked down. The sand beneath his feet was now dressed in silk, smooth and shiny. The stars suddenly sparkled in a multitude of colors in a way that he had never seen. They were always uniform, distant white dots, some brighter, others dimmer, constantly shimmering. Even here, in this made-up world. Now they shone steadily and distinctly red, blue, yellow, orange, white, even purple. Were there actually any purple stars? What about green ones? Why not green? Ah, he was trying to flee again. His mouth twisted. The wind prompted the chimes suspended from the eaves of the clubhouse to begin a song. He did not believe in divine signs, but . . . perhaps he was getting one right now?

Wasilla was right; he was a very lucky bastard. However, no matter what he did, someone was going to be hurt. Mirielle would have time to heal. His mom was a psychiatrist, she would help. Elise . . . it was her last day in this world. Her last chance to experience intimacy. His nails dug into his palms. Damn! Why was he trying to rationalize?

Leo clenched his teeth, kneeled, and started to pull the torn stockings down, pausing often. The being looked at him, they crossed gazes, and a gentle smile was then displayed. Was her body glowing? He checked Wasilla; she was glowing too! He laid his eyes on his empty hands, then moved his gaze back up. The being, Elise, was now entirely exposed. And the ocean breeze caressed his bare skin.

He wiped his sweaty palms onto his thighs, his heart pounding in his throat. He desired her so badly. He yearned to embrace her glowing frame, to stroke her hair, to gently touch her face, to kiss her eyelids. And he also wanted to run away, hide in a deep cave, and seal the entrance with a boulder he could move only once. His fingers raked through his hair, while he stared at her belly button, adorned with a silver stud, and cringed. It was his daughter, not Elise!

His hand rose, shaking. "Come closer . . ."

Elise complied. She joined him on the ground. Her hands rested on her thighs and her gaze found his. The corners of her mouth twitched a few times, then she installed a straight face. Behind her Wasilla started playing with her hair.

Leo gulped and caressed her cheek. The touch set off a meltdown in his chest. She tilted her head, pressed his palm against her skin, and shut her eyes, instantly reminding him of that treasured moment on the bridge near their old school—the moment when they met again. He scraped his lips, his mind racing. Elise flicked her eyes a few times, glowing and breathing shakily through her mouth. Maybe he was glowing too. Suddenly, as the moon delivered light upon her face, she playfully stuck her tongue out, her eyes smiling. He raised his brows, and they threw themselves into a fiery embrace. Their lips parted, their tongues entwined, their hands could not find a spot to rest, and their hearts danced to a throbbing beat.

"Damn!" Leo swore between the kisses.

"I love you too!" Elise huffed and exposed her neck.

Leo paused briefly, grabbed Wasilla, and yanked her down, then drew both women in his embrace.

*
**

As dawn broke, the sun cast its rays on Leo's eyelids, but he kept the shutters closed, basking in last night's memories for a while, then sighed and drew his eyes open. Elise had snuggled up to him with hands clutched tightly at her chest. Wasilla had wrapped her arms around Elise's waist. The sand had shed its costume, looking ordinary and feeling rough.

Leo stroked the wavy locks.

"She-she should have . . . taken over this body," Elise said with a wobbly voice.

Leo froze and his eyebrows furrowed. "What do you mean?"

Elise revealed her face and looked at him with puffy eyes. "Mom . . . she should have stayed. This body, it will grow old."

Wasilla scrambled up. "Lizzy? Er, shit! Mirrie?"

Leo clenched his jaws so hard that he heard a crack, and a piece of broken tooth bounced inside his mouth. He winced, propped himself up, and pushed it to his cheek. His thumb hesitantly wiped a tear from their face. "Negative. She had her days, her life. Now it is your turn."

Then he nibbled on his lip and mumbled after a while, his ears burning, "I-I am sorry." As much as he wanted to look away, he kept his gaze on target.

"What for?"

"Er . . . because . . ." He gave up and hung his head. "For last night. You know."

"Ah . . ." Mirielle wearily rose up and tried to smile. "No need. It—I don't remember much, only that it felt good. Exceedingly good."

Then she squatted and wrapped her arms around his head. "Don't worry, Dad. Seriously! No need."

"OK." Leo shook slowly his head and both stood up.

"Lizzy!" Wasilla screeched, staring at Mirielle with enlarged, unblinking eyes.

"Wass. This is our, er, kid. Now, let's go." Leo placed his arm on her shoulders and tugged, glancing occasionally at his child as they walked.

Wasilla kept her gaze downcast.

Mirielle braked suddenly and said sharply, "Dad!"

Leo pouted and hesitantly nudged his eyes toward them. They stepped nearer and grabbed his hand. The jolt reverberated throughout his frame.

"Shake off the guilt, old man! Forget it! Will ya?"

"I'll try."

"Listen, Dad—"

"Not now, please." Leo drew them closer and mumbled, as they continued to walk, "That was gross."

Wasilla abruptly pulled away from him and knitted her brows.

"Gross! What the fuck are you talking about? That was the best time we ever had! You narrow-minded prick!" She kicked his calf. "You!" She hissed and kicked again. "You cannot see further than your cute nose!"

Wasilla drummed on his chest with her fists, angrily whipping her head, her long, disheveled hair flying, twisting. "You still live in the damn past! You aren't made of flesh! You are a turd!" She swung her hand.

Leo skipped backward toward the clubhouse, waving arms in unpersuasive self-defense. "Hey, calm down. Ugh!"

"The hardest turd!" She tried to deliver another thump but missed. "These few hours were absolutely the best! Come here!"

"No!" Leo ran, as Mirielle's laughter rang in his ears.

"Idiot!" Wasilla grabbed the door leaf and bent down, breathing heavily. "Don't you understand?"

Leo cautiously stepped closer, weighed his chances, and then drew her in his arms. "I guess you are right. Come, let's have some coffee. Or you want a stronger drink?"

"Coffee's good." Wasilla looked up through the strands of hair covering her face. "Try to think outside the box, please."

"I was in the mold for much longer."

"Yeah, I know." She blew her hair and pensively traced her lips. "I know. Now, where's the brew?"

Mirielle pushed a mug into her hand, took an apron from its hook, and put it on. "I'm gonna tidy up."

Leo looked at them and his face scrunched. Just like their mom! There was no relief!

"Why did you growl?" Wasilla squinted.

Did he? "I . . . ah, never mind!"

"No, go ahead."

"Memories. Recall."

"You mean cooking naked?"

He nodded.

She slurped from the mug and said, "Yeah, I remember too. Anyway, there must be clothes in these lockers."

Leo followed her nod.

"What are we going to do with the cake?"

"Mirrie! Wanna cut your cake?"

Mirielle glanced in from the back door. "OK, hard work shall not go to waste."

"There's your answer."

Leo donned the shirt and kilt he found, fastened the belt, took the cake to the big table, and put it in the middle. Then he fetched the candles, leaned in, and started piercing the crust. One, two, three . . . eighteen. He sighed and his shoulders slumped again. Eighteen! He had lost her twice now at this age. In a way. But existence had to go on. Leo drew in a ragged breath and called, "It is ready! Shall I light the candles?"

"Not yet!" Mirielle shouted.

Leo leaned against the table and fidgeted with the lighter. Weirdly, he had no urge to smoke. He could go for months without cigarettes, unlike in his old life. But yes, this world was different; he was not the same being. Expecting the same experiences was naïve. He struck the lighter and ran his index finger through the flame. What were they indeed? He shook the little gadget in his hand, listening intently, then flipped it upside down. If this world was built out of memories, could they be so detailed?

His thoughts were far away when the door opened and his parents stepped in, followed by his stepmother. He quickly put his unanswered question on the mental shelf and a goofy smile on his face.

"Hello! Apologies for last night. Something urgent came up." His eyes leaped across the faces that were filing into the large room. Steve, Margot, a young Japanese man. Ayumu perhaps?

Mirielle bumped into him and said quietly, "I called them back."

Leo glanced at them. They had changed into fresh attire, and their hair was now held off their face with two polished metal clips shaped as human skulls. Their style was weird in his eyes: striped stockings, laced red skirt, those big boots. But it was fresh, he had to grant them that, if not a bit over the top, and not at all distasteful.

"Sure." He did not move when they touched his hand. He just raised his voice. "Before you ask, I am not the one pulling magic tricks this time around. It is Mirrie. They are making you see, and, well, it won't last forever. For it to work, they must be around. So, get to know each other while you can."

Uncle Boris turned to Margot, dipping his head. "Boris Loeve here, ma'am."

"Margot Stein." She curtsied. "Hm, you are not that old!"

"You do not want to see."

Steve laughed.

"Did you undergo breast reduction at some point?" Annette chimed in.

"I had a double mastectomy," Margot answered calmly.

"Oh, sorry!"

"It was a relief. You are Leo's mom, right?"

Leo suppressed his urge to pinch his mother and counted the guests. They must all be here now. His father was looking at the new people with furrowed brows, as if they were going to deny him a slice of the birthday cake. The elderly woman, certainly Wasilla's mom, appeared shocked. Walid, her youngest son, was talking in her ear. Ruth gave Boris a slap on the rear and stuck out her tongue. Aha, that was whom Lizzy inherited the silly habit from. Lizzy . . .

Mirielle pulled his shirt. Leo remembered his duty and searched his pockets for the lighter. Then he saw it lying on the table, but Beatrice had already pushed another one into his hand and lingered, letting go.

"You don't look festive, and I was disinvited. Must have been very serious. Care to tell?" she whispered in his ear.

"Later."

"Sure, as you wish. Where's Wass?"

"In the kitchen, I suppose. But don't pester her with questions. I told you I will let you know."

"I won't. Sometimes you take me so wrong. Come down!"

Leo leaned. She pecked him quietly on the cheek and whispered, "Dickhead!"

"Cunt." He smiled.

THE UNTOUCHABLE

Leo hurriedly shuffled the papers on his desk and shoved them in the drawer under the puzzled gaze of his child. Then he stretched his mouth, feeling the blood rising to his face. "Er . . . hi, Mirrie!"

"What are you hiding?" Mirielle stepped into the study.

"A project. I am working on something, but—"

"OK, I get it, keep it under wraps." Mirielle approached and placed their palms on the desk. "Mm, I-I am gonna have a haircut."

Leo nudged up his shoulders. "Fine, but why so formal? It is your hair." They did look very nice right now, especially after Beatrice had successfully tamed the normally wild growth, but as he said, the growth was theirs to do with as they pleased.

"I'm gonna get a bob, like Mom."

Leo blinked and stared at a point. Neither Wasilla nor Beatrice wore short hair. Then his throat tightened. They meant Elise. "O"—he held his breath—"kay!"

"Are you sure? This is why I came to ask." Mirielle poked his hand with a finger.

Leo retracted it swiftly and clumsily scratched his flank.

"Dad! You promised!"

"I did." Leo returned his hand to the desk.

"If you knew what she felt, you would be happy."

"I am." The answer rang hollow. "Anyway, go ahead, but why a haircut?"

"A way to remember her. There are no pictures of her in this world, no photographs. You were unable to draw her portrait. So, being her copy is, well, reminding us that she existed."

"I will never forget her for as long as I exist! Now go!" Leo snapped, then quickly reversed course. "Sorry, Mirrie! My bad."

Mirielle came around the desk, kissed him on the cheek, and headed for the door.

Leo rubbed the spot. "May I ask where you are going? Your attire is not what I have become accustomed to." Indeed, they wore normal shoes, a denim skirt, and a red blouse with long sleeves, not any of their goth ensembles.

"To see Walid."

Walid? As in Wasilla's brother? Leo remembered the skinny youth with curly brown hair and the scar. He must be how old—Leo did a quick mental math—almost one hundred. And those close to him were all dead. Then why was he still around? Ah, their older sibling . . . but then Walid was the youngest, and at ninety-eight, how old was Jaques? He would consult Wasilla. Perhaps Walid had a sweetheart.

***

Walid was standing at the corner, holding a flower and a box in his hands. When Mirielle approached, he offered the flower.

She pecked him on the cheek. "*Arigato.*"

"Ah, cut the Japanese. You know that I'm not good."

"OK. What's in the box?"

"Fried chicken."

"Huh?" Mirielle raised her brows.

"If you were a boy, I'd have offered the food."

"Wanna see a boy in drag?" She giggled.

Walid nodded and his heart raced. Mirielle shape-shifted. Walid cracked a laugh; the tall boy did look funny in the short skirt.

Mirielle changed back. "Which one do you like more, me or my male 'moi'?"

"Both. I like both. It is still you."

"OK, then which one do you prefer to make love to?"

Walid blushed instantly as the memory from the shower room hit him in the face. He cowered. "Er . . ."

"Well, him"—Mirielle transformed—"or her." She switched back.

"Please don't play games with me!" Walid wailed.

"OK, sorry!" She gazed down, then held his hand and looked up again. "But you don't have to be ashamed! I understand that you were raised in a certain way, that your programming is not the same as mine, but we exist in a different world with different rules, and here you are free to be yourself. You admitted to wanting to be a girl; there is nothing wrong with being attracted to boys. Or both. You know that Mom was like that and—" She stopped abruptly.

Walid remained silent. Mirielle looked around, then pulled him into the bushes, found a secluded spot, and disrobed quickly.

"Like this"—she spread her arms—"or this?" She became a "he."

"*Aaaagh!*" Walid screamed silently, then took off his shirt. Mirielle came closer and helped him with the pants. Then they rolled into a ball.

Mirielle posed the same question to Ayumu, too, as soon as they met and in exactly the same way. His face lightened up at first at the sight of the slim, neatly groomed female body, then he scoffed.

"OK, girl then," Mirielle said, switched shape, and stepped closer.

Ayumu looked down as his dick went up. He grunted angrily and turned away. How did she dare? This was not the way.

"Hey!" Mirielle called. "You want me, I can tell!" Then she added softly, "But you are confused and somewhat repulsed." She slipped back into her clothes and took his arm. "Traditions, eh?"

His eyes traveled over the horizon as he searched for an answer. She behaved like a whore, undressing like that in front of him! But she was pure; she had to be pure. Or not—that other man, Walid, she mentioned, the one he could not see. Should he ask? No, that would be unbecoming, rude.

"I am of this world," he heard her saying.

"And?"

"You all carry too much baggage, which for some reason you are refusing to offload. But you—when did you die? How long ago?"

"About forty, I didn't count."

"You see? Over four decades and you still want things to be the old way. What about accepting change, adapting? Are you not supposed to evolve? Like from beings of flesh and bone into something else? I don't know what exactly you are. I don't know what I am, but as far as the people from the other world are concerned, I think that being here is a step up in your development as a species."

"What a speech!" Ayumu scoffed.

"What is wrong with it? Point it out or shut up!" Mirielle's face was taking on a shade of red.

Ayumu wondered what to say, if anything. It was annoying that she made him speechless again. He didn't have to be drawn into her little game. The wisdom of youth. Ha, what nonsense! She thought that eighteen could compete with sixty-eight or so. She believed that she could understand a world she had never lived in! She was convinced that she had access to his thoughts. He stared at Mirielle for a while, then pivoted, stuck his hands in his pockets, and walked away.

Mirielle rushed and grabbed his arm. "Hey, Ayumu, try to think outside your box! Please!"

"Let go of me!" Ayumu said sharply.

"What are you angry about? What are you ashamed of? Is it because you had touched yourself—"

Touching oneself! What did she know! He pulled his arm free, then swung it. The back of his hand met her cheek, then went right through with no resistance. She jerked backward and grabbed her face, took a few steps away, squatted, and looked up. Her eyes were enlarged. He didn't have to be a strong empath like her to tell that she was stunned.

Ayumu's heart sank. He landed on his knees and pulled her into his embrace. "Sorry! I'm so sorry, Mirrie-chan! I didn't mean it, sorry!"

Mirielle let her knees touch the ground, face still buried in her hands. Ayumu felt her frame shiver, and his anger turned to guilt. He should not have reacted so violently. She annoyed him with her speeches, but she meant no harm. She was born here, she was raised here, and all she was doing was trying to understand the world he came from.

"I'm so sorry, Mirrie-chan!" he repeated. Holding her in his arms gave him goosebumps. It was enchanting! He had dreamed of that moment for ages and was terrified of how it turned out. He didn't want to hurt her; he loved her for the nonexistent emperor's sake!

Ayumu gently peeled her hand from her face and kissed her palm. Then leaned and kissed the cheek the hand had just revealed. Mirielle remained still, her mouth ajar. Only her eyes moved and followed his gaze. Ayumu brushed her hair aside and touched her forehead with his lips. Then anew drew her into his embrace. "My bad, Mirrie-chan! I know you meant well."

"But how?"

"How what?"

"How did your smack not affect me? All I felt was the air whoosh."

Ayumu furrowed his brows. Indeed, he did not land a hit; he also felt nothing at all.

Mirielle wriggled out and leaned backward. "Try again!"

He looked at her with raised brows.

"C'mon, try again!"

"Try what?"

"Hit me, dummy!" She turned her cheek at him, wrinkled her forehead, and tightly squeezed her lips.

"No, I didn't mean it—"

"Cut the excuses! This is science! Hit me!"

"I don't want to! I can't!"

Mirielle growled. "Ah, wanker!"

Ayumu raised his arm and swung it unconvincingly. The strike still sent the girl tumbling. She gasped, showing her gums, then rose partially and held her burning cheek. "Shhh . . . what do you make of this?"

He shrugged, his heart beating loudly. "I . . . how the heck would I know?"

She sank in thought, then mumbled after a while, "Does it mean . . . does it mean that I am untouchable?"

THE STALKER

Mirielle was still a virgin in a way. When she made love to Walid, she was in her male form. Walid seemed to be like her mom—drawn equally to both, not discriminating between her yin and her yang. Then there was Ayumu. At times, he worried Mirielle. There was anger in him that she could sense yet was unable to decipher the source of. He was wanking, but so what? He was ashamed. And so was Walid. But they both had the need; this is how they were made. Why was it such a big deal in their world? She had to find out if she were to stop making the two men feel awkward.

When Beatrice entered the room, Mirielle opened her mouth to ask a question, but then changed her mind, went upstairs, donned half leggings and a tutu, went over the windowsill, and climbed down. Then she hurried to the house where Walid lived with his mother and knocked on the door.

Fatimah answered. The woman was also hopelessly stuck in the old world. After all these years, she still wore dark clothes and a head-scarf and refused to shape-shift. Wasilla lamented sometimes for being unable to change that. But Mirielle's grandmother had changed. Ruth had accepted the perks the realm offered. However, Ruth could see her other grandmother, the doctor, whereas Fatimah was unable to. Mirielle pouted—maybe she could facilitate a session, make Fatimah and Annette meet.

"Hi, Auntie Fatimah. Is Walid home?" Mirielle chirped as soon as she transferred the idea to the back burner.

"No dear, could you not sense?"

Well, Fatimah had adapted to this world to a degree. "I do actually sense a presence, which is not yours, and that's why I asked."

"No, Mirie. Check the theater."

Mirielle looked at her, puzzled. "You know that I can't enter without him. The theater is his domain."

"Ah, yes, yes . . . I am so accustomed to his hideout that I keep forgetting that he is also the doorman."

The theater was Walid's dreamworld. Just as her mother had one, so had Walid—the venue where they prepared and presented their shows. It was time for a gala, now that Mirielle was able to make people see each other; however, she had to pull double duty—perform and keep invisibility at bay. Indeed, if he was in the theater, she wouldn't be able to sense him. But then who was emitting the itch?

"Bye then, Auntie Fatimah." Mirielle pivoted and walked to the street. She twirled her hair, thinking, then turned slowly, eyes tracing every window and every door. Nothing. Mirielle saw a wooden bench in front of a house across the narrow street, crossed, sat, and buried her face in her palms. Maybe it was Walid after all; maybe he was at home and Fatimah was unaware.

Mirielle returned to the house, sneaked to the small backyard, and made her way up the drainpipe. She hung sideways, pressed her palm against the glass, shielding her eyes from the reflection of the sky, and peeked inside. Walid wasn't there. She saw masks decorating the walls, a clown costume on a stand, and a short red dress thrown over it. Nothing unusual. Mirielle returned to the ground, dragged fingers through her locks, and sneaked back to the street, crouching as she walked past the kitchen window. The sense of being watched returned. Mirielle ran.

Fatimah caught the movement and peeked out. The girl was gone. The old woman pushed the headscarf back, lifted the teacup, moved to the couch, and turned the TV set on. Not that she could understand a word, but the moving pictures entertained her. She would often doze off until it was time to cook a meal. Then she would spring into action, pull fresh produce from the pantry and spices from the pots in the garden, chicken or beef from the fridge, and start slicing and dicing. Cooking was what she loved doing. The satisfied faces of her kids and husband after a good meal made her content.

She was raised to be a housewife and subservient to her man, and she had no objections or divergent ambitions. She had been happy with Tarek for many years. He had been caring and kind. He was educated, spoke four languages fluently, and had a good job teaching at university. He started as a junior associate when they got married in '63 and steadily rose through the ranks.

But then, when they moved from war-torn Lebanon soon after the civil strife started, Tarek changed. He became angry and extremist, demanding adherence to religious rules and his own. He forced her to dress "modestly" as he called it—subdued colors, long sleeves and skirts, no trousers, always headscarves—after being quite relaxed for many years. She liked flowery dresses, light blouses, and pleated skirts, and she wore them with no objections from him until they switched countries.

Same with Wasilla—he liked his cute girl in minidresses and big silk ribbons in her hair until she spoke her first words in the language of their adopted homeland. Walid had it the worst, perhaps. His father seemed to hate him from day one. Jaques was a large and confident boy, their firstborn, the chosen son, and Walid was skinny, shy, and small. Compared to Jaques, that is. And he liked his sister's dresses and playing with dolls. That infuriated Tarek. He regularly beat up his child, and she was unable to stand up to him. She should have reported him to the police when he imprinted the scar on Walid's face, but she was too afraid, as he was the provider, after all. What would she do without him with three growing kids?

She knew that she was free here to do whatever she wanted with herself. She could be young again, throw the scarf away, and run naked on the beach, feeling the air with her skin. She could dive in the warm waters and swim, squinting and blinking, facing the morning sun. But it wouldn't be fair. She had to pay for her weakness, for her failure to defend Walid, to defend her dear Wass. And she lived the afterlife she chose; having her two kids near her was all that she needed. She was immensely glad she had this opportunity.

Somebody knocked on the sliding door. Fatimah shifted her gaze. It was Mirielle. Ah, this kid, she was a blessing. She changed Walid with her mere presence. He looked so happy nowadays. Even before that, when she was still young. They played with dolls. Walid shrank and wore a dress and laughed. Fatimah accepted him for who he was, unlike his father. Fatimah had accepted her Wasilla too. They were her children, and they never did anything bad. They hurt nobody besides their father's fragile ego, his expectations for his offspring.

"You back, sweetie?" Fatima asked and stepped aside, letting Mirielle in.

"Mmm."

Just like her mom, the old woman thought, and said, "If you are here for Walid, he is still not back. Do you want some tea or juice?"

"A glass of wine would be fine." Mirielle splashed in the armchair, then sprang back up. "Auntie Fatimah, can I help?"

"No worries, I am coming." Fatimah had also learned not to judge. If Mirielle wanted wine, wine would be it. In this world there were no drunkards, and she knew that Mirielle was allowed a glass or two from time to time.

"Here, sweetie." Fatimah handed her the drink.

"Shukran!"

Ah, and she had learned Arabic too! Where did all that ambition come from? Not that Fatimah objected. Her Walid was the teacher, and he was happy and highly motivated and that was good.

Mirielle took a gulp, placed the glass on the table, and said, "Something is after me; I can't shake it off."

"What something?"

"Something's following and watching me. I can't get rid of it. It's unlikely to be Walid. Inside here—it's not burning my neck anymore. It's unsettling, though. Your kind cannot be hurt here, but I don't know about me."

"Then stay here until Walid is back, and he then can walk you home. Or, if you are in a hurry, I can do so. I wonder why is not the space folding—"

"No, no, space's not folding, because I am not trying to escape. I am trying to confront the thing, my fears . . . I just popped in for a short break. Thanks, Auntie Fatimah." Mirielle saw the bottom of the glass, burped quietly in her hand, and jumped out.

Fatimah smiled. *Oh, how I envy you, girl, for your courage. Why was I not like you?* She pulled the scarf back over her head and took the empty glass to the kitchen sink.

Mirielle inserted her toe in the joint between the blocks and pushed her body up. The tutu got caught in something and pulled her sharply back. She stepped on the ground. The threaded bracket the pipe was fastened to the wall with was sticking out quite far and had grabbed the laces. Mirielle traced the route to the roof. There were more brackets like this one; if her dress got caught in another, she might fall. Mirielle pulled the tutu over her head, looked around, suspended it on the very same bracket that had caught it a moment ago, and prepared to return to the climb. Getting on the roof would allow her to scan the area from a vantage point and possibly locate the stalker.

Luckily, climbing had become second nature to her, and the locked warehouse doors were no obstacle. Knowing that she may get hurt if she fell made it even more attractive. She had to concentrate and pay attention to her every move, which relegated all thoughts to the back seat until she triumphantly reached the top or had set feet on the ground. Having a head full of buzz was not always great. The buzz sometimes hurt—the fear of losing the people she loved, the self-doubt, the uncertainty of her future. The normals knew where they came from and what was coming next. With her, nobody had even the slightest guess.

Once on the roof, Mirielle crawled to the edge and peeked over it. She was not afraid of the height; the idea was to not be noticed by the stalker. She shut her eyes—the presence was still there, but the itchy feeling of being observed had gone. So far, so good. Lying on the corrugated sheet, she crossed her hands under her chin and slowly moved her gaze across the landscape below: roads, streets, houses, tiny backyards. In the distance there were two apartment buildings. Ayumu lived in the taller one, on the sixth floor. She eyed the railway tracks and the shopping mall with the pedestrian bridge across the road that led to the train station. She checked the immediate vicinity again. Nothing. The wind was animating the signs in front of the minimart. Wait! Something moved under the canopy shielding the row of vending machines! Mirielle focused her sight on the area and waited patiently. A cat emerged and slowly crossed the street. A cat. Must be somebody's memory of their pet. No animal was native to this world as far as she knew. A world made of memories. Whose memory was she?

Mirielle crawled backward to check the other side. The itch returned. She twisted her neck, then rolled and stood on all fours.

The silhouette in front of her laughed. "I scared you, didn't I?"

"Ayumu, you prick!" Mirielle let her fear pour out. "What's the fun in stalking someone? It was you all along, wasn't it?" She rose, pounced, and started banging her fists on Ayumu's chest. "You stupid donkey!"

Ayumu clasped his arms around her. She tried to break free from his rough hug, but he squeezed tighter. Mirielle looked up, her molars making a shy peek from the corners of her mouth.

"You scared me, bastard," she growled and stopped squirming.

Ayumu realized that his hands were touching bare skin. He glanced down. She was wearing only her purple leggings. How had he failed to notice before? Her hands were clutched close to her chest, her eyes still trained on his face. Her anger was gone. She appeared so defenseless, and her wrinkled nose was so cute.

Ayumu opened his mouth, then closed it, holding his breath. His heart was drumming, and his groin was tense. He desired this miracle! He dreamed about her. She made him angry, and she made him glad. Ayumu loosened his grip and cautiously bent his neck until their lips met. Her breath was hot. Was her heart racing too? Hard to tell. Ayumu flexed his knees, and his lips reached her nipples. He kissed the little knobs. They stiffened and the areolas shrank. He drew them one by one in his mouth, his craving for the girl growing. Mirielle's hands combed his hair; he heard a sigh. Ayumu eased her leggings down, then kissed the flat belly and caressed her thigh.

Mirielle quivered briefly and grabbed his head. He continued kissing, while reaching up and gliding his hands over her hills. His fingers rolled the nipples, she moaned quietly, then both kneeled. Their lips met again. She slid her hands under his shirt and pinched his nipples; he felt a mild jolt in his crotch. Her hands came down and pulled the drawstring knot. He gently lowered her on the roof and let his rigid pride out. His knees scuffed the corrugated sheet, but he gleefully ignored the pain.

Mirielle would have preferred Walid for her first female foray. Ayumu was a bit of a wild card with his changing moods and violent streak. But when he held her, the butterflies in her groin fluttered their wings. The desire bubbled up, and she chose not to resist. His touch rippled throughout her body. She felt the pulses of her heart reaching her head. She wanted him to rub her breasts. She pulled his shirt over his head and threw it to the side.

Ayumu planked over her; she ran her fingernails down his bare chest, then rolled his tiny nipples with her thumbs. Ayumu flexed his arms, and his penis touched her mound. Mirielle laid her eyelids low and spread her legs, taking noisy breaths and anticipating pain. All she felt, though, was a mild prick and then delight as he settled in. Her lips shivered. She moaned quietly as he rocked, each rub of his penis casting pleasurable sparks.

She grabbed his arms and wrapped her legs around his hips. Ayumu's thrust intensified. The sensation was amazing! And now it was entirely her own, not just the memories of her mom. She felt an urge to shed tears; she let them roll. She sobbed as the fire inside her went wild. She felt the squirt and then, a moment later, her groin exploded; her body quivered, rolling in delight. Mirielle waited for her heartbeat to slow down with her eyes closed. Then she flipped them open, looked at Ayumu, and smiled. His face was long yet glowing.

Ayumu went on a hunt for words but caught not even one strong enough to express his emotions. He'd made love to a girl for the first time since he had died. She loved it, didn't she? She sure did. Her tears, they did not speak of ache; they were cries of joy. Her face . . . it was wet yet illuminated; her eyes sparkled. What a story! What a turn of events!

Ayumu wanted to continue, but the fit of his appendage had become loose. He extracted it and noticed what looked like a bloodstain.

Unbelievable, she was a virgin! He gazed up and said, "Wow! Am I your first?"

Mirielle shook her head and chirped, "No."

Something inside him growled. He rolled to the side and pulled his shorts up nervously.

Mirielle sat. "What is it? You were ecstatic and suddenly your mood went dark."

Ayumu clenched his teeth. He was not supposed to expose his emotions; he was a man. And, yeah, he was disappointed that he was not her first, but so what? Damn, the indignation was so hard to control!

"N-nothing really. I thought that I was your first, you know. You are young and I saw some blood. Anyway . . . may I ask who was the lucky one?"

Mirielle looked at him and pouted. "I'm not sure I understand."

"I mean, who—ah, never mind!" Ayumu waved his hand and reached for his shirt.

"Walid," Mirielle said simply.

The beast inside him growled once more.

"You two should meet. But you caught glimpses of each other at my birthday bash, did you not? I was the one who made people see."

MEN

Beatrice leaned against the doorframe and watched silently as Mirielle pulled the wax strips from her calves, grimacing and breathing noisily through her teeth. When all strips were gone, Mirielle rubbed her legs, applied some lotion, pursed her lips, and returned the jar to the shelf. Then she stepped into the bathtub, removed her shirt, exposed her back, and transformed. Beatrice laughed.

"Happy that you get to torture me?"

"Oh, yeah!" Beatrice pushed the pitch of her voice down. "Seriously, though, I know that waxing hurts, so why do it? Nobody in this realm would care. If I wasn't just a memory of myself, I wouldn't bother."

"Does Dad like hairy women?"

"Mm, probably not."

"Correct!" Mirielle grunted. "But I am not doing it for him. I don't like body hair myself, I mean on a girl, and doing just legs and armpits would be enough. The thing is that when I transform, my yang looks weird. Smooth legs and a hairy chest. And I cannot have that, can I?"

"Since when does it matter?"

"Since I became self-conscious to the required degree."

"When you mention yang and yin . . . do you realize that you are complete? You are both." Beatrice was hurriedly spreading the wax, yet she found a resource in her mind to also run her mouth.

"It is not always fun and makes me very confused at times, but it is part of my nature, whatever that nature may be, and it has its perks." Mirielle squinted in anticipation. Beatrice ripped off the first strip.

"Ssss . . ."

"Ho-ho," Beatrice said then added, "Maybe I should get your dad to follow your lead. But . . . seems I don't care; I don't feel compelled."

"Mom liked him as he is. In fact, she loved the version with the long hair and the beard for some reason. She found him very sexy."

"I don't remember that version of him from the other life. When we got divorced, his hair wasn't particularly long, and he was cleanly shaven. But, yeah, the look appeals to me too. Must be something primal, from before razors were invented, a vestige from the Stone Age."

"I am often afraid to look at him— Phew!" Mirielle hissed. "Sorry, continue please."

"Why are you afraid?"

Mirielle kept mum. Beatrice shrugged. If the kid didn't want to talk, that was fine. But being afraid to look at Leo? That was strange. He was a lovable old dude—who could also make himself look young—and they had plenty of good times. Perhaps to make up for all animosity and heartache. Ah, that was a poor choice of word—he died from a heart attack. But it didn't matter. They were happier with each other as ghosts.

Beatrice heard the sobbing and laid hands on the young man's shoulders. "Hey, what is it, daisy? Want to share?"

"No, Bea, sorry." The young man wiped his cheeks.

"Well, if you change your mind, I'm always here."

"Thanks. I appreciate it." Mirielle caressed the hand on his shoulder. "Now, can we finish my back?"

"Sure!" Beatrice pulled another strip.

"Ssss . . ."

Beatrice squinted when Mirielle reverted to a girl and stood up. Was she having déjà vu? Mirielle's tummy looked rounder. It was normally flat.

"Hey, can you shift a few months back?"

"You know that I can't. Why?"

"Ah, nothing. Your resemblance to your mom is astounding. I sometimes mistake my memories of her with you."

"I *am* her."

⁂

The small, secluded beach at the bottom of the temple forest looked like a suitable place to turn the vision on. She had been there with both. Mirielle set the time—at noon—the day before, then arrived early and waited in the trees for her friends to show up.

Ayumu was first. He leaned, expecting a kiss. Mirielle pecked him on the cheek and smiled. "How are you, Ayumu-kun?"

Ayumu's gaze moved to the waves. "I'm good, and you?"

"Nervous."

"Why?"

"Well, you two are men, and I have read a thing or two. So, I don't know. Dad says that only good people make it to this world, and I concur. Yet you, Oshikiri, worry me sometimes."

"I'm so sorry, Mirrie-chan!" Ayumu blushed and bowed. "No more will I try to hurt you. I am so ashamed!"

Mirielle rose from the rock she had sat on, came closer, and pecked his cheek again. "I am certain of that, Ayumu-kun." Then she turned her attention to Walid, who had just emerged from the forest path. "*Assalamu alaikum!*"

"*Salam.* Is he here?"

"Mmm. You stand there." She pointed, then counted, "One, two, three, now!"

Ayumu checked the other guy head to toe. Yeah, he had seen him in the clubhouse—skinny, curly hair, facial scar. And short, but he himself was not a tall man either. He bowed down. "Oshikiri Ayumu."

The other man also bowed. "Buhari Walid."

Mirielle laughed. "You don't have to follow Japanese conventions. Anyway," she cross-pointed, "Oshikiri, Walid, Walid, Oshikiri." Then she grabbed their arms and swung them. "My best friends!"

Ayumu spoke first. "Shall I call you Buhari? We are not on first names yet, as far as I am concerned, but Mirrie-chan here . . . she used my last name but your first. So, I don't want to be disrespectful. If this is the custom in your land, I shall follow it."

He was polite, but his eyes pierced the other and he couldn't help it. So, this was the guy who was her first! What a weakling! She was weird. What did she see in him?

"Walid is my mom's baby brother."

"I'm not a baby." Walid sounded offended.

"OK, younger brother—"

"Huh?" Ayumu gasped. So, she slept with her uncle? "How old are you, Buhari, if I may ask?"

"Ninety-eight. And you, er, Oshikawa?"

"Oshikiri," Mirielle corrected. "Why don't you just stick to Ayumu and Walid? I'm getting tired of your old-world rules. Considering how few people we can see, we can be on first letter, not even first name. Do you agree, A?"

"I am younger," Ayumu said.

Walid munched his lips. This Oshikiri Ayumu, there was something about him—he was polite yet felt aggressive. His demeanor reminded him of Tarek, his father, and he shivered. There were no bad guys in this world, yes, but what about Peter, her father's nephew? Did he not try to do a horrible thing? What if this guy tried to hurt Mirielle? Would he be there to defend her? Would he be able to raise his hand and throw a punch? He knew that he was weak.

He sighed quietly and glanced at the other guy. She was so trusting. He had a bad feeling, but he could think of no way to caution her. He could not just start trash-talking Oshikiri, as the guy was also her friend. One of two. That was the deficiency of this place, very low availability of potential friends. Even Mirielle, who could see far more people than he on his own, had just the two of them. Therefore, he had to try to get along with the dude somehow. For her sake. Sake! "Hey, guys, what about some sake to seal the friendship?"

"*Hai!*" Ayumu grunted, but Mirielle lifted her hand. Walid followed her movements with raised brows as she walked around the large boulder and a moment later emerged on its top.

"I . . ." she began, glancing sideways, "I . . . must give a speech."

It looked like Ayumu was also intrigued now. He turned and looked up. His hand came out of his pocket, and he wiped the palm onto his pants. Walid wanted to prompt her to continue; however, his mouth only moved without making a sound.

Mirielle squatted on the rock and began poking it with her finger. Then she lifted her gaze, weighed him, then the other guy and said, "Once upon a time my mom had someone she loved dearly. That was Walid's big sis, Wass—"

"Hang on!" Ayumu interrupted. "Did you not say that Buhari's sister was your mom?"

"Yes, she's my mom too, because she raised me."

"Ah, I see. So, she's not your biological mother then."

"And neither is Elise," Mirielle said calmly. "Is there anything biological here?"

"Hm!"

"Anyway, there was someone else she also loved. Someone she almost lost, because she withheld a truth. I learned the lesson. If someone is dear to you, let them know even if there is a risk of losing them. So—"

Ayumu threw another question. "Who's that other person?"

Walid shot an angry glance at him. *Will he not shut up!*

Mirielle's round hazels found Ayumu's stretched almonds. "Father, it was Father."

Ayumu blushed and cast his gaze down. Walid was impressed— the dude felt shame!

"I want you to know the truth, that you two are my dear friends. However . . . well, you know that you like me in more ways than one." She paused, then finished quickly. "I want to let you know that neither one holds exclusive rights over my affection."

Walid understood. He was prepared in a way. He remembered the anxiety his sister went through when Leo showed up, but then things settled, and she grew happier with a man in her afterlife. An oddity for a lesbian. But Ayumu? Walid turned his head. Ayumu had parked his gaze on something on the ground—a pebble or a seashell. His hands were clutched behind him, and he was obviously busy digesting the statement. His lips seemed to move.

Ayumu raised his head and said, "OK, I understand!" Then he faced Walid and extended his hand. "Good to know you, Walid-san!"

"Great!" Mirielle stood up. "Now let's dip!" She ran down the spine of the boulder, kicked off her shoes, and dispensed of her scant attire, sending it flying and landing in the soft white sand. She splashed in the sparkling waters of the high tide.

Walid scratched the tip of his nose, hesitating. Then he also kicked his shoes off, threw his shirt, and ran toward the water. Ayumu followed suit.

Splashes, some grunts, and Mirielle's laughter filled the air. The deed was done! She was worried that her friends would not take to each other kindly, Ayumu in particular, and seeing the smiles on their faces, exchanging embraces, being caressed by both, made her heart sing a jolly song. Selfishness, rivalries, jealousy. She understood where all this came from—evolution by natural selection—but it belonged to the old world. Yet, she was also acutely aware how clingy that old world was—everybody she knew struggled to shed it. She detected her dad's sense of guilt almost always when the two crossed paths. But she also detected his unflinching love and . . . she loved him too!

Ayumu tried to kiss her, but she dodged. "Let's go out now. I'm getting cold." Mirielle sank, reached the bottom with her feet, then pushed forward toward the shore. Her mind went dizzy for a moment. The sun blinded her when she surfaced, then she squinted, turned away from it, and walked toward the shore. Something was amiss. This was not the same beach. The dizziness struck again, and she squatted in the shallow surf.

"What is it?" Walid's voice reached her ears.

Mirielle twisted her neck and crossed eyes with him. "I jumped."

"Ah, OK." He helped her stand.

Mirielle looked down and touched her breasts—they were bigger and softer and—was that milk? Her heart sprinted.

"Er . . . er . . . how long?"

Walid's expression turned blank.

"What took place since I introduced you to Ayumu? D'ya remember, we also swam?"

"Ah, I see." Walid stretched the silence. "Well, not sure how to deliver it, but . . . hm, the most important is that you gave birth."

Mirielle's legs turned into a soft, gooey rubber, and she slumped back into the warm surf. "Shit!"

ELIAN

Walid ran after Mirielle, holding her clothes in his hands. She'd probably set a new world record. Walid had a hard time keeping pace. Had she turned male, he would have stood no chance perhaps.

Mirielle opened the front door, jumped the step, not bothering to clean the sand from her feet, and looked around, then popped back and galloped upstairs.

Walid heard a bang, then silence. He diligently cleaned his soles and climbed the stairs. Mirielle stood at the door of her room, panting and staring inside. Walid heard cooing, then his sister's voice. "You jumped, didn't you?"

Mirielle nodded slowly, lifted her hands, and wiped the water and the sweat dripping from her face. Then she turned and headed back downstairs. Walid trotted after her with his extended hand still holding the clothes.

She reached into the fridge, popped a can open, guzzled it, then bent over the sink and retched. The beer had not had time to froth in her gut. Mirielle put her elbows on the countertop and buried fingers in her hair.

"Here." Walid held out her shirt. Mirielle glanced at it, then walked past him saying nothing and returned upstairs. Walid followed and stuck his head in the room.

Mirielle stood by her old crib, looking inside. He could sense the medley of emotions—curiosity, confusion, fear, even hostility. He was about to open his mouth when she bent over and took the baby in her arms, then brought it close to her chest. When she turned around, the little creature had drawn a nipple in its mouth. Mirielle began pacing slowly across the room, flinching and biting her lip, occasionally looking up and rolling her eyes. He had seen these grimaces before. She hated breastfeeding but for some reason kept doing it. He was itching to ask why yet never gathered the courage.

"Who is the father?" Mirielle asked suddenly.

"Strange question coming from the mother," his sister replied.

"Well, I behaved like a cat in heat to be honest, and with the memory block, how could I know? Maybe I told you. Please, don't make me wait!" She flexed her knees with furrowed brows.

"You didn't know. You said you had sex with both Ayumu and Walid. Elian has no Asian features, so he must be my bro's."

Walid's legs trembled each time he heard that.

"Elian?" Mirielle asked. "Did I pick the name?"

"Yep. You asked us to write proposals, then read them out loud, then named him Elian."

Some memories started crawling slowly back into their slots. "And Grandmom asked, 'But isn't it Spanish?'"

"Yes, and you answered, 'So what?'" Wasilla smiled.

"Where's Dad?"

"With Shinji. They are up to something. They have been for a while."

"Yes, I noticed that long ago. How did he take it?"

"Calmly. There are no careers to worry about here, I guess, but even if there were, he'd still be supportive, I am sure. And such things happen in the old world too; it is anything but extraordinary."

Elian pushed the nipple, spat a few bubbles, and prepared to nap. Mirielle placed him in the crib, stretched, arched her back, and clutched her hands on her head.

"Here it is. I am a freak and my having a baby proves it again!" She dropped her hands, grabbed the crib, and closed her eyes. Then she grunted, "Ugh, seems I am now stuck in my yin. Perhaps he stole my yang. Even so, that doesn't make me less of a freak."

Walid stepped closer and laid a hand on her shoulder. "You are not a freak, Mirrie. Different from the rest of us, yes, but freak—no."

Mirielle looked at him and smiled wearily. "Oh, yeah, Daddy?"

Walid blushed.

Suddenly, she turned around and her eyes framed the baby. "He is not premature, is he? Like, he was inside me for all nine months?"

"Heh, time here . . ." Wasilla scoffed. "He did not look premature, no. A fully developed, healthy boy. Why?"

"Nothing, just asking." Her face had certainly turned white. If the baby was not premature and had no semblance to Ayumu, then . . . she did not remember having intercourse with Walid while female early on! He preferred the boy! Was it possible to be impregnated this way? Orally or in the bum? Who knew, this world was wild! What if . . . Cold sweat popped on her temples. She went to the closet, pulled out a pair of leggings and a shirt, and finally clothed herself.

"You should use a bra; you keep staining the shirts," Wasilla noted.

Mirielle pulled the shirt over her head and threw it in the closet. "As if I care! Happy now?" She went to her bed and collapsed on it face down. Propelled by her hand, the pillow traveled and came to a rest over her head. She heard Wasilla sighing, then a pair of departing steps, then the door shut.

*
**

The memories began piling up like unpaid bills after Christmas as soon as she came out of her stupor. She pushed the pillow aside, sat on the edge, and brought the baby into focus between the slats of the crib.

She was scared and confused when the signs became undeniable. She was not ready. She had no intention of ever getting ready. Why would anyone procreate in this realm? It was not the way. She was an abnormality, a prank this world had played. Once was enough!

She went wild with her friends, trying to unburden her mind. Eh, they had a threesome for the first time! Ayumu resisted initially, claiming it was undignified. Then she began describing pictures of herself and another girl, fellating him or making love to one another as he watched. He could not conceal his arousal, neither physically nor emotionally.

"You see?" she said. "When it is a girl, you are ready."

He mumbled something in response and cut the conversation short then, but a few days later he begrudgingly agreed.

She enjoyed observing their red faces, standing naked and hard next to each other and waiting for her to take the lead. She had no idea what thoughts rummaged through their minds; however, the emotions—shame, discomfort, resignation, keen interest, strong desire—she was amazed that there was room for so many. And as fired up as them. They would roll on the tatami mats or her mattress or on the lush green grass and come together. She would draw Walid's penis in her mouth while Ayumu was swaying his hips behind her, then the men would switch. She would give them hand jobs. They'd suck her nipples cheek to cheek, and she'd experience her first tit orgasm. However, they never touched each other. Walid was keen, but Ayumu—not at all. Understandable. What she couldn't quite get was him agreeing to participate. She didn't want to hear a "because of you" and she forewent asking.

Then she grew much larger. She wondered what a pregnant man would be like, but she failed to transform when she tried, she recalled. She began practicing meditation, guided by Mayumi, aiming to empty her mind from uncomfortable thoughts. And she played her keyboard for hours on end, angry that she was unable to climb with that giant sack at her front.

When, despite all distractions, one day the tiny creature popped out and ended up in her arms, she inspected it coldly, as if it were a plastic doll that had just been gifted to her without consideration of her preferences. She didn't bother to pretend that she was happy. Everybody knew that she was not.

"Shit happens," her dad commented and took his grandson from her. His face was dark, tense.

When they asked her to choose a name, she shrugged. She had no preference at all. She did ask them to write proposals indeed, then made them read each one aloud, thought, and uttered, "Elian." The name was not on the list; it just popped on her tongue.

Feeding Elian became a chore. She tried to abscond, but the thing kept sounding the alarm. Beatrice helped her fill bottles a few times; however, the milk in them did not last. It disappeared soon after the deed. Illusion, that was what it was. So, she had no choice but to suffer pulls and bites, just to keep the volume down. Her mom enjoyed it, the memories revealed, making Mirielle scratch her head.

"Did you like breastfeeding?" she asked Beatrice.

"Mixed bag. In a way, it was gratifying, I felt closer to the kid, but to be honest I was more concerned about the shape of my boobs."

"Should I care?"

"I'd say that this is up to you."

Better bonding with the child. She decided to try that and endure the discomfort from that moment on.

The baby moved, spread his fingers, and then stuck his tiny thumb into his mouth. Elian was not at fault here; she would accept him. Even if he were, there would always be room to forgive and give another chance. But he was just a newborn baby; she was getting way too philosophical. In the old world, he'd be considered the product of someone's loins, she mused. Not here, though. Here, she didn't know. She grabbed her head and started rocking. What had she gotten herself into?

"Life, this is your life."

Mirielle looked up. Who was that? Goosebumps popped up on her skin. No other person was in the room besides herself and Elian.

"Er, who are you?" That was her world, after all.

Silence. Her world did not respond. Perhaps it was a thought, one of the many rushing through her mind right now. On consideration— the thought was not wrong. Another being like herself born into this world. She was not unique, and not alone. She had a mission: to raise this child. Realistically, what else was there for her to do?

The baby opened its eyes and moved its limbs, then made an angry face and screeched. Mirielle pursed her lips and rose. She retrieved the kid from the crib, clenched her teeth, and offered it a nipple. Elian drew it greedily and suckled.

What is the point? Mirielle wondered again, as a grimace momentarily distorted her face.

THE CONFESSION

Over two hundred days had passed, and Elian's eyes remained blue. Then Annette uttered, "Heh, he looks just like you when you were a baby."

Leo let it pass at first. Then he felt the blood draining from his face. "Are you sure?"

"Yeah, look." She smiled. "The nose, the eyes—" Then her jaw dropped. "No, you didn't . . ."

Leo wailed inside. "It was Elise, Mom."

Annette called out, "Wass! Will you please take the baby and give us some space? And call Mirrie, please!"

Wasilla trotted in, took Elian, and said, "She's coming . . . but . . . I think that I shall also stay."

Annette pulled her hair and reached for a cigarette, then remembered the baby and just bit the filter of the stick.

"What is it, Grandma?" Mirielle chirped from the door, then sensed the angry vibe and squinted quizzically.

Leo rose from the couch. "Don't drag them into this, Mom. Let's go out."

"Seems you are all involved in this travesty! Why talk to just you?"

"What travesty, Grandma?"

Leo raised his hand. "OK, we can talk here, but you promise that you'll keep your mouth shut until you hear the full story."

Annette growled, "Fine!"

"Elise did not drift away all these years ago, just after Mirrie was born. She, her consciousness, transferred to Mirrie's body, and she existed there until Mirrie turned eighteen."

"Bullshit!"

"You promised to keep your mouth shut!"

Annette tried to cut her son in half with her gaze but remained mum. The lighter kept spinning in her hand.

"They, Mirrie and Lizzy, shared the body. Mirrie had it most of the time, but her mom manifested herself on occasions. Then they could share no more, one of them had to go—the consciousness, I mean—and Lizzy offered herself." His eyes became moist. "Before she let herself die again, she asked for one last love dance and . . ." Leo paused and wiped a tear. "We indulged her, me and Wass . . ."

Annette wanted to voice her indignation but just moved her mouth like a beached fish. It was wrong, very wrong! She dropped her attempts at speech and just shook her head slowly, struggling to digest the story. *What have these morons done!* Yet, she was somehow touched.

Her hand reached for a cigarette, then squashed it angrily and threw it on the floor.

"It is all true, Grandma!" Mirielle chimed. "It was Mom that night, not me! I was fast asleep!"

Annette looked at her granddaughter. The girl's face was wet, the eyes—red. So, she'd been crying too.

"And you? How are you, sweetie?"

"I told you; I was asleep."

"But you remembered, didn't you?"

Mirielle nodded and snorted.

"And?"

"Well, everything has consequences. I could not escape them either. But I am not harmed in the slightest, believe me! It was beautiful! I envy them!" Mirielle thumped her feet.

"What are the consequences for you? I mean, besides Elian."

"I . . . I fell in love." She took a deep breath, pouted, exhaled noisily, and then added almost inaudibly, "With Dad."

The thick silence took a victory lap; the room belonged to it!

Leo recovered first, stood up, and beckoned his child. "Let's have a private talk, Mirrie."

Outside they sat next to each other on the narrow wooden bench in the middle of the small garden. Mirielle squinted again at the bright light and shielded their eyes with their hand. Their face was red, but their lips no longer trembled.

"Love is a complex emotion, Mirrie," Leo started. "I am also mad about you, so, let's try to frame our feelings in a way that would make us understand what we expect from each other. I-I, for example—"

"Don't worry, Dad. I do not want intercourse."

"I must admit that I was a little worried after what transpired that day, so, thank you! My other concern is that you will compare every other man you meet to me, and they will always fall short due to no fault of their own. But I am not exceptional. I was, and I still am, an average man. I was never particularly good as a designer and as an artist. I failed Bea and Eric. Physically, I know that I am not ugly but don't have thick biceps and a six-pack." He scratched his belly. "Yep, just an average man." Then he cowered. "Ugh!"

Beatrice blew air on her palm, then bent and wrapped her arms around him. "Nobody's perfect. It is a matter of which personal traits prevail, the positive or the negative. And also, what is considered good and bad? To some people material wealth is good. 'Money, money, money, always funny in Otto Starmer's world . . .'" She sang ABBA's tune, shoving her last husband into the song. "I became one of them. It is not bad indeed, being wealthy, but you were middle class, quite a reasonable station in life, and you made up for the lack of fabulous wealth with your other traits. Which, now, after my death, I find very valuable. Even more so in a world where money does not exist."

"Thanks for the praise, Bea, but I asked for a private conversation; no need of extra ears."

"Sorry, I did it again, didn't I?" She sighed and headed toward the house.

"Maybe we should also go back, Dad. We are a tight nucleus. We should be able to bare our souls to each other, right?"

Leo tested his palm over his child's hand. The contact jolted both. Mirielle clutched him in their arms and buried their head in his chest. "I love you, old man! Damn! But I understand."

Leo let some time pass before saying, "But I don't."

"What is it that you don't get? I am also Mom. She was head over heels for you, and the emotion, it never went away."

"No, not that. What do you remember from the night? Were you really asleep?"

"Not exactly. It was like being at the bottom of a lake, looking up. You see what is happening, you hear, you feel, but it is all dulled, remote. It gets to you with a delay. It was beautiful, though. Your bodies were like made of frosted glass, only alive, shimmering, glowing. Your eyes . . . your eyes were all dark, like windows to the sky above. You sometimes merged, like you would hold hands with Mom or Wass, and they would melt and mix, and tiny streams of light would flow between you."

"But . . ." He sighed, took a breath, and said confidently, "I did not go inside your mom. I couldn't bring myself to do it, knowing that it was also you."

"Ah, yes, you did not. But you have a playful tongue." Mirielle giggled, sat upright, and offered a smile.

"Well, that is probably irrelevant as far as Eli is concerned. This world is different. Even you, if the rules were the same, you should not exist. But you do and I am glad!" He drew them in his embrace.

"Hey, Dad!"

"Mm?"

"You should probably stop using the fluidity pronoun."

"Why?"

"Because I can't transform anymore. I stay a girl. My hypothesis is that Eli stole my yang."

"You absolutely sure?"

"Well, no, I may reacquire the ability, but at the moment I am stuck with the boobs. Ah, Walid liked you so much!"

"As in?"

"He's bisexual, like Mom, but with a slight preference for men, and, well, my yang was a copy of you."

Leo chuckled. "Ah, I get it. Do you like him?"

"Yes, he's a gentle soul, caring, considerate. You share traits. He annoys me at times, though, with his low self-esteem and indecisiveness. Nothing like you in this department. He demands constant validation of his actions, and it can get old really quick. But he is otherwise OK, and we are having fun. And then there's Ayumu . . ."

Mirielle grew animated, probably because they hadn't shared anything about their boyfriends before. Leo sharpened his ears.

"He often looks mean and grunts a lot, but that I guess is because he is Japanese. Anyway, I like him plenty too. He has a great sense of humor and somehow manages to dig up new jokes. Do you know the one about the horse and the whiskey bar?"

"Nope."

"Well, a horse sticks its head into a bar, swings its gaze around, and calls the bartender, 'Double bourbon, please. On the rocks.'

"'Sure, sir, but why don't you come sit at the bar?'

"'I can't, I'm harnessed up.'"

Leo smiled and got up. "Yeah, now let's go inside, shall we?"

He turned around and crossed gazes with Beatrice, then Wasilla. The two had glued noses to the sliding door's glass, eyes trained on Mirielle and him. His mom was peeking over their shoulders with Elian in her arms.

Ah, shit! Leo cringed.

"Hey, Mirrie, I've never asked you this, but now that your grandmom is here, she triggered a reminder," Leo said as the two stepped inside the house. "How do you see us? Like, I am nineteen years old to Wass, thirty-five to Bea, and sixty-one to your grandmom. But what about you?"

"Ah, this . . . unless you are projecting a different age, I always see you true. Like, you are pale and creased right now."

Beatrice shrieked.

AFTERPARTY

Ayumu tossed and turned in his bed, breathing heavily, growling and grunting. Then he flipped his eyes open and stared in the dark, catching his breath.

"Whore!" He put his feet on the floor, went to the kitchen, opened the refrigerator, and retrieved a can of iced tea. He had way too much whiskey last night. Whiskey was strong, and he got drunk much faster than with sake. And he was so horny and wanted to do her in the bum, but she flatly refused. He popped the tab, chugged the contents, squashed the container, dropped it on the countertop, and reached for another.

Why was she always saying no to the fun? Alcohol loosened him up, lifted his inhibitions. He wanted to lick her pussy and stick his tongue up her anus, but when he was sober, he was way too self-conscious, and these things . . . they were bad.

This is how he was programmed to think, and as he himself said once, in the old world these parts had to be squeaky clean. In this world they always were; their entire bodies always were. Yet, the houses had bathtubs. Mirielle told him that in Europe the apartments had no bathrooms at all, not even ones with just tubs as was the case here. And no trains.

Ayumu sipped from the cold tea and swirled it in his mouth. It was so funny when they, the three of them, boarded a train here and stumbled upon her father banging, well, her mom, the one with red hair and green eyes, who he used to salivate over. Mirielle seemed to have lost the ability to turn the vision on or off. When she was nearby, regardless of whether she was looking or not, people could still see each other. When she saw the scene, she turned and shut her eyes, but nothing changed. Then she smacked him on the neck. "Stop looking, you pervert!" But he couldn't pull his eyes from the redhead. She looked about thirtyish, as was the father, as they had obviously shape-shifted, and she was gorgeous. Mirielle looked like a child compared to her, and he got goosebumps at the thought.

"Mom, Dad!" Mirielle shouted after he refused to look away. The couple did not stop immediately. Then they embraced each other, looked at her, and made goofy smiles.

"Oops!" the father said and laughed awkwardly. Mirielle then grabbed Ayumu's arm and dragged him away. Buhari followed with a red face.

Ayumu took another sip and looked at the moon outside. Why did he call her a whore in his dream? Because of Buhari? Ayumu twitched his lip and admitted to himself that jealousy indeed often raged inside him, but the argument she made was sound. And he was in love, and any argument the person one loved presented was probably sound. No, she was right about that, despite his feeling—too few of them in this world; everybody needed some intimacy; they had to adapt.

She was so smart and wise, this eighteen-year-old skinny girl! She spoke fluent Japanese, English, German, Arabic, French, and even Swedish! Not that he could understand anything. She could have tricked him easily, but she was not that kind of girl. Her pronouncements were deep and fitting. She made him feel good! She was his— what was the best word to describe her—his superstar! She wanted to make people happy, but that was impossible without these people also being generous. If he succumbed to the desire to keep her exclusively for himself, she wouldn't be happy, and she would probably leave him or abandon Buhari. Buhari would then be sad. Now everyone compromised a bit, even Mirielle, because she sensed the emotional conflicts in her friends, his occasional anger, and he could see the worry in her eyes. Ayumu rested his chin on his crossed arms and gazed at the moon again. Maybe one day he will have his own child. From her. Now it was Buhari's turn. Ah, the lucky bastard! Ayumu smiled.

*
**

Walid was fighting insomnia again. The bastard! Ayumu wanted to do anal with her! By whose decree? He never brought her flowers or a small gift. True, these things cost nothing here, but they were tokens of appreciation, nevertheless. All he did was take, consume! He would pant and moan when she sucked but would never bend down and run his tongue on her! As if she were dirty! She sparkled, always! And she had to take baths, because she was not a ghost. Perhaps this was why her father chose to settle in Japan.

Why, indeed, did houses here have bathtubs? He would have enjoyed taking baths at home. Even just a shower! He liked the water spray. He had to dream up the shower rooms in his theater. Or maybe he dreamt them up because there were none in his other world? She said once, "Why don't you go out when it rains?" She did that—she would shed her clothes and go out on the roof terrace and swirl, and the raindrops would fly away. He could only envy her. For that and being able to transform and . . . everything else. Even though her mom was gone, the people she grew up with loved her. Her father— Walid sighed. He knew that she had a half brother and sister in the old world and that the sister was queer and their dad never turned his back on any of them. Not to his children in the old world and certainly not to the one here.

If Tarek was like Leo, Walid would probably still be alive, maybe married, maybe married to another man. He might have transitioned to a woman. Mirielle's dad explained once that it was possible now. Hm, "now" was almost a quarter of a century ago. Who knew how far medicine had advanced . . . although new arrivals and the visuals they brought along spoke of punishments and bans. Two steps forward, one step back, sometimes more. Tarek was en vogue again. But his father was not here, he was, and she and the other guy. Walid's thoughts returned to Ayumu, and his eyebrows furrowed. The jerk took her climbing as if nothing had happened! What if she fell again? She was obviously not immune, not like them. What if the fall was fatal and she died! Like, really died, ceased to exist. She had a kid now, his kid, whom she had to live for and take care of.

His kid. Elian. Walid turned on his stomach and grunted. Mirielle . . . she should have told him; she should have asked what name he wanted for his son. Perhaps she had no idea that he was the dad, indeed. However, the baby bore no semblance to Ayumu, so . . . but where did Elian get his blue eyes from? Walid knew of no blue-eyed people amongst his relatives. Everybody had brown eyes. Must be this world somehow mixing things. And why was she resisting the two of them, Walid and her, moving to a place of their own with the kid?

He'd understand her unwillingness to share a house with his mother, even though it would have been very handy. His mom had raised three children, and Mirielle was already sharing a house with his sister, but Mirielle was opposed to choosing another place, another home. In this world, there were plenty of options—if the home was not locked, they could take it. Perhaps she didn't want to irk the Japanese guy. Almost certainly so! Ah, that bastard!

Walid began picturing Ayumu. The prick was attractive; he had to grant him that. Well built, muscular, moved like a cat. He was a climber, after all. Walid felt his groin getting tense, desiring, when he watched the guy naked. He wanted to suck his dick; he wanted Ayumu to suck his.

Arousal sneaked in the dark and entered his mind. Walid rolled on his back and rubbed his penis, then held it in his hand and pumped, picturing a mix of partners. The person in his head morphed— Wasilla, Mirielle, Ayumu. He imagined that Mirielle had straddled him, with his happy member inside her, and Ayumu, kneeling over him, driving his dick into his mouth. They could try it, if only Ayumu would agree. He moved his hand more vigorously, his lips trembled, then the pleasure briefly overwhelmed his mind.

⁂

Mirielle was again worried about Ayumu. Sometimes he could not hold his liquor and could get angry and rough. Ayumu had a violent streak in his character, and sadly, it often came to the foreground after heavier than usual consumption of spirits. Or sometimes it was just the type of drink that got him. Last night, he drank whiskey and laughed and sang some silly songs, then he wanted to make love, demanding her bum, and became mean when she refused. Luckily, he maintained control and ended up hiccupping an apology. Him getting drunk was, frankly, also a rare occurrence as of late, so she didn't bitch about it.

She was more annoyed by Walid badmouthing him after that.

"See, I tried to warn you. Ayumu is a loose cannon. He can fire at any time, and I am not talking about, you know, his dick. You must be cautious; don't move too close to him," he said, not for the first time. Perhaps she should tell him that she was untouchable by anger, but knowing that Ayumu had tried once to punch her would give Walid even more reasons to be worried.

Elian moved next to her and sighed. She flipped on her side and looked at the child. The curtains weren't drawn, and the moonlight was bright, pouring its cold rays over them. She had become accustomed to his presence; he had grown on her. Maybe that breastfeeding thing Beatrice mentioned did work.

She smiled. So, this was what her dad was like as a baby. This was what a brand-new human looked like. Was Elian not just a breathing doll? He never woke her up for food during the nighttime. But during the day he was sometimes greedy. She remembered her mom being bitten many times by her, often quite painfully, yet her mom liked squirting milk into her little mouth. But she herself still wanted to opt out if they could find a substitute. They tried water and also milk from a carton; however, the baby spat it out each time and screamed. Elian would not perhaps starve if not fed, but he would be uncomfortable and cry a lot. So, she kept offering her breasts. Strangely, though, when he wasn't biting, that act began giving her butterflies, as the euphemism went.

Or not so strange, humans had evolved in a certain way, and she undoubtedly carried that programming in some form. Why would she otherwise enjoy sex? Straight, oral, whatever, she loved rolling in it. Her mom went wild after dying, as apparently sexual things were very complicated in the old world. Mirielle asked her dad to elaborate on fragments of his memories, and he tried to explain—the selfish gene, diseases, religion, the weird intertwining of reproductive functions and waste discharge.

Or the growing attachment to the little creature. Another borrowed human program running, no doubt. She was not a flesh-and-bone human, and neither was Elian. Yet she went through the rites as any other woman. As she discovered, her initial aversion was not unusual. Her Grandmom Annette told her that the condition was called postpartum depression, and that she had had it too.

Mirielle turned on her side and dove into the sea of dreams.

DIETRICH

Elian made his first steps in Europe. One day after feeding him, Mirielle steadied him between her legs and then let go, while her grandmother beckoned him from the opposite side of the room. The child lurched forward and promptly tumbled down. She pulled him up. He grabbed and squeezed her finger, eyes still trained on his great-grandmother. Mirielle waited patiently, but he just rocked in place, showing no desire to try again. She rose and led him forward until Ruth took over. When he eventually succeeded in trekking between them unassisted, Ruth began clapping with a wide grin on her face. Mirielle retreated to the chair, thinking that this was bound to happen sooner or later, so what's the big deal? She then glanced at the newcomer. "Hi, Uncle A!"

Anton stretched his mouth. "Hi, M!" Then he stepped aside and let a woman enter. She appeared younger than Wasilla, so about thirty? Blonde hair, blue eyes—pretty standard fare for this neck of the woods, a bit on the plump side, but she was cute and produced a charming smile when she greeted Mirielle. "Hi, er, Mirielle. I am Renate, your uncle's girlfriend, past and present."

Mirielle rose to her feet and bowed. "I am Mirielle!"

"Huh?" the woman exclaimed.

"Ah! Sorry, a habit from Japan," Mirielle said. "Call me M, as Uncle does, if you want. He's too lazy to utter even six letters." The woman blinked a few times with her sight anchored on Mirielle. Mirielle sensed her confusion. "What is it?"

"What is what?"

"You . . . I can detect people's emotions. Everybody can after a while, but seems my receptors are more adept. You were surprised by something." Then Mirielle waved her hands. "But keep it to yourself; it was perhaps rude of me to ask."

"Er, no, it is OK. You see, your uncle had pictures of his sister all over his apartment, and you . . . you look just like her. She was your mom, right?"

"Yes. I could look a bit different if I let my hair grow, but since there are no photographs here, I-I do it . . . I keep it short so we remember her. Works perfectly every time!" She smiled again.

"Hey, Mirrie!" Ruth called. "Who made Eli's clothes?"

"Me and Dad, why?"

"My bet is on your dad designing them and you doing the sewing. Do I have that right?"

Mirielle nodded. "Yes. Care to explain, Grandma?"

"The stitches are not straight for a starter. Your dad learned to sew very well. Leo and your mom, they created many pieces; they enjoyed making things with their hands. Damn, I miss her . . ." Ruth sighed. Elian spun, surrounded by her arms. Then he seemed to get dizzy and sat on the floor.

"I could have designed them myself."

"Yes, and there was the lucky guess!" Ruth looked up and stretched her mouth.

"Dad still does. He's been up to something with Uncle Shinji, but they're keeping it under wraps."

"And you? Do you like it? Designing, sewing?"

"Not particularly, but do we have a choice? The realm is not supplying children's clothes, as you know."

"You can let him run around naked. Like your mom."

Mirielle squinted. The implication was ambiguous to her. Her mother ran around au naturel, but so did she when she was very young and even later. But then her mom was dwelling inside her, and it may have been her . . . Ah, very complicated.

"Well, he can't yet run, can he? He just walked. But since he is naked most of the time, would it not be odd if we never put him in clothes? If we did that, I wouldn't have to sew anything."

Ruth gave Elian a mild acceleration in the direction of his mother. He made several wobbly steps again before falling and reached his destination crawling. Mirielle chuckled, raised him to his feet, and sent him back. The child approved of the exercise—he giggled and clapped clumsily each time he reached his end point while managing to stay upright.

In a while, when he ended anew between his mother's legs, he looked up and emitted, "Uh . . . uh . . ." Mirielle pursed her lips; the child wanted a tit. She tried to dodge—she pushed him toward his great-grandmother, but Elian was having none of it; he sat on the floor and wailed. Mirielle grimaced, then bared her breast and called, "Come, Eli!"

Elian quickly crawled back and climbed onto her lap.

Ruth moved to the couch and sat next to them. "Listen, Mirrie, er, I need your help."

"Sure! What for?"

"Making me see someone."

"Certainly! By the way, I don't have to move a muscle anymore. When I am around, everybody can see, and I can't prevent it. You know what happened a few months ago? I was with Walid and Ayumu, we boarded a train, and guess who else was riding it and what they were doing?"

"Well, this world is kind of small—must have been your dad and, hm, Bea?"

"Yep! Enjoying themselves."

"Good for them! I want to enjoy myself too. Simon and Boris are doing their best, but you know gays; I am not their cup of tea. But there is a man, Boris's brother-in-law. His name is Heiko Dietrich. We met briefly when you were here the last time, and Boris brought him along. I don't know if you remember. I like him. It seems he likes me too, but it is weird to communicate via Boris. So, if you . . . you get the idea, I hope."

"Just let me know where and when."

"What about now?"

"Wow!" Mirielle laughed. "Just tame your expectations. You two have met only once so far, right? He may be disappointing or be disappointed. Let me just finish feeding this little mouth. He doesn't need food, I am sure, but he gets fussy when denied. Same as us, I guess. We don't have to eat and bang, but we do it nevertheless, because it gives us pleasure." Elian abruptly pushed the nipple out, as if angered by her words.

"Hey, A, will you please take care of your nephew? Your mother needs me," Mirielle called.

$$*\!*$$

The place Mirielle was taken to by Ruth was familiar. It was in her outer memory—the memory that belonged to her good parents. Elise had a room here—on the last floor. A room full of toys. "I think I've been here," she said, looking up at the first window on the last floor.

"How come?" Ruth furrowed her brows.

"Well, not me, I meant Mom and Dad."

"They've been here?"

"Yes, why not?"

"But it is a—" Ruth stopped.

"A brothel? Perhaps, in your old world. Here it is just a place where ghosts play."

Ruth blushed.

"Nana!" Mirielle smiled. "Relax. Where's the guy? Ah, there . . ."

Her grandfather, Simon, Uncle Boris, and a very tall blond man, all in their thirties, stood by the door. Simon and Boris were almost naked, wearing just lederhosen and Tyrolean hats. The tall man was dressed casually—a pair of blue jeans and a navy shirt. His hair was short, and he sported a moustache and goatee, both considerably darker. And his eyes—they were brown, almost black.

"Mirrie!" Simon opened his arms.

"Jerk!" Mirielle replied. "You should have come to meet us."

"I asked them to set up the meeting; don't apportion blame." Ruth rose to the defense of her husband.

"I see. But why clad in lederhosen?"

"Do you prefer naked?" Simon winked.

"You are unusually horny for your extremely advanced age," Mirielle said.

Simon nodded unashamedly. "We all are!"

"Keep talking. Grandma is already with the guy . . . what was his name?"

"Dietrich. Heiko Dietrich Braun, but he hates his first name."

Boris chimed in, "Hello, kiddo!" He offered a high-five.

"Don't call me 'kiddo.' I don't like it."

"OK, Mirrie, as you wish. In the old world, I would have asked how the trip was, but here this is pointless."

"Not entirely. We again came via the airport."

"You mean you were not teleported directly from home to home?"

"No, for four days. Then Dad got pissed and we went to Chūbu." She glanced at her grandmother. Ruth and Dietrich had sat on the couch, talking. Her grandmom, having long shape-shifted into her twenty-year-old self, seemed excited. Her arms were flying around as she was talking, perhaps hoping to accidentally bump into the guy and have him hold them.

Simon followed her gaze and chuckled. "This is not my old Ruth. For good! She was way too shy, and she wasted decades, even here. Let's hope that they click indeed. But then you will be leaving soon."

"We'll see. If they click as you said, I can stay, or they can join me in Japan. For now, just take me to a bar or a café. It is tiresome and boring standing with you two here."

Simon grinned as if she had uttered a compliment. The two men led her to the establishment next door and sat at the bar. The realm served her a piña colada, and the men got beers. She had three drinks in a row, then switched to just piña; she got tired of the burning taste in her mouth. And she had to stay sharp. Probably.

Her grandmother's excitement was pulsing vividly in her mind. Mirielle had no idea what it was feeding on, though. She could not read thoughts, only emotions. The guy was sending good vibes too. So, they seemed to have clicked. Maybe she should start making preparations for staying. Call Ayumu and Walid. The loft at the warehouse was replaced by somebody else's memory of the place, but she could stay with her grandmothers or find an empty home. Hey, she could even squat in any of the glitzy office buildings downtown; it would be fun.

"How are they doing, if I may ask?" Simon said. "I think that they are fine, but, you know, my senses are not as sharp as yours."

"Why don't you let them tell you?"

"Because I am impatient. Ruth deserves happiness. She's a great woman, your grandmom, but when it comes to intimacy, I struggle to deliver. I can do it once, er . . . weekly, and that's all. We started playing games, you know, with ropes and stuff, and I do get aroused and she likes it, but she needs a man. A straight man, that is, like Dietrich. I hope that it works."

Mirielle took a sip from her juice and began swirling the glass. She should have taken a book with her, or perhaps brought Elian. Waiting in a bar with her grandfather and his boyfriend was definitely boring. She fidgeted on her stool, then put the glass down, jumped onto the floor, and went behind the counter. "Gentlemen, would you like to order something?"

"Two double espressos, please!" said an unfamiliar voice.

Mirielle followed the sound. Dietrich and her grandmother had entered the joint, with smiles plastered on their faces.

The man, Dietrich, approached and said, "Thank you, miss."

Mirielle nodded politely.

"I wish that this world let us see each other easily. Now you are like the sun," Dietrich continued. "Without you, we are blind."

"My dad made people see my mom. Maybe if your shared feelings are strong enough, you will get to keep the vision."

"Maybe. I am already strongly attracted to Ruth, I must admit, but being old and wise, I would not say that I am in love, just that I like her a lot."

"She's hearing all this." Mirielle looked him in the eyes, still smiling, and pushed the espresso shots across the countertop.

"I share his feelings, Mirrie," Ruth said. She sat on the stool and placed her hand over his. Then she turned to her husband. "You OK with this, Si?"

"Sure! Even if I was able to respond to your needs, we've been together for eternity, and you have been extremely generous! I wonder why you even bother asking. It is your right!"

⁎⁎

Mirielle lifted Elian and kissed him on the cheek. He made a grumpy face and began kicking. She returned him to the floor and approached the window. On their way back, Ruth reported the encounter. Dietrich was younger than her mom, but that didn't bother Ruth in the slightest. He was a dentist, married once, then divorced, with three kids—a girl and a set of twin boys, she learned. They had dared show their true selves to each other and, Ruth said, they had both laughed wholeheartedly. Congratulations! Beatrice screamed when she found that Mirielle saw her aged. Ruth had shared her own story.

"Then what did you talk about before?"

"Mostly the same, but we were brief. It was very awkward with us not seeing each other and Boris relaying. He knew both and he was bored to his core, I could tell."

"OK, I get it."

"And we, er, we just talked."

Mirielle shrugged.

"I mean, we did not try other things."

"Ah!" The bell finally rang; they did not have sex. This is what her grandmother meant. "That's fine, you know. I don't even know why you think that you should mention it."

Ruth crossed arms at her chest, sending her gaze flying. "It was like in the old days, so romantic. I want him, but I can wait! He gave me flowers!"

"I saw that. But what old days are you talking about? As far as I know, your marriage to Granddad was arranged."

"Still . . . Simon courted me for a while, brought flowers and sweets, we went to the movies . . ."

"Why don't you do the same now? There are movie theaters in this realm."

"But we will have to bother you; you know that we can't see each other on our own."

"Well, we will have a majority vote on which flick to see, that's all. And I think that I can sleep now and you'd still be fine."

"Damn, thank you, dear!" Ruth drew her granddaughter in a tight embrace.

FIRST FUCK

Ayumu slowly swept the curve of the horizon with his gaze, hands entwined behind his head. Mirielle was somewhere beyond that arc. Or was she? Was this world a ball? She may be just a whisker away or even occupy the same space. Whatever the case, there was an emptiness inside him he was desperate to fill.

He undressed, tossed his clothes on the boulder, and stepped into the water. It was warm as usual. Ayumu dived and swam leisurely, marveling at his ability to see clearly without a mask and wondering how that was at all possible. How surviving the depths without any sort of breathing apparatus was possible.

He learned that he could not drown after he discovered that he could fly. He reasoned that there had to be protection against it, as there was against falling. He then came to the beach, swam to a deep spot, and dived. The survival instinct brought him back to the surface. He tried a few more times; however, he was unable to prevail over the drive to stay alive. He laughed at the irony of the situation; he was already dead.

Then he loaded rope and a sack full of gym weights on one of the small paddleboats and went back to sea. He put a knife in a bright red nylon bag, lowered it to the bottom, tied the heavy sack to his feet, sat on the edge, clenched his teeth, and pushed it overboard.

The weights pulled him down fast. The pressure on his chest increased. He remembered trying to fight it, but eventually it prevailed, forcing the air out of his lungs and with it, expelling every bit of confidence in the success of the endeavor and replacing it with unmanageable fear. Then he fainted.

When his consciousness returned, he found himself back at home, lying in bed, fresh out of the arms of Hypnos. So, yes, the realm would not let him drown. But he wanted to be like a fish, swim, explore the depths. He began training by holding his breath and counting. Eventually, he discovered that breathing in this world was optional. Time for his next underwater attempt.

Then Mirielle told him, "Ah, but you can breathe water. My parents did."

"What about you?"

"I don't know. When we jumped from the tower, you floated, and I fell. So, who knows. I must try it, but I am afraid."

"You can try holding your breath for a start. I learned to not breathe."

He didn't know if she followed his suggestion. He saw her with puffed-up cheeks a few times, but she always quickly let the air out after catching his gaze.

He missed her. If he could see Buhari without her, he'd drag him on a trip. He needed some courage to show up in her homeland uninvited. But wait! Buhari was from the same place, was he not? Perhaps he was already there. Ayumu surfaced and spat the water out. Which way was Europe?

*_**

"Come on in!" Mirielle smiled and stepped aside. Ayumu lingered, then outstretched his arm and shoved the kokeshi doll in her hands. She recoiled before laughing. "Ah, sorry, thanks! Come, come, don't be shy. Is that me?"

"*Hai*! In your female form. I-I . . ."

"You made it yourself. I can see." Mirielle wrapped her arm around his neck and burned his cheek with a lengthy kiss.

"Er, sorry for the intrusion."

"Au contraire! I am so glad to see you!"

"What is that? *Akontre*."

"*Gyaku ni, sukidesu*. You being here, that is."

"It is amazing how many different languages you can speak. Hey, Eli!" Ayumu opened his arms for Elian. "Wow, he walks!" The child latched onto him for a moment, then turned and wobbled away toward a pile of obviously homemade toys.

"I heard that your smart devices have become so good at translations that people no longer have to learn a foreign language." Mirielle had fetched two cups of green tea. One found its way in front of him.

"You didn't have to learn so many either. Japanese, I get. But Swedish, for example, why did you learn this one?"

"It came with Mom."

"Huh? Which one, Wass or Bea?"

"No, Elise. She learned it."

"And you decided that you would learn it too?"

"No! It came with— Ah, forget it. It is complicated."

"*Konnichiwa*, Ayumu-san. *Ogenki desu ka*?" Leo's face graced the doorframe.

"I'm fine, thanks, Leo-san!" Ayumu rose and bowed.

"Well, see you around," Leo said. He stepped inside, bent down, pecked Mirielle on the cheek, and headed out. He had shape-shifted to a much younger self for some reason.

Ayumu's eyes became narrow slits as his gaze shifted quickly from Elian to Leo and back. The kid resembled his granddad for sure! A lot.

"No offense, but so far there's nothing from you in Eli-chan"—he turned to Mirielle—"but plenty from your dad. The hair, the eyes, the nose . . ."

"Yeah, whatever genes are in this realm, they work in mysterious ways." Mirielle chuckled and took a sip. "Listen, would you like to go out for a walk? It is time for him, and I promised something to Grandmom."

"That would be great, Mirrie-chan! I've never been to your city, as you know!"

"Grandma! Get ready!"

*
**

"May I ask who he is?" Ayumu inquired quietly after they opened some distance between them and Ruth and Dietrich.

Mirielle briefed him.

"Ah, I understand. You make them see each other."

"Yeah. I wonder what my range is. Let's find out! Slow down a bit, will you?"

"But that will not be polite!"

"Ah, sometimes you are so righteous." Mirielle scoffed and braked. Ruth and Dietrich continued to walk.

"They surely like each other a lot. I think that they are in love but are either oblivious or ashamed, refusing to recognize it. I've been watching them for a while and . . . they remind me of Dad and Mom—Elise, that is."

"I am in love with you, do you know?" Ayumu suddenly blurted out, unable to resist any longer, then cowered silently, blood rising to his face.

Mirielle just held his hand and gazed down. What did this mean? He tried to read her emotions, but he was no match for her.

Then Elian pulled his leash.

Child on a leash! That was new! When Mirielle took the leash from its hook, Ayumu thought that they would also be walking a dog. But then she squatted, wrapped Elian in an altered pet harness, and clipped on the leash. She held the child in her arms until they reached the park.

Mirielle dropped his hand and followed her son, trying to keep the child steady with the line as he swerved from side to side.

"Er, I haven't seen a kid on a leash," Ayumu said.

"Well, normally I let him run and crawl around, but when I must follow Grandma, I need him to stay close, so I came up with this idea."

"In the old world, people would laugh and point. Not in Japan, though. There, they would just make long faces and talk afterward."

Mirielle shrugged.

Ayumu threw a glance at the alley. It was deserted. "I think that your grandmother and her companion went out of range. I can't see them anymore."

Mirielle looked up, then furrowed her eyebrows. "I don't see them myself. This is strange." She grabbed Elian and accelerated her pace.

Ayumu followed suit.

"If they went out of range, they should have stopped seeing each other. The normal action would be to reverse . . . ah, there."

Her grandmother and the man, Dietrich, had swerved away from the path and were locked in a kiss under a willow tree, Ruth balancing on her toes and him bent down like the handle of a cheap walking cane.

Mirielle stopped. "But if they were out of range, how did they see . . . Maybe I can reach much further than expected." She let the child down and detached the leash. Elian ran toward a patch of flowers, tripped and fell, then finished the stretch crawling. Once there, he grabbed a tulip and ripped the flower from the stem.

"Eli, no!" Mirielle ran toward him. He giggled and ripped another.

Ruth and Dietrich looked at them, still embraced. Mirielle tapped the kid's hand. He took it as an invitation to play and slapped back. Mirielle grunted, then turned to the approaching couple and said, "I was wondering how big my range was. Can you help me find out?"

"What range are you talking about?" Ruth asked.

"How far away you two can go before you lose sight of each other. That thing."

"Ah, yes! Sure, sweetie!" Ruth nodded.

"OK, then we will remain here, and you and Herr Dietrich walk until you two can no longer register your lovely muzzles. Then you come back, counting your steps."

"Skip the 'Herr.' You don't have to be so formal, Fräulein Mirielle." The tall man smiled. "Sure, we will do it! Ruth?" He offered his arm.

"Yeah, that would be interesting," Mirielle murmured, following the couple with her gaze. Elian ripped another tulip. "No!" she barked and snatched his hand.

Ayumu failed to keep his laughter to himself.

Ruth stood by the ornate wrought-iron gate set between two rustic granite posts and voiced her thoughts. "Interesting! Her range must have increased. Look how far we went."

"What was her range before?"

"Not sure, really. A few rooms' worth?"

"But the pond is at least a kilometer away!"

"I know. Shall we continue or go back?"

"Maybe cross the boulevard? I am intrigued." He looked over her head. "Then we will head her way. It is getting late, and the kid probably needs to be fed."

"Ah, don't worry about Eli. She feeds him anywhere. But he may want to take a nap and will get cranky."

On the other side of the wide boulevard, they still could see each other.

"Well, she's grown powerful." Ruth tilted her head backward, trying to catch Dietrich's sight, then licked her lips, grabbed his shirt, and pulled him down, unashamedly seeking his lips. The man offered them promptly. She drew him closer, rubbing her body hard against him. Her heart grew impatient; she wanted to rip his shirt and bury her face in his bare chest. Her granddaughter may leave soon and then what? Fantasies and toys. And gays . . .

She felt his rigid member under his jeans. Was he aware of her stiff nipples? She detached herself slowly, puffed up her chest, and put on a disarming smile. Did he see? Perhaps not. He kept looking straight into her eyes.

"Hey, Didi!" Ruth held his hand as they walked back. "Take it as you wish, but . . . erm, maybe we shall do it one of these days? I am very willing."

Dietrich glanced at her, his face straight. "What are you talking about?"

"I . . ." But he was also willing, she was sure! She was no Mirielle and at that moment she didn't have to be!

"Well, you are, erm, you have an erection, so I thought—"

Dietrich braked and his mouth nudged into a smile. Then he burst into laughter, grabbed her, and swung her around. "Gotcha!"

"Bastard!" She tried to free herself with a furious grin. "You have no idea how hard it was to utter these words! I am old, very old."

"Sorry!" He deposited her on the ground. "Didn't cross my mind. Looks are definitely deceiving. Well, I desire you too, pointless to deny it." He nodded at his groin. "But then wouldn't your grand-daughter have to be present? I-I would feel very awkward." He raised his hand and touched her breast. "I guess there is no way around it, and, thinking about it, she could be in another room, right?"

Ruth nodded and snuggled into him. Had his little Didi grown?

"Hey!" Dietrich halted again. "Let's do it!"

"You mean now?"

"Yes, why not!"

"Wow, you are bold!" She considered the suggestion, looking around in search of a spot. Her heart began to race. She took a deep breath. "OK! There!" She grabbed his hand, and they sank into the sparse bushes.

Mirielle rubbed her nose pensively. Where did the pair go? It was taking way too long; they should have returned by now. Maybe this world had pulled another prank and sent them to who knew where. But then what was that faint buzz in her head?

"Maaa," Elian said and grabbed her leg.

"I think that he's tired. Shall we not go home? Your grandmom should have already returned, I think. I wonder what happened."

Mirielle nibbled on her lip. The only explanation was that they were all over each other and forgot about the task. "OK, let's go."

Ayumu lifted Elian on his shoulders. Soon the kid fell asleep, the little arms wrapped around Ayumu's head.

"Ayumu."

"*Hai?*"

"You should know about Eli. He . . . he is not Walid's son. He is, well, how shall I put it . . . not even mine."

"Now you've got me confused but continue."

"You know how weird this world is. So, you know how I could transform, shape-shift into a male."

"Hai."

"And that male was a copy of Dad?"

"Hai." Ayumu grunted again.

"Well, I also have their memories from the time before I was born."

Ayumu sighed and smiled. "You are a weird creature, Mirrie-chan, but . . . shall I confess again?"

This time, Mirielle held his shirt instead as both his hands were supporting her son. Should she tell him everything now? Probably not, as it would be too much and certainly disappointing. Besides, her feelings for her father did not stand in the way, just that she was unable to say, "I love you too."

"So . . ." She opened her mouth.

"Hey, what is that?"

"What is what?"

"There's someone there, in the bushes." He leaned slightly and pointed.

She closed her eyes. Then her face lit up. "Ah, I know who that is. Ha!"

"I know too, I see them! Oops! Sorry, Mirrie-chan!" Ayumu pivoted and looked away.

Mirielle guffawed. Loudly. On purpose. Elian twitched, blinked awake, and turned the siren on.

FURIOUS BOND

Ayumu knocked on the apartment door. Mirielle answered instantly and let him in. He removed his shoes and bowed to the gleaming Ruth. "Good morning, madam!"

Ruth stretched her mouth. "You can dispense with the formalities, young man."

"I'm seventy-five."

"Still young. I'm five quarters of a century. But I feel as just one!" She looked up dreamily. Then her gaze returned to him. "And you don't have to remind me, because if you think my teen granddaughter having a seventy-five-year-old man for a boyfriend is creepy . . ."

"Sorry, mad— er, Ruth."

"That's better!" She stroked his cheek and gave him a playful smile. Ayumu blushed and rubbed the spot.

Mirielle returned, carrying Elian. She offloaded him on the floor in the foyer and reached for the harness.

"Leave that. I'm gonna let him hold my finger," Ruth said and lifted the child.

Mirielle opened the front door, letting them pass. "See ya!" She then carefully closed it, looked around with a goofy smile, and grabbed Ayumu's hand. "Come, let me show you something!"

She led him to a bedroom, her grandmother's for sure, opened the wardrobe, rose on her toes, and pulled two books from under the pillows on the top shelf. She put them on the dresser. "See!"

Ayumu peeked. *Kama Sutra* read the title of the first one. The second was entitled *Fifty Knots of Love*. "What are these?" he asked.

"You haven't heard of *kama sutra*? Well, not necessary. It is an ancient Hindu text about sexuality and relationships. People like the illustrations, I guess, not so much the text." She paged through the book. "Look."

Ayumu stretched his neck. "Hm, I see why." His groin tensed as she flipped the pages. His eyes moved to her face. She traced her lips; her mouth remained ajar. Was her skin also changing hue?

"What about this one?" Ayumu pointed at the second book.

"I don't know. Let's check it out!" Mirielle left *Kama Sutra* and opened *Fifty Knots of Love*. "Ah, bondage."

"Kinbaku?"

"I haven't heard the term." She glanced at his face, then down. "It turns you on, right?"

"Er, I . . ."

"All right, let's see . . . we have some time." Mirielle dropped the book on the mattress and left the room. She returned holding a run of clothesline.

"Here, we can try with this." She tossed it on the bed and paged through. "Yeah, the beginner section looks easy, simple stuff." She pulled her blouse over her head, sat on the edge of the bed, and began wriggling out of her jeans.

"OK, it turns me on, but . . ." Ayumu spoke quickly.

"Then indulge yourself with a willing partner. Another leftover from your world, I suppose." She removed her panties, got up, and raided the wardrobe again. "We can make use of this one." She tossed the dildo she held onto the dresser.

Ayumu tried to maintain a respectable composure. With measured moves, he neatly stacked his shirt and underwear on the nearby chair and placed his trousers on the backrest. Then he turned and spread his arms. "Well?"

Mirielle climbed on the bed, sat, put her hands behind her back, and nodded at the page. "Follow the instructions."

Ayumu began threading the rope as shown, his penis stiffening further with each pull. Mirielle was breathing through her parted lips; her cheeks were red, and her nipples had popped out. Goosebumps covered her skin, and she growled.

Ayumu stopped. "Er, something wrong?"

"Er, no, I . . ." Her voice quivered. "Hurry up, will ya?"

"This is an art; I can't hasten it." As Ayumu leaned to pull the rope ends over her shoulders, he felt her drawing his penis into her mouth. He tugged the ropes lightly and swayed his hips. "Ah, you are so impatient. I'm gonna finish fast."

"Uhuh . . ." she grunted and carried on.

He could feel the pounding of his heart in his throat. This girl was insane! She had no inhibitions whatsoever! But why would she? Why would he himself foster any? She was of this world, and he had been dead for decades. If she wanted it, that was fine.

Mirielle spat his dick out and drew breath through her mouth while smiling. Ayumu kneeled and kissed her. Her tongue greeted his own, as she moaned quietly and her hot breath mixed with his.

His hands moved over her body, uncertain where to settle. Ayumu arched his spine; Mirielle rose on her knees, leaning forward, unwilling to let his lips depart from hers. Then, both lost balance and tumbled to the floor, laughing. Mirielle rolled and scrambled back on the bed, exposing her modest derriere. Ayumu moved fast and nipped her buttock. Mirielle giggled. Ayumu rubbed his cheek against the skin, then his tongue entered the split, sending her silent. She gasped when the tongue reached her ring and fluttered over the orifice, then the tip pushed in. Ayumu held the ends of the rope while doing so and pulled gently, eliciting a soft moan from his partner. He rose, transferred them in one hand, wrapped the rope around his wrist and, almost shaking, introduced himself. Fire erupted in his groin, and he twisted his mouth, his brows nudging closer. He began rocking, holding her hip with one hand and the rope in the other, unsure what to do with it. The visual alone made his heart race. He moved deliberately slowly, dragging the flutter of his receptors for as long as possible.

"Faster!" She huffed, swirling her rear. "Ugh!"

Ayumu was in no hurry; he knew he would not last if he heeded her request. Still, he accelerated, his piston feeling almost no resistance in the well-oiled hollow. He pulled the rope up; Mirielle squeezed her eyes shut and relinquished control of her vocal cords. Each thrust produced a moan, adding to his elation. He dropped the rope and grabbed her hips with both hands, moving faster, his penis on the verge of bursting. He clenched his teeth when the spillway gave way and paused, powerful reverberations shaking his frame, then grabbed the rope, pulled it straight up, and resumed. Mirielle quivered, tears of impatience rolling down and staining the wrinkled bed-throw. Her face was bright red, her noises—loud.

"Bastard!" Walid shrieked and pounced over Ayumu. "What are you doing? Have you got no shame?"

Ayumu plummeted to the floor, his scalp splitting as his skull met the corner of the dresser. Mirielle, yanked by the rope, crashed next to him.

"All you do is use her as a sex doll!" Walid landed a punch on Ayumu's face. "A pleasure robot!" Walid grabbed the loose end of the rope, wrapped it around the neck of the stunned Ayumu, and pulled. The veins on his temples stood out and his opacity decreased.

"Wal! Walid!" Mirielle shouted, twisting her body like a trapped lizard. "Stop!"

Walid ignored her and pulled harder. The rope cut into his hand. Ayumu began gasping for air as he clutched the rope and tried to yank it free.

Mirielle rolled on her back and launched out her legs, delivering a blow with her feet. "Stop!"

Walid rolled on the floor, bumping into Ayumu, then, ignoring the pain, sprang back and swung his hand hard. It passed through her head without resistance. Dragged by the inertia, he swirled and landed on one knee, his molars peeking through his mouth slit.

"There you have it! I cannot be hurt! Now stop!"

Walid finally obeyed; his molars retreated out of sight and his shoulders slumped.

Ayumu crawled closer to the girl and began untying her, blood dripping from his cracked scalp.

Walid began shivering. What had he done? He tried to hit her! Unforgivable! All because of this punk! He clenched his teeth, his hands rolling into fists anew, his heartbeat gaining pace once more. Now what, beg her for forgiveness? So utterly humiliating! All because of the damn punk! Walid looked up, his lips trembling, then he sprang to his feet and ran out, slamming the door.

Mirielle caught a glimpse of the theater lobby before the door snapped shut. So, he had retreated to his dreamworld. She rubbed her wrists and followed Ayumu into the kitchen. He bent, inserted his head under the faucet, and turned the water on. The wound had already closed, and the water rinsed off the traces of blood.

"Wow! That coming from the quiet guy! We need to talk to him. I mean, both of us. I also have things to say, and I don't want you to handle everything alone. I'm a man, a man from the other world, and I understand how he feels. I tried to hit you too, for which I am infinitely sorry. Well, I actually did land a punch."

"I asked for it." Mirielle huffed a chuckle. "OK, you have a point about being a man from another world." She headed back to the bedroom, then stopped, turned, and smiled. "Ah, it was exciting! I mean, before Walid showed up. We shall try again. And thank you!" Then she pushed the door handle down, mumbling, "I wonder what Walid is doing here, anyway?"

ELIZABETH

Mirielle leaned against the doorframe, waiting for her head to cease spinning. When the dizziness subsided, she forced her eyesight into focus, let go of the door, and protruded her head into the space behind it. She had jumped; the locale was unknown. She took a step back and scanned the hallway: off-white walls, doorknobs instead of levers, framed dry flowers on the walls. All vaguely familiar. She searched inside her outer memory. Was this her dad's American home?

"Dadadadadada . . ." came a child's voice from downstairs. Elian? Were they visiting? She pivoted and descended the steps. Leo was sitting on a navy-blue sectional under a large green plant with massive leaves, which she could not name, and playing with their kid. Both had become accustomed to calling him that. It was a fact in a way. He raised his gaze.

"I jumped," she announced.

"When were you?"

"If I tell you 'in the past,' that would be meaningless. I was at Granny Ruth's, playing matchmaker. Or rather seemaker."

"Ah, that was last year, almost to the day."

"I can tell. Eli's grown."

"You too." Her father smiled.

"Seriously?" She knew that unlike the others, she was aging, but without mirrors it was hard to tell.

"Yeah. I'm starting to see what your mom would have looked like had she not died. I love you, Mirrie!"

Mirielle stepped closer, sat, and snuggled up. "I love you too, Dad," she said quietly, then drew Elian into her arms and added, "And you." She then sat upright and said, "Anyway, remind me why we are here. It is your home in the States, right?"

"Yep. We came to visit."

"How does it come? You never took us here before. By the way, are just the three of us here, or did we all come? I can't detect Bea or Wass, but they may be out somewhere."

"Just the three of us. Bea's spending time with—what was his name? I think it was Rudy? Wass . . ." He looked at the floor and sighed. "Walid drifted away, and she's still upset."

Mirielle's heart sank. Did she manage to talk to Walid, to bring him from the brink, or had he become even more unhinged? She sensed his burning anger and the hatred mixed with love. She had to do something about that. *Did* she do something about that? He had it all wrong. He wanted to protect her, she understood, but there was nothing to protect her from. She mishandled the situation, but where did she step wrong?

"You were close friends," her father said.

"Oh, good to know. Did I tell you about our problems or did you guess?"

"You sought my advice."

"Ah, OK, that would be me indeed." She started crying. The short, skinny guy with the scar on his face certainly had a place in her heart. She was going to miss him! "And Ayumu?" Her voice trembled. "Is he—"

"Your Ayumu-kun is still around."

"Mamamama . . ." Elian looked her in the eyes and giggled, then he wrapped his arms around her leg and delivered a smooch on her knee.

Leo spoke slowly. "I-I didn't bring you here earlier because I couldn't find the place. I tried several times, I wandered around, but I was unable to reach the street; space always bent away from it. My guess is that the house was inaccessible because Elizabeth was alive. And she may still be. She's twenty years younger and was very healthy, exercising regularly. Something must have changed, though. I was drawn here; you know the feeling. When Walid drifted away, you were also very miserable, and being a strong empath, you merged your grief with that of Wass. You two were shedding tears nonstop— honestly, it was seriously getting on my nerves—and I offered the trip as a distraction. Wasilla refused to leave Fatimah alone, though."

"That's understandable. What was I doing upstairs?"

"You wanted to see Abi's room."

"I still do."

"The second on the right. I hope that it is barren; it would be bad if otherwise. I—"

Mirielle caressed his hand. If the room was not empty, that would signify that her half sister was dead, and Abi should be in her early fifties now, provided the mental math was correct.

She got up and climbed the steps. Second on the right, he said. Yes, the door was ajar; she left it this way. Mirielle pushed it open and ascertained—the room was indeed empty! Her half sister was still alive, hopefully for good. Mirielle was aware of the hardship and discrimination Abi faced and that she was now living in Europe, in their father's real old home. But maybe Europe had changed too, going backward on queer rights. Her dad said that was a strong trend when he passed. Leaders who had once promoted it had reneged, siding with mainstream sentiment. She still struggled to understand. Why did mainstream care?

Mirielle turned back, ready to deliver the good news, when her eye caught the door at the bottom of the corridor. A narrow gap was apparent between the leaf and the frame. She made it wider with her finger. The leaf swung silently.

It was a bedroom. The curtains were drawn, letting sparse light through. She saw a bed, a nightstand, a door—probably a walk-in closet—and a chaise in front of the window. There was the usual mirrorless dresser with a stool. On the wall, there was a flat-screen TV on a swivel and in the corner, another large plant. Mirielle approached it and touched the leaves. It wasn't artificial. She had yet to see a fake indoor plant. Leo's memory stated that in the old world there were plenty of these. But not in this place. According to him, Elizabeth hated fakes, and all plants in the home were real.

Mirielle opened a gap in the curtains and looked outside. Motion caught her eye. An old woman dressed in half leggings and a tight shirt dismounted a bike and pushed it in the driveway. Then she looked up, and their gazes crossed. Mirielle dropped the curtain and stepped back. She heard the bike crashing on the ground. Mirielle pulled the curtain and looked out; the woman was hurriedly walking away. Her senses detected worry and confusion.

"Hey, Dad!" Mirielle ran down the stairs. "Abi seems to be OK, but I think that Elizabeth is here! I just saw an old woman pushing a bicycle."

Leo rose to his feet. "Where?"

"Outside, but she ran."

"Take him." Leo navigated around their son and rushed out.

"Elizabeth! Liz!" Leo called, turning his head in either direction. The street was deserted, except for the occasional car. Cars! Yeah, these were the United States. And what were the United States without cars? The vehicles were old Chevrolets and Buicks and Cadillacs from the 1950s, shiny though, the chrome parts bouncing sunlight into his eyes. What a weird place. Why had there been no cars in Vegas? And where did his wife go?

"Liz! What the hell is going on? Why are you hiding?"

His voice rang lonely in the quiet neighborhood. He blocked his ears, as if that would help, and tried to sense her. Nothing! Leo pouted. What was his wife's problem? Was she ashamed that she died? He tried to broadcast peace: *Liz, please, gal, this shouldn't be you.*

She was always troubled. She was smart and educated; she stood above him in this regard, a doctor of science versus the lowly master of arts, but he cared not. He was proud to be her husband, but did she believe him? She was constantly on edge and tried to always be rational. She went overboard sometimes, as if having emotions were a crime. He was the one who cried in the family, and he was not ashamed. Crying was a simple physiological reaction to relieve stress.

Maybe she had too much on her hands. For a woman to prove herself as a scientist was harder than it was for men, even in the 2020s, and it was also the onset of the anti-science movement. Knowledgeable people were labeled crooks. There were unethical scientists for sure, but everybody? Not by a long stretch. But emotions overrode logic and the mob went wild. Chemtrails, flat earth, plenty of rubbish to choose from. Malicious players and raging fools were spreading unhinged ideas on social media, and later in the meta-space. It likely had gotten worse after his last day.

Leo walked back with slumped shoulders. She kept a secret, maybe more than one. He was depressed by the militant stupidity around them and personally touched—he was a CGI specialist, tired of hearing how everything was CGI. He could often spot the fakes just by looking at the video; he had developed a seventh sense.

Elizabeth, she worked on life-saving medicines, and she had to deal not only with the shame of the exuberant greed of the pharmaceutical corporations, but also with the morons who praised Godfrey when it was her and her colleagues' hard work that saved somebody's life. He tried to draw her into a refuge—be kind to each other, make love, then face the world again—but she resisted. There was no problem, she said.

"Dadada . . ." Elian grabbed him when he stepped inside.

"Dadada, indeed." Leo tousled his son's hair. They could just leave, as Elizabeth had succeeded in alienating him to an almost uncaring degree; however, he still held a soft spot. And he was still curious.

"Describe the woman, please."

"She was old; you know that I see true age. Her hair was certainly dyed, as it was blonde. I didn't notice her eye color, probably blue. She was slim, and her face was somewhat long." Mirielle tugged at her chin.

"Must be Liz. We liked biking, it kept us fit, and walking for leisure in the USA is not a thing. You must be on some kind of wheels."

"Will you tell me more about her?"

"Sure. Let's go out on the lawn. I think that the pool is also present in this reality of ours. Eli!"

Mirielle tried to set her nose straight, but her thoughts were on the way, and it kept wrinkling at the root. Why would Elizabeth behave this way?

"Did you ask Grandma Annette? She's a shrink."

"No, by the time I started worrying, she was already dead."

"What about now? Now she's around."

"I will. When we get back."

"You can summon her here."

"And what, hunt Liz? No." Leo relaxed in the lounger while keeping an eye on Elian, who was flapping with his little hands in the water.

Mirielle floated closer and looked up. "But you found the house this time. Maybe her repeal is weakening?"

"Maybe . . . but I think that we must give her space, let her come home. We'll leave a note."

"OK." Mirielle pulled Elian by the leg and pushed him on the edge, then lifted herself up. She brushed the water off her skin, took the toddler under one arm, and grabbed her clothes with the other. "Where are we going to go?"

"To a motel. There's one four streets down. Or there should be one. Not the best place but not the worst either, and in this world it ought to be clean."

Leo went to the study adjacent to the living room and returned with a notebook. He sat, opened it, and wrote with large letters: "Liz, please! See you at Barbeque Inn. Left, 4 xings, then left again. Leo." He centered the open notebook on the coffee table, stood up, and said, "Let's go." Then he thought for a moment, took the notebook in his hand, and added next to his name: " + Mirrie + Eli."

"Hm! That's better." He grunted, Japanese style, and returned the notebook to the table.

"What is 'xings'? Something in Chinese?" The word irked her for some reason.

"Crossings. There are no traffic signs here, but in the old world, pedestrian crossings were demarcated with a XING painted on the road and written on the warning sign. Also used for street intersections in vernacular."

"Ah, I think I've seen it in pictures in books and magazines I read. But I paid no attention."

"Well, here's the first." Leo pointed at the intersection. "In the old world, there'd be a yellow, diamond-shaped traffic sign with the silhouette of a walking person and a plate below it reading PED XING. And same on the asphalt. That was California. In other places there was no plate."

"I think I see that."

"See what?"

Mirielle laughed. She could indeed see PED XING painted on the road.

Leo squinted.

"You can't see, can you?"

"No." He shook his head. "But I was not born here. Anyway, I disliked these markings."

"Why?"

"The wording was unclear even for English-speaking people, for people from other states, and PED always reminded me of the word *pedophile*."

Mirielle checked inside her. "Pedophiles—individuals sexually attracted to children. Yuck, that's horrible!"

"I think that all men are pedophiles."

The young woman's jaw dropped. That, coming from her dad? Her eyebrows traveled upward. "Including you?"

"Yes, I am a man. I was a man. Well, if I am pedantic, we are not *all* pedos, but we all carry the seed. I don't know if this is an evolutionary trait, from the days when the survival of the species overrode everything else. Pedophilia was sadly normal centuries ago. Muhammad, the Muslim prophet, was married to a six-year-old girl and consummated the marriage when she was nine, shit like that. In many places it still is; young girls become brides to aged men. Don't get me started on old-world horrors, please. Point is, at the end it is a question of intelligence, integrity, and self-control. Some people don't want to exercise it; others simply can't. In the West, pedophilia is considered a mental illness, but so was homosexuality. The major, crucial difference is that a child cannot give informed consent, and a child will be physically and emotionally hurt, whereas two or more adult individuals can consent and enjoy the experience. I'm certain that you do."

A pause followed. She caught her father's worried gaze. "Well, I indeed do enjoy said experience. Please continue."

"Homosexuals often get lumped together with the pedophiles, and your sister got flak about being queer. But it is worse for men, because pedophiles are preponderantly males, and the poor, consenting gays are hated and often hurt because of that. But I've heard of—"

"Female pedophiles. Yes, I know."

"Of course you do. But seems that opinion of mine I just presented was lost to you."

"Yep."

"Let's swing him!" Leo grabbed Elian's hand.

"Sure." Mirielle grabbed the other and they ran, swinging the kid. "Wheeee!"

Elian laughed and demanded, "Mmo!"

Absorbed in the game, they missed the rings of the bicycle bell. They halted only when Elizabeth shouted, "Leo!" and braked hard. The tires screeched and left a short trail on the road.

"Come home," she said quietly. She was still old, perhaps not yet able to shape-shift.

Leo narrowed his eyes and shook his head. "Hi, Liz." He wondered whether to step forward and hug her. Her hands holding the crossbar were twitching occasionally, and her breathing was ragged. She lifted her arm and wiped her cheek. Leo noticed the fingers trembling.

"Sure, thanks."

She didn't move.

"Well? You said I should come home. What about them?" He nodded at Mirielle and little Elian.

"How come I can see them? And . . . who are—wait! I remember her face! Is she your—"

"No, this is my daughter, Mirielle. They're local. And this is, er, Mirrie's kid, Elian."

"Isn't it Spanish?" Elizabeth blurted out.

"So what?" Mirielle furrowed her eyebrows.

Leo lifted his hand. "Yes, it is. It is a nice name."

"I-I am sorry," Elizabeth stuttered. "Well, let's go back; there's plenty of space."

"Gracias!" Mirielle chirped.

"Mirrie!" Leo raised his voice. Mirielle cowered and took Elian's hand.

"Na . . ." the little boy said, pointing at Elizabeth. Then he laughed, grabbed his mother's skirt, and pulled it down.

"Eli!" Mirielle restored the garment to its position.

"When did you die?" Leo asked his wife. "And can I push the bike for you?" He reached for the crossbar.

"No, when I hold the crossbar, my hands don't shake."

"There are no diseases here; therefore, you must be stressed out, overexcited. Is it us or something else?"

"Over a year ago, 401 days. I keep track."

And he had detected her only recently. But why? Why was she hiding?

"That's a lot. I wonder why I sensed attraction only a few days ago. Bea found me on her first day."

"She's dead?" Elizabeth voice was still unsteady.

"Well, she'd be over a hundred if she were still alive. So, yes. And . . ." Leo sighed.

"And what?"

"There's too much to tell, and you may get overloaded."

"I've been here for a while, don't worry."

Leo sought her eyes. "Why did you hide? I mean, shit. Do you hate me, Liz?"

She violently shook her head and shrieked, "No!" She then lowered her gaze and added quietly, "Why would I hate you, Leo Hans? Why would I?"

"Sorry, but—"

"Dad!"

Leo turned. Mirielle moved her hand side to side. He bit his lip, thinking. Elizabeth was under a lot of emotional stress, which was practically visible. He didn't need Mirielle's enhanced empathic ability to tell. But why?

"Liz, Mirrie here is a strong empath, and they signaled that you are not OK. I can see that myself, so maybe the three of us should go back to the motel and give you space to calm down."

"Thanks, but no. This is your home too, and I am still your legal wife, am I not?"

"Legal wives can and do kick their husbands out of their homes," Leo said with a faint smile. "And there are no courts and lawyers here, so I will have no recourse."

Elizabeth grabbed his wrist, still looking down. "You are coming home. Period!"

"OK!" He continued. "Also, you should know that sometimes Mirrie's guesses derived from the emotions of the person are so accurate that people reckon them a telepath, but they are not."

"Are they non-binary?"

"Not in the usual way. They are more like trans on demand. They can switch from female to male form and back. At least they were able to. They lost the ability some two-thirds into the pregnancy, just like their mom was unable to shape-shift at that time. Then, when she stopped breastfeeding, she reacquired the trait."

"Their mom . . . was she your girlfriend? They look just like the pictures."

"Yes, but Elise drifted away shortly after Mirrie was born."

"I'm sorry."

"Don't be, this is the afterlife. We all continue our journey sooner or later." Leo opened the front door and let everybody in.

DOUBTS

Leo pulled a bottle of whiskey and three glasses from the cabinet in the kitchen, poured, added ice from the fridge dispenser, and handed out the drinks. Then he glanced at Elian. The child was quiet, clutching his mother's leg while she was leaning against the wall.

"You know what pisses me off the most?" Leo turned to his wife. "You not sharing news about Abi. And maybe even Eric. They live in the same city, but I wouldn't go that far. You could have told me: 'OK, this is how they're doing' and then sent me away if you didn't want me around—"

"But I don't want to send you away." The ice in Elizabeth's glass kept clanking as she held it in both hands.

"OK." Leo sat on the couch and beckoned his son.

Elian clutched his mother's leg even tighter and said, "Ape . . ."

Leo squinted. What did the kid mean, what ape? He swung his gaze across the room; maybe Elian had seen a picture or something. Leo twisted his torso. The African figurines were there on the shelf behind him, as in the old world. One of them, carved from blackwood, represented a large Indigenous woman with huge breasts. Perhaps it gave the idea to the kid. Racism was built into people and had to be consciously shaken off. His son was born in this world indeed, but he was obviously not immune. Leo sighed and sipped from his drink.

"Abi is OK. She stopped coming home some eight years ago after she and Susi were arrested at DJT International on suspicion of traveling abroad to get abortions." Elizabeth's voice was still shaky. "This happens very often now. They had to undergo invasive examinations and were both pissed. The kids became adults. Both went to University, Aerin—to your Neues Polytechnic—which I guess shall be called 'Altes' now. We have a great-grandson, Rohan Phillip."

Elizabeth sipped from her whiskey, then scoffed, placed the glass on the table, and buried her face in her hands. Leo waited patiently.

Elian said "Ape," again, this time, pointing at Elizabeth.

"Eli, this is rude!" Leo furrowed his eyebrows, surprised by the lack of reaction in Mirielle.

She had trained her eyes on Elizabeth, squinting slightly. Then she looked down at the kid and back to Elizabeth.

"Eli, let's go outside," she said finally and took the little hand. They headed to the backyard. Just before crossing the door threshold,

Elian turned back and pointed again at Elizabeth. "Ape." Mirielle yanked him out.

Elizabeth uncovered her face. It was white, much whiter than it should normally be. Her shoulders had slumped low. If Leo could see her true visage, the wrinkles around her eyes and mouth would appear deeper and more numerous.

He got up, left his glass on the countertop, went behind his wife, and silently laid his hands onto her shoulders. He then caressed the golden hair he remembered from their last days in the old world. She had a secret, he was absolutely sure. She was troubled, even more apparently so now. But would she tell?

"Liz, I am certain that you carry something very heavy inside your mind. I struggle to understand why you are refusing to confide. Ultimately, it is your choice, but am I that untrustworthy? Did you ever feel betrayed by me?"

She laid her hand over his and shook her head slowly. "It was dangerous."

Leo twitched. What was dangerous? Her secret? Did she work on bioweapons? Was she involved in clandestine biological research?

"But now it isn't; we are very dead."

"It still is, in a way. It will bring you hurt."

"Try me."

Elizabeth sighed and buried her face in her palms again. Her shoulders started shaking.

"Speak up!" Leo raised his voice sharply, sending a jolt throughout her frame.

She turned at him, exposing her wet eyes, the desperation on her face having morphed into surprise.

Leo moved in front of her and squatted. "You are not helping me, and you are not helping yourself. You made me really pissed when we were still alive by denying the obvious. Unbecoming for a smart woman like you! If you continue to insist, then fine, have it your way. I'll be out of here by tomorrow, and you will enjoy your solitude."

He rose to his feet, grabbed his glass, and downed it, then out of habit looked for the dishwasher and, failing to locate the machine, abandoned the glass on the countertop.

"It is about Abigail."

"What about her?"

"She may not be yours."

Leo squinted. Did Elizabeth mean that he was not Abi's biological father? She bore resemblance—his nose, his wavy dark hair, the shape of her eyes.

"As in, you slept with somebody else?"

His wife nodded.

"She is mine! It is irrelevant whether we are biologically related or not. She will always be my girl. I raised her, we raised her, and nobody else was involved. She is ours!"

"Elizabeth was raped, Dad. Elian meant 'rape,' I think," Mirielle said and leaned on the folded door.

Leo froze and his jaw dropped. Then he gathered his composure, waved Mirielle out, and laid a gaze on his wife. "Is that so?"

Elizabeth nodded.

"Oh!" He frantically searched for words. Then he spoke fast. "But you should have told me! We should have gone to the police, sought justice!"

"It was Roger. And not just once. It's complicated."

"Roger Weiss? Your stepdad?"

"Yes. It started shortly after he married Mother. I was fourteen. I am ashamed because I-I liked it. It was an adventure; this is how he framed it. Sneaking out, having sex in the dungeon of the mansion or on the beach . . . he was a very classy man, slick. And I was also taking revenge on Mother for turning her back on Dad. Roger paid for my education, my PhD, and he got me the job. He also left me alone for several years, so I thought that it was over. It is crazy, but back then I missed him. He found himself a younger mistress. Get me more." Elizabeth suddenly outstretched the hand holding the empty glass.

Leo took it and went to the cabinet, unscrewed the bottle, and poured.

"No ice," Elizabeth said.

Leo complied and skipped the fridge.

His wife swirled the glass, sipped, hissed, and then continued. "No offense, but I was attracted to you because you reminded me of him— much older, tall, dark hair, blue eyes. I found you very sexy."

Ah, that would probably explain our initial good run, Leo thought.

"Then after we got married, he was back. He said that it was time for him to have another child. I refused, and he beat me up. Remember the bicycle fall?"

Leo nodded almost invisibly, his mind still crunching the news.

"Well, that wasn't a fall at all. He beat me and forced himself on me. Several times. Why do you think I started pushing for a kid? I was afraid that I was pregnant, and I had to act fast to conceal the origin of the child. I was indeed pregnant, but to be honest, in my confusion I underwent the screening after I slept with you too, and I am not sure who Abi's father is. I never dared to run a test, even though we had sequencers in the lab. I hoped that it was you."

"I still think that you should have told me. We could have reported him to the police—"

"And be destroyed? He was a state senator, for God's sake! He had connections everywhere. The police, the goons. We could have easily become involved in a deadly crash. You were always an idealist; you believed in the good in people."

"Well, let me reiterate. Abi is my daughter, regardless of whose genes she propagated! That aspect of the story you must stop worrying about. Even if I found out earlier about the whole affair, she would still be my girl. The kid has no guilt."

"I wasn't sure. Sorry, Leo. And you may have blown the horn and gotten all of us into trouble. People like Roger are ruthless."

"I understand."

Elizabeth took a gulp and hissed again. "People believe in divine justice. I deserve punishment, but what did I get? The same comfy home, the same balmy weather, the same sense of guilt. Maybe that is my punishment—the remorse I am unable to shake off. But if he is also here, he has no conscience, no integrity. He'd still be smug."

"He's not here."

"How do you know?"

"Because this world does not tolerate human monsters. Years ago, my nephew Peter, you know him, he tried to rape Elise, and he was expelled."

"Expelled where?"

"That I don't know."

"Maybe he was expelled to a luxury yacht somewhere off the coast of paradise. Maybe Roger is in such a place. Maybe he bought himself an afterlife!"

"You are so cynical—"

"Is my cynicism unjustified? People like Roger ruled the old world, and they might be ruling this one too; it's just that we can't see them."

"That's still something." Leo laughed. "Or else this place would indeed be hell."

"Yeah . . . these people are truly unbelievable, their total lack of humility and self-awareness. They took the insult and turned it into a gain. Oranyeland . . ." Elizabeth scoffed and downed her glass.

"I don't get it."

"You have not heard it, eh? The Great American Confederation of Oranyeland and Canuck—this is what the expanded country is called now."

Leo pouted. Yeah, nothing new under the sun. The so-called leaders never had a trace of shame. And the masses still venerated them. Elizabeth had a point: Maybe it was just a matter of who they could see, and they in fact shared this world with the assholes. He hoped not. Cold sweat covered his temples, and he shivered. Was there a way to find out?

SUICIDE

Mirielle and Elizabeth were rolling down the shallow incline, saddled on their bicycles. Mirielle had reverted to her androgynous appearance from her adolescent days, drawing curious glances from her father's legal wife. Elizabeth had calmed down considerably since the other day.

Elizabeth finally succumbed to her curiosity. "So, what is it like to be born here?"

"I age."

"Just that?"

"Well, I am also both yin and yang, or rather I was. Time will tell if I become whole again." Mirielle looked around. "There are cars here. In Japan, there are trains. Back home only Steve has a car, and Dad built a motorboat and a light airplane."

"I have seen no trains. But cars—yes, there are many. Just that they are all very old models from over a century ago. Don't you find this place weird?" Elizabeth asked.

"This place is all I know. To me, your old world is weird."

"Yes, right, good point. And since you are local, do you know what this place is?"

"It is made of the memories of the dead, of people like you. Look around—houses, cars, streets, skyscrapers, all things that people remember, only not quite identical to the ones in your old world. Here they are clean and idealized. All these cars are now considered classics, right?"

Elizabeth hummed. "Yes."

"I am myself a memory."

"You? A memory of what?"

"Of affection, love. My mom's and my dad's," Mirielle said softly.

"I see." Elizabeth sounded unconvinced.

"And you? You don't love Dad, do you?"

Elizabeth braked sharply. Mirielle followed suit.

"What do you know about love, little girl? Or little boy. I don't know what you are."

"I have their memories, and I have feelings of my own, so I am of the opinion that I know a thing or two. I don't want to be aggressive. I apologize if it came out this way."

Elizabeth dropped her gaze. "Yeah, seems there's no hiding emotions from you. No, I was never in love with Leo, as in being totally devoted, lacking sound judgment, head over heels. I was never in love with anyone in that way. I was afraid to let my guard down. Too many broken hearts, too many betrayals, and too much rationalization, I guess; love is just an evolutionary trait, mindless attraction designed to make members of the species desire each other and thus procreate. Because this is what it is at the end of the day. Even here. I know that Leo never stopped loving your mother, and when they met again in the afterlife, see what happened? They procreated. Sorry, I'm just stating a fact; I'm not being cynical."

"Let's ride. I want to give more thorough consideration to your words."

"Sure." Elizabeth pushed the pedals. "I don't know how far your experience goes, Mirrie, er, may I call you that?"

"Course."

"But can you make yourself experience the emotion purely on the qualities of an individual? You may know that he or she is an exceptionally good person, trustworthy, caring, reliable, courageous, and wholly deserving of your affection, yet all you have is respect, and you'd rather be cuddling in the arms of the bad guy next door."

Mirielle squinted.

"Because this is when your heart pounds and your blood boils—"

"Stop!"

Elizabeth again braked hard.

A second set of tires screeched. "Sorry, I'm trying to digest your words, and you keep adding more and more."

"Apologies."

Both resumed the ride.

"Er, are you all alone here?" Mirielle asked.

"No, I can see my father and my stepmom. My half siblings, they are younger and either still alive or invisible."

"And your mother?"

"My mother I cannot see. And I don't want to."

"If you wish, you can come with us, with Dad."

"I was under a lot of stress indeed, but I nevertheless heard him mentioning the faux redhead. If he's reconciled with Beatrice, what am I supposed to do there? Stir up animosity? Mischief?"

"I get it. But I also don't want people to be lonely."

"There are plenty of lonely people; you can't take care of them all. Also, do not worry about me. I'm coping quite well. Take care of yourself and your kid. Who's the father, by the way?"

"Dad."

Elizabeth veered sharply to the left and promptly plummeted to the ground.

*
**

Leo peeked through the window. Mirielle was in the pool, playing with Elian. Elizabeth followed his gaze and frowned. "Your . . . er, children, why are they naked?"

"Because they are in the pool."

"Normal people wear swimsuits."

"Depends. It is a cultural thing. When I was a kid, I ran around naked on the beach until I was, what, six or seven. Other kids too. Ladies sunbathe topless. It is not a big deal. Even less so here, where there is nobody to see you." He turned toward her. "You are grumpy, I can tell. Why? You've been like that since yesterday, after you returned from the bike ride. Did you have a fight with Mirrie?"

Elizabeth avoided his eyes. Her face was slowly changing color, as if her blood had defied gravity. Leo peered; a quarrel between Mirielle and his wife was a very plausible explanation. He couldn't think of anything else.

"We did not!" Elizabeth grunted and relocated to the side of her desk.

"OK, so if not that, what is it? You know how awkward one feels in the face of obvious ire, and the best way of settling issues is by talking."

"Your daughter told me."

"Told you what exactly?"

Elizabeth said, "You know what—do I have to say it?"

"They could have told you many things," Leo pushed. "I am not a telepath."

Elizabeth's face had now fully taken the color of the Chinese national flag. "The boy, Elian, he is your son, isn't he?" She was breathing heavily. "You slept with her, your own daughter!"

"In a way, that is correct." Leo had no intention of defending his actions or extending excuses. He had long found peace with himself for the events of that day. An uneasy one, but still . . . how could he make his wife understand? One had to experience it; words were insufficient, weak. He shook his head.

"And you show no remorse! Look at you, just look at you!" Elizabeth screamed.

"Liz, try to calm down, please, and I will do my best to explain."

"Pervert, damn pervert! Now I know that Abigail is your daughter for sure! That's why she's damaged! Her illness, it came from your fucked-up genes. Damn it, why did I marry you!"

"Don't call our kid sick!" Leo said, his voice coarse. She was wrong, so wrong!

"Why? She's the same! I slept with my stepfather indeed, but he was not biologically related and a straight man. I am straight! You are sick! Your darn children are sick!"

Mirielle filled the doorframe, dripping water. "Elizabeth, I beg you to calm down." She dropped on her knees and brought her hands together. "I truly beg you!"

The old woman's lips nudged up, exposing her teeth. She laid her gaze over the pious nude, then grabbed the wooden pencil holder and hurled it at Mirielle. "Abomination!" she screamed.

Leo quickly glanced through the window. Elian was sitting on the lawn, stuffing grass into his mouth. Sensing the gaze, the child looked up and laughed, then chewed on another batch of fresh greens.

Leo's gaze promptly returned to the room. Mirielle had crawled closer to his wife. Elizabeth held one of her trophies like a bat, her opacity fluctuating. Leo recognized the symptom.

"Liz, I beg you too! You will be expelled."

She trained her blazing eyes on him. "What if I want to be expelled? Heh? Maybe life on the other side is better. No lesbians, no gays, no drag queens, no . . . transgenders, no incest!"

Leo felt like a fish swimming in foreign rapids without a guide. This was not his Elizabeth. Where did all this hatred come from? "But I want you to stay! What . . . what will I tell Abi one day when she asks for her mom?"

Elizabeth's upper lip twitched again, and she growled. "Why would I care? For another pervert!"

Leo's fingernails dug into his palms, his knuckles emitting a cracking sound. Why did she keep insulting their kid? Perhaps he had to rush and embrace her, show affection, but at this moment she repulsed him.

Mirielle had crawled very close. Leo was aware of their intentions. They wanted to hug Elizabeth and drain the anger and the hatred. They did it once with Beatrice. Their mother did the same to him; Elise always brought him peace with her embrace.

Elizabeth noticed and swung the trophy. Leo leaped. The marble base cracked his skull and sank in. Elizabeth flickered away with a contorted face.

FATHER

Mirielle snuggled more tightly into Ayumu and caressed his chest. Then she kissed him and rested her head where she could hear his heartbeat.

"And Leo-san? He recovered, obviously, but how bad was it?"

"He disappeared too, and I panicked. Then I heard Eli screaming. It was a mess. I ran up and down, searching for them, primarily for Dad. I had no idea what I was doing. I couldn't sleep at all, I was shit-scared, as you say in your world, and Eli also didn't stop crying the whole night. Then Dad returned in the afternoon. He had been tele-ported back home, and Liz . . . I tried to save her, extract her anger, but I reckon that she committed suicide. She had trained herself to control her emotions, yet she refused to do so at that instant. I don't believe that she would have really hit me with that thing. She smashed Dad's skull by accident, as he threw himself in the way, unaware that she was just trying to prevent me from touching her. As if she knew.

"Her feelings, there was so much guilt. Anger too. She was oozing hatred, but I think that it was directed at herself, at her inability to accept her daughter for who she was. I later talked with Dad. Seems Elizabeth always struggled with Abigail's identity, and when she found out that Elian was also Dad's, she lost it. By the way," Mirielle raised her gaze, "how do you feel about me, Eli, and Dad, now that you know? I sense mixed emotions, hard to tell them apart."

"Mixed indeed. But I understand that it was not you he made love to; it was your mom. However, a vessel was required to carry the fruit of their affection, and since the body was shared, you ended up giving birth. From this perspective, Eli is not your son; he is your brother. Can I make love to you now?"

"I had that same idea a while ago, about Eli being my little bro. And of course!" Mirielle tugged herself up and found his lips. Ayumu gently rolled her to his side and dragged his hand over her breasts, then the abdomen, then the mound. Mirielle smiled and gasped quietly when his fingers found her sweet spot. She kept rolling her tongue inside his mouth as he split her petals and slowly moved his pinched fingers upward, then rolled them over the clitoris. She twitched when the fingers went inside her, pushing on the walls, and she smiled.

Ayumu kissed her cheek, then her eyelids, one by one. She liked his touch. His fingers abandoned the warm, slippery cavity and crawled further down. Ayumu probed her ring. Mirielle giggled, then rolled on her back and said, "Come . . ."

Ayumu planked over her, and his eager soldier dived head-on. Sparks traveled throughout the bodies on the crests of the waves, set in motion by the splash. Ayumu let the waters calm down. She savored the feeling, then asked for more with a shy gasp. Ayumu swung and rolled his hips, delivering joy. He was a good guy. He changed so much. He grew on her, his kisses, his touch. She wanted him. She needed him and she was not ashamed. More waves of delight rushed to her head, engulfing her mind. She raised her arms and caressed his face. Ayumu smiled, his hips swayed, she moaned.

"Where do you want it delivered?" Ayumu huffed.

"Between the boobs. If you can . . ."

Ayumu stretched his lips sideways and sped up his dance. The waves grew taller. She pinched his cheeks, then drew his head closer. They kissed. "Faster," she whispered and drew her eyes closed, emitting shy moans as the frothing crests chased the prior lot throughout her frame. She muffled his ears with her palms as he rocked, her face turning angry. Her body quivered in anticipation of the pleasurable surge.

Ayumu's aim was off. She felt the stream splash on her mound. Her hands traveled to the location, and she spread the fluid, then grabbed the melting soldier and squeezed it in her hand. "Ah, I want more."

"Soon."

"Sure. Come . . ." She tugged at him again, and her tongue parted his lips. Then Ayumu crawled down and pushed her legs up. She felt a kiss.

"Your pussy's usually smooth," she heard her friend saying, then his hand warmed the mound.

"Ah, yes, I became sloppy. It is boring and it hurts, the wax thing."

"No worries!" He kissed her pussy and drove his tongue inside. She sighed, then raked his hair with her fingertips. Ayumu found the clitoris and fluttered his tongue. She took a deep breath. She wanted more of him, not just a fleshy tip. Ayumu's fingers glided inside; he pushed and rubbed. Just a bit harder, she begged, languid tears departing from her eyes. Then her body quivered, she arched her spine with a loud and wavering moan, stood still and breathless for a tiny fragment of eternity, and then slowly lowered herself and resumed her oxygen intake.

Ayumu's tongue retreated. He crawled back up, dispersing tender kisses along the way. He rolled next to her and drew her closer. Their bodies intertwined. He carefully pulled her hair over her forehead and brushed the young skin with his lips.

She snuggled up and rested for a while, rubbing slowly her cheek against his chest, then asked, "Ayumu-kun, tell me, who amongst the living do you think still remembers you?"

"Sis Tsubame and her kids. And her hubby too. And I had a girlfriend, as you know, Keiko. Ah, she must be old now." He sighed. "Why? The drift?"

"Yeah. I don't want to lose you. I think I am also in love."

"Appreciated, even after so many years." Ayumu gleamed and looked at her.

They exchanged a lazy kiss and Mirielle continued. "But then there's a complication. I am aging and I cannot make myself appear young, and you cannot go past twenty-nine. But even if you could, would you still like the old me?"

"Probably. I don't want to make promises that I cannot keep. Feelings change, but there are many examples of people adoring each other even at an advanced age. So, chances are—"

"What about your parents?" Mirielle cut him short, unwilling to consider this future right now. "Each time I hint at them, you broadcast reluctancy to talk. Now I am asking you directly. I want to know more about my boyfriend, and I bared everything about me, Eli, Dad, so don't you think you owe me, even if it is just a tiny bit?"

Ayumu pouted. "Yes, I do. Well, they are both here, Mother and Father, but there's a caveat."

"Like?"

"Father was the typical salaryman, on the job twenty-four/seven, always overworked. He died while I was still in Mother's womb. Karoshi, it is called, dying from exhaustion. So, I don't really remember him. I can't see. The photographs we had did not help. Mom relays all the time. And cries. She says that he cries too. I don't visit often, because it makes them sad. He died young, I died young, he cannot see his son, I—"

"Why didn't you tell me earlier? I most certainly can help!" Mirielle jumped and began rapidly putting her clothes on.

"Oh! I was, er, well, to be honest, it didn't cross my mind."

"Dummy, dummy, dummy!" She slapped him on the head. "Rise up, let's go."

Ayumu set a new personal record on getting dressed fast. Soon they were on their way, running.

"Hey, not this way!" Ayumu shouted.

"Ah, sorry, then you lead."

Ayumu sprinted. She had a tough time keeping pace. Then she transformed.

⁎⁎

The old woman checked the tall young man head to toe who was wearing a layered ruffle skirt and a tight white blouse and holding a pair of sandals in his hand, her eyes almost round. Then she shifted her gaze to her son, her mouth ajar.

"Mom, call Father!"

The old woman remained frozen with a quizzical expression on her face.

"Mom." Ayumu shook her shoulders. "Where's Dad?"

Mirielle looked at the sandals in his hand and became a girl. "Sorry!"

The woman took a few steps backward and sat when her calves rubbed the chair, her eyes still firmly trained on Mirielle.

Mirielle bowed and said in Japanese, "Mirielle. It is my honor!"

"*Otousan!*" Ayumu shouted.

The screen slid open and revealed a man in his thirties, short and sturdy. Ayumu turned toward him, then bowed deeply. "Otousan! I am your son! Ayumu."

The man's eyes flicked from Ayumu to Mirielle, then to the old woman. He stuttered, "But . . . how?"

Mirielle bowed deeply again. "It is me, sir. I make people see. My name is . . . miracle." Behind her she heard a loud thud. She squeezed her gaze through the gap between her legs. Ayumu's mom had slumped to the floor, her eyes closed.

"Ammonia," she mumbled, still bowing.

"Huh?" Ayumu grunted.

"Ammonia, have you got any?" Mirielle stood upright. "And stretch her on her back."

The old man sprang into action. He rushed to his wife and tried to roll her as instructed, but she recovered and gathered her legs underneath her.

"Yumi! Are you OK?" the kneeled man said.

She nodded, then moved her gaze to Mirielle questioningly.

Mirielle rolled her eyes and turned to Ayumu. "So, seems I am the secret of the ages. You haven't told them about me, have you?"

Ayumu was inspecting the tatami mats, rubbing his hands. He shook his head briefly.

"OK, that's fine. Just unexpected. I will be outside." She treaded backward, careful not to miss the step, made a quick bow, crossed the threshold, and closed the front door.

Ayumu pulled it open again, grabbed her hand, and tugged her back inside. Then he faced his parents, bowed, and said, "Otousan, okaasan, this is Mirielle, my friend, and I love her, and ... er, she is indeed a miracle. She was born here, in this world, and she makes people see. Otousan, you can see us, can't you?"

The other man was silent, his gaze focused on the couple. Then he bowed and said quietly, "Yes, I can. I just cannot believe."

"He is Ayumu, your son, Takeo," Yumi, Ayumu's mother, said. "The one you never saw."

"Yumi, Takeo," Mirielle repeated silently, trying to store the names for future use. Then she freed her hand and gently pushed Ayumu forward. *Japanese are so reserved,* she thought, *but they also have feelings. And they are in my world now.* She slipped out as quietly as she could and sat on the small bench by the door. The wait was long. She tried to pay no attention to the powerful emotions streaming from the house behind her, wondering instead how to break the news about Stella.

STELLA

Back in the days before Elizabeth's departure, while they were still staying with her, Elizabeth's unhappiness had been getting hard to bear. The woman was not grumpy or rude; she was smiling and calling her and Elian "sweetie." She was friendly, but Mirielle's enhanced sensors withered under the duress. Elizabeth was sad.

Elian took a nap and Mirielle quietly snuck outside and borrowed one of the bikes residing in the garage. She rode around the neighborhood with Elizabeth a few times. There were rows of almost identical-looking houses with garages taking most of the façades and footpaths ending abruptly, only to resume a couple of streets later. Sometimes there were cars parked in front—Fords, Cadillacs, Chevys, and others—which her dad said were anachronisms, some sixty years too late, compared to the homes.

Mirielle rode a few blocks, then braked and removed her shirt. She wanted her skin to breathe; she missed the sensation. Elizabeth was openly throwing disapproving glances when Mirielle was playing au naturel in the pool with Elian, but it was a swimming pool, and that pool was in her world, so she chose to ignore the hints. Yet flaunting her mammary glands in a different setting would have been too much for the embattled old woman, and Mirielle opted to indulge her. Maybe Elizabeth would change. At this point, she had no idea what was going to transpire several days later.

She strode across the saddle and rode along the street again. The PED XING markings were missing now. Perhaps she needed the memories of a non-native person like her dad or his wife to see them. She took a note to confirm when she rode again with Elizabeth. Soon she reached an intersection, past which was the expanse of the shopping mall parking. It was empty. She wondered why. If there were cars parked in the streets, wouldn't there be cars in the parking lots too?

These vast, open spaces with nothing but tall lampposts were horrifying to her. So unsightly and soulless. The mall itself was ugly. A massive box with some glazing and mostly beige concrete walls otherwise, with signage that spoke nothing to her—Walmart, Binghamton, Macy's, Sharell, The Rouge, Hobby Lobby. Past the mall was a highway—eight lanes of concrete nothingness, certainly burning hot in the other world during sunny days.

How did people stand these things? Why did they exist here? Didn't people want to forget? She raked her fingers through her hair, then made a U-turn and pushed keenly on the pedals.

In the residential area, she slowed down her pace. Her heart rate decelerated too. The mall frightened her. She didn't want to go inside. She knew that there was nothing scary or remotely dangerous lurking between the walls, as she'd been to shopping malls before. But this one, it was humongous and such an eyesore that she was afraid of even contemplating what the interior might be like, let alone seeing it. Pink and beige and gold trim perhaps. Yuck!

Mirielle swung her gaze. A house on the right drew her attention. It was somewhat different. It was painted navy blue whereas all others were in some shade of gray, and it had wind chimes suspended from the porch ceiling. And a colorful weathervane toy, which was trying to turn at the mild blows of air but failing with a disappointed screech.

Mirielle leaned the bike against the picket fence and flipped the garden gate open. The wind greeted her welcome with a gust, which animated the chimes. She climbed the three steps and glued her palms and nose to the front door glass. On the other side there was a lobby and a staircase leading to the upper floor. On the left seemed to be the kitchen and on the right the living room.

Mirielle stepped back. A brass horn with a rubber blower served as doorbell. She squeezed the blower. "Quack!" the horn sounded. Mirielle smiled; it was humorous. "Quack!" She squeezed again, then slowly turned the doorknob. The door yielded.

"Hello! Anybody here? My name is Mirielle." She stepped inside and looked around. She was certain that the house was devoid of presence, as she felt nothing but introduced herself just in case.

The house looked different inside too. The kitchen cabinets were not of the common variety she'd seen around; they were like the ones they had in the warehouse loft. She pulled a drawer. It was empty to her, but she knew that it was not for the inhabitants of this home. This is how her world worked. The stove was also different—electric, just a flat black slab. The other homes had gas burners. They had no stove in the loft, but then it was purpose-built. In the houses people had what was featured in their old-world homes except toilets, which her parents' memories defined as a means of disposing of bodily waste also known as pee and poop. Nobody in this world that she knew of, including herself, produced anything of the sort. There was a difference, though, between her and the regulars. She was not self-cleaning insofar that she could get dirty, and she had to wash off that dirt—

from her hands, from her legs, from her face. That was an inconvenience—she had to use the kitchen sinks and in Japan—the bath spouts. But Japan was better; it had bathtubs. And here too. What was wrong with old Europe? She loved the showers, and she often danced under the warm faux raindrops.

The living room sported a massive flat-screen entertainment set, a TV of some sort. She browsed her father's information store. Rear-projection TV, it said. Popular when he was a man in his early forties. Opposite the large box were two leather recliners. Mirielle went to the set and looked for the on-switch, but it was not readily apparent. She turned around and spotted a remote on the small table between the recliners. She took it and pressed the button, while pointing at the set over her shoulder. The set chimed and began talking with a trained male voice. A narration of some sort. Mirielle sat in a recliner, pushed the lever for the footrest, and stretched. Soon the dark surface lit up and displayed a jungle—lush green trees surrounded by water vapor halos. Low, puffy white clouds swam leisurely across the screen. At the corner there was the letter H in gold.

The view changed. Now she saw naked people with brown skin, dense black hair, and long wooden plugs piercing their lower lips. The adult men had white wraps around their private parts. The women and the girls often wore white feather headdresses. The men walked with bow-and-arrow pouches on their backs, and some women were beating dense purple fruits inside wooden bowls, while others were breastfeeding, weaving baskets from palm leaves or playing with the older kids. All adults seemed to have bad teeth. Mirielle listened to the narrator. So, this was the Zo'é tribe, living in the Amazon rainforest jungle. They were egalitarian. The sexes enjoyed equal rights. Polygamy was practiced but so was polyandry.

That reminded her of her world. There were no leaders, no hierarchies, and people were free to be with anyone for as long as they could see. Perhaps only vestigial customs and inhibitions stood in the way.

Nudity also didn't seem to bother these tribespeople. But they were living in the forest. She remembered Beatrice talking about that—how she felt perfectly fine, baring all amongst the woods or on the beach, but highly apprehensive when doing it in town and persisting only to dislodge the conventions of the past from her own mind.

Interesting—was there a correlation? Her mom had no such problem and neither did she. She simply respected the sensibilities of others. But then Elise lived almost her entire life here, and she herself was a native.

Mirielle imagined herself without clothes amongst a mob of strangers on a public square in downtown. The faces were identical, and all people were dressed practically the same. Some men held briefcases while others had no neckties, but apart from that they were all clothed in formal suits. The ladies wore long, straight hair draping over their shoulders, faded-yellow calf-length dresses with orange spiral patterns, and were balancing on high heels. All of them were slim. The upper bodies were often dark, emitting thick black smoke.

She flipped her eyelids open. She'd been watching too much anime with the boys. The vision was plucked right out of a zombie scene. Her gaze returned to the television screen. It had gone dark.

Mirielle closed her eyes again. She missed Walid and Ayumu. Ayumu was still in reach, but the shy, skinny guy with curly hair and large, worried brown eyes was gone. She sighed and recalled how much he liked spending time between her legs regardless of her form. How he got mad thinking that Ayumu was exploiting her and the difficulty convincing him that it was not the case. She had to get Ayumu tied up and with a vibrator in his bum to get her assurance across. Then Walid wanted to be tied up too. And then his sister-in-law showed up, and soon after that he was gone.

She failed to notice when her hand had traveled to her groin. They used to play this game. She would lie on her back, spread her legs, and rub herself while he was watching, kneeling in front of her. Then he would dive and lick. Where did her leggings go? Perhaps she wished to be naked, and the world indulged her. But it would not bring Walid back. She pinched her fingers and began rubbing leisurely. The labia parted and she touched her sweet spot. Walid's face would lighten up as she looked at him through languid eyes and scrape her upper lip, while breathing through her mouth. Now he existed only in her imagination, but the sensation her hand produced was real. She cycled air slowly, twitching her eyelids from time to time as her busy fingers cajoled her receptors to generate pleasurable sparks.

Mirielle briefly fondled her breasts, rolling and pinching the excited nipples. Soon her hand returned to her crotch. She warmed the mound with her palm, then let her index finger slide inside and roll. She squeezed her eyes shut and rubbed herself vigorously with the side of her palm. A cascade of delight left the spot and splashed in her head. Her voice hesitantly joined the game. Her moans were quiet yet intense.

When the dam broke, she stiffened, unwilling to let go, as her entire body bathed in the ecstasy of the release. When the waves subsided, she withdrew her hand and brought her knees together, her palms resting on the leather recliner. She was fond of touch, and she was not ashamed, unlike the ghosts. But, admittedly, it was much better when it was someone else touching her. Was she missing just his touch? Walid, that is, was she missing just his touch? No, she missed her friend, his insecurities, his worries, his excitement staging the plays, his desire to be the perfect mime, his demons, his longing to have had a normal life. Mirielle let the tears roll. She missed the whole damn scarred, annoying prick! She curled up in the recliner, wrapped arms around her knees, and let her shoulders shake.

Then a buzz she knew so well trickled in her mind. Someone else had arrived! Mirielle raised her head and looked. A teenaged girl, a few years younger than her by the looks, with thick straight blonde hair, a fringe, and deep blue eyes just like her dad's, was sitting on her calves with a bunch of daisies in her hand. She was also naked, her pale skin making her reminiscent of an ivory statue. Her body was wrapped in a barely noticeable white halo.

The girl extended the hand holding the daisies. Mirielle's heart, if she had one, began pounding loudly. Her muscles tightened. Suddenly, all she wanted was to launch herself from the recliner and pull the girl into her embrace. Instead, she clenched her teeth and hugged the armrests.

"I . . ." The girl nudged her mouth open. Mirielle shook her head. The girl stopped.

Mirielle started counting to five on each draw of breath, then exhaling likewise. She loosened her grip on the armrests, but resumed it immediately, sensing the shaking of her hands. Her mind struggled to stay sharp as she pushed it to seek answers. How could she be so attracted to a complete stranger, to someone she had just seen? Was *that* love? Blind, irrational, incomprehensible, elating, scary?

The girl rose to her feet and transformed. Mirielle whimpered. The girl was just like her!

The teenaged boy stepped closer and outstretched his hand. "Here, I hope you like flowers . . . Er, my name is Stella."

Mirielle jettisoned from the recliner and wrapped her arm around the boy's neck. She reached blindly with the other hand for the improvised bouquet, retrieved it, glued her cheek to his, and stuttered, "I-I am Mirielle! T-thanks!"

FOLLOW UP

Stella's parents bore the uninspiring names of Sarah and Yidel. When they entered the room and introduced themselves, Stella had reverted and shared the couch with the flabbergasted Mirielle. Mirielle forgot the bow. She just mumbled out her name, unable to move her eyes away from them, her mouth ajar.

Stella giggled. "Hey, breathe! Are you really that shocked?"

Mirielle vigorously shook her head.

Stella elbowed her lightly. "C'mon, I knew I was not the only one." She then wrapped her arm around Mirielle's and shifted closer.

"Er, I know, I have a son," Mirielle mumbled some more.

"A son? Must be very young."

"How'd you know?"

"You are lactating." Stella reached and touched Mirielle's nipple. She gasped as a jolt traversed her body. Never before had these sensations been so intense. Stella licked her finger, tilted her head, and stretched her mouth into a smile. "Yummy!"

"Er, it has no taste as far as I am concerned." Mirielle wiped her breast with her forearm and looked to the side. "So—"

"Tell me more!" Stella interrupted with excitement in her voice and snuggled into Mirielle.

Mirielle shivered. The burning urge to draw Stella in her embrace, caress her, taste her lips, returned. Her hands rolled into fists. She had just met this other girl and her parents, she knew absolutely nothing about them, and she had never experienced an attraction so difficult to resist. Mirielle pumped up her chest, wriggled free, measured the blonde, and said, "Well, why don't you go first?"

"Sure! We, my mom and dad . . . well, why don't you tell her?" Stella turned to her parents.

"We were Jewish," Yidel started. "Hasidim, a very religious, insular sect. Do you know anything about religion?"

"Religion, yes, belief in supernatural beings pulling the strings. I . . ." Mirielle turned to Stella. "Do you have their memories?"

"Yeah."

"Same here. So, I know about Christianity and Islam and that other religions exist. And Jews. But I am afraid I know nothing about Hasidim."

Yidel sighed. "Hasidim are a group of very religious Jews living by a set of strict rules—how you dress, how you talk, how you fart." He chuckled. "I won't go into detail now; suffice to say that we could not walk more than a few yards without head cover, and our women had to shave their hair." He nodded at his wife. She shape-shifted, revealing a stubbled scalp. Her soft features became somewhat more pronounced.

Interesting, Mirielle noted. Now she wanted to run her hand over the woman's head for a change. "Why so?"

"For stupid reasons—so no other men beside their husbands saw their hair. Imagine that, my dear Sarah here with her shaved head and wearing a wig. Why?" He rolled his eyes. "And foreskins. God hates yeast and loves foreskins for some reason."

Mirielle raised her eyebrows, but Yidel seemed to have missed that hint.

"Anyway, me and Sarah, we were married in our teens—I was nineteen and she was two years younger. Arranged marriage; we had no say in who we'd spend the rest of our days with. That was and probably still is the norm. Not always a bad thing, by the way, but I digress . . . We, we were lucky. We fell in love with each other." His hand rested on his wife's. "We were both kind of rebellious souls. We found life in the community constraining, the rules pointless, and the reasons behind them often outright bizarre. Can you imagine that— raised to love Hashem, yet full of criticism and doubt? Wasn't easy. Anyway, the pros were that the community also provided security and comfort in the knowledge that there was always somebody to lean on for as long as you abided by the regulations. So, we did our little acts of dissent in secret. Like holding hands, kissing, touching. We made love naked, then hugged and waited for Hashem to strike us down. It was awkward and fantastic at the same time." He signaled to his wife to continue.

Stella again wrapped her arms around Mirielle's and rested her head on Mirielle's shoulder. Mirielle clutched her hands in her lap. The desire to draw the other in her embrace was overwhelming, and her resistance began showing cracks, ready to crumble. Perhaps she should seek a way out. But, then again, she was also quite intrigued.

"Well, in our community, having children, lots of children, is the norm. Mandatory, I'd say." Sarah took over the narration. "This is what God ordered us to do, be fruitful, multiply. We also had to make up for the losses. But I was unable to conceive. This puts a lot of pressure on relationships. Yidel was patient, though. I think I was the one panicking, and we were more than content with each other, to put it mildly. To the point that we received warnings that we . . . we were immodest. Anyway, we had tests done. Yidel had a very low sperm count for some reason; the doctors never settled on a cause. We could have tried in vitro at this point, but Yidel's parents didn't want to admit that the problem was with him, and the two families began bickering. Things turned ugly. People started sending long stares, talking. They took us to the rebbe, and he said that it was a test from God and . . . Do you know what a rebbe is?"

"Later," Yidel said. "In a nutshell, we grew tired of the bickering, and crazy as we were, one day we packed and left. We were terrified— two young people with no skills and no idea how the outside world worked—but we managed somehow!"

"Yeah! We were crazy. We still are!" Sarah added loudly.

Mirielle sensed pride in the little woman's voice. Her doppelganger next to her moved.

Stella's hand caressed her cheek, gently turning her head until their gazes crossed. She smiled softly and ran her finger down Mirielle's dense locks, then grinned goofily, her eyes sparkling. "Show me your male form, will ya? Your dad!"

Mirielle shook her head. "I can't."

"Why?" Stella said and turned male. "You can do that, can't you?"

Mirielle gasped. The penis of the teenaged boy next to her was erect, and she was sure that his skin now cast a mild glow. Her heart jumped; she drew air through her mouth. "I-I think it is because I am breastfeeding."

She blinked a few times, raised her arm, and touched the boy's face, her hand shaking, blatantly disobeying her command. Then she sharply straddled his lap, and their tongues intertwined. She buried fingers in his hair, willingly oblivious to her surroundings, irresistibly driven to become one with the being in front of her. She leaned back, breathing heavily, and surveyed the boy's face; her fingers touched his lips. He looked odd with the bunch of beaded braids inherited from his female form decorating his now curly hair, yet innocently cute. His hands glided shakily over her arms, barely touching, yet electrifying her skin; his lips were trembling, his mind pushing her away, yet screaming for them to merge into one.

"How old are you?"

"Sixteen," Stella huffed out.

"Ah, the hell." Mirielle rose a bit and let him in. Her body quivered as she took a massive gulp of air. His fingers dug into her frame then shyly spread. She drew her eyes closed, savoring the stream of delight flowing between them. She didn't have to move; he stood still. They had become one, but the circuit was still incomplete. Mirielle grabbed his head, leaned closer, and their lips met again.

"Beautiful! This light they emit . . . is it caused by their love?" Sarah exclaimed quietly while looking at the two glowing bodies, her fingers digging into Yidel's thigh.

"Perhaps. I love you madly, as you know, but we never luminesce," Yidel whispered.

"You do . . . sometimes," Stella purred, almost breathlessly, with Yidel's voice, when Mirielle opened the circuit for a while.

Yidel blushed and moved his gaze away, then smiled. Of course, Stella had seen him and Sarah making love. The pendulum of modesty had swung all the way away from their strict past and had become entangled in the fabric of this realm. When Stella was still tiny, they didn't care that there was a kid around. There was no one else to take care of their child, so they had to keep an eye on her. They lost the sense of shame somewhere along the way. They tried to be discreet when Stella grew up a bit, but the kid would often stumble on their hiding place. Then it was Stella's turn to look away, but Yidel and Sarah could often feel her gaze from between the leaves or through the keyhole. Then they discovered Stella's outer memory.

"Come." He rose to his feet, holding Sarah's hand. "Let's give the space to them."

Sarah heeded the prompt, and they quietly slipped out of the room.

"I can sense their emotions; the attraction is aplenty. But will it last? Stella needs one of her own kind. They both glow now, and it is beautiful to look at and absorb indeed, but their glow is . . . it feels shallow," Yidel said thoughtfully and sat on the pool's edge. "What is love like here? We, me and you, we were lucky to be able to keep it intact, but in the old world, that is one in a million, maybe rarer. I have no idea how we succeeded after all we went through. A miracle of sorts."

Sarah sat next to him and played for a while, splashing the water with her feet. "Well, her parents must have also been amongst the one-in-a-million couple. I wonder about that child she nourishes. She must be in love with the child's father for the kid to exist, don't you agree? So, where does our Stella fit in this picture? Will this person accept her as equal? Would you?"

"You doubt me? You know how tired I became with all that hatred and mistrust. Here I will love even a jellyfish. Hey, Sarah." He looked at his wife and leaned toward her. They touched their heads and released their youthful looks. The shadows of the two timeworn yet loving ghosts grew longer as the sun declined.

"Yeah, these are Mom and Dad." Stella had switched to a girl and had again wrapped her arms around Mirielle's as both were looking out in the backyard through the glass of the French door. "What about yours?"

Mirielle came out of her thoughts. "Huh? Ah, Mom died when she was eighteen, and they met again here, she and Dad. But I think that I must go now; Eli is certainly missing me."

"Eli?"

"Yes, my son."

"Ah, OK. Will you come again?" Stella's eyes resembled those of a kitten begging not to be abandoned on the street.

Mirielle sensed despair. "Sure! Why don't you come with me now? I will introduce you to Dad and his wife! And to Elian! I can make people see. I-I guess that you can do that too."

"I don't know. I have never seen anybody else except Mom and Dad, and now you."

Mirielle was quick to raise her eyebrows. "Never? But don't they have dead relatives? Parents, siblings?"

"They certainly do, but we can't see them. We went to Brooklyn, to their old neighborhood. It looked weird, like an unfinished painting. And we saw nobody. One would think that we would see plenty of people in a community like theirs; they had their parents, aunts, uncles, siblings, a lot of them. Yet it was a desert. Mom and Dad, they have no idea why. They even got dressed."

"Oh! So, you grew up alone?"

"I did indeed." Stella sighed, then chirped, "But it was great! Mom and Dad would transform and we played games! We traveled around! We went to many other places! We lived on islands! It was so much fun to run around in the sand and dive in the sea!"

"OK, let's go then! The sun's about to set."

The two ran outside. Mirielle lifted the bike and offered it to Stella. "Wanna ride?"

"Not now, thanks."

Maybe she didn't know how, Mirielle surmised. "I can teach you—"

"No need, I can handle it." The blonde girl smiled. "I . . . well, it would be odd if one of us rode and the other walked."

"Agreed." Mirielle pushed the bike.

Stella looked happy at first, skipping and chattering; then her demeanor changed. She became quiet, glancing nervously around and avoiding crossing sights with Mirielle.

When they turned yet another corner without reaching Elizabeth's place and Mirielle saw the navy-blue house, she looked at her companion. "What is it? You are bending space, aren't you?"

Stella gazed down and nodded almost unnoticeably.

"Why?"

Stella sat on the curb and wrapped her arms around her legs. "I . . ." she started, then halted and buried her head.

"You are afraid, I can tell."

"Yes. Sorry, maybe some other time." Stella looked up, tears balancing precariously at the corners of her eyes. "I-I was so attracted to you, but now I am . . . I am s-scared." Her face was turning paler as she stuttered.

Mirielle dropped the bike on the pavement, squatted, and wrapped her arms around the shivering body. Could she understand? She was accustomed to being surrounded by people, but until today, Stella had never seen another person in her life besides her parents. The perspective of being seen was perhaps as anxiety inducing as it was desired to someone like the petite blonde girl in her embrace.

"OK, some other time," Mirielle said softly and helped Stella get up. "I think that I understand."

"Thank you!" Stella hung around her neck and imprinted her lips onto Mirielle's, then ran toward the navy-blue home. She halted at the door, turned, and waved goodbye.

Mirielle straddled the bike and pushed on the pedals. Her lips were burning, yet she was unwilling to extinguish the fire. The air was cold, however, she was perspiring. The urge to turn back and be reunited with the blonde girl/boy grew proportionately to the distance she put between them with each turn of the wheels. Mirielle clenched her teeth and stayed on course.

SHOES

Mirielle continued shelving the reveal, unable to find a solution to Stella's raging fear. Each time she gave the petite blonde girl a mild push, the other clammed up with a tearful visage. The condition seemed to be contagious to some degree, as Mirielle kept Stella a secret even from her helpful cuckoo doc, Grandmom Annette. She embarked on her daily routines, occasionally swerving from the settled paths to hold her new friend into her embrace and taste her or his lips. And other body parts. But the aftertaste was always sour—Ayumu deserved to know. So, she spilled her mind at Stella's feet, touched the tip of the little nose, decorated with a few freckles, and asked the blonde to lend her a hand. Then she went climbing. The exercise always kept the unsettling thoughts at bay.

When Mirielle and Ayumu reached the top of the cliff, they sat next to each other and bumped shoulders. The view was breathtaking, but they had plenty of breath. Both were seasoned climbers now, with her trying not to think of the dizzying heights and Ayumu drawing the equivalent of adrenaline rush from his fear of her meeting an untimely demise.

Recently, they went to the mall to get new pairs of climbing shoes and recalled how they reconnected. Back then she could tell that Ayumu wanted strongly to end his self-imposed exile. On her sixteenth birthday, he finally showed up but kept avoiding her, always looking away and mumbling incoherently when she approached to greet him. When she tried to hug, he stepped back and chuckled awkwardly. Ayumu had feelings for her. Just like Walid. In those days, her mom was still alive inside her and helped with the determination.

Mirielle had feelings for both men too. They were dear to her. She grew up with them; they were her childhood friends. As she matured, the rest of the picture revealed itself, one little fragment at a time. Finally, the childhood friends transformed into a pair of attractive young-looking men. They wanted to be with her, and she wanted to be with them. Walid was easy, but Ayumu resisted. Was it the culture or the guilt?

When one day she and her folks visited Shinji and Mayumi in their seaside home, the nephew happened to be hanging around. Mirielle did not waste time:

"Ayumu, we shall climb together yet again. I like it, you like it. I climbed by myself, you know? On roofs and the rock wall in the dispensary mall. What happened occurred years ago, like what, six, seven? Now we know that I am as dense as a rock, and I can't fly, and we will also take precautions when climbing—safety lines and stuff." She tried reapproaching.

"Maybe . . . I don't know."

"Are you still feeling guilty?"

Ayumu lingered. "Yes, I do."

"Then it is time to stop. The only context feeling guilty about something makes sense in is learning what not to repeat and how to make amends."

"Who's saying that?"

"Dad."

"Leo-san is a wise man!"

"Then take it from him. We learned what we had to learn from the event."

"Leave me alone!" Ayumu retorted, rose, and left the room.

Mirielle sighed. She sprang up and ran after him. "Ayumu, I know!"

"You know what exactly? What is there to know?"

She blushed. "I know that you have feelings for me. The feelings of a man. And I am not a child anymore!"

Hearing that, Ayumu had sat on the landing between the floors and grabbed his head. What was she trying to tell him, that she was also in love? How could she be in love with a seventy-year-old man, with someone who could be her grandfather?

Mirielle climbed the steps and laid hands on his head. "I am not seeing an old man, if that is what you are thinking. I see a guy in his twenties, and I love his stretched eyes!" She pushed his hands aside and glided her thumbs over his eyelids.

He wanted so much to embrace her and kiss. His palms were sweating profoundly, and he was desperate to find a reason to give in, but drawing a blank, he said, "Give me some time, Mirrie. To me you are still just a kid, and it . . . it feels wrong."

In a few weeks' time, she tried again. She knocked on the door of his apartment, and when he opened it, she shoved a pair of climbing shoes in his face.

"What do you think of these?" she demanded.

Ayumu tried to keep the pounding of his heart under control. He took the shoes and had a careful look, then bent the sole a few times. "These are not for you; you are a novice. These are aggressives."

"Not quite a novice. I did climbing while you were, er, how shall I put it, avoiding me."

"Where?"

"In the dispensary mall."

"It is called a *shopping mall*."

"Don't try to sell me that. Nobody does shopping here; you just go and pick things if you can even be bothered to go, hence 'dispensary.' Different world, different terminology."

He handed the shoes back. "I would still recommend neutrals."

"How would I tell the difference?"

"Neutrals have stiffer soles and are more comfortable to wear. These are aggressives." He took the shoes back. "Do you see how thin and flexible the sole is? The idea is to feel the rock. But your toes will start to hurt soon."

"Mm. Listen, why don't we go to the mall, and you help me get the right ones."

"And then climb?"

"And then climb!" She smiled widely, and her hazel eyes increased in size.

"No!"

"I got it! Whatever then. Bye!" Mirielle rose, took the shoes, and quietly closed the door behind her, as she left the apartment.

Ayumu recalled his heart falling to his stomach. He was rude, and he hurt her feelings. He could have been diplomatic, not just bark out a denial. That was not part of his upbringing; the Japanese people were polite! He rushed outside, but the corridor was empty. He shouted, "Mirrie! Mirrie-chan!" and ran to the elevator. He glued his ear to the door; the machinery was quiet. He closed his eyes and tried to sense her. She was definitely somewhere near; he could still detect the warmth. But she was also elusive. She left no trail, no hint for him to follow. He ran all the way down to the street and swung his head, then closed his eyes and screamed in his mind. *Sorry!*

Somebody pulled his shirt. Ayumu turned sharply and there she was, smiling. "Apology accepted."

"B-but," Ayumu stuttered. "You cannot read thoughts. How did you know?"

"Correct. I can't tell what somebody else is thinking, but I have a very high success rate dealing with emotions, and you feel guilty, right?"

Ayumu dropped his head. "*Hai.*"

"Well, when you are feeling guilty, you seek to apologize, is that not so?"

He nodded. "I get it. The way you tie your reasoning to your empathic trait is impeccable. Yes, you are right."

"But my reasoning can't tell me what exactly you wanted to apologize for. Because you turned me down, or because you did so in a manner unbecoming for a Japanese person. Or perhaps both?" She continued, "Ayumu-kun." She raised her hand and touched his cheek. "Can't you meditate and get rid of all your worries? Pray at a shrine? Is there no way?"

He couldn't believe what was happening; it was right out of his dreams! A beautiful, gentle girl with big eyes was extending her arm. He watched thousands of anime series, he dreamt of being a lucky boy, then he returned to the reality of his existence and went solo with his hand. But she, the embodiment of his dreams, was here now, and he couldn't bring himself to touch her with his dirty paw.

"OK, will do my best. When do you want to go to the mall?"

"Tomorrow morning?"

"Sure, I will pick you up." He turned and prepared to walk back to his apartment but felt another pull on his shirt.

"Hey, not so fast! Let's take a stroll."

"You know that I have nothing else to do, and I have no Japanese excuse at hand. Therefore, may I just ask for your kind permission to go back home? Until tomorrow, that is."

She smiled. "Of course!" They both lingered, then Ayumu walked backward to the building's door, his gaze focused on her slim frame, waved goodbye, and sank inside. So far, so good! When he got back into his apartment, he undressed, lay naked in his bed, jerked off and cried, then washed his hands at the kitchen sink. He needed a bath. He took a towel, opened the door again, and stepped right into the locker room of the nearby onsen.

Mirielle remembered that after the encounter, back at home, she piled a few manga books in her hands and went upstairs to her room. She dropped the books on the floor, sat, and started paging. Battle manga, mostly. There were heroines wielding swords and other weapons here and there. Would he be impressed if she showed up wearing a metal exoskeleton and dragging a katana? This could probably be arranged with management, but it would be weird, considering that they were going to be choosing climbing shoes and possibly going up the wall.

She opened another book. This one was closer to what she was after—romance stories, plenty of cute schoolgirls in miniskirts. That was boring; Mirielle wore those at school. She continued to page through. Did men really care so much about female underwear? She closed her eyes and consulted her archive. Her dad had made a special place for an image of her mom on their first date—white skirt, red blouse, hoops—but absolutely nothing on underwear; he didn't seem to care.

Her mom, nothing there either. She had once tried to look under his kilt, but it was her doing that, not him, and what left a far deeper impression was his kneeing her in the forehead by mistake. *Must be a Japanese obsession*, she concluded and drew a plan.

Leo was cutting veggies when she descended the stairs and entered the living room. He lifted his gaze, and his face grew longer. He put the knife down, scratched his chin, and leaned against the counter, eyes glued on her.

"Er . . . the skirt is too short and the blouse . . . she was wearing a sleeveless shirt, but, damn it, Mirrie, you are really her. Sorry, I know you hate being reminded of the fact; however, you challenged me with this outfit right now. You must have dug the look up right out of my mind. So, what are you up to, if you fancy sharing?"

"I'm going with Ayumu to pick climbing shoes. And it is not a blouse; it is a leotard."

"Ah, so you two are friends again?"

"I hope so. I've been trying hard. He's a very nice guy, he's lonely, and I don't want him to be. His self-imposed exile is stupid; he is still blaming himself for the tower accident. I wish you could tell him to stop worrying."

"Without seeing him?"

"Yes, Shinji-san will relay."

That was before her mom transferred the ability to her. And indeed, in those days she was still irked by the "spitting image" thing.

"He has relayed it many times already." Leo sighed. "But if you insist."

"I do! Bye now!" She sent him an air kiss and ran out where she bumped straight into her friend.

In the mall, Ayumu tried hard not to stare and concentrated on the task at hand—the climbing shoes. He selected a pair. "Sit!" he said. "Let's try this one."

She kicked off her shoe and stretched the leg he touched briefly. He was reluctant to continue. Why were men so stirred up by a certain type of female lower limb? Why did she come dressed like that? Like a whore? No, that was wrong! Ayumu mentally chastised himself. But the question remained—why were slim female legs such a turn-on? He clenched his teeth and tried the shoe. "How does it feel? Comfy?"

"Yeah."

That was all. They picked the shoes, then drank Irish coffee, but the whiskey inside did not untie their tongues. They split when the awkward silence dragged for way too long. Upon returning home, Ayumu took a beer from the fridge, popped it open, and chugged it in one go. He then burped, popped another can, and sat. He couldn't think of anything else but her—her big, round eyes, her shiny hair held off her face by the cute Neko hairclip, her long legs, exposed by the miniskirt, which the heels made appear even longer, and her hard breasts under the stretched fabric of the leotard. He felt embarrassed back in the mall—he stuttered and tripped often. Strange, though, she never laughed; she ignored his clumsiness completely. Most people he remembered—his old friends—wouldn't have been so kind. But they were not here now; she was. He wanted her. She liked him too, he had no doubt, but did she want him?

Ayumu tried to picture her with her clothes off. No, not that skinny kid he saw once on the beach! The young woman from today. He lit a cigarette, smoked it with his eyes closed, carefully extinguished the butt, undressed, and lay flat on the mat. He wished that she was here with him. The area between his legs felt warm. He closed his eyes again, sighed, and reached down. His hand bumped into a face.

⁂

Ayumu gasped and opened his eyes. Mirielle, still with his penis in her mouth, was looking at him questioningly. She was bent low over him on her knees, and another young man with a scar across his face he'd never seen before was right behind her.

Ayumu scrambled backward. "Eghh!"

Mirielle rested her head on the mat and sighed. "Ayumu jumped."

"What is going on? Who are you?" Ayumu pierced the other man with his eyes.

"You jumped, relax, you will remember. We are having fun," Mirielle said softly and sat. The other man joined them.

"Yes, apparently! But what is *he* doing here?"

"We are having a threesome. Not the first time, you will recall."

Threesome! Not what he wanted! Did he really agree to this? And who was the other man?

"I'm Walid, Ayumu-kun."

Kun? We are friends? Close ones? Ayumu tried hard to beat his emotions into submission.

Mirielle moved closer and caressed his arm. "Just shut your eyes and relax. I can sense that you are very angry. You went ballistic when I first suggested this, and without the memories you are back at square one."

Ayumu pushed her hand away. Threesome! How could he have accepted that! That was gross! She was a whore! He buried his face in his hands, hiding his tears. She was a flower, beautiful and pure, the girl of his dreams. His girl! What happened? What spoiled her? He felt that he was beginning to shiver. He jumped, grabbed a towel, and shouted, "Get out!"

Mirielle sprang up, stepped in front of him with hands on her waist, and shouted back, "No! Man up! Don't make it harder on yourself!"

"Get out!" he screamed.

"Fine! Walid!" She stormed through the front door, followed by the other man.

Ayumu panicked. They went outside naked! He grabbed the handle and pulled the door. The corridor was quiet and empty; they had folded space.

*
**

Yeah, those were the days. His recall arrived after he had already consumed several bottles of sake and had vomited repeatedly in the kitchen sink for lack of a more suitable outlet. It was not the first time he had abused alcohol on his journey through existence, and that made him feel bad. He returned to the present:

"I'm sorry, Mirrie-chan!"

"Huh? What for?"

"My drinking."

"It is over now." Mirielle left the comfort of his chest and sat. "There is something I must tell you."

"OK."

"When I went with Dad to California to seek Elizabeth, there I met another one like me, a child native of this world—"

"Really! I am so glad!"

"Her, er, their name is Stella and . . . and I love them too."

Ayumu's largesse shrank immediately. Walid before, now this Stella.

"Sorry, Ayumu, I am aware that it hurts, but you must know the truth. I learned that from my mom. But if you can't accept Stella, I will let them go. The two of us, me and you, we have been together for much longer—"

"No! It hurts indeed, but I have no excuse to be selfish in this world. They are welcome!"

"Are you sure?" Mirielle looked quizzically at him.

He pushed her flat on the soft grass and answered the question with his lips. He then breathed in her ear, "Shall we go down now? The sun's about to set."

INTRODUCTIONS

The introduction of Stella was anything but forgettable. Elian was taking a nap in the shadow of the trees, and Mirielle had sat on Ayumu's face, marveling at his tongue's drilling skills, with her hands raking through his lush hair. Her slow sways and quiet, sensual sighs turned him harder yet. Then she stopped abruptly and snapped her eyes open. Ayumu looked up.

"I think they are coming," she whispered.

"Who?"

"Stella."

The thick bushes to his left rustled. He targeted his eyeballs. The branches separated and a petite girl with long blonde hair and blue eyes, shielded from the sun by dense eyelashes, emerged, clad as her mother had her on the day the girl was born, wearing only a necklace made from seashells. He felt Mirielle's body twitch. He realized that he was aroused and performing cunnilingus, but to his surprise, he felt no embarrassment or shame. That somehow made him feel proud.

The girl came closer and without a word transformed into a boy of matching vintage, also light hair, still long but with an orange tint and curly this time, and similar to his female version eyes. He was eager too; his penis was likewise excited. The boy positioned himself in front of Mirielle and offered her his ripe fruit. She drew it in her mouth and savored the taste. Ayumu held her thighs and rolled his tongue. The quiver of her body reached him too. His gaze climbed her torso and lingered at her breasts before proceeding further up. The boy was looking down, quiet, still, his hands, kind of unnaturally for a man, clutched together at his chest. Mirielle held his scrotum in her palm and swayed her head unhurriedly, tilting it occasionally as she moved.

The boy delivered the syrup silently and let Mirielle linger before resuming his female form. The girl crouched briefly and pecked Mirielle, then moved behind her and straddled Ayumu. Mirielle rolled to the side, kneeled, bent over him, and her juicy lips met his. Her fingers pinched his nipples, then she glided her palms over his cheeks. His heart was giving gun salutes. He glanced past Mirielle's head and met the blonde girl's sensual eyes as he became her guest. She swayed slowly for a while, then she leaned forward, locked her hands behind Mirielle's neck, arched her back and moved her hips.

His delight was immense, also spiced with some shame for resisting the threesomes with Walid. Observing Mirielle and the blonde girl kiss amplified the elation that ran throughout his frame. When he reached climax and ejaculated, it felt like a dormant geyser finally erupting after countless years collecting vigor deep underground. He couldn't help but arch his own spine and convulse.

The blonde girl bent forward, elbows flexed, her breasts touching his chest, and whispered in his ear, "Hi, I am Stella."

"I love you too." Ayumu smiled.

"You still don't know me," the girl said, dismounted him, and sat on her calves.

"Love is blind."

"I guess so." She looked at the ocean behind him, then at the sleeping toddler. "This is Elian, right?"

"Yeah, my little bro."

"Your brother?" Stella's eyebrows went up.

"Brother, son, both. It is complicated."

Stella's mouth went ajar.

"You know that this place is weird," Mirielle started. "I-I was my mom."

Any trace of comprehension left Stella's eyes. So much so that Mirielle guffawed. Then she rolled flat on her stomach in front of the other "they," propped her head with hands, and proceeded to tell the story of Elian's conception.

"Ah, I see." Stella's face lit up, and her lips stretched sideways. "That is fascinating! So, you were in love with your dad?"

"Kind of, for a while, but I grew out of it. I still adore him as a parent, though. That said, now I have Ayumu and you. My other friend, Walid, drifted away shortly before you and I met for the first time. His drift was one of the reasons we came to California. Dad wanted to diversify the days for me and also find his wife, who he sensed had passed."

Stella said, "My parents died almost together. Mom passed at eighty-three, and Dad followed her some two months later. He said that he had become exceedingly frail after her cremation—angry, sad, in constant pain—and had no desire for that to change. He wanted his little Sarah, and sensing death on the doorstep had actually made him glad. He had been taken to the hospital for care and passed soon afterward in his sleep."

Stella rose to her feet, approached Elian, and kneeled. Her shadow crossed the toddler's line of sight, and he opened his eyes.

"Stea!" The small mouth produced a smile. The child rolled on all fours and crawled to her. Stella drew him cautiously into her embrace and looked questioningly at Mirielle.

Mirielle nodded. "It's OK. Erm, are you ready now?"

Ayumu nudged his eyebrows up.

"I believe so. You see, I met Ayumu and little Eli here." She hugged the child, then let Elian go.

The toddler ran to Ayumu and pulled his arm. "Swim, Yumu!"

"No, it is getting late." Ayumu then asked Stella, "What must you be ready for?"

"Meeting other people. I-I am torn to shreds when it comes to this. I am drawn almost irresistibly to Mirrie, and somehow, I am OK with you. I'd say that I am attracted to you too. But when it comes to other people, I am the complete opposite. I panic, I want to run, and I can hardly breathe. I don't know, maybe you being one with Mirrie in that moment helped us meet."

"Don't tell me that I must make love to people so you can see them all." Mirielle giggled.

"No!" Stella waved her hands. "I must toughen up. I grew up alone, just me and Mom and Dad," she told Ayumu.

Ayumu nodded. "I see. All right, you have the support of two. I have no magic traits to speak of, but at least you can see me now, and my goofy smile, when you are afraid."

"Thank you!" Stella touched his arm, then took a deep breath and huffed out, "OK, let's go!"

Mirielle had slipped back into her clothes. "I think that we shall get you something to wear. The folks are very accommodating but may still be shocked. Ah, what a contradiction."

Stella bowed her head and dragged her palms down her abdomen. "OK."

Ayumu buttoned up and installed Elian on his shoulders. Then the conversation reached his brain. He put the child back on the ground and offered his shirt. It, however, failed to provide adequate cover for some parts from the girl's physique; he himself was not a large man.

"Dispensary mall?" he suggested.

"Yep, let's go!"

At the mall, Mirielle pulled out a pair of denim shorts and a crop top and tossed them at the blonde girl. Stella diligently put the pieces on.

Ayumu squinted. The garments made the petite girl more attractive compared to her unaugmented look. He remembered how

Mirielle drove him crazy with her white skirt and her red leotard and chuckled.

"What?" Mirielle buzzed him with her eyes.

"Nothing! She looks great."

Mirielle moved her gaze to the obviously uncomfortable Stella and propped up her chin. "No, not these!" She pivoted and scanned the rails and racks. Then she sank deeper into the store. Upon her return, she delivered a pair of loose denim trousers with machine embroidery along the leg, a formal white shirt, and a black necktie. Ayumu tried to scratch his scalp and landed a mild blow on Elian, having forgotten that the kid still rode on his shoulders.

"Yumu!"

"Oops! Sorry!"

"OK!" The kid shuffled his hair. "Put down!"

Ayumu did as asked. The child ran to Stella, lifted the shorts she had just discarded on the floor, and tried to put them on. Ayumu laughed. Elian raised his gaze and looked with a grave expression straight into his eyes. His hair took a much lighter shade, his eyes turned hazel, and his weenie disappeared.

"Ah, Eli is now a 'she'!" Ayumu smiled unperturbed. That was expected; it was just a matter of time before the kid presented the trait. Then he checked Stella head to toe. She was still female, wearing the new outfit Mirielle chose for her. He understood; it was androgynous in style.

"Stella's not a kid," he remarked.

"I know, but I still sometimes transform involuntarily. Perhaps it is the same for her."

"True," the blonde girl confirmed. "For some reason when I am with Mirrie, I feel compelled to take a male form. And you saw it— when I was with you, I turned back into a girl. I don't give these conversions much thought; they simply happen." Then she became a boy. "How's that? You know that I can't see much of myself."

Mirielle said, "It is good. I learned to pick the right clothes as I was growing up." Then she squinted, went to the shelves, and returned with a small skirt and a blouse featuring an embroidered yellow duck. "Here, Eli, wear these." The little girl grabbed the clothes and promptly put them on, then reverted to a boy. Mirielle rolled her eyes and huffed, and Ayumu guffawed silently, feeling the blood rising to his face as he squeezed his lips.

Only Stella stood silent, continuing to look uncomfortable and tense.

"What is it?" Mirielle asked calmly.

"I-I have never worn clothes before. It feels weird."

Mirielle comically wrinkled her nose. "Never? How come?"

"We . . . we live alone, and Mom and Dad never bothered. Until today, I didn't know that it was a thing, to be honest. A thing in this world, that is. I know that nudity was unacceptable in the other world, even more so in their community. But once they woke up here, they were free to do whatever they wanted, and they took full advantage of that. They enjoy it. I know!"

Now that it was mentioned, Mirielle recalled that Stella's parents were indeed naked when she met them that day, wearing only light canvas shoes. She paid no attention, as she didn't care. She saw no one bare or clothed. Only sensibilities of immigrants. She remembered the Zo'e tribe.

"That is because no outsider could see. I don't know." Mirielle pouted and looked at the ceiling, engaged in thought. "My folks would certainly not mind but will also be surprised. There's that convention that we don't walk around naked unless it is on the beach. Ah, at the same time, my parents bang on the train." She shook her head. "Yeah, it can be confusing with a larger group of people."

"Stella," Ayumu said thoughtfully, "you being as you are, with your phobia, you certainly don't want to draw more attention to yourself than what you can take. Clothes will act as a dampener, in other words, beneficial in this case."

"You don't have to convince me about anything, I understand. Just that I need to get accustomed to fabric constantly rubbing into my skin." She displayed a smile.

"Hey, Mirrie, what about a loose gown or something?"

"No!" Stella was adamant.

Ayumu chuckled and extended a hand for a high-five. Stella looked at him quizzically. He dropped his arm. Mirielle glanced at him with a nod. Enough novelties for the blonde girl.

"Your parents? I thought that your mom drifted away."

"She did, but she was in a polyamorous relationship and left me with another mom, and then Dad reconciled with his first wife, who I also consider a parent of mine."

"It *is* complicated," Stella mumbled, her face turning white.

"Indeed. Now, let's go meet the lot!"

Elian pushed the front door open and ran inside the house. "Daddy, see Stea!" The living room was empty. "Daddy, come!" Elian raised his voice.

Leo emerged from his study on the second floor and peeked down. "*Konnichiwa*, Ayumu!"

"*Konnichiwa*, Leo-san!" Ayumu greeted back and bowed briefly.

"Dad, meet Stella!" Mirielle announced triumphantly and stepped aside.

Leo moved his gaze from side to side, then raised his brows.

At this moment, Elian appeared in the hallway, having switched to a girl again. "Daddy!" The kid ran up the stairs. "Stea's here!"

Leo smiled. "Mm, I can see! Hi!" He wrapped his arms around the little girl in oversized skirt and kissed her head. "And where is Eli?"

"I am Eli!" The kid wriggled out of his embrace.

"But you said that you were Stea—"

"No, it is Stella, Dad. They are here." Mirielle pointed at the frozen girl next to her. "They are like me."

Leo sat on the platform and rubbed his head with a knuckle, then sucked in his lips before speaking. "Hm, I am afraid that I cannot see them. My apologies."

Mirielle poked Stella.

"Ouch!"

"Hm, you *do* exist." She grunted. "Ayumu?"

"Yes, I can still see her."

"Where are the moms?" Mirielle glanced into the living room.

"I am here." Wasilla extracted her frame from her room. "And Bea went to the Nakagawas. I think that they are having fun."

Ah, another threesome, Mirielle thought. It had become popular amongst close dead friends. Then her thoughts shifted back to the case at hand. "Can you see a person standing next to me?"

"Nope."

"OK, give me some space!" She spread her arms and closed her eyes, trying to isolate Stella's emotions. Anxiety, that's what she thought. So, fear could stand in the way of seeing, it seemed.

"Stella, please relax!" Mirielle implored. "They can't see you like that."

Stella's lips were turning blue, and she had started to hyperventilate. Mirielle grabbed her hands. "Stella, baby, please." She kissed the hands one by one, still intently crossing gazes with the other girl. Then she turned to her father. "Dad, I think she's having a panic attack. She's been living with just her parents, and she's seen no one else; she knows no one."

"Damn, I have no idea how to handle that." Leo rose to his feet and pointed. "Lead her to the couch, make her sit, and give her some water to drink, I guess. Your grandmom is too far away."

Stella abruptly pulled her hands free and rushed toward the front door. At this very moment, the door swung open and squashed her against the wall. She managed to turn her head an instant before the door could flatten her nose.

Yidel barged in. "Stella! *Var a man! Herstu? Var a man!*" he shouted, staring straight forward, not even trying to locate his daughter. Then he flicked his eyes from side to side, inspecting the space, and installed a puzzled look on his face.

Ayumu silently pointed behind him. Yidel turned and saw the pinned Stella. He let go of the door handle. "Be a man, Stella," he repeated in English in a now tired yet firm voice.

Stella hiccupped and transformed. His pale face began regaining color, albeit washed out, and his gasps turned into measured draws. He rubbed his eyes and brushed his curls away from his face. "S-sorry!" he succeeded in saying, then gazed worriedly at Mirielle, followed by Ayumu, and hiccupped again. "*Tate*," he greeted Yidel, took a few steps toward the living room, looked up the stairs, and said, "Sir! Ma'am! My apologies! I am S—," another hiccup, "Stella."

DREAD

Stella fed Elian another spoonful under the watchful eyes of Mirielle, who had planted her elbows on the table, cradling her head with her hands.

Yidel drank from the beer offered to him by Leo and sighed. "This is the story. We saw no one. We were eleven kids in my household. Sarah had four brothers and three sisters. There were more relatives than we have fingers. We were members of an insular community in our youth, and we existed alone in this world until now. Always in some sort of isolation. And Stella—we noticed her propensity to panic when she was still a young kid and the effect of the sex transformation. No offense, ladies," he swung his gaze around, "but it is a fact; our boy is braver and stronger than our girl."

"I use the pronoun 'them' for Mirrie," Leo said and tasted his own brew. "They are physically stronger in their male form, but as to bravery, I see no difference. They cannot fly, yet they climb towers and cliffs without hesitation—"

"What do you mean by 'they cannot fly'?" Yidel wrinkled his forehead.

"Like us—float in the air after we jump."

"But Stella can! We've seen her!"

All eyes turned to the blond boy.

"What?" He looked up. Elian took the spoon from his hand and put it in his mouth, spilling most of its contents over himself. He giggled, transformed into a girl, and spread the puree with her hands.

"I can't fly," Mirielle confirmed. "Your dad said that you could. How?"

"Ah! Yes, but I can't control it. I must be very calm and cozy and then I feel weightless, and I float in the air. When I was a little kid, I would cuddle up with Mom and that feeling would come—"

"And she would glow as well," Sarah chimed in. "She had a teddy bear, a large, fluffy one. She still has it. She would hug it and snooze and start glowing and lift off. Only hugging the bear kept her anchored. And with me, I had to wrap my arm around her so she would not float away."

"He is so soft and cozy!" Stella crossed his hands at his chest. "My Bawl!"

"The teddy bear," Sarah clarified.

"But you have never jumped from somewhere high, have you?" Mirielle said.

"I have."

"And?"

"I have jumped into the water from trees and cliffs."

"And?" Mirielle repeated.

"What do you mean?" Stella said sharply.

"Did you levitate, or did you fall?"

"Ah! No, I did not float, I fell. But it was fun! You know, splashing in the water!"

"That's not what happens when you fall from a seventy-five-meter tall communications tower," Ayumu scoffed.

Stella looked at him. "What's that in yards?"

Ayumu shrugged.

"About eighty-five," Leo guesstimated.

"No, not that high. Ten the most, I'd say," Stella said.

Mirielle shut her eyes and pulled a memory. The memory of the night. The three bodies were also glowing, she recalled, and didn't they also float in the air from time to time? She remembered her mother feeling weightless. But she was barely conscious, detached, a remote observer despite being physically part of the small group. Maybe it was not the same.

Elian transformed again. "Mommy, look!" He grinned, undoubtedly enjoying the newfound ability to change shape. Mirielle smiled. "Great!" Then she focused on her new friend, who was playing with the child. Her heartbeat rushed. Desire warmed her cheeks. She wanted to hold her, him, in her embrace, feel the smoothness of the skin, rub her body into his. It seemed she preferred the boy, but she wouldn't mind the girl too. The being in front of her was the object of affection, regardless of its form. The being ... what were they? Would they float if they kissed? Mirielle itched to lead the being to her room upstairs and probe the soft lips with hers, caress the strands of gold, feel the smooth skin under her hand, see the glow. Stella looked up and their gazes crossed. Stella smiled, turning Mirielle's heart into a blob of molten wax. Her mind wailed.

"Come." Mirielle extended her arm. "Moms will take care of Eli. I want to try something."

"My Wass will soon be gone," she overheard Leo saying and froze. The molten blob of a heart solidified in an instant with a jolt. Mirielle turned sharply and wheezed, "What did you say?"

Leo twitched and looked up but remained silent.

Mirielle dropped Stella's hand and, tight-lipped, turned slowly, checking every face in the room. Elian, Beatrice, Sarah, Yidel, Ayumu, Stella, her dad. She shook her head. Wasilla may have gone upstairs or . . . no, why would she doubt her father. She drew a shaky breath and stared into her dad's eyes, silently begging.

Leo raised his shoulders and shook his head unenthusiastically. "Sorry, Mirrie. It had started. Her nephew's been dead for what, six years now, and her niece joined recently as you know. Auntie Fatimah is certainly also departing."

Mirielle felt a pair of arms surrounding her. Stella tightened the embrace, saying no word. Mirielle dragged her feet awkwardly with the transformed Stella in tow toward the door, but before they could reach it, she spun sharply, buried her head in his chest, and let her tears roll.

"Mommy, no cry." Elian tugged on her dress.

Mirielle crouched and took the little hand. "Why not, Eli? Mommy Wass will soon be gone. Aren't you going to miss her? This is why we cry, I guess, the irreversibility of the event."

"He's a kid, Mirrie." Leo massaged the root of his nose, then turned to Yidel and Sarah. "I hope you don't mind my shedding tears. I feel no obligation to act macho, pretend to be tough. I . . . well, I'm gonna miss her. Unsurprisingly . . ." he murmured.

"Not at all, same here. Just that we have no one to cry for yet."

"Have you got other kids? In the old world?"

"Josiah and Esther, twins. We hope to see them one day. And the grandkids," Sarah answered. "We, er, we wanted children. Not that I dreamed of popping one every couple of months or so, no. Two, three max. By the time we had enough money to get treatment, Yidel had no viable sperm left, so we used a donor."

Mirielle sensed considerable discomfort and turned to confirm the source.

Sarah continued, "We asked Yidel's brothers to donate, but they . . . they did not even reply. As if we were dead. Anyway, we took advantage of the wonders of modern medicine. I gave birth. A girl and a boy. 'Beautiful' some would say, but the reality was that they were just red, wrinkled sacks of meat." She cracked a weak smile. "Beauty is in the eyes of the beholder. Anyway, we raised them, we loved them. It hurts sometimes that— Er, well, what about you?"

Mirielle wondered if her father detected the sadness. It was even in the woman's voice. There was no indication that he did, though. He was perhaps too deep into his own foul mood to notice. Leo set out to tell them about Eric and Abigail.

Why was Sarah sad? Why did she suddenly abandon the narration? Was it apt to ask? *And when will Eric come?* Mirielle's thoughts finally found refuge. Eric was in his seventies now. Hopefully, not in at least another decade. She was keen on getting to know her otherworldly siblings, Eric and Abigail, yet in no hurry to meet them, for her joy would mean sorrow for somebody else, as no awareness of this realm existed in the place the ghosts called Earth.

But then all those who had drifted away or were about to leave her world, where did they go? Did they disappear forever? Perhaps not! Perhaps there was a third stop? She might meet her mothers there. But then she was different. Her shoulders slumped again.

"Mommy!" Elian tugged on her dress again. "Stea, Yumu, walk."

Was he trying to take her mind off the subject? She tousled his hair. "OK." Stella resumed the usual shape. Elian weighed her, transformed, and his laughter rang out.

*
**

When they returned, Wasilla was leaning quietly with her forearms on the island countertop, her hair draping around her face as if trying to conceal the glass of whiskey in front of her. She took it, swayed it so the ice cubes clanked, and took a sip, then returned it to its prior spot. Mirielle didn't know whether to rush forward and embrace her mom or pretend that nothing serious was taking place. So, she herself became a block of ice. Wasilla looked at her and dispatched an air kiss.

Beatrice tried to be playful and patted Leo's bum, but then threw her hands in the air. "Ah, fuck, Wass!"

"No vigils this time around," Wasilla said, as if reading minds. "This is how it goes, and this place gave us such a wonderful time if you think! I had Lizzy, Mom, little bro. I still have you all, particularly that thing over there." She pointed at Mirielle with her thumb. "Do you remember what we did before Lizzy drifted? We traveled; we had fun! Time to repeat! Now we have Sarah and Yidel as guides; they've been to places. Right?"

Yidel blinked before reacting. "Sure. Let's go to Northern Queensland. Great beaches there and a coral reef, the Great Barrier Reef in case your geography is poor. In the old world it had completely bleached at the time we died, but in this one it is still alive, full of vibrant colors."

"By airport or just bend space?"

"What about a boat?" Yidel squinted.

"What boat? I built one, but it was a small speedboat to have fun on the river."

"A big sailboat. Trimaran. There are ocean-going trimarans in LA; we can borrow one from there."

Leo voiced a concern. "Yeah, but will Wass be able to materialize on a boat?"

"You traveled with your Elise, didn't you? Did she not return where you were?"

"She stayed with us the whole time."

"We're going!" Wasilla announced. "It is my call, isn't it?" She smiled.

*
**

Later in the evening, Mirielle glanced at the sleeping Elian next to her, turned the illumination off, and rested her head on the pillow. The clouds outside were in a hurry to reach some unknown destination and were annoying the full moon as they sped across the sky, making its light wobble.

Wasilla was not in a hurry to leave, but as with the clouds, there was no opposing force, and she would eventually also disappear into the unknown. Mirielle joined the moon in anger. Losing a loved one hurts. But what was life without pain? A life with no joy either, right?

Not quite. The horrors she had found in her outer memory made her shiver. And these were not lived. Neither of her parents experienced them; they only knew. Her dad considered himself extremely lucky to have had an uneventful, peaceful life. But she saw in his memories suffering on a grand scale, humans, animals, tormented and killed by natural and unnatural disasters—raging bush fires, tsunamis, earthquakes, chemical spills, radiation leaks. Creatures, domesticated and in the wild, living in constant fear and dying in excruciating pain, slaughtered, starved, consumed by diseases, torn apart. Pictures of war, people blown to pieces by others just like them on some madman's command. The dear leader. The orange king. The Russian turd. Some guy named Adolf. These "leaders" were horrible human beings inflicting irredeemable suffering. Why were they leaders? Who put them there? She could not understand. It was all so messed up. She flipped on her back, sweating, and stared at the ceiling. And what was that? The ones who preached love were often the worst offenders—the tormentors, the haters, the oppressors, the murderers. Why? Why?

She had missed the moment when she started sobbing. Something soft and warm snuggled into her. "Mommy. You . . . sad." Elian's little arms hugged her.

Mirielle halted her breath, biting her lip. She didn't want to upset the child. She knew what it was like to feel somebody else's dread, but she struggled to set her thought train on a different track. It veered back. Desperate, she tried to rid her mind of buzz, imagining a large pink balloon.

"Good . . . people. Come . . . here." The little guy seemed to have read her thoughts before she inflated them away.

Mirielle swayed her head slowly. "No, Eli, no, love, they do not. This world is not real. It is just some dude's wet fantasy, a written dream. We are all figments of somebody's imagination."

"No, Mommy, sis . . ."

Mirielle popped her eyes open and swiftly turned. A young man was staring at her in the milky darkness, the moonlight engraving the features of her dad. Then the face morphed, and she looked straight into her mother's eyes. Or were they her own? Why couldn't she move? Was she dreaming? She took a gulp of air through her open mouth.

The other young woman outstretched her hand and wiped the tears from Mirielle's cheeks. "Mom, sis . . . cry as much as you want, but rest assured that we are real."

Mirielle flipped back, closed her eyes, and followed the advice. She sobbed, her shoulders shook, the pillow silently absorbing the stream of tears. She turned, clutched the little hands again, and cried more. For Elise. For Walid. For the impending loss of yet another ghost she dearly loved.

The world? It was too big for her.

FIRST TIE

At daybreak, Wasilla changed her mind, realizing that her mother might also depart soon. They both died within a few years of each other; maybe they would bow out of existence together, hand in hand. Fatimah was in Europe, surrounded by her grandkids, glad to be with them and sad that her older son did not make it.

What was the deal with men? Jaques was brutal, unsupportive of her, Fatimah, and Walid, instead looking down on them, and, as reported by his kids, he had become a zealot in the fading years of his life, seeking heaven and trying to save souls. Just like Tarek, their father. And he was not with them now, only a sad memory imprinted on the canvas of their minds. Leo's half brother Carl was allegedly a zealot too and was also unaccounted for. But he was much younger, so he might still be alive. Ah, Leo . . . she could not imagine loving a man, yet she loved the dude in more ways than just as a very close friend. Would she still have emotions and be capable of missing him where she was going? Would she meet her, no, their old love Elise?

"Sorry, folks, I'd rather be with Mom," Wasilla said to the little crowd gathered in the house. "I'm not suggesting that you go by yourselves, because I know you well enough. So, let's move back to Europe for a while. We may go to Beirut, though; Mom may want that. It used to be home." She then turned and left the room.

Stella was holding Mirielle's hand, occasionally rubbing the palm with her fingers. When she heard the announcement, she let go and approached her parents. "I'm staying with Mirrie," she said quietly.

"I understand." Yidel nodded and hugged his child. "We are just a strong thought away," he whispered in her ear and pecked her cheek.

"*Vi du vilst,*" Sarah concurred.

Stella returned to Mirielle's side and clutched her hand again. "I suppose I could join?"

Mirielle snapped her head. "But of course!" she said and squeezed the hand she held. Then she blushed and added calmly, "Yes, Stella, thank you. Ayumu is coming too. We must tell you what happened when he first visited the old continent, if it is a continent at all here. Probably not."

"What happened?"

"Well," Mirielle leaned closer and continued in a quiet voice, "when he came to my grandma's place, and we were trying bondage, Walid barged in—"

"What is bondage?"

"Ah, you don't know?"

Stella browsed her outer memory and shook her head. "Negative."

"To some it is a sexual travesty; to others it is an art form. I must show you a few books, and from there you can make up your mind. It is OK to dislike it as much as it is OK to practice it. I found it enjoyable, but then I was with people I trust absolutely—Ayumu and Walid. I think that trust is a big part of it. Without confidence, it is abuse."

"Gets complicated, doesn't it?"

"Everything in their world is complicated." Mirielle nodded at the ghosts in the room.

"Seems so, yes."

$$\overset{*}{*}{*}$$

"Let's start with something simple," Mirielle said after Stella paged through the books, blushed, licked her lips a few times, and gave her informed consent.

"Again, are you sure you wanna try?" Mirielle repeated.

"Yes, I am already dripping wet. Weird, though, what makes it so arousing?"

"No idea. The kinkiness of it perhaps? Or the surrender?"

"Mm. What do we do now?" Stella asked.

"Will you be a girl or a boy?"

"My native shape is that of a female, same as you, so let's start with that and then we can switch."

Mirielle visited the cupboard and returned with a leather harness fitted with Velcro strips. "Something simple, I said, easy to put on, easy to remove if you dislike it. Jump in." She gathered Stella's long hair and wrapped it loosely around her neck. Next, she held the harness, then pulled sharply and started fastening the straps. Stella gasped as her breasts popped through the holes.

"Gimme your hands. Behind your back. That's it!"

"Ugh!" Stella grunted.

"Something wrong?"

"No, it turns me on actually. Why did you not let Ayumu join? Don't you trust him?"

Mirielle ensured that Stella's arms were properly tied and moved to the legs. "I trust him completely, but it is your first time, and with your anthropophobia . . . just the two of us is much better."

"Phew!" Stella's face had become red, her mouth ajar, and her heartbeat could almost be heard.

Mirielle closed the padded restraints of the metal bar over Stella's ankles and ran her fingers up Stella's groove.

The blonde girl moaned, breathing impatiently. "Damn, I want something in . . ."

"Would you have told that to Ayumu?" Mirielle lifted the large feather she had fetched from the cupboard and positioned herself in front of her friend. She moved the feather between Stella's legs and fluttered it.

The girl tilted her head backward and moaned again. "Ah . . . I-I guess so, I am about to explode!" She huffed.

Mirielle took a piece of cord and tied knots around Stella's nipples. She was getting aroused herself, tempted to attach the cord ends to her own tits and pull, precipitating the pleasurable tingles she'd grown to look forward to. The massive feather then fluttered anew, followed by the delicate probing of an elongated metal toy.

Stella swallowed hard. Each touch sent strong ripples of delight throughout her body, followed by a calm she was not content with. She wanted a stream. When Mirielle tugged on the line, she clenched her teeth, trying not to scream for a stronger pull. When the toy split her labia and tickled her sweet spot, she hissed, swallowing a call to push. She arched her back, brought her hips forward, and tried to rub against the toy. Mirielle produced a sinister grin and withdrew it. Stella grunted. Mirielle put the toy aside, took a banana from the bowl that was waiting for them when they arrived, peeled it slowly, and ran her tongue along the fruit, staring straight into Stella's eyes.

"Bitch!" Stella produced a tortured smile.

"Here." Mirielle offered her the fruit.

Stella drew the peeled half of the banana into her mouth and rolled her tongue around it. Then she pushed it out a bit and chopped a piece. Mirielle smiled and rubbed her vulva with the toy. Stella squashed the piece and gasped. Joyful yet angry tears appeared in her eyes. She tilted her head.

Mirielle dragged the toy all the way to her belly button. She lingered there, then rose to her feet and transformed into her yang. Stella drew a ragged breath and twisted her mouth. The muscles in her groin contracted. Mirielle went out of sight. Stella quivered— what was in store for her now?

A mild push sent Stella face down on the soft mat. She raised her rear in anticipation of something making an entry, but time passed quietly. Then Mirielle parted her petals with the toy. Or maybe not. The blonde closed her eyes, filtering out unnecessary sensory input and concentrating on the pleasurable flashes brought about by the swaying motion. She gasped and squirmed as Mirielle moved faster.

Mirielle held her hips and thrust harder, turning the flashes into a stream of endless sparks. Stella lifted the constraints on her vocal cords, and her moans filled the room. Her head was spinning, and her body was restrained yet abundant in ecstasy. She started shaking uncontrollably when the pleasure roared. Her mind was shrouded in delight, suspending all thoughts, leaving room only for desire. She craved more!

But she also sensed Mirielle's grief returning. Wasilla had been gone for yet another day.

"Come here, Mirrie! Closer."

Mirielle complied.

"Kiss!" Stella pouted.

Mirielle smiled and they touched lips.

"Thank you!" Stella whispered and rubbed her cheek against Mirielle's. "You want to go now, I think."

"Yeah, I wonder if Mom has come back. And how beings like me and you die. And if there is a second time for us ..." Mirielle sighed and released the leg restraints, moved behind Stella, and ripped the Velcro strips open. She returned the harness and the accessories to the cupboard, donned her sweatpants and her top, and opened the door. Stella walked past her, lost in thought.

"Hey!"

"Yes?" Stella turned.

"Your body mask. You forgot." Mirielle handed her the baggy dark blue shirt.

"Ah, yes, sorry." Stella dived into the garment headfirst.

"So, you really wore nothing up till recently? And your parents?"

"We didn't. We were like cavemen. Mm, no, more like animals; cavemen wore skins and fur. Sometimes we wore flowers and fig leaves for fun. I think that they were mocking their book."

"What book? Ah, never mind, I got it." Mirielle had retrieved the info from her store.

"I remember what Mom and Dad did in their lives, their upbringing and how nudity was, well, shameful, horrifying. When they died, there were only the two of them in this entire world, so why cover?

Hide from what? God? Truth be told, they were apprehensive for a while, not expecting to continue existing and unsure of the nature of this place, but they chose to challenge it in their own perhaps silly way. They undressed and stepped out on the street. Then they had sex in the next-door yard, on the lawn. Funny, it was. I remember Mom's fear and desire intertwined. So, they dropped the cover. And when I was born, things did not change much."

"Clothes are the equalizer."

"What do you mean?"

"I found that in my outer memory. A thought from Dad."

"What outer memory?"

"This is what I call the memories that are not mine. You just quoted your outer memory in my speak."

"Ah, I get it. Equalizer how?"

"Well, not all people are naturally good-looking, and clothes give them the ability to improve their appearances, make themselves more attractive, objects of desire. But it is not just that; there's much more. Only, I struggle to understand the many nuances. Clothes as a protection against the weather or other environmental conditions is easy to comprehend. When I cook, I wear aprons. I wrap myself when it is cold. Their world is also dirty. By the way, you have never been to a cold place, it seems." Mirielle glanced at her friend.

"No. But I am aware that such exist."

"We shall visit one. There's a place nearby called Köennendorf." Mirielle wrapped her arm around the other girl's shoulders and drew her nearer. "Anyway, women dressed in a certain way can be found to be more sexually appealing than if they were au naturel. Ayumu told me that you were like that to him, but he didn't know why. Men like to watch naked ladies, yet they do not want to bare themselves. They have that thing called the Internet, and at some point, people were posting fake nude pictures of ladies, often former girlfriends, and it was shameful. But it had become so prevalent and widespread that the natural response had been to stop caring and even publish real nudes. Jamima, Mom's niece, told me that. She had been a victim, and after she had cried out her heart, she had taken a bunch of pics herself and challenged the shamers. But she grew to be distrustful of men and never loved again."

Mirielle retracted her arm and sent her gaze away. "Damn, I'm gonna miss her, Stella! Wass . . ." The tears bubbled up. She used her palms as a handkerchief and put on a brave face. "But this is life! Could be far worse."

SURPRISE

Mirielle was observing Wasilla with complete indifference. Just a few days ago, her emotions were tormented by the impending departure of the beloved being who raised her. And now? Nothing. As if the woman was a supporting movie character, augmenting her reality. She cursed this realm. It was unfair! Why would it not let her grieve?

Wasilla was no longer aware that her drift had begun. Each time she returned from a hop into the unknown, her memories were lacking, scrubbed clean of the trip. As soon as he figured that out, Leo jumped at the opportunity to spare Wasilla the anguish and promptly told people to keep their mouths shut. She always disappeared together with her mom, and that made the ruse easy. However, Mirielle's dad almost got a bald spot on his head where he kept scratching it, seeking to understand why they were flashing out and returning at the same time. The realm would wait for the two women to be simultaneously out of sight before acting. He was tempted to relaunch the vigil, just to see if one of them would go on her own, but Beatrice talked him out of it.

Mirielle was grateful for the amnesia and the censorship. Walid's drift was still fresh in her mind—the anxiety, the ache, the dread, the last spectacle they played in his dreamt-up theater, the last love dance. Had she known that she was leaving the afterlife, Wasilla might have been hurt by the blank expression on Mirielle's face and her cold stare. Maybe this indifference was her private coping mechanism.

"You are angry, Mommy. Why?" Elian's crisp chirp delivered her from her thoughts.

"Because you are a bad boy." Mirielle smiled and hugged her son.

"I can be a girl!" He instantly transformed.

Mirielle laughed. "Ah, you are smart!"

Smart indeed. His vocabulary was unusually rich for his age, and his speech quite eloquent. She wanted to know who resided in his outer memory, but he was still too young for that. She herself was unaware until her early teens that the strange recollections she harbored inside her were not actually hers.

"I can also sense your anger. I know that it is not Eli, so may I ask who it is directed at?" A soft voice sounded next to her ear, and she felt fingers combing her hair, then a warm breath and lips brushing against her cheek. She quivered. Stella's touch, no matter how light it was, always stirred desire, perhaps too much of it. But she was unable to send her away even for a short while, as the petite girl appeared so fragile. Mirielle was afraid that avoiding her intimacy might break her petite heart. She'd been alone for so long.

"Yes, I am angry at myself. But it will pass."

"Turn into a boy," Elian advised very seriously.

Mirielle squinted, then laughed again, when the meaning of his words became clear. She promptly transformed. She'd begun to appreciate the trait since she reacquired it a while ago. Her guess was correct—it returned when she stopped breastfeeding the no longer little mouth.

"Hah, hah, you are wearing a skirt." Elian pointed at the young man.

"And you are stark naked!" the man replied.

Elian shrugged, squeezed herself between the table and the couch, and trotted in the direction of Wasilla. "Grandma!"

Stella breathed on the cheek again. "Shall we sneak out now? I think that you need to lie down and relax. I will give you a treat." Her lips touched Mirielle's unshaven face. "And you shall use a razor; your beard is still sparse."

Mirielle reverted.

"No, no, stay male! I haven't given you a blow job for some time." Stella giggled.

"But I am wearing a skirt."

"So what? Isn't it fun?"

Mirielle threw a glance at the room and became a man again, shook off the slippers, got up, and the two quietly left.

Stella pinned Mirielle to the wall and rose on her toes as soon as they reached the ground floor. Their lips touched. Mirielle's heart pounded as usual, the attraction made him squirm, but he took hold of the arms wrapped around his neck and tugged them gently down. "Not now, baby. Let's just take a stroll." Mirielle dropped the male form.

"Nooo . . ." Stella stepped back. "Can't you stay a boy for a while?"

"Why? My native form is that of a human female."

"I wanna have a boyfriend."

"Well, what about Ayumu? He's a proper male ghost."

"Ayumu is your boyfriend. I want mine. Please!"

Mirielle sighed, morphing into the tall, unshaven young man dressed in a crop top and a denim skirt. "So, you don't like the girl in me—"

Stella hung on Mirielle's arm and looked up cheekily. "I do! I love you! But . . . Well, yeah, I prefer your yang as you call it. But it is still you inside! What difference does the shape make?"

"Look at yourself. The girl in you tends to panic, whereas the boy stands firm. There's a difference. And when I switch shapes often or stay male longer, I get confused. My body gets confused . . . When I fall asleep while male, a girl wakes up. This is my native shape. Don't tell me it is not the same for you."

Stella dropped her head and sighed. "Yeah . . ." Then she cheered up. "OK, be yourself; I don't want you to be uncomfortable."

"I will indulge you for a while." Mirielle smiled. "Now, let's go."

Outside the day was on the decline; the sun was dressed in brass, and the shadows stretched to infinity. Mirielle tried to imagine the other world. The place there was probably noisy, crowded, and packed with vehicles, most of which she had seen only in books and on screens.

She took a few steps, stopped, and adjusted her attire. "You see, I have no problem wearing a skirt as a girl, but I find it uncomfortable as a boy. I'd rather don a pair of trousers. Explain that."

Stella inspected Mirielle. "My outer memory says that skirts can be uncomfortable regardless. But maybe it is your weenie, it is like a stick of pepperoni now."

"Pepperoni, indeed. Your touch always turns me on."

"Then why resist? I am more than willing! I am hungry!"

"Because I want us to do more than just bang. And also, because it feels weird, you know, not being sad about Mom. Worse now, I am no longer indifferent! Now I want her and Auntie Fatimah gone; I want the whole drift-away shebang to be over. And I am full to the brim with guilt about feeling this way. Angry even." Mirielle shook his head, then abruptly changed the subject. "Hey, do you play an instrument? Or sing? We can form a band. Something meaningful to do."

"I learned the Hawaiian guitar when we lived on an island somewhere. I'm not very good at it, but I suppose I can improve. And I do sing when I'm alone."

"I play claviers. Both my parents did, and I somehow knew how to do it when I tried. And Ayumu thinks that he can play drums. Maybe this way he'd actually learn."

"Cool!" Stella hugged Mirielle tightly, forcing him to stop.

Ayumu's gaze followed his friends until the branches of the willows stepped forward and obscured the view. He'd grown on Stella too, and she reciprocated with no hesitation, yet he couldn't convince himself to be happy. Lately, Stella and Mirielle had begun spending much more time as a couple than they had been with him. Even when the three of them were together, he often felt out of place, a guest. The three had their shared moments of elation. The girls went wild and spared nothing. He was living every man's dream, yet he was still an outsider. An old-world ghost, mingling with the locals. Being surrounded by magical creatures yet lonely.

He went inside and pulled a can of beer from the fridge. The room was empty. He could hear Elian chatting with his grandmothers somewhere down the hallway. He chugged the brew, dropped the can into the bin, and proceeded outside. Mirielle and Stella went east; therefore, he was going west.

"Why is your name Stella?" Mirielle asked, attempting to revive the conversation. Chatting kept his dark thoughts at bay.

"'Cause I like it."

"How does it come? Your parents chose it, so—"

"No, I did. My name was Miriam. Bland, boring. I complained and Mom and Dad told me that I could be called anything I wanted."

"I see. Interesting! It never crossed my mind that I could pick another name. But I like mine. Mirielle. It allegedly means 'miracle.' You know, a baby in this world."

"Mine means 'star.' I found it in a book Dad brought once. He likes to read; we all do. Dad said that in their old world, reading had gone out of fashion. I wonder why. It makes you fantasize. No two worlds are ever the same, even if they came from the same book. Everybody imagines things differently. The stories in those films are too condensed, flat. I guess by necessity. Er, I veered off topic, sorry. So, I pranked them. I said I wanted to be called Khah-rah."

"Sounds legit. Where's the prank?"

"It means 'poop' in Hebrew."

"Oh!" Mirielle guffawed. "And?"

"They pranked me back. They said that it was a fine name for a Jewish girl. So, for a while they called me that, barely keeping their faces straight. I gave up and switched to 'star.'"

"Here." Mirielle pointed at a heavy wooden door, then pulled it open. Stairs led down to the basement. "My outer memory says it was a Greek tavern, but now it is a jazz club, I'd say. It has musical instruments—grand piano, electric organ, drums, double bass, a saxophone. No steel guitar, though, but you may try a regular one."

Mirielle remembered his parents' escapades in this joint. It was fun to be them in those days. He was tempted to pull something of his own with his petite sweetheart in tow, who'd been tormenting him in a way since they began the stroll, but that would have demolished the point he was trying to make—let's do something else, not just bang. Unless the banging was on the bongos, of course.

"Ah, it is cozy!" Stella swayed her gaze around. She climbed onto the podium and picked an acoustic guitar from its stand. It looked enormous in her hands. She sat on a stool, placed the instrument in her lap, and plucked the strings.

"No, it is not the same. Even if I had a bar, this one has frets." She then held the guitar the proper way and tried a few chords. "I will have to learn. But that's OK!" She smiled.

Mirielle had sat behind the grand piano, massaging his hands. Then he hit the keys. The melody flowed, not quite effortlessly, though. Was it the male shape?

"What was that?" Stella asked when the last note faded.

"Rick Wakeman, a composer and performer from the twentieth century of the other world. I wonder if he's here. Is there a way to find out?"

"Erm, I don't know. But there must surely be more of our kind. We must search for them, don't you agree?"

"With your anthropophobia?" Mirielle laughed, then put on a grave face. "Yep, that is something we must do. We ought to travel, me and you. I have so many questions about our world; there must be answers! We must, after Mom's drift, though . . ." Suddenly his head dropped. His emotions. It was a roller-coaster ride.

Stella rose from her stool and came close. She straddled the young man in the miniskirt in front of the piano and placed her hands on his shoulders. Mirielle looked away. Stella caressed the young man's cheek, scratched his beard, smiling, then pulled his head and aimed at his lips. Her tongue parted them and pushed deeper. Mirielle offered no resistance; just shut his eyes.

Stella wriggled out of her baggy garment and tossed it inside the instrument. Their tongues became entangled again; the hearts they didn't have thumped loudly. Why did he want this girl so much? Was it because they were alike? Sentient products of zombie love?

"Leo?!" A voice wedged itself between the two. Mirielle's eyes flipped open and traced the source. Stella cowered and snuggled up tightly. She glanced backward with enlarged eyes, then buried her face in Mirielle's chest. Her faint halo faded away.

"Grandma?!"

Ruth, with her mouth agape, had trained her eyes on the couple on the stool. Dietrich stood beside her, appearing far less impressed. He was barefoot and bare-chested, wearing only a pair of oversized shredded jeans, and Ruth, not to be outdone, was topless, clad in just an embroidered apron and accessorized with a coral necklace.

The attire was of no concern to Mirielle, though. The two more than obviously had come together, and there was no way for them to have known that she'd be around. Stella had begun drooling on her chest. And she herself was still aroused and male. She promptly switched shape.

"Grandma?" she repeated. "You can see Dietrich on your own?"

"Oh!" Ruth clutched Dietrich's arm. "Mirrie, I saw your dad."

Mirielle scoffed. Of course she did. "Since when? Since when can you two see each other? And can you see Stella?"

"Since that day in the park. Remember, when you caught us in the act in the bushes. And I can see your friend."

"Then go away!"

"Ah! Yes, of course!" Ruth dragged the puzzled Dietrich out.

"Stelly, calm down, we are alone now." Mirielle caressed the blonde. "Be a man, if you will."

Stella clutched her even tighter.

Mirielle kissed her head and spoke softly. "C'mon, baby, relax; it is just me and you."

"G-give some t-time," Stella stuttered.

"Of course."

Stella continued squeezing tightly, but the quiver stopped. "I-I wanna fight it. It makes . . . no sense." She took a deep breath and slowly peeled herself from Mirielle. "I don't want"—another deep breath—"to be a man right now."

"Sure, I agree . . . bitch!" Mirielle laughed and pinched her friend's cheeks.

Stella looked down. "I don't know where this panic comes from, but it happens when I am in a tight spot, and I cannot escape . . ."

"My other grandmother is a shrink. She may talk to you if you so wish."

"Shrink?"

"A doctor, psychiatrist. They deal with mental issues. Not saying that you are crazy . . ." She waved her hands. "She performed a miracle with my other grandmom, the one that was just here. Did you notice something odd about her?"

"N-no. I saw just two silhouettes in the doorframe."

"She was topless."

"So?"

Mirielle sighed. Wearing clothes was optional for Stella; of course she saw nothing unusual. "People normally cover themselves, as you know. Some are very strict about it—"

"Yes, I am aware. My parents were Hasidic Jews."

"Well, she used to be like that and also very shy."

"Ah, I get it now. And you are saying that it was your other grand-mother who helped this one change?"

"Yep!"

"All right, then I will talk to her." Stella leaned closer and whispered to Mirielle, "But now, can you turn into a boy again? Please!"

Mirielle shook her head, stuck her tongue out, and complied with glee.

TWINKLE, TWINKLE LITTLE STAR

Ayumu crawled from underneath the table and hiccupped. That was all. His head should have been killing him after the quantity of booze he consumed before he passed out. But he threw up at some point during the binge, that he recalled.

Why did he drink? To forget, of course. To forget that he was on his own again. Mirielle was with Stella now; he was just an extension of the relationship. Today, yesterday, the day before . . . sometimes they'd remember and call him to join. And it was good, the experience. But when was the last time he and Mirielle climbed? Ages ago, still in Japan. Maybe he should climb instead of drinking. Good idea! But then without danger, his mind was not dedicated to the task of staying alive up high. He would keep thinking of her. Still, worth the try.

Ayumu pushed the door open and checked the street. It was, as expected, devoid of human life. Mild wind, birds, and that distant hum, as if coming from a busy highway. Same as in Japan. Except for the trains. There were no trains here, just shiny tracks. He remembered when they stumbled on Mirielle's parents having fun in the carriage of the Meitetsu Nagoya Line. Weird, at any other time, he would have wished for the redhead. She was a gorgeous woman, but now he wanted his Mirielle. He wanted the slender girl with unimpressive boobs and angry hair in his arms. Was she getting shapelier with age? Probably. She seemed curvier now, but she was unable to shapeshift like them, the regulars, no way to compare her appearance from a few years back.

Ayumu passed by another bar. He hesitated. Maybe get another drink? He pulled the door, then let go. Then he opened it again. Climbing without Mirielle and danger was dull. He entered and sat at the bar. He imagined a bartender. A girl, Japanese, dressed as a maid. He missed these also. Thinking about the past, his other life, it was lonely at times too, despite the crowds. But it was not bad. He had friends; he had Keiko. She was a nice girl, and they had sex. So many young people in his country had none of this, sharing their lives with a computer, buying used underwear from vending machines, and probably masturbating. He didn't know for sure. Sad. Yeah, he was a jerk with all this self-pity. Stella was around, yes, but so what? There were so many positives about it. It was a pleasure to observe the two ladies making love—they glowed in the dark, their movements were so incredibly graceful, like an intricately choreographed dance, and sometimes they did float in the air, as if weightless, twisting and turning in slow motion, faint streaks of light in a multitude of colors running through their bodies. Then they would become one with him, their elation would transfer, and his ecstasy would be supreme! Those moments alone were priceless.

Ayumu downed the glass and headed for the door. Shoes! He had to find a sports goods store to pick up some climbing shoes and gear. They could climb the fortress wall. There may be some good cliffs too. He wasn't familiar with the area, but he saw the mountain peaks. Where there are mountain peaks, there shall be cliffs as well. Stella may choose to join them or . . . he had no idea. But it was worth trying. He and Mirielle might hoist her up for the fun.

*
**

Mirielle gasped when the front door opened with a bang. She quickly walked the short distance to the corner and peeked around. Ayumu squeezed in, loaded with gear—climbing ropes slung over his shoulders and three obviously heavy backpacks packed to the brim.

"Sorry! I didn't mean to startle you. My hands were busy." Ayumu looked around and raised his eyebrows. "Where's everyone?"

"Eli was crying too much. They dragged him out." Mirielle sighed. "What is it?"

"Why did he . . . wait! Don't tell me your mom is gone!" He dropped the gear on the floor.

Mirielle dragged her repeated nods.

"So sorry, Mirrie-chan!" Ayumu got closer and tried to hug her. She pushed him away, then changed her mind and wrapped her arms around his neck and drilled into his mouth with her tongue. She wanted him! Right here! Right now! Her hand crawled and rubbed his crotch. Would he be able to perform? She rubbed harder. There was some excitement under the fabric. She unbuttoned his pants and pulled the zipper down. The liberated member popped out, still unsure what to do. She rolled her palm, pressing firmly. The member chose to expand further; its owner, though, stood still.

Mirielle looked into his eyes, traced her lips, and found his mouth again. Her hands crawled under his shirt and pushed it up. She pinched his nipples, rolled them with her thumbs, then pressed her palms against his chest. The thumps of his heart—could she really feel it? She stepped closer, grabbed his hair, and kissed him on the mouth again. Her arms encircled his frame.

Finally, Ayumu moved. His hands crawled around her waist and greeted each other. He tilted his head and pushed his tongue into her mouth. Mirielle loosened her embrace. Ayumu did the opposite. Mirielle wriggled out, breathing heavily, and relieved herself of her shirt. Ayumu followed, then took her hands and brought them up. His eyes danced over her face, shy of looking down where her stiff nipples were screaming at him.

She grabbed his wrists and pushed his palms against her breasts. "I want you. I need you," she whispered. "Please!"

"But . . ."

Mirielle bit her lip and let go of his arms. "Come, I'll show you."

The room Wasilla had occupied was empty. All the furniture was gone. The large floor-to-ceiling window was bare, as if never having seen curtains. Even the pictures and trinkets had disappeared without a trace. There were no nails and no discoloration on the walls where they used to hang. As if they were never there. Only the rug lingered but looked pristine, untouched by a foot.

"I want you, Ayumu," Mirielle said quietly. "I want us to be one. I don't know why. It seems inappropriate, I know, but . . ." Her throat stiffened.

Ayumu gently gathered her into his arms. "I don't understand, but this is OK, I guess." He stepped out of his pants, tugged her to the center of the room, kneeled, and unburdened her of the remainder of her clothes.

She came down on her knees too. He was as confused as she was, he had just admitted it. Why did she want to make love in this moment? Was she grieving? She should be relieved, for her wish from the last few days was granted; the shebang was over, but . . . being so unfeeling was wrong! She pulled Ayumu and glued her lips to his. She wanted her mind to be blank for a while, free of questions, free of doubt. Her hands descended and encircled his penis. She tugged on it. She wanted this stupid thing inside her. Now! Mirielle rolled on the soft, jolly rug, dragging Ayumu with her. Wasilla liked bright stuff.

Wasilla . . . Mirielle shook her head, straddled Ayumu, and pinned him down. His eyes did not stop following her face. She spread his arms, leaned forward, and pressed her lips against his. Her breasts rubbed his chest, and she gasped. Ayumu's hands grabbed her buttocks. She could feel the silly rod rubbing against her petals. Where there are sparks, there will be fire! Mirielle sat upright and let the penis glide in. She loved it! That thing . . . She began swaying, her eyes closed. Amazing! She could not only feel the dance, but she could also see! Inside her! Her heart beating, her chest rising at each breath, then retreating, her hips rolling, even his penis gyrating as she swayed. Yet the pain lingered. She flipped her eyelids up, crossed gazes with her man, and moved faster. Their hands intertwined. The fire, she wanted fire! Maybe it would incinerate the pain. More sparks flew. It felt good, so good! Yet not powerful enough. She clenched her teeth; her face turned angry. She knew that it was red. She felt the blood. Then the eruption shook her frame. She froze, basking in the aftershocks, pleading that they never stopped. But reality was quick to follow. Her eyebrows gathered closer, and her lips trembled.

"Mom!" Mirielle wailed. "Mommy! Fuck!" She collapsed over Ayumu, and her lips moved. "Please come back ... please!" She scratched the rug, then dug with fingers into her hair, sobbing, "Mom!"

Ayumu cradled her shaking body in his arms and waited. Mirielle sent her hand exploring—his chin, his lips, his nose ... He was like an obedient big dog at this moment, being poked and probed. She traced his eyebrow with a finger, then patted his cheek and let the hand rest. Then her soft voice disturbed the silence.

"How are you, Ayumu-kun?"

"Er, sad, but otherwise OK."

"Do you think that I will drift away like you all do? Or simply die."

"How would I know? How would anyone know? You are a miracle, remember? The first one."

"I hope that you are not going to drift away any time soon. I'd be devastated, now that Mom is gone. I love you, Ayumu-kun!" Mirielle sat upright and found his gaze. "I love Shinji and Mayumi too, and Yidel and Sarah and your parents. They are all good people!" She turned her head and added quietly, "Maybe that's why this place is so empty." Then she stared at him again. "How did you exist in your old world, Ayumu-kun? I see nothing pretty there. Well, maybe some, but overall, it is awful, isn't it?" Her voice rang clear. "I want to find others! Others like me, so they can make me see! I want to know! Are there any former politicians here? Are amputees whole in this realm? Are conjoined twins separated? Are rape victims compensated? If this is paradise, then what about all that?"

He grabbed her wrists and crawled his thumbs into her palms. "I—"

She interrupted. "You know, I went to the sex toy shop, the one opposite the hotel. They dispense sex dolls now. They look so real. And all girls, beautiful girls. Why? Why no men? And why do you have them in the first place, in a crowded world? Are there not enough people? I get it here—you lived without another person's touch for a very long time, longer than I've been alive, and so did Mom, I mean Elise, but there? I don't understand."

"I am not a wise man, Mirrie. I was, I *am* a shallow person, a climber with a short temper and a penchant to show off."

"You are a wise man, Ayumu-kun, since you call yourself all that. This is what Dad thought. Your temper is no longer short, and I have never seen you showing off."

"Well, you should have seen me when I bought my Kawasaki bike." Ayumu frowned at the memory. "The number of humans is not important; what matters is how they relate. We were never good at that. Always at war with each other. As nations, as groups, as individuals. Over possessions, over control, over pride. You learned about kamikaze at school, right?"

He continued without waiting for her answer. "People went to kill other people and themselves died, for what? The emperor. An old fart. Well, maybe not old at that time, but still a pompous fart. Traditions drag us down. The woman must be submissive; the man rules the world. And when men have no power, they cower in dungeons, watch porn, play video games, and think of revenge. Women, sorry, they are not much better. They see men as cash cows, especially if they are pretty. They betray each other at the blink of an eye. But I guess this is how things go in a world with limited resources. I guess it is a primal instinct—to dominate, to manipulate, to expropriate, to hate the outgroup—"

"But would it not be better if humans cooperated, if they showed compassion and restraint?"

"Certainly! However, you would not believe what we are capable of. We, many of us, we would accept to personally suffer if we could make someone we hate suffer more."

"I don't think that I'd be able to survive in your world. You are heroes!"

"No, we were lucky to not be pushed against a wall. And I died young, so who knows what I might have become had I lived to old age. I have that violent streak, you know. Combine that with low self-esteem, and some people become abusers. I might have turned into one. I never fully trusted anyone in the old world besides my mom."

Mirielle sensed that the mood had become way too dark. Yet, she'd started it. She had all these questions, and she wanted answers, but maybe it was time for a break.

"Hey, wanna eat something sweet? Chocolate? And our crowd may be back soon. I hope Eli has calmed down." She sighed. "He sensed it first. He screamed 'Grandma!' and barged into her room. Then he couldn't stop crying. Only Stella somehow managed to soothe him a bit. Perhaps because she is of our kind." She shivered. "Sorry, it sounded bad; I mean it just technically . . ."

Ayumu got up and outstretched his arm to help her do the same. "Don't worry, I know. I am Japanese, after all, a yellow guy, and you are not, yet we get along quite well with each other."

"We sure do!" Mirielle clasped her hands behind his back and rested her head on his shoulder. "I love you, yellow guy, I truly do."

⁎⁎

The grief made a comeback in the evening, when the sun was well below the horizon, if there was one. She held up her tears when Elian broke free from Beatrice and ran to Wasilla's room:

"Is Grandma back?"

She put on a smile. "Not yet, Eli." Then she reprimanded him firmly when he began sobbing again. "Why are you crying? Your grandma can't take a dump because of you!"

"What's that?"

"It's complicated and not quite right. Do you wanna hear?" She bet on his impatience and won. For now. But the youngster sensed the dreary mood around him. He probed each person and again chose Stella. That made sense. She and Ayumu were the least affected, if at all; their auras were perhaps bright.

For the first time, she felt a need for a cigarette or a joint. She lit up occasionally in the past, experimenting, playing roles, then stopped. Ayumu was still puffing when nervous or upset. Her parents, though, the whole lot, had moved on. Now she was a parent short, one less mom. Mirielle considered Beatrice a mother too. She joined the club relatively late indeed but was so affectionate and caring. One day Beatrice would also be gone. And her dad too. And Ayumu.

She found a pack of cigarettes and a lighter on the table. She pulled a stick and sniffed it, then pushed it back. It broke in two. Mirielle tossed it over the railing, pushed the pack into her pocket, and looked at the stars. Were they even real? Some people in the other world believe that the deceased become little twinkles in the night sky. Romantic and nonsensical.

She started sobbing quietly. She missed her mom so much! She didn't know why. Wasilla was no different than Beatrice, and Beatrice was still around. Yes, they had distinct personalities. Wasilla was stricter and somewhat obsessed with cleanliness and order, whereas the faux redhead was more like her, or she was rather more like Beatrice. If her attachment to them both was purely utilitarian, meeting her survival needs, she shouldn't care who the provider was.

Mirielle pulled out a cigarette and lit it this time, then leaned on the railing and gazed up. They had to make a plan—she and Ayumu and Stella. They had to search for others! But how? She squirmed on the inside.

Stella stood next to her and said quietly, "Elian's asleep."

Mirielle drew her closer. The petite blonde grabbed Mirielle's arm and snuggled into her. She had that habit. She'd do it with Ayumu too.

"Where's yellow man?"

"Right here," Ayumu said and pulled both ladies into his embrace.

Stella held his forearm and squeezed it lightly. Mirielle smiled at the sight. Then her thoughts returned to Wasilla. Driven by ancient stories and beliefs, she again looked up at the cloudless night sky, chose two random bright stars shining close to each other, and thought: *Goodbye, Mommy. Goodbye, Auntie Fatimah. Farewell.*

The distant sound of Elian crying pricked up her ears. "Damn! There's no peace with kids around." Mirielle threw the butt into the dark and trotted toward their room.

WTF

Mirielle removed her gloves, put them in her pouch, cracked her fingers, rubbed her palms into one another, and looked over the edge. They'd done far more impressive climbs, but today the plan was to hoist Stella and Elian to the top, once she and Ayumu got there.

The abyss challenged her. "Do you dare jump?"

Over ten years after the accident, she still had no idea what would happen to her if she did. Both Ayumu and Walid failed to land a punch on her, when they swiped at her in anger. Therefore, it was very likely that the fall would not be terminal. She might bounce off the ground like a rubber ball or simply get up and walk away. There were no laws of physics here, no kinetic energy to contend with. Just illusions. She wanted to find out, but the primal fear inherited from her parents was still way too strong. She peeked over the edge once more.

"Mirrie-chan, stay back," Ayumu said calmly. "You may slip, or the rock may break."

She didn't want to challenge him unnecessarily and moved away from the abyss.

Ayumu checked the tackle he had set up one more time and said, "I am still worried, though, hoisting up Stella and the kid. What if they panic?"

"We can give them a bite of bread soaked in wine."

"What do you mean?" Ayumu twisted his neck and aimed his eyes at her.

Where did this idea come from indeed. Mirielle shook her head. There it was—when her dad was a small kid, Babette, his great-grandmother, would sometimes give him a piece of bread dipped in red wine to calm him down and help him fall asleep. He didn't like it and often spat it out, but Babette persisted.

"Nah, ignore me. It was something from my outer memory, doesn't make sense. We don't have wine anyway."

"Hey, Stella! Here it comes!" Ayumu shouted and threw the rope over the edge. "Attach it to the large tree over there. Yes, that one. Use the carabiner." He pulled the rope. "Good, that's it. Sending the harness. Eli goes first, OK!"

"Of course, I am not that dumb!" Stella shouted back.

Mirielle stepped forward and peeked down again. Stella was putting the harness on the child, while he was looking up. Mirielle waved her hand. Elian responded with both of his. He had just turned four, according to their dad. She rarely accounted for time. Years meant nothing in a world that was certainly not circling a star. Years were a vestige from pre-life, because from her perspective, unlike her, the ghosts had lived once before.

Lately, their father had often been observing her with fascination. She wondered why. She checked his memories but failed to find a probable cause. One day she caught again his stare and asked, "What?"

"*What* what?"

"Why are you looking at me with that face?"

"Ah! Because of your mom."

She understood at that very instant. Her mom died aged eighteen, and she had now existed for over twenty-two of the vestigial time periods. Sporting an identical appearance in the past, she probably now looked as her mom would have been like at this age. She voiced her guess.

"Correct," Leo had confirmed with a smile and sadness in his heart, which he was unable to conceal from her. He still missed Elise after all this time and now—Wasilla.

"You have become a young woman. Your mom remained an old kid on the outside for all her days here."

"Seems I am no longer her."

"No, now you are you. And someone she never got a chance to be herself." Leo had stood up and taken her into his embrace.

Yeah, a girl forever young, forever smiling and doing wild things. Well, not quite indefinitely, just for the duration of her stint in this world. Had she stayed in this body, she would have understood what it was like to grow old. But Mirielle would have done the same—let her child continue to exist.

"Mom!" Elian grabbed her leg. "I am here! Incredible! I want to learn to climb!"

"You will, Eli, but you need to grow a bit more and become stronger." She pinched his cheeks. "Now, let me help Ayumu; Stella's heavier than you."

When Stella reached the top and Mirielle dragged her over the edge, her face was white and her lips blue. She crouched motionless on all fours.

"Stelly." Mirielle poked her with a finger. Nothing. Normally the blonde girl would have giggled. She was having a panic attack again, it seemed. Mirielle aimed and gave her a mighty smack on the rear.

"Ouch!"

"You better now?"

"Yes." Stella finally moved. She crawled further away from the cliff's edge, then sat on the grass and looked up. "Damn, that was scary."

"What's scary?" Ayumu asked. "You cannot die."

"How do you know?" Stella retorted.

"Sorry, I don't know indeed. I just presume. You are different. But, you see, this is part of the challenge and the fun. The risk. Nothing serious can happen to me here, but Mirrie . . . she fell once and as crazy as it may sound, the risk to her is what drives me. I must ensure that she's safe. Same goes for you."

Stella rose to her feet, went to the squatted Ayumu, bent forward, and delivered a long smooch.

Mirielle caught a glance of her son walking along the edge and looking down, and her heart jumped. She had lost track of him while dealing with Stella. She clenched her teeth, then took a deep breath and said as calmly as she could, "Eli, come here, baby, you have grass in your hair."

He swerved and came to a halt in front of her. "Why are you suddenly afraid, Mommy?"

She rolled her eyes. Of course, he sensed her fear. "Because so close to the edge, you may have fallen and been badly hurt. We—me, you, Stella—we cannot float in the air like Ayumu."

"But I've seen you and Stella float. And you also glow if it is dark."

Mirielle wondered how to respond. He'd seen them while engaged in intimacy, when they indeed could sometimes become weightless. The sensation was challenging to describe. Extreme attraction, rivers of delight flowing between them. Just kissing Stella was enough for a liftoff. The thought of the experience stirred desire, and the grown-ups would have been all over each other by now had her kid not been present.

"Sometimes we do, that is true, but it is spontaneous; we cannot control it. Also, have you ever floated yourself?"

The kid shook his head.

"Well, that's it. If you don't know how to make yourself float, you can get hurt."

She had to find out what would happen. What was the highest she could jump in water before being injured? Her outer memory informed her that water could be as hard as rock if the fall exceeded a certain height. But what height? The comms tower? This cliff? Should she take a chance? Perhaps.

She looked at the still-shivering Stella and asked, "Hey, babe, what's the deal with your siblings? Josh and Esther, right? Keep mum if it's too private."

Stella squatted and sent her gaze to greet the peaks. "Mm, my siblings hated each other. Josiah in particular, he wanted his twin sister dead. Mom and Dad are very sad. They fault themselves, but looking into their memories, I don't know why. They did not have a favorite; they treated them both the same. Hey, Ayumu, can you hold my hand? I want to look over the edge."

She rose, took a few steps, then dropped on all fours even before Ayumu could grab her hand. Then she switched sexes and crawled decisively forward. Nobody prompted him to stand.

Mirielle sank in thought. Why would siblings hate each other? Evolutionary pressures? Resource fight? The pre-life world and its people were intriguing yet scary. She had to find out more. So much to do! So much to discover!

⁎⁎

Leo was jolted by emotions he had not felt for a very long time. He reacted as before—threw everything, jumped over his desk and rushed into the hallway, then leaped with open arms. The house shook when he smashed into the staircase wall and slumped on the landing, bruised and with perhaps broken fingers. His forehead was cracked and bleeding. He grabbed his shoulders with his aching hands and wailed, "Mirrie! Fuck! What did you do?"

Elian ran screaming out of the room where he was playing with Stella and Ayumu. "Mommy! Mommy!"

Stella wrapped him in her arms. "Hush, baby! Mommy's fine." Her face was paper white, and her hands were shaking as she caressed the little boy.

"Ugh, fuck!" Leo staggered up, holding his broken fingers with the other hand. "Fuck . . . Ayumu, something happened to Mirrie. Something . . ." He threw a glance at his crying son. "Do you know where they went?"

"No. She said she wanted to conduct a test, the results of which might embarrass her, so she'd rather do it on her own and left."

"What test?"

Ayumu shrugged.

"Stella?"

No response. Stella had kneeled and hugged Elian tightly, her gaze affixed to a point on the wall. Her hands were still trembling, and she was drawing air through her mouth.

"Stella!" Leo raised his voice.

She stuttered, "S-s-s-orry . . ."

"Be a man!"

Stella lingered before changing shape. The young man took a few deep breaths and answered, "Sorry, Mr. Hackensack, no idea. She's been thinking about something lately, and I sensed mood changes and emotions—curiosity, uncertainty, fear. But you know that we are empaths; we can't read thoughts."

Leo moved his fingers. They felt restored and his forehead was no longer dripping imaginary blood.

Elian broke free from his gentle captor and ran to Leo. "Mommy's gone, Daddy!" He started crying again. "Mommy's gone!"

Leo kneeled and hugged the child. He had the disturbing feeling that the little one was right. He could see no path forward, yet he knew that he had to lead. Where to? He desperately needed a compass of some sort.

"We'll find them, Eli. You can cry, of course, but we will find them. They're my child too."

Ah, how he wanted to start crying himself. But not before he was absolutely sure!

Beatrice barged into the home. "What happened? Are you hurt?"

"Mirrie went missing."

"How'd you know?"

"Can you sense them? I was jolted into action just as when they fell from the comms tower—"

"I sensed her fear, desperation, and then nothing," Stella-boy interrupted. "I can't sense her anymore. You know how strong our link is. It is a void now where she used to be." His voice trembled. "I'm afraid to revert to a girl; I'd probably faint."

Elian wailed again. Leo gathered him in his arms and stood up. Should the kid listen to the discussion that the adults had to have? Perhaps not, because they had to consider the worst.

"Ayumu, Stella, please try to guess what she might have been up to. I will take a stroll with Eli and Bea. I need to collect my thoughts."

He tried to mount the kid on his shoulders, but Elian grabbed his shirt. "No, Daddy . . ."

Leo wrapped his arms around the little body. "OK, but walking like that is a bit tough; you will start slipping."

"Then a horse," Elian agreed.

"Bea." Leo nodded invitingly.

Beatrice held the front door open for him and then followed as asked. Leo looked at the redhead. He had no regrets in letting her back into his life. His regrets went deeper into the past—when he had failed to consider her needs and had let her go. They walked along the shore, exchanging no words. Elian had wrapped his arms around his father's chin, his head bowing. Beatrice snuggled up into Leo. The sky was cloudy, gray, and the ocean looked angry with its tall waves crashing on the shore. What did his girl do? What had happened to her? His heart sank to his stomach, and a stone settled into his throat.

Elian began sobbing again and squeezed his head tightly. Damn, hard to have bad feelings with a young empath around. Leo looked at the ocean and imagined calm, balmy seas and bright sun. And his kids running happily in the white sand and diving in the surf.

"Hey, Bea, come here." Leo stopped and turned. "Kiss."

Beatrice answered the need. She smiled and they locked their lips. She wrapped one hand around his waist and offered Elian a finger, which he grabbed instantly. For a moment they forgot about the trouble; for a moment they were content. Then Leo sensed disturbance.

Beatrice stepped back, her face losing color, her green eyes enlarged. "Did you feel that?"

Leo nodded.

"Eric?"

"I think so. Who else?"

"Shit!"

APART

Mirielle lost all her carefully cultivated bravery as soon as she became airborne, as the primordial horror tied her throat into a knot and sealed her facial expression in a grotesque mask—brows drawn close, eyes enlarged, almost popping out of their sockets, mouth agape. Her fingers fanned and arched, as if there was something else besides whooshing air for them to claw into. She frantically tried to imagine herself passionately kissing Stella and the weightlessness it sometimes induced. Then a blinding flash drove her eyelids violently shut. Her ears rang loudly, as if whipped by a supersonic blast. Water gushed into her gaping mouth. Blind instinct slammed her jaws together and held her breath.

Then she popped to the surface, like a fleck of wood submerged in a puddle. No large pool of air bubbles, no impressive splash, just lazy ripples. She flipped her eyes open, spread her arms, and drew a gulp of air in her lungs as the dam holding back her thoughts collapsed. She dipped briefly and resurfaced, then floated, trying to contain her wild heartbeat and to think. She had survived!

Mirielle cheerfully replenished the contents of her lungs. She was alive, unhurt! She sealed her mouth and took another deep breath as her heart continued to race. The air carried a strange scent, something she was unaccustomed to. The night sky was littered with stars, more than she had ever seen—a silent, lasting burst of fireworks congratulating her success. The moon was firmly out of sight, though. Had she jumped?

Certainly, she had no doubt! It was around noon on a bright sunny day when she leaped. It was dark now and the cliffs had disappeared. She spun slowly in the water, tracing a circle with her gaze. There! She made out rugged treetops. Mirielle scooped the water and propelled herself toward the presumed shore.

She had jumped, OK, but why was she so far from land? Why would she swim to the deep in the middle of the night? Where were the others? Or was she halfway through another secret experiment? Something that she didn't want to share for fear of being stopped.

The distant trees approached leisurely as she swam toward them, so much so that she had to take a break. She flipped and floated on her back. What was that bright flash that she saw? Did she hear a crack? And was she naked? Mirielle grabbed her tits, then her hand checked her crotch. She was. The leotard had disappeared. Did she lose it during the impact? Strange. She felt nothing. But then she was hardly paying attention. She dragged her palm over her tummy. The belly button stud was missing too. She puffed her cheeks—it was a gift from Beatrice. Damn! Back to swimming.

When she sensed that she was close to shore, Mirielle dropped her feet and immediately floated anew, grimacing. Her heels had broken through some gooey layer before reaching surface. She swam still nearer to the shore and then treaded out of the water, careful not to slip on the uneven, slimy rocks.

She gazed at the sky. The starlight was in abundance, brighter than a full moon. Which part of her world was that? Or whose memory?

Mirielle nudged her lips into a smile. So, she'd leaped from a great height and was still whole. True, she'd never gathered the courage to perform her experiment over dry land, and she dived into a deep gorge, but she got a result, nevertheless. She had not fallen apart on impact or else she would not have lunged through time. Eventually, she would get her recall and find out how the adventure ended.

She felt grass under her feet, sat down, and stretched her legs. The grass—it was different. Not the usual blades, more like cooked spaghetti with a substantial spring to it. She sought an answer from her parents. Neither one remembered a place with such growth, but then their old world was huge, and they were not botanists. The sensation was pleasant, though. She rolled into the growth like a piglet in soft mud. She spread her limbs. She had found the courage to leap! Wherever she was now, there was no reason to be tense. Space would bend in the morning and reunite her with her folk.

And the air . . . it was fresh, sweet, with an unfamiliar yet uplifting fragrance. She inhaled and licked her lips while playing with the stems under her palms. The sensation nudged upward the corners of her mouth. She must come here with Stella and Ayumu. She smiled at the stars, closed her eyes, and imagined kissing Stella's petals while Ayumu observed. Then they would both kneel, bend forward, and offer their friend a choice, or compete for his ripe fruit. Stella would transform into her male self and reenact the experiences from the times with Walid, only somewhat more exquisite.

Mirielle reached between her legs. Who was there? Ayumu or Stella? She liked both. She loved both. Her yellow man, as he called himself, and her little star. She didn't quite understand why yellow. Apparently, this was a derogatory reference to his race in the other world. His complexion was darker indeed, but yellow? No. Unless she was color blind.

She touched herself, imagining his playful tongue. It had taken him ages to abandon his macho stance and kiss her pussy, but then he threw all his passion into it. She spread her legs further and rolled her finger over her ring. Ayumu would push in with his dick before he dared do it with his tongue.

Stella had no qualms. She would do anything that generated carnal pleasure. Carnal . . . flesh in an immaterial world. Mirielle chuckled and introduced her pinched fingers, then vigorously rubbed. Her free hand visited her breasts, pressing and swirling, making her nipples throw sparks. She gasped and suspended all thoughts, keeping only the hazy image of her Japanese friend hovering over her, then her hand guided him inside. As her palm moved in unison with his hips, she started seeing tiny flashes at the corners of her shut eyes. Then the fuzzy silhouette dissolved. Her crotch celebrated in solitude, only in the company of her hand. Lonely but satisfactory, nonetheless. The elation finally arrived, spilled throughout her body, and made her quiver as it traveled to her head.

Mirielle relaxed, letting thoughts crawl back into her mind and push the uplifting dizziness away. She rolled on her side and curled up. Another day would come soon, and she would head home. There she would be reunited with her friends. Her memories would return, and she would know what she was doing here and how she had arrived.

The grass was comfy—warm and springy. Would it feel the same lying in a giant spaghetti bowl? Perhaps. They shall try that, she and her friends. Something tickled her leg. She scratched it, lay flat on her stomach, and spread her arms. A curious strand entered her mouth. She spat it, shut the orifice, and drew air in through her nose. The aroma was still pleasant and still alien to her. She rolled on her back, her head getting lighter. Maybe she'd try to get home now. Or maybe not, she was in no hurry. Her eyes focused with some effort on the sky. The stars, the twinkling little dots, they were beautiful. And so many! She scanned the dense spread for known constellations but drew a blank. Yeah, some part of the world. Her vision blurred and her eyelids slowly shut. Time for some rest. Her hands twitched a few times, then her muscles relaxed. A few faded faces drifted across her sight, followed by calming darkness shrouding her, as strands of the growth stretched and bowed.

Beatrice opened the front door and entered the apartment. She glanced at Leo's room then checked the kitchen. Eric was sitting on a chair with a coffee mug in front of him. They crossed gazes.

"Mom?"

Beatrice rushed toward him and hugged his head before he could rise to his feet. "Baby, welcome to the afterlife!" Then she twisted her neck. "Hi, Ann!"

"Hello, Momma!" Annette extinguished her cigarette and stood up. "Wanna coffee?"

"Yeah, please!"

"Mom! I can't breathe!" Eric said, his voice muffled.

"You don't have to breathe here."

Eric pushed her away. "Whatever, it is still uncomfortable." He got up and embraced her. "Unbelievable! The afterlife! With you here! And where's Dad? Grandma told me that you two have reconciled and have been living together for almost two decades."

"He had an emergency to take care of."

"What emergency?" Annette asked.

Beatrice bit her lips, then parted them with difficulty. "Mirrie went missing—"

"Who's Mirrie?"

"What? How? Ugh." Annette turned sharply, spilling ground coffee on the floor.

"Mirielle, your half sister from this world. Yesterday. We can't detect her presence anymore."

"Half sister?" Eric slumped back into the chair.

"Yeah." Beatrice proceeded to brief him and Annette. The grandmother in the room deposited the coffeemaker on the countertop, reached for another cigarette, then swore and pushed the packet away. Her face had become pale. Beatrice could see droplets of sweat forming on her temples.

"Ayumu found her gear missing. Now they are checking their climbing spots. Trouble is, with space bending, she could be anywhere, and he could not find a single clue."

Eric's jaw dropped.

*
**

Mirielle opened her eyes and tried to move but found herself restrained. Only her head would swivel and turn. The reddish strands had coiled around her arms and legs; some had crawled over her chest and abdomen. She cursed and reeled inward, ripping the tenta-cle-like growth. The broken stems squirted a warm, gel-like substance as they lost their integrity. She scrambled to her feet and ran toward the trees, crushing stems and leaving a wet trail of destruction behind her. She saw a rock, climbed on top, and clutched her hands close to her chest. Her teeth chattered. She squeezed them and began taking deliberate deep breaths and counting to three before exhaling.

The growth beneath her appeared alive. The stems were capped with white bubbles with a dark spot on top, resembling miniature eyeballs. In the immediate surroundings of the rock, the minute eyes appeared fixated on her, whereas further away these gazed at the sky. Further still, the water of the lake was covered with what was probably red algae near the shore, then turning black where the surface was clear.

The sky was cloudless with a purplish hue she did not remember either seeing or reading about before. But the other world was big. The sun was still lurking behind the tall trees. The water was very calm, almost glazed. Gray haze obscured the horizon, and she was unable to discern a distant shore.

The trees. Their conical shape resembled pines, but the leaves were large, like the ears of an elephant, attached directly to the trunks with no branches to speak of, and getting smaller as they approached the tops.

She had no memory of such trees either, yet she read a lot about the world of her ghosts and looked at many videos and magazines. Nothing like that existed in the Amazon jungle. No baobabs. Still, she was aware of how little she knew.

The spaghetti field ended abruptly in a straight line a short dis-tance from the trees, cut from the rest of the landscape by what ap-peared to be a waist-high glass barrier. So, the place was civilized.

Mirielle turned back at the shore. The traces she left had disap-peared; the grass had now healed. Her gaze glided over the undulat-ing field of tiny eyeballs blossoming from reddish stems, swirling and waving as if there was a wind blowing. But the air was strikingly calm, as if she was inside a shelter of some sort.

Then what was animating the strange growth? She squatted on the rock and tried to get a closer look at the plants. The darn things were observing her, she was sure! She moved her hand over them, and the eyes followed, as the stems leaned and stretched. She pulled back, sat, unfolded her legs, and sent her gaze chasing the invisible horizon, sucking in her cheek. Something inside her had raised a red flag about the plant, but she couldn't put her finger on it. Her world was safe, why the worry?

Ah, perhaps she was afraid that she would crush a lot of these stems under her feet as she aimed for the fence. The plants did look alive, almost sentient, as they followed her movements with their tiny eyes. But she didn't have a choice.

She cautiously slid down from the rock and tiptoed toward the barrier. She felt stems still breaking under her reduced footprint. Then her thighs tickled. She halted and looked down. The stems in the immediate vicinity had become longer, leaning, twisting, swirling as if trying to envelop her. Some of them succeeded in coiling around her calves. She bent her knee, tearing the tiny tentacles, and balanced like a stork, wondering what it all meant, while more spaghetti strands wrapped around her leg, stretching, reaching as high as her crotch.

She had to move, or else . . . she had no idea what that "else" was. It could go either way. The young woman pressed her lips together and ripped the tendrils that were attempting to hold her captive then continued tiptoeing hurriedly toward the glass fence, followed by the somewhat disappointed gazes of thousands of tiny eyeballs perched on top of stretching, waving tendrils.

Mirielle grabbed the top of the fence and jumped over the waist-high translucent panel. She felt lighter than usual, but the barrier was taller than she calculated, and she landed on her side on the squishy surface. *Could have been worse,* she thought while getting up. The thick carpet of dead leaves had cushioned her fall. She glanced at the glass. There was writing she did not see from the other side. The letters, or rather glyphs, for the lack of repetition, were unknown to her, and their appearance did not ring a single bell. She shrugged and squinted at the sun, which had finally climbed high enough to overcome the resistance of the forest. It carried a reddish tint and . . . did it not look larger? Much larger! She gazed away and bit her lip.

⁎⁎

Ayumu lifted the harness from the ground. A lump had found a welcome home in his throat. It had become so difficult to push out sounds. What happened here? What had she done? The safety line was still in place, and her backpack was lying in the shadow of the pine tree, with her hat and sunglasses tucked in it. The rest of her equipment—the helmet, the pick, the pouch—was also there. Even her purple shorts and her climbing shoes. Only Mirielle was missing.

There were no indications of a fall—no disturbances along the edge. He checked for footprints and squashed grass. Perhaps she went inside the forest for some reason, leaving all her things behind. Ayumu's mind could not settle. Had space bent right here, and had she been teleported to some unknown place? That seemed the only reasonable explanation in this bizarre world. But then how would they find her if she did not return? And why, why this sense of emptiness? As if she were dead.

He sat and wrapped arms around his knees. His gaze crossed the canyon and grazed the trees, then ventured further and paid a visit to the snowy mountaintops. The view was breathtaking, but he was already short of breath, fearful for his friend. His heartbeat was uneven, fast. He scraped his lip so hard that it started bleeding. Where was his Mirielle? He loved her! He adored her! She was such a massive part of him! She was his first true love, not Keiko! And Stella was no substitute. The young man transformed into a small boy, curled up, and sobbed.

REFLECTIONS

Mirielle followed the fence until she reached a paved spot. She couldn't shake the feeling that something was not quite right with the sun. That reddish hue, its size. But how? What part of the other world would show it like that? She could think of none. And the water—why was it black? It was usually a shade of blue. Was she on the equivalent of Mars? Nah. In somebody's dreamworld which was Mars? But Mars was cold and dry and dead. And here, there was a group of animals in the distance, grazing. The forest had ended and had become a field. There were patches of dark green, almost blue, growth and trees, different ones, with multiple trunks and wide, flat, sprawling crowns. Fog obscured the view in this direction too.

The animals . . . were they giraffes? Perhaps. No other animal had such a long neck. But the color . . . she had never seen or heard of a pink giraffe outside children's books. And also, the necks, they were not actually that long. Some of the creatures seemed to be eating leaves from the trees, and others were bingeing on the dark green grass, if it were that.

Mirielle dragged her gaze over the surface. It was clearly artificial. Light gray in color, similar to concrete, but it had a squashy feel to it. More like rubber. It encompassed a large semicircle; then there was a footpath made of big, square pavers, three abreast. The pavers looked hard and dry, but once she stepped on them, she discovered that they were like a very dense sponge. A small amount of liquid rose to the surface under her weight and cooled her soles. She smiled; the sensation was pleasant. It would feel great to the bare feet on hot days, when the red sun had scorched the surface. The red sun indeed. She was unable to look straight into the star; it was too bright. And white, but with a reddish tint. If she were a kid, painting the scenery in color, she would use a pink crayon or paint, not yellow.

The footpath entered the forest. The pavers changed color and no longer squirted water. She heard a buzz behind her, turned and ducked right before the large insect would have collided with her, or so she thought. The insect resembled a dragonfly, a giant one. It hovered in the air just out of reach, as if studying her, then it abruptly flew away.

Mirielle looked around and saw more insects of the same kind, hovering over what looked like the blossoms of some exotic plants— shaped like cones, with fleshy brownish petals and cyan stigma. There were ferns too and some other vegetation climbing the large tree trunks, trying to steal some of the sunrays for themselves.

The path reached a slanted clearing in the forest. An angular structure resembling a pile of large glass shards stood at the top. Another novelty for Mirielle. Her mother wanted to be an architect, and even after her passing, she continued to dream, sketch, and collect impressions from magazines, books, and videos. There was no stylistic match. Mirielle pouted and proceeded along the path. As she drew closer to the structure, the wild vegetation became tamed—terraced strips of uniform color radiated from the footpath. Some of the terraces were shallow ponds with large maroon leaves floating on the surface.

Mirielle introduced her hand into the water. The action precipitated a desire to step inside the pond and thread between the leaves. She dismissed the urge and continued toward the structure. The pavers became pedestals rising from the bottom of a seemingly deep, moat-like pool. She looked at her reflection in the water. As usual, her face was imperceptible; the otherwise smooth surface was shimmering at this spot. A lot of guessing had gone toward this phenomenon— why they were not allowed to look at their own faces. The non-scientific consensus seemed to be that acne was to blame. It would be unfair to those who had it to be reminded of their misfortune.

Did she have acne? She nervously touched her face. Her skin felt smooth. She sighed, squatted, and pierced the clear water with her gaze. The bottom was sandy with what looked like starfish dwelling there. Only these had four arms, not five. She craved a closer look at them; she sat and carefully submerged herself into the pool, then dived. The creatures curled up into balls as her hand came close and hurriedly buried themselves in the beige sand.

Mirielle surfaced and flipped on her back. Inside her chest, she hosted an excited pump! So many things she saw today were new. But there was also that cold, silent void inside her she only noticed now. Suddenly, she wished to be reunited with her folks—Elian, Ayumu, Stella, Beatrice, her dad—without delay. She had never been completely on her own for very long. Where was she? Where were they? Goosebumps popped up on her skin. Why was space not folding?

She counted silently to ten and moved her gaze toward the structure. It looked like a house, a luxury one. She'd seen them in magazines and in her outer memory. She recalled that Beatrice used to live in homes of this kind; however, she was unable to find their afterlife equivalents. Beatrice said her days there were not jolly, and there were things she'd rather forget. She probably did, hence the inability to locate the mansions.

Mansions. Perhaps today was Mirielle's chance to set foot in one. She began searching for an ingress point. The footpath ended somewhere behind a corner on her left. Maybe there was a door there. She swam and peeked in. The footpath terminated abruptly at a pane of frosted glass with no visible doorway.

The glass next to her appeared clear. She pressed her forehead against the smooth surface, fighting the shimmering blob that was the reflection of her face. The blob was overpowering, and each time she tried to shield her eyes from the bright light with her palms, she sank.

She looked around. A large and deep niche was breaking the monotony of the glass pane. Mirielle swam and climbed onto the platform fronting it. The blob had followed her, but now she could isolate it, as she was able to press the fleshy side of her arched hands against the glimmering surface without sinking into the water. The glass seemed to be one-way. Only barely distinguishable silhouettes of objects could be seen. Mirielle stepped back, lips sagging. And then she saw them. The reflections of two humanoid creatures looking at her from the other side of the moat. Looking at her! The reflections had eyes. She pivoted hastily. The creatures stood staring, and she could sense they were curious and confused.

"Hi!" Mirielle greeted and waved. Then she bowed deeply. "I am Mirielle!"

When she resumed upright position, the creatures had disappeared. Her shoulders dropped. Why did they go? She was glad to meet them. Couldn't they detect that? She sighed. Perhaps they were not sharing her enthusiasm.

Her outer memory did not provide classification of these beings. While humanoids at first glance, there were also substantial differences. Spirally shaped dark bone ridges resembling horns ran from the temples backward, circled around the ears, and terminated at the roots of the sideways-pointing, triangular earlobes. The eyes were large, shiny black raindrops embedded into the heads on either side of flat, elongated noses with wide, pointed tips. There were no lips to speak of, only a slit. The beings sported a coat of slick fur—one golden brown and the other gray. The trunks were somewhat disproportionately short, and the legs were reminiscent of those of animals made for speed. The creatures seemed to be standing on their toes. Maybe they *were* animals. But then why wear clothes? Yet many people dressed their pets. Maybe the creatures were somebody's pets.

Mirielle kept browsing through the records in her head. What kind of pets were these? She realized that she was naked. And sucking on her thumb! Her mother's childish habit had stuck around. She withdrew the thumb, inspected it and plunged it into her hair. What if they saw her as an unknown species of wild animal? But then why unknown? She bore the outward appearance of a human, and she was one to a great degree, and humans—their memories made this world tick.

"Hey!" she said hesitantly. "Please come back. I am Mirielle, a harmless girl."

Only the sound of gurgling water and the shuffling of leaves up high in the crowns answered her call. She dismissed the answer with a sigh, turned, and tried to move a pane. She marveled for a moment at the intricate patterns engraved in the side panels, then grunted and dived into the pool. A few strokes and she was on the other side. She extracted herself from the water, stood up, and looked around, wondering what her next step should be.

Space was overdue to fold and lead her home. These shortcuts never manifested in open areas, as far as she could recall, so she chose to head into the forest. She noticed dark clouds quickly gathering in the sky, then she saw flashes, followed after a while by loud bangs. A thunderstorm was coming. She glanced at the structure, then rushed for the trees. Large drops of rain descended upon the land. She found shelter by the massive trunk of one of the cone-shaped trees, shivering, as the lag between sight and sound shrank to almost nil.

Somewhere at the back of her mind rang a warning—don't hide here, move away. Mirielle heeded it and swiftly abandoned the protection of the layered crown. An instant later, an explosion of electric light, accompanied by an ear-splitting crack, took her sight away, leaving her with screaming sirens in her ears. The tree trunk split. She ran. Something bashed her head, as her foot got caught in the crawling growth. Mirielle spread aimlessly her arms and crashed face-first on the carpet of giant, disintegrating leaves. Her consciousness had already slipped away. The raindrops kept splashing onto her skin and forming streams. The streams became tiny waterfalls, promptly delivering their moisture to the ground.

Soon myriad spores sprang to life and spawned long stems in all directions. The fungi bloomed and a sea of red, beige, and green caps surrounded Mirielle's unconscious frame. Then the rain stopped, and the red sun returned, but the large tree leaves spared the mushrooms from its undiluted rays, giving them a chance to procreate.

Mirielle twitched. The daylight reached her mind and turned it on. She grunted and drew open her eyes, then frowned. Her head felt heavy but otherwise fine. She staggered on all fours, then sat and rubbed the spot where she was hit. She was not supposed to get hurt, so how did it happen? Why did she lose consciousness? Ah, amazing! All these mushrooms. Were they edible? Probably, as the realm was not known to offer poison to its inhabitants. Her stomach gurgled. She could go without food, she knew, but she would feel hunger, nevertheless. Mirielle picked a beige mushroom, resembling an upside-down pear, sniffed it—it smelled like a sweet fruit—and opened her mouth.

A loud screeching sound nearby made her gasp and turn her head.

The creature was waving its hands, and she sensed distress. She put the pear-shaped mushroom aside and rose to her feet. The creature approached, having calmed down a bit. Mirielle tilted her head backward, her eyebrows raised and her mouth ajar. Then something touched her breast.

How rude! she thought and traced the source. Then chuckled as the puzzled face of one of the creatures she saw earlier could not be helped. She was not repulsed or afraid. She felt a desire to ruffle the mane she failed to notice when they first met. The creature swiftly withdrew its hand.

Mirielle smiled. "No worries!"

"I'iyaa'i," the creature screeched and flickered its long eyelashes.

Mirielle looked at the larger specimen, then back at the two smaller ones. These were not animals! They acted intelligently; they spoke.

The large creature crossed its hands at its chest and said, "O'i'omp'o. P'a'ame o'i'omp'o." Then it pointed at the smaller ones. "Imii'i, aom'eai." Then repeated pointing at itself, then the other two. "O'i'omp'o, imii'i, aom'eai."

Must be their names! The young woman shoved her index finger into her chest and said, "Mirielle!"

"Mii'ee," the big guy tried to replicate the sound.

"Mirielle!" she confirmed. "Oiompo, Imii, Aomeai," she said, pointing with her palm. The creatures twitched their heads when she spoke what she presumed were their names.

She then performed another round—she stared for a moment at each creature before moving to the next. *Must be the guy or gal who touched me!* she concluded. Each time she laid eyes on the being with the tall mane, a spark flared inside her chest. It must be the child of big love, another one like her. But there was no way to seek confirmation from the small group.

"A'iip', e'a!" the big creature said, "a'uiim." The hand gesture that followed the screech was unambiguous. It meant "Let's go."

The second small creature transformed. It grew larger, its coat became darker, and its tummy popped a bit. The slit under the nose bent. Was it smiling?

Mirielle pointed at it, then at the creature roughly her size and gesticulated: small, big?

"Emo'a." The head twitched again. Was it the opposite way?

"Imii'i?"

"A!" The being moved his head again.

Her supposition seemed confirmed. Left twitch meant "yes" and right twitch meant "no." She tried to memorize that.

"Imii'i, a'iip'!" a call came. The two large creatures were already jogging away.

The smaller individual took her hand and ran. Mirielle, jolted by the unexpected pull, tripped and fell, murdering a bunch of fresh mushrooms in the process. She scrambled back to her feet, gave a thumbs-up to the startled furry guy, and jogged, following the smashed fungi trail. The furry creature caught up instantly with her.

CLOUDS

Mirielle gave up trying to keep pace and halted, wheezing, her heart ready to pop out. These guys, they couldn't walk, could they? They had to trot, and she was not made for that. She kept gasping for air and attempting to shake off the pain.

"Mp'o m'eai a'ay!" the smaller being screeched.

The two large ones braked and gazed back. Then they approached briskly.

"A'mo aa'a?"

"Imo'eo e," said the small guy.

I will never master this language, Mirielle thought, but chanced a shot nevertheless. "Imo eo e."

One of the big creatures began huffing, imitating shortness of breath, then screeched, "Imo'em." Then it crouched, lifted Mirielle, let her straddle its shoulders, and stood up. "E' ep'oya."

Mirielle shrugged and produced a smile. She had no idea what the sounds meant, but she had no objection to riding. The group resumed their advance toward some place.

Mirielle wrapped her arms around the creature's head. Her dad used to carry her like this, and she loved it. Then she grew too big or maybe not—Ayumu was now sometimes the horse. Or the donkey— she smiled. That was before she met Stella. Ah, these guys . . . She squeezed her lips, eyes flicking, taking snapshots of the path. Where were they? Would space bend with these creatures around?

They came to another clearing and entered a paved ditch. Soon she saw openings in the walls—windows, doors. The ditch was a street! There were intersections! The walls became taller, five or six stories, with strips in varying styles and colors. Sky bridges linked the roofs. She was certain that the cones suspended upside-down below them were streetlights.

The group crossed a wide "avenue" with two paved lanes, vegetation in the median, and two rows of lights. They entered a building, where they ran up a steep ramp and stopped at a door. The door slid open. The creature crouched again and carefully transferred Mirielle from its shoulders to the floor.

"Thanks!" Mirielle briefly touched the creature's hand. These guys had long, slender fingers, four in total, on each hand. What were they? She'd never read, seen, or heard of such beings anywhere in the old world or in hers. And as far as she knew, dreamt-up realms could not feature intelligent beings, which these three clearly were. She followed the outstretched arm of her new friend and walked through the large door.

The room was wide, tall, and well lit. The entire wall opposite the entrance consisted of a grid of square windows with thick rustic mullions. Mirielle approached and peeked outside. She saw the street and the buildings on the other side. A drapery of dark blue plants graced the perimeter of the roofs. It seemed that the city they were in was carved into the ground, not built above it. Where did they have cities like that on Earth? Petra? In a place called Jordan. But it was ancient, uninhabited, and this place was definitely populated and alive. Where else? She didn't know.

The front door chimed and opened after someone issued a screech. Two more large beings came in. Mirielle sat on the windowsill and looked at them. One was white, and the other brown. They turned to her, crossed their hands, and shook heads. "A'aaey!" Obviously, a greeting.

Mirielle rose and bowed. "Hi!" Then she looked up and pointed at herself. "Mirielle."

The white-furred creature came close and squatted. "Op'ue ii'ua, e'e." It extended its arm, and the long fingers gently glided over Mirielle's hair, then continued down, tickling her skin. "E' io'ap." She suppressed the urge to laugh and instead studied the being in front of her. The giant wore a nose hoop, three necklaces, gemstone-encrusted blue-and-purple armbands, a sheer black skirt, and numerous anklets. The fingertips probing her were reminiscent of the feet of a gecko, only without the claws. Perhaps the claws were retracted.

"Uu'i a'o!" The small guy showed up with an object resembling a rectangular mirror attached to a handle in his hand. It stood between Mirielle and the white one and shook the object. It was some kind of device; the surface lit up. A tablet? Mirielle had never seen one anywhere else except in her outer memory; her dad had used them extensively. However, those had no handles. The creature used its finger to draw a circle with some blots, then a cloud, then four stick figures in the circle.

"Imii'i?" Mirielle asked.

The head twitched to the left. The creature pointed at those present in the room except Mirielle and itself, then at the stick figures on the screen. "Aya'e ia a'a."

Mirielle shrugged.

The creature changed the tool, selected the four figures, and dragged them from the circle to the cloud.

Mirielle tried twitching her head left.

"A!" The being seemed to smile.

"A!" She repeated. Seemed that it meant "Yes."

A fifth, smaller figure appeared in the cloud above two of the existing ones. Imii'i then drew two lines, connecting them with the new member of the group.

"Imii'i." The creature pointed at the small stick person, then at the two figures underneath, turned, and pointed. "Aom'eai i o'i'omp'o. I ya'a i ya'o." The delicate fingers connected the remaining two stick figures with the recent arrivals, the white one still squatted, observing the interaction, its eyes following each move and trying to read each grimace.

Mirielle understood—the other world, then this one, the ghosts. But why were they so jarringly different? Her eyes framed each face. She then reached for the tablet. The creature hesitantly released its grip on the device. Dimensionally it was on the larger side for her, but it was very light. The handle was made of some dull red, non-slippery material and felt comfortable in the hand. There were no buttons that she could see; however, the neck of the handle was pressure sensitive—a square on the screen changed color as she pushed with her thumb. Why was she paying so much attention to the device when there was a larger question to be answered? Perhaps because she was scared of the possible answer, she had to admit to herself.

The young woman took a deep breath, moved the device to her right hand, and added another circle and another cloud. She saw a color selector, picked green, and introduced a fifth small stick figure inside the second cloud. She pointed at the figure and then herself. "Mirielle."

The broad heads with triangular, pointy earlobes twitched to the left and exchanged words she could not understand. She then dragged the blue figure from its cloud and dropped it into the other. She noticed how the skin above the creatures' noses wrinkled and their earlobes fanned. They exchanged words again.

The being who had carried her on its shoulders crouched so its head could be at the same level as hers and looked at her intently. "Aa'i'i om up'p' yaa," it said while slowly shaking its head.

She tried to guess the meaning by the emotions that were reaching her but gave up and chose not to chance a head twitch. Somebody's hand crawled over her skin. The little one!

"O'aa'iyo!" The larger creature's voice sounded sharp, and it slapped the arm that was probing her. Then the creature stood up and took her hand. "E'a."

⁂

Thirty days had passed since Mirielle's disappearance. Thirty comings and goings of the light, marked with red pencil strokes in Leo's timekeeping notebook. He wanted to shape-shift to his early childhood, curl up next to his mom on the couch, rest his head on her thigh, and cry. But Annette perhaps wanted to cry into somebody's arms herself. And Ruth. Perhaps everybody. So, he sobbed a few times between the walls of his study, then put on a brave face and presented a sad but reassuring personality to the lot. Elian needed it the most. They wanted their mom. For reasons that could only be a guess at this point, Elian maintained a female shape most of the time, which drove Leo almost insane. His child had no idea that it was her—Elise, Mirielle—who everybody saw albeit as a young girl.

Leo pushed his chair back, lifted his legs on the desk, and crossed his arms behind his head. What had happened? Ayumu reported finding her gear at the cliff's top. And how could he still see Ayumu and Stella without Mirielle? Maybe Elian? He had to ask Beatrice or one of their grandmoms to take the kid to some place a considerable distance away, while Ayumu and the blonde girl remained with him. But then Ruth and Dietrich had been able to see each other without a medium for several years now.

Years. Another remnant from the old world. The time it took a planet to circle its star. But they weren't on a planet here; he was convinced of that.

His thought flipped back to seeing. Maybe it was the united power of the love kids, Mirielle and Elian, which made seeing permanent. Now there was also Stella. Or perhaps it was the fact that Ruth and Dietrich were in love. Yeah, Lizzy's mom found her big love in the afterlife. The wonders of existence.

Leo cleaned his nose with a pinch, snorted, waited for the mucus to dissipate, and rose. Time to go. And he should perhaps let Beatrice make love to him again. All she wanted to do was give him some pleasure, provide much needed relief. There was no betrayal in the act. It was not Elise he lost this time. Or was that so? Leo cursed and opened the door.

Another short but powerful thunderstorm had refreshed the air outside, and the clear sky resumed its purplish tint. How long had she been here? Eight days? Ten? Mirielle didn't count them. She seldom did. There was no point. There was no planet revolving around a star, the seasonal changes were random and unpredictable, there were no fields to seed, and there was no harvest to collect. Ghosts were sailing through existence with no goals and no deadlines to meet.

The ghosts counted, though. It seemed to matter to them. To them their existence was a continuation of a prior one where keeping track of days, months, and years was important. How many years in the afterlife? Fifty? Ah, good! Had her world been populated only by beings of her kind, they'd probably have no concept of time.

Mirielle left the windowsill she had been sitting on, took the tablet, and headed for the really big room. These creatures, her hosts, were considerably larger than humans; stretching her arms above her head, she could reach no further than their chins. And everything around them was made to accommodate their size. Rooms, furnishings, doors. But the sensor picked up her insignificant frame anyway—the automatic door opened and let her out.

"O i omp o." She approached the big guy, who had stretched on a thick, soft yellow mat on the floor with another device in his hand.

"A." The creature left the tablet aside.

Mirielle sucked in her lips, then drew a small circle and shaded one half. She then added a star and an elliptical arrow indicating that the small circle orbited the sun. She showed the drawing to the guy. "Planet, sun, you understand?"

O'i'omp'o took his device, pinched something on the screen, and turned it at her. He'd understood. There was an animated diagram of a star system. Mirielle counted the planets. Six, and the fourth one was purplish-blue, similar to the other world, Earth. But Earth was the third planet from its sun, and the total planet count was eight. And the planets themselves looked different—sizes, colors—from what she could recall.

She nodded slowly. It seemed she had crossed into some other species' afterlife. But how? The free fall? She started a new drawing— a star system with a yellow sun and eight planets. Then she enhanced the third one with blue and showed her host the result. It seemed the dark, shiny raindrops became larger. O'i'omp'o clicked with his tongue. She had observed during these few days similarities in body language—smiles, wrinkled noses, enlarged eyes.

She wanted to cuddle up in one of these creatures—their fur looked so soft and inviting—but had so far refrained. She presumed that it would be impolite. Imii'i, the little one, the child of big love, he or she, was very curious and inconsiderate. He kept touching her hair, her breasts, even her rear. They shared a room; one day she leaned over the wide windowsill to glance down at the street when the rascal sneaked and split her cheeks.

"E!" She swung around swiftly. "E!"

Imii'i retracted his arms and mumbled something. He looked embarrassed. Then he turned and lifted his little rear flap, exposing what was probably his anal orifice.

"Yamma' o'aap'a." He pointed.

Indeed. Nor did she have a front flap. The creatures sported these on both sides. The adults had much longer, lighter strands of fur around the perimeter of their crotch flaps. Same under the noses and a large, well-groomed, triangular patch covering the chest and upper abdomen. From that perspective and dimension-wise, Imii'i was certainly a child. But how old and was it male? The sex was her assumption. She had not observed obvious sex-specific features in her hosts. Perhaps some extra facial and front flap hair in O'i'omp'o but in no way indicative of anything. Mirielle transformed.

Imii'i gasped, then checked her head to toe, and in his typical inconsiderate manner, he reached and pulled the penis. Mirielle rolled her eyes, pushed his hand away, and then prompted him to shapeshift, if he could. His mouth slit stretched and he shrank a bit and his fur became lighter. And his face, there was a noticeable change. So, he could transform too.

"Aom eai?" she asked.

"A. I O'i'omp'o." The creature changed its appearance again.

So, he was just like her. She reverted to her native shape and drew him into her embrace, her heart melting. Another one! Confirmed!

Imii'i stood still, confused, as she could sense. Indeed, she had no idea if hugging was appropriate amongst their lot. She let go.

They crossed somewhat embarrassed gazes. Then Imii'i grabbed her head, brought his face a whisker away, and drove briefly the tip of his hard, long tongue into her mouth. Then stood back and kind of smiled—the ends of the mouth slit arched upward. It felt like a kiss. The kiss of a child.

She rolled her fists and inhaled deeply. She missed her Elian; she missed him so much! And to think that there was a time when she didn't want him. She turned her head away, trying to hold the tears which suddenly popped up in her eyes. They failed to heed her wish and rolled down her cheeks. Mirielle covered her face with her palms, tilted her head up, and cursed silently. She missed Ayumu and Stella too. Her yellow man and her yellow head. And her dad. And everybody else. She missed her home. She wanted so much at this moment to just jump through time and move the present into the past.

She felt the touch of soft fur and arms encircling her frame. Imii'i. He was awkwardly holding his arms around her. Then he tugged on her ears and massaged her earlobes; then, as if realizing that it may not bring her comfort, he hugged her clumsily again. She returned the embrace.

WORMS

The animal that entered the room issued a loud "Baaah." It had a large, flat snout and eight legs. The fur was long, thick, and wavy, and the eyes—faceted half-spheres. The tall, plump being with reddish fur, dressed in a long blue-and-purple overcoat and yellow leather "pants," that followed it leaned and exchanged licks with Imii'i, flicked ears at the others, and verbally addressed Mirielle. "Ay Mii'ee!"

It was Grandpa. Or Grandma. The otherworldly visitor was still uncertain. Mirielle shortened it to "Gran" in her mind. Gran reminded her of her own grandmother, Annette, more precisely, two of them—both obese and stacked on top of each other. And the bleating animal was Sylvester, Annette's dog. Gran was not obese, though; they were just very large.

Mirielle wrinkled her nose at the greeting. The language barrier was still in place. The creatures' way of talking sounded horrible to her, consisting primarily of a fast, screeching sequence of vowels with an occasional consonant, mostly "m" and "p," thrown in. She struggled to make out the words despite having a trained musical ear. Speaking was even harder. Speaking in vowels required a very large lung capacity or a different throat design, neither of which she possessed.

The tablets came in handy, though. Aom'eai programmed one to map words. They'd look at pictures and then say the words and then use this map. Mirielle and Imii'i spent a lot of time expanding this translation tool, and now they were able to have some basic conversations.

O'i'omp'o and Aom'eai were indeed the youngster's parents. They had been separated in their other world, or not allowed to be together, she did not quite understand. Eventually in advanced age they finally united and then died. As their afterlife rolled on, amidst their ecstasy, the little one was unexpectedly conceived. Same as her, a miracle, an event so far unknown. He was about two-thirds in on the way to maturity, as indicated on a chart Gran drew. In human years, Imii'i was perhaps around thirteen. And that often showed.

Mirielle turned her attention to Gran. Gran was the matriarch or patriarch of the group, the oldest related person still around. All were interested in Mirielle, but Gran stood out. Gran would come every day and try to talk to her, drawing pictures on the tablet she received, asking questions. Mirielle tried to ask questions in this way too; however, the large individual was somewhat overbearing. Gran made

Mirielle feel like a little child. The creature would draw sketches in the tablet and take notes, then flick its ears and sometimes lick the tip of its nose. Mirielle would then laugh, causing the creature's earlobes to fold back and the eyes to turn angry, confirming the emotional broadcast.

That said, Gran was the first one to take her on a short tour of this world. They went to a much larger settlement with highways, bridges, pompous, chiseled in the soft rock, edifices, and much smaller ones, often erected on the roofs. Some buildings were beautiful and others bland, even outright ugly. There were no vehicles, but she heard noises, a distant hum. This city reached far deeper underground. There were numerous levels with vast, brightly lit halls connected by tunnels with moving floors. As was often at home, the city felt bustling with life, yet she could see nobody else besides Imii'i and Gran.

Then there was more—an island with a tall metal and glass tower with the view from its top reaching far away. It had beautiful paintings and other artwork and a knowledge vault with stereoscopic screens showing stories, but Gran dragged her away like a misbehaving child before she could take a decent look.

"Let me go! I am not a child!" Mirielle objected, to which Gran responded with an uncomprehensible whistle and nothing more.

Mirielle had become bifurcated in a way. She was now convinced that she had crossed a boundary of sort between realms when she leaped. She was fascinated by what she had found. Her curiosity had reached a fever pitch, yet she longed for home; she craved human company and touch. She wouldn't mind being here if there was a clear path back to her world. Without one, she felt trapped. Maybe if she leaped again? But she arrived here in the middle of, as it turned out, a large lake, so there was nothing there to jump back from. And there was no guarantee that she'd land or surface in the right place.

What if she jumped in another spot? The tower on the island? She bounced the idea in her mind, then concluded that she lacked the will. The fear of emerging in yet another foreign world stood firmly in the way.

The front door chimed and moved, letting more visitors in. These three she had never seen before. The whistles and screeches flew abundantly. Mirielle turned her interpreter on, but it was rudimentary, unable to keep up, spitting out random words. The newcomers moved toward her, appearing dumbfounded, with Gran encouraging them with mild pats on their backs. Mirielle cowered, sweat polished her skin, then she sprang forward, sneaked past them toward the entrance, touched the contact, and ran out, heading down the ramp and onto the street.

She didn't want to be a freak show exhibit or be treated as a rowdy kid. She gulped the air as she dashed down the deserted street. Somebody was coming after her! These beings could run fast; she stood no chance. Her hair swirled around her as she pushed to outrun the pursuer. Tired claws began tearing into her chest. Tears rolled down, some entering her open mouth. The salty taste lingered on her tongue. Her muscles joined in the pain. Finally, she could sprint no more and curled up on the pavement, wheezing and sobbing. Then she started coughing violently.

Nobody approached to pick her up. She raised her gaze and looked around. She was not in the city anymore; the expanse of the lake greeted her instead. The space must have folded. Mirielle wiped her mouth, took a deep breath, and pressed her lips together, her heart still pounding. But the view had brought her calm. Here, on the shore, she felt closer to home. She kneeled and wiped the tears with her palms, then sent her eyes gliding over the dark waters. There had to be a way. An airplane, something flying that she could leap from. This was the afterlife of a developed species even more advanced than her own. But then her dad built the plane himself. Could she do the same here?

Mirielle laid her sight on the spaghetti growth and crossed gazes with the many minuscule eyeballs trained on her. It felt as if they were calling her. She stood up, approached the glass barrier, bent over it, and dangled her arm on the other side. The spaghetti sprang into action—the stems stretched, reached her hand, and began coiling around her fingers, then around her wrist. She didn't feel threatened this time. These things were so fragile. She tore and squashed so many of them that day.

She dropped the other arm over the fence and let the stems crawl and wrap around it too. The touch was pleasing. And the scent . . . she took a deep breath and smiled, when the optimism the scent injected reached her brain. She was going to find a way home, she was sure! And here—life here was not bad. So much to explore! The creatures were big, yet friendly, gentle. Even Gran. The way Gran treated her was like a real grandparent. A bit rough indeed, but so what? She wanted to be a kid again. A small girl. She wanted to run naked in the soft grass and have colorful butterflies land on her palms.

Now, she wanted to be a grown-up. Still naked. She was naked. With Ayumu. And Walid. And Stella. And her dad. No . . . yes . . . she didn't know. What happened all these years ago, it felt so enchanting. And so wrong . . .

Walid . . . she saw Walid kneeling in front of her, enjoying her male form to the fullest, his hands crawling all over her abdomen and flanks, his tongue rolling around her glans, his head swaying. Then he rose to his feet and kissed her lips.

It was Ayumu now, not Walid, and she was a girl again with tense boobs, firm nipples, and looking forward to accepting his eager magic wand inside her. What was Ayumu doing? Why was he lingering so much? Ah, he came in from behind. She rose on her toes and arched her back. The magic wand . . . it glided in and Mirielle rocked. Where were his hands? She wanted him to fondle her breasts. Her eyes were closed, yet she could see the light, all colors, red, purple, yellow, green, blue . . . then a shadow . . . was that Stella? Her face was glowing! She offered her a tit. Mirielle drew it in her mouth. Ayumu was dancing behind her, rubbing the sensitive petals her female body was fitted with, eliciting delight. Stella . . . why were her breasts wet and sticky? Was she lactating? She never had a child. Mirielle looked up and switched tits. Stella smiled and tugged her head gently. Mirielle's tongue fluttered.

And Ayumu . . . ah, he was so nice! Or was it Walid? His pelvis rolled and his wand was truly magic, rubbing against the little knob. She was almost there . . . Ayumu! The thrusts he delivered threw sparks, yet . . . why were they unable to ignite the flame? She was so close! Where were her hands? She wanted to embrace her petite blonde friend, feel the silky skin, entwine her tongue. Maybe then . . . her breasts begged to be caressed . . . where were his hands? Where were *her* hands? Was she home? Yes, she was, or where would all these people otherwise come from?

Then Walid . . . no, Ayumu abandoned her. Why? She was almost there, her exaltation was near the ignition point. Why did he do that? And Stella—her chest changed; it became hairy and flat. Did she transform? Why? Why now! And where did she go?

Mirielle grunted, her mouth twisted, and she tried to reach between her legs. Somebody or something had clamped her in a tight grip. She squirmed, seeking to elbow the arrestor. Her gaze brushed her shoulders, and she shrieked. She had no arms! They were gone! No arms! Not even stumps! She shrieked again, her body shaking. Then the light went out.

Mirielle took her time opening her eyes. The eyelids seemed to screech as she pushed them up. Breathing in required effort. She tried to raise her arms, but ran out of steam, so heavy were her limbs. She fanned her fingers. At least her arms were still attached. Her mind hummed, "Good!"

"Worm, bad." She heard her own broken voice coming from the tablet Gran held in their hand. "Must, no, touch, I, sorry, I, bother, you, much."

Mirielle moved her eyeballs. Her head was very heavy too. She was back in the room she shared with Imii'i.

"What . . . happened?"

The tablet whistled, then it was Gran.

"Worm, poison, change, mind, make, see, things, not, here, make, no, force."

"But I liked what I saw . . . and felt."

"All, like, joy, fear, want, more, no, stop, die, end."

"Die? Here?"

Gran's ears twitched, then pointed backward, somewhat defensively.

"Here, we, no, old, world, we, yes. Mirielle, Imii'i, no, we. Mirielle, Imii'i, live, die. We, no, know."

"I get it." Mirielle sighed. "These 'worms,' are they not plants?"

"Worm, no, plant, worm, anchor, animal, live, wet, land. I, bad, I, sorry."

"What are you sorry about?"

The tablet struggled. Gran screeched. Tablet said, "No, understand."

"You, sorry. Why?"

"Mirielle, run, away, I, make, Mirielle, cry. I, bad." Gran's ears retracted fully backward, and their thick eyelashes came down. "I, want, know, many. I, make, Mirielle, cry. I, come, friend, show, Mirielle. Mirielle, run, away."

"I ran from them indeed. You . . ." Mirielle hesitated. "You are curious, inquisitive. I understand." She succeeded in lifting her hand and touching Gran's. "Please slow down. Please!"

"Good. I, no, many, question. Mirielle, sleep." Gran reached and very gently guided Mirielle's eyelids closed. "Sleep."

Mirielle complied. She sank into a restless dream. The spaghetti tugged at her hands, and behind her, Ayumu and Stella pulled her away from the greedy tendrils. Her arms stretched like elastic bands, then snapped, but there was no pain or blood. Then her dad appeared and drew her in his embrace. And it was cozy, until he suddenly grew fur. She recoiled and saw O'i'omp'o. But the eyes, the eyes were human. Blue. Stella. However, she had local legs and dense brown fur from the waist down. A word started cycling in her mind: *satyr, satyr, satyr*. She turned and saw Elian. Still a toddler, yet large, towering over her. Then darkness came and cast a soothing spell.

DIVERGENT SPEEDS

Leo kissed the plump lips of the redhead, only that she was a blonde now. Beatrice had shape-shifted to her late teens. Leo was still around thirty-five, but this time to everyone. In these moments of intimacy, he kept Mirielle out of his mind. He knew of the many cases where the loss of a child tore couples apart. Perhaps there were good reasons for this to happen, perhaps not. And in his case, there was nobody to blame. Just that the grief took his mojo for a while. He wanted no food, no drink, no love, no pleasure whatsoever; he wanted his kid back. But then he had a fight with Beatrice, a different one. She was right, his foul mood solved no problem at all and had begun alienating Elian, who cowered each time Leo was in the same room. "Grieving can be selfish," Beatrice said. True. "Everything we do is selfish," he replied, admitting to himself that he had to make a choice—continue savoring the pain from the loss or return to appreciating the people that were still around. Elian was now without his mom and was certainly in need of a jolly vibe. And he was glad that Eric made it to this place, albeit perhaps a bit prematurely. Still, it meant that his son was a good man. But then there was the memory of his nephew Peter and the doubts sown by Elizabeth, his wife.

"We must keep an eye on Eric, just in case. He's a decent person, yet—"

"Why?" Beatrice crossed her arms on his chest and rested her head on them, inspecting his chin.

"Peter. I don't want our son to turn bad. Loneliness and isolation, they eat into one's mind."

"I am not worried. I know bad people, and our Eric is not one of them. I don't want my other offspring here, and I am sure that they will not arrive." She pushed up, straddled him, and sat. "Eric's just fine."

"I don't know. He grew up with you and your mom. I . . . shit! Sorry, it came out bad. I meant that I don't know him as well as you do and—"

"Ask him how he is."

"I did. He said he was fine."

"Then that's it."

"Can I tell him about Peter and why I worry? Would he not be offended?" Leo asked.

"Jerk! It is up to you. Seems you are afraid."

Leo looked past her. "I am. What if he is? Last thing I need right now is pushing my other kid away. I almost succeeded with Eli."

Eric opened the door. "Mom?" His eyes framed his parents. "Ah, sorry!" He turned around.

"Come here," Beatrice said. "Your father has a question."

"But . . ." Eric mumbled. "You are, well . . ."

"C'mon, you should be used to seeing us like that by now; we didn't hide much when you were a kid." Beatrice grinned.

"Perhaps. I have no recollection of those days and scenes. I was a toddler. What do kids at this age remember?"

"Yeah, nothing mostly . . ." Beatrice pursed her lips. "But now we are all dead and this is a different world. And do you know how we picked your name?"

Eric turned. "No. How?"

"It comes from 'erotica' with three letters removed!" Beatrice giggled. "So, don't be shy. Or are you afraid that you may take a liking to your old mom?" Beatrice raised her hands and shook her young boobs.

"Bea!" Leo barked.

Beatrice cowered. "Ah, sorry. Sorry, Leo." She blushed and crossed tightly her hands at her chest.

Leo rolled her suddenly stiffened body on the mattress and sat on the edge. He scraped his lip, then rose and slipped into his pants. "We better talk with me clothed; otherwise, it will be weird. Come."

Eric followed.

"You know about your cousin Peter, what happened to him here, right?"

"Yes."

"Well, he was not a bad man, but the loneliness changed him, I think."

"Probably. Where are you going with all this?" Eric asked.

"I am worried that loneliness may send you where you should not go. Sorry if I am off the mark. I probably am. Sorry, son."

Eric stepped closer. "Now, revert to true."

Leo heeded the request. In his son's eyes he shrank, his stomach popped, and what was left of his hair turned white.

Eric hugged the old man. "No worries, Dad! I passed away much older, and I have dead friends, so I am not lonely. But even if I were, I would never turn violent. Peter, I think, was an oddity. Walid was lonely yet not violent, right? And Ayumu. And, well, there's little Stella. She's not shy, is she?"

"Sorry, I'm dumb."

"No, you are not! I appreciate your worrying about me!"

"No, I meant Stella, I didn't get it."

"Ah . . ." Eric remained mum for a moment. "Well, me and her, we are intimate."

Leo's face twitched. Stella was Mirielle's lover and a close friend. And his son . . . wasn't that a tad too early?

"Ugh, she's your sister's—"

"Dad, it has been three years since Mirrie disappeared. You were celibate for over two of these, but now you and Mom are back naked in bed and who knows where else, aren't you? And me and Stella, we had just started."

"I understand. OK, fine, that's good to know. Stella!" Leo roared unexpectedly.

The blonde girl emerged from Mirielle's room shaking, her eyes open wide.

"I just heard that you were banging Eric."

She pressed her lips into a straight line and nodded nervously.

"Well, I wanted to say that you should not feel guilty doing that. It's been over three years; existence must go on. Now excuse me." Leo rushed back to his room, shut the door, and buried his head in Beatrice's lap.

"Fuck, Bea! Fuck! I can't always hold my nerve. I managed far better when I was alive." His tears ran unrestrained. In the big room someone played a record, Queen's *Innuendo*, "The Show Must Go On." Then there was a knock on the door.

"Yeah."

"Uncle Leo?" Stella shoved her head in the gap. "I will never forget her. I am still in love with Mirrie. Did you stop loving her mom? Come. Bea, you too. Let's remember our Mirrie. She may still be back one day."

"OK, kid, thanks." Leo wiped his face with his palms before he noticed the towel in the hand of Beatrice. He glanced at her. "Ah, thank you too." He repeated the operation with the towel, while Beatrice put on her long sweatshirt. Then he rose, pulling his ex-wife, and the two wobbled out of the room.

Stella lit a candle and pushed it to the middle of the table, then closed her eyes and started mumbling something. Praying? Leo hadn't seen a person praying in decades. What a useless thing! Never made a dent. Never fed a hungry mouth. Never saved a life. Never grew a limb. He scoffed.

Beatrice pinched his butt.

Freddie . . . was Freddie here, in this world? The guy seemed nice. Was there a way to find out, get to meet him? He was loved by enough people to keep him put for eons. Leo listened to the song, trying to ignore Stella, and then he snapped.

"Stella!"

The girl looked up.

"Are you praying?"

She nodded quickly a few times.

"To whom?"

"Leo!" Beatrice tried to intervene.

The girl's eyelids flickered worryingly, her palms still pressed together at her chest.

Leo shook his head. "Go on," he prompted her with a dry screech.

"I-I don't know," she stuttered. "To some . . . higher power. It makes me feel better, gives me hope."

"Yeah? And where was that higher power when Mirrie went missing?" Leo hissed. "Shouldn't that higher power have intervened then?"

Stella lowered her gaze.

"I'm sorry, Stella!" Leo stepped forward and pulled her in his embrace. "Higher powers never did anything good, never, ever! Am I not right? Where was the higher power then? Where is it now? Where was the damn thing when that car hit Lizzy? Where was the damn thing when I screwed up my relationship with Bea? It hardened Pharaoh's heart, and it kept me in the dark when it came to the needs of my loved one."

He let go of her and sat on the couch. "Sorry, guys, it was a pointless rant. Eric, will you please play 'Delilah'?" Leo smiled.

*
* *

Mirielle slapped Imii'i's hand. Yeah, she hadn't groomed herself since her arrival, and the guy seemed fascinated that she also grew some hair here and there.

And she had started counting the days. She never felt a need to keep track until she joined this world. Now she wanted to know how much time had passed, and she asked Aom'eai to program her personal device. This world also had no calendars and clocks. Paper here seemed obsolete. So, her host added a button to the home screen, which increased a counter each time it was pressed, and Mirielle diligently pushed it every morning. Now the counter stood at 274. How long was that? Nine months. She scraped her upper lip. Nine months. It felt as an eternity away from home.

"Imii'i." She held up her tablet. "I want to go to the lakeshore again. You know, the worms. Will you come to pull me away when it is time?"

Imii'i hesitated. "You, know, it, bad."

"Bad in old world. Here we don't know. I need the visions. I miss home."

"OK."

"And tell no one."

"A!" He twitched his head to the left.

**

The spaghetti waited patiently on the other side of the fence. She recognized some of the glyphs etched on the glass—STAY. NO. ORGANISM—but she was unable to join them into a sentence. The locals had two writing systems: an alphabet and a logographic like the Japanese kanji consisting of thousands of symbols. The logograms were used worldwide. As on Earth, there were many languages, and with the logograms, everybody could read the text regardless of what language they spoke, whereas the alphabet, albeit much easier to learn, did not support this universal understanding.

Mirielle approached the barrier. The cooked spaghetti greeted her; the strands stretched and swayed. The tiny eyeballs seemed to have framed her in their fields of view. Her lips parted. She yearned to crawl amongst the tender stems and let them draw her into a tight embrace and deliver a delightful dream. But they were so fragile, how could she do that . . .

She leaned over the rail and outstretched her arm. The stems quickly coiled around her fingers and her wrist and started crawling further up. She grabbed the rail with the other hand, closed her eyes, and tried to flush her mind. For a while there was nothing besides muddy darkness. She huffed, let go of the glass, and dropped the arm. The spaghetti wasted no time; stems quickly took hold of the friendly limb.

She shut her eyes anew and painted Stella's face. The blonde girl became alive, wavering and shimmering, then her face came very close, and Mirielle felt her lips touching hers. She parted them and traced the guests with the tip of her tongue. She craved to lay hands on her friend, but she had no arms. Again. Yet, this time she continued to breathe with a steady rhythm. She imagined her upper limbs restrained. She surrendered herself to Stella, let her lover take the lead. Stella morphed. She was now a boy. A boy with long, curly hair accessorized with beads. Mirielle loved him. His fruit was ripe. Mirielle had not tasted it for so long. She whispered, "Come." Stella understood. His lips trembled; he started swaying slowly, his hands barely touching her shoulders, his gaze downcast.

Where was Ayumu? Mirielle wanted him as well. Or Walid. The taste was good; it made her hunger grow, though. She was hollow; she needed a reprieve. She moaned. Then she felt somebody's hands hold her derrière and a warm breeze between her legs. She quivered. Ayumu! Must be him! He stopped moving. She grunted—what was he waiting for?

Then she sensed a change. She was weightless now. Stella raked her hair, then became a girl and floated. Their cheeks touched, then their lips. Stella clutched her hands behind her and wrapped her legs around Mirielle. Her skin rejoiced at the touch. Ayumu tugged her waist and glided in. The warm greeting of the welcome guest made her squirm. She chased her breath as the jolly ripples spread.

Stella spun into the air and found her breasts. She rolled the nipples, then squeezed the bulbs. Mirielle gasped as the pleasure spread. Ayumu swayed faster. Mirielle drew her eyes closed, yet she could still see Stella's body as a shapely cloud of tangled rainbow lights. And Ayumu! His dance! He was injecting so much delight with each stroke! Stella flipped and they kissed once more. Salty droplets departed from the corners of her eyes. She was almost there! She was yearning for the burst! So close! A few more strokes, a pair of hands holding her breasts, another kiss! *Ayumu! Stella! Please!*

Then, suddenly, her friends dissolved away. The colors withered. Her heart pounded, her desire screamed, she begged, yet there was no one to heed her plea. Mirielle sobbed and cursed. Gravity returned with vengeance. Her bones creaked. Mirielle tried to open her eyes. Her eyelids, though, stayed shut. She chanced a scream, but only a gargle came out of her mouth. And drool. That must be the aftermath; Imii'i must have acted. Couldn't he wait? She was with her lovers, her dear friends, she was bathing in ecstasy, and she was so close . . . she grinded her teeth.

Soon the spasms subsided, and her mind was engulfed in thick fog. In a clearing, she saw a naked woman. Dead. The skin was gray and slick. The woman was lying in a puddle of a dark, oily substance. The hair was dry, though. And bright red, like a clown's wig. And . . . she could see the face. It resembled that of her mom, which was also . . . hers! The eyes flicked open. A pair of bloodied marbles converged on

her. Mirielle tried to put some distance between herself and the creature, but she couldn't move. Only her mind squirmed. The gray body
began convulsing. White frothy liquid poured out of the mouth. The
being coughed violently and sent spatter her way. Then it stood still,
spread its arms, looked her in the eyes, and smiled. Mirielle started
throwing up.

"Mii'ee, Mii'ee!" A distorted voice reached her mind. She ignored
it, gathered the remnants of her strength, rolled to the side, and snuggled up. Whoever was calling her would have to wait.

ANOTHER DAY AWAY FROM HOME

Gran threw her a suspicious glance but whistled nothing. Mirielle looked down. Was it the new hair? Or some dirty spot? Unlike the ghosts, she had to wash and groom herself. She was clean. She dismissed the glance.

Maybe she should try dressing like the locals. Or a medley of some sort. The locals were not at all concerned about their pelvic flaps, which she now knew protected their private parts. So, wearing "pants," which were just two soft cylinders fitted with pockets and suspended from a belt around the waist, or the popular tailcoats exposing their front flaps, were not particularly suited for a cultural exchange.

But they also wore skirts and loincloths. And they liked accessories—necklaces and bracelets in particular and nose hoops. Nothing on the ears, though; the lobes were probably too sensitive.

They also often styled and tinted their manes in a multitude of colors. However, as with her own ghost folk, the mane styles were what they wore at some point in their lives. Still, for her it was different. If she dyed her hair, the colors would stick for a while, well past her next awakening.

"Imii'i, how do your folks color their manes?"

"Color, what?" The interpreter had failed.

Mirielle reached and pulled his own mane. "This."

"Come!" Imii'i led her out. They descended to street level, then sank into a tunnel and rode on the moving footpaths until they reached a wide, multistory atrium. It bore an uncanny resemblance to the interior of a shopping mall. Were all civilizations plagued by these?

Her companion took a moving ramp to the second level and then stood in front of a row of large, swiveling straddle-chairs with tall backrests. Over each there was a hollowed-out, semispherical device with several buttons and a few steadily glowing green and blue lights. Strewn on a shelf were numerous tablets and . . . there were mirrors! Mirielle immediately checked her reflection in one and pouted. No, these were screens cycling through style selections. Probably the stylists punched in some codes and the overhead devices took care of the rest.

She climbed on a chair and looked up. Inside the device there were nozzles and some wheels and small levers. The thing was not designed for humans, so who knew what might happen if she tried to use it on herself. Her hair had grown long, nearly reaching her waist. It may get entangled. No.

Imii'i had disappeared. He returned with two tall and narrow cones. His tongue was dipping into the contents of one of these, and his face was oozing delight. The long eyelashes flickered over his half-closed eyes. He pushed the other cone into her hand. She got it—a delicacy of some sort. Too bad that local delicacies did not excite her. Unbearably sweet or equally unbearably salty or sour, served in cylindrical or conical containers and consumed in the manner of an anteater having lunch. Her tongue was too short and lacked the tiny suction cups which helped lift the food.

"E." She tried to be polite and accompanied the denial with a smile. Oh, how she craved some human food. Fried sweet potatoes with sour cream, Viennese schnitzel with rice and boiled baby carrots, spring mix salad with green apples, broccoli, sunflower seeds, bacon, and grated parmesan. Only here she realized that she had never conjured up food. It was always the ghosts. Several times since emerging from the lake, she pushed her mind, salivating; however, all she tasted was disappointment. This is how the afterlife so often behaved. But she could cook! If she had ingredients . . . spaghetti. Spaghetti Alfredo with chopped thyme and plenty of mushrooms!

Her thoughts returned to the worms. She had to go again, but it had become tough convincing her roommate to tag along, and going alone—something held her back. And Imii'i—he said that he didn't know when to pull her away and sever the link. So far, he was doing that when her body started contorting and her moans became too loud, he explained. He had no idea that it was a sign of euphoria, of her rolling in delight, a whisker away from a powerful climax. How could she put that into their words? Even if she knew, he was young, and talking about such experiences might be inappropriate as it was in many earthly cultures. She sighed, grabbed his arm, and pulled him into what was probably a clothing store, judging by the three-dimensional images traveling across the giant screens suspended from the ceiling.

Inside the store she saw no clothes, only several large cubes with lights dancing on the white walls. A surface faded as she walked past one of these and revealed long rails with garments suspended on thin rods. She swerved and stepped inside. Her companion followed. The wall resumed its opacity, and Mirielle saw herself less her face, wearing a yellow skirt.

"How's that?" She pointed at the screen, smiling. Then she looked at the matrix on the side wall and directed her index finger at another garment. Her reflection changed; it was now wearing a purple loincloth.

"Hey!" Mirielle wrinkled her nose. "I asked you what you thought."

Imii'i stared at her with a blank expression on his face, his ears slumped, dipping his tongue in the cone from time to time. If he were a human, he would have probably shrugged with complete indifference. When the cone was empty, he squashed it, tossed it into a receptacle at the corner of the cube where it disappeared with a whoosh, and moved to the second one. He seemed grateful for her turning down the offer—his ears folded backward and then sprung straight. She heard a slurp. Kids.

She tried on a few more items, then addressed her roommate via her device. "How do you get the real thing?"

He looked around, tongue in cone, then pointed. "Touch there."

She did as she was told. The faint square on the screen changed color with a muffled ding. Mirielle waited, then snapped, "And now what?"

He stepped back, causing the wall behind him to dissolve, turned, and literally dragged his feet toward a large counter near the exit, on which she saw a bag. Mirielle shook her head, suppressed her urge to accelerate him with a kick, and followed him instead.

"Imii'i," she said, "I want to go to the lake again."

The creature crossed gazes with her and screeched in the microphone: "Why? You, get, hurt."

"No, not really. It may look this way, but . . ."

The creature pinned his ears.

"I am almost there." She wrinkled her forehead. "Each time. You break the link just before, well, just before I get there. And talking to the worms, it feels good. But it is exhausting, that I grant you."

"Say, again."

"Ah!" She scoffed. "You pull me away too soon. You must wait longer before you do that."

"How, long?"

A good question, how long indeed?

She took the bag and retrieved its contents. The predominantly purple loincloth unfolded in her hands, revealing the geometric patterns in contrasting colors that tickled her fancy in the cube. She tried it on. Not a bad fit. Garments on demand, perhaps. She had noticed that the clothes here had no visible seams. Were they 3D printed? Or was it the magic of the afterlife?

Her attention was drawn by an accessory display on the far wall of the hall. Thumb in mouth, she approached, still chasing answers to the question and ignoring the bored vibes emanating from her friend. The necklaces and bracelets looked handmade. There were body chains in silver and gold, some with gemstones, and a multitude of richly decorated collars draped the shoulders of headless mannequins. She'd never seen any of her hosts wearing a collar. Certainly, a matter of personal preference.

She reached for a chain, and her knuckles scraped the wall.

"Ouch!" The accessories were projections too. She heard an excited high-pitched whistle behind her—the equivalent of laughter.

"Shut up! Mmuy'i!"

"You point, not touch."

"I got that, OK!"

The mirage in front of her split in two, revealing her twin wearing the chosen chain. She added armbands to the look, then furrowed her brow and punched two holes in the bag. She then pulled it over her head. The high-pitched whistle sounded anew, much louder this time. Mirielle checked the altered image of herself and laughed. Why had she not thought about this earlier? Wear a full-face mask. The distracting shimmer was gone, and she could have a good look at the rest of herself. But the appearance was funny, there was no doubt.

Then her thoughts shifted. An hourglass! If she could make an hourglass! Or maybe ask Aom'eai to program her tablet. That would be easier. But what if she was interrogated?

She switched the body chain and added bracelets and embroidered gaiters she had seen her locals wearing on their calves. The bag departed and returned to her hand. She turned at Imii'i, tilted her head, and smiled. "How's that?" Then, remembering the still-limited capabilities of the translator, she added, "Do you like my attire?"

The creature looked at the simulation with a bored expression. He retracted his tongue from the cone and chirped into the microphone, "You, still, ugly. I, like, you."

She pulled a lock of hair, looking at him. What did he mean? Ugly, yes, she could understand him considering her to be unsightly. Even amongst her own kind, or rather, the humankind she was a derivative of, the same person can be seen as both beautiful and not quite so.

She liked these creatures, the local folk. Their large, dark, raindrop-shaped eyes, their long, dense eyelashes, their cute, playful ears. She wanted to cuddle up in one of them, preferably a specimen with a flat abdomen. Funny, she also had preferences. She wanted to kiss their closed eyelids and stroke their broad shoulders, burying her face in their hairy chests. These gentle giants. Except Imii'i, of course!

"Why am I ugly?"

"Your, skin, bare, no, fur, only, head, there . . ." He pointed at her crotch.

She transformed. "What about now?"

Imii'i's ears flickered and he choked. He began coughing, then spat into the cone and hurled it in the nearby trash hole. His ears looked appalled. "Worse."

Indeed, her male version, while hairier and unshaven, was also far from the ideal of this world and perhaps looked ridiculous dressed and accessorized like that. She reverted and waved dismissingly. "Whatever . . ."

What if she talked to the worms in her male form? It had never crossed her mind. Maybe the exhaustion would be less severe. But also, how long should she maintain the link? What would "a bit more" be in real terms? She beckoned, "Let's go now."

To the lakeshore? She sighed. Not today. Gran was here and their glance . . . were they sensing? Gran warned her about the worms, yet she went again. But why did nothing happen the first time? She had no visions; she experienced no exaltation. On that occasion she was just afraid.

They walked past a large glass pane. Mirielle glanced at the reflections. Hers was shivering and the face was the usual smudge, but his image was sharp.

"Stop!" she said in the microphone.

Her companion glanced at her. "Why?"

"Can you see my face in the glass?"

"A."

"Can you see your face?"

"E."

"Why do you think that is?"

He seemed to have taken the question seriously. His ears flickered, then stood still, his stare fixated on something behind her. Then he announced: "I, no, know. Mother, Mother, no, know. Good question. Hard question."

"Do you want to meet another one like you?"

"I, meet, you."

"Another one of your own kind. A girl perhaps?"

"My, kind, yes. Meet, what?"

"Girl."

"You, girl. I, meet, you."

There was a misunderstanding. Mirielle pointed at herself. "Girl," then transformed, "boy. Do you understand?"

Imii'i's head twitched to the right.

"Girls can have babies. Boys cannot." She changed her approach. "I have a child, Elian." A lump formed in her throat; she swallowed with difficulty as she took a deep breath.

"You, boy. You, have, child. No, understand."

She rolled her eyes, sighed, activated the sensor of the front door and stepped inside.

O'i'omp'o moved his gaze slowly from her head to her toe, then said, "No, nice. Must, put, decoration, from, your, world."

"I cannot make any."

"Can, not, make, with, mind?"

"E." She twitched her head to the right.

"Can, make, with, hands?"

"I could try!" Her face glowed. Not a bad idea! Something to keep her mind occupied! With thoughts of home. She swallowed hard again.

"You, sad," her big host said.

She nodded repeatedly while removing the borrowed attire. "I *am* sad. Sorry." She wanted to rush to him and seek comfort in his arms, but instead she carefully suspended the body chain and the loincloth in the large, shared closet by the front door, removed the gaiters, and stashed them on the shelf. She then lifted her tablet from the floor and went to her room. There she dropped face down on the thick mat and tried to sob. But her eyes were dry. She may never see home again. She had to adapt.

INTERSPECIES LOVE

Mirielle began pestering her roommate as soon as he emerged from his lair at the corner of the room, her sweaty palms rubbing into each other. "Imii'i, we shall go to the lake today. Please, please, please!"

"You, know, worms, bad."

"And you keep repeating that like a broken record! Has anyone died here?"

"Yes."

Mirielle gasped. In her world nobody did. They all drifted away. Was he talking about their kind, those born in the afterlife?

"How? Were they like us? Born here?"

"No. They, like, O'i'omp'o, Aom'eai, Ee'mimii."

"Who is Ee'mimii?"

The creature looked at her, puzzled, his ears twitching, "Ee'mimii, big, stomach, light, fur, he, tell, you, worms, bad."

"Ah, Gran!"

"No, understand."

"I call Ee'mimii 'Gran.' I didn't know, er, his name. How did they die?"

"They, here, they, not, here."

"But did you see them dead? Lifeless?"

"No, I, see, no. Nobody, see."

Mirielle held her chin, head tilted, cheeks puffed up. That was the drift; they were here, then they were gone. She sighed as the stone in her chest disintegrated.

"They did not die. They moved on."

"Moved? Where?"

"I don't know exactly. My mom moved to this place, but I don't know where it is."

"This, not, dead?"

"No."

"Why?"

"Death—body here, doesn't move, doesn't breathe."

Imii'i rubbed his ear, then ran his hand through his mane, the cogs of his mind spinning. Then, just like Gran he licked the tip of his nose, eliciting a chuckle.

"They, dead. Other, world, they, move, here. They, not, know, this, world, here. Here, they, move, other, world, we, not, know. They, dead."

She wished the translator worked better. But as she interpreted them, the words made sense. He seemed to understand dying as moving to another world. To him it was irrelevant that there was a body that had to be disposed of in the old world and here, people simply disappeared. Maybe her take was too detailed. At the end of the day, contact with that person was lost in either world. So, death it is.

She changed tactics. "Do you know someone the worms killed?"

"Me, not. Everybody, else, know."

She tried a cute face. "You see? This is because nobody gets killed here. Now, let's go, shall we?"

"Mirielle, first, killed, here."

"Nooo. Nobody gets killed here." She stood behind him and gently rubbed his earlobes. "Come on, Imii'i, don't worry."

Imii'i twitched but did not object to the touch. She had noticed that the locals liked these rubs, liked them a lot. Then she wrapped her hands around his neck, and they nuzzled cheeks. "Please!"

He whistled in the microphone. "Last, time."

"Thank you!" Mirielle pecked him.

Imii'i wiped the spot with his palm as if she had deposited dirt on his shiny coat.

"Sorry," she mumbled. "But you like this, don't you?" Mirielle massaged his ears again. The purring sound he emitted confirmed it. But he was also worried, she could tell. Was it about her or about being reprimanded by Gran, if their defiance came to light?

*
**

The spaghetti appeared excited to see her again. A multitude of eyes trained on her as soon as she leaned against the translucent barrier. The stems swirled in a welcoming dance. She wanted to dive straight in and be again with her loved ones, even if it was just an elaborate ruse. The familiar human faces, the melody of the voices, the tactile sensations, the euphoria the combined stimuli induced, the reprieve from the desperation of existence in this alien world—she needed all that and she needed it now!

She yearned to feed her child and play with him and encircle him in her arms and take him for a stroll and let him rip tulips along the way. She wished for a humble serving of ice cream. In a cup. No cones! Some fresh, crispy bread with butter and soft cheese. And fruit! Strawberries, bananas, watermelon. There was no other way to experience all this but by hallucinating, courtesy of the so-called worms. Her regular dreams were chaotic, the imagery—random and lacking color and detail. The worms showed her vivid visions of the past and let her interact with her memories in most exquisite ways. Up to a point, though, when making love, she could never reach the end, that magical moment where her body would rejoice.

Maybe this time, she would instruct Imii'i to wait another twenty ticks of the counter on her device. Or if she was lying down? Could it be as simple as this? She was always in that uncomfortable pose, flopped over the barrier like wet laundry, kneeing the glass and with dangling arms. Where was the end of the damn fence?

"Come, beauty?" She waved at him.

"Beauty? You, find, me, beauty?"

"Yes, why not?"

"You, ugly."

Mirielle scoffed. "Why do you keep saying that? Yes, I know that you think that I am ugly. A slug. But I find you cute, with your big, moist eyes and your shiny coat. You are like a pet."

"You, see, me, domesticated, animal?" The device expressed no emotion, but his screech was upset.

"Yes. Our pets are furry. You have fur. Therefore, you are a pet." She could not help injecting some sarcasm. His insistence on her being ugly—what if she really was? Her dad adored her mom, and she was her, their, copy, but both her parents felt insecure when they were young—small biceps, small boobs. What if there was a reason? What if they were ugly in the eyes of their peers and so was she?

The fence terminated at a rock formation, which extended all the way to the water. She climbed the rocks with ease and looked back. Imii'i made no attempt to follow.

"Come here. Don't you want to?"

He tried. He hooked his tablet on his belt, lifted one leg, and sought support. But his foot kept sliding down. Mirielle realized that these creatures could not climb well. Their legs were made for speed. They ran fast, but climbing rocks was very hard for them, and going up trees, perhaps impossible. She returned to the ground. The spaghetti growth was calling her. There was a scent in the air that had not been there before. It tickled her nostrils, amplifying her desire to be caressed by the tender stems.

She detected that Imii'i felt the same way but was afraid. He took a step back. His running away was not what she needed. She turned, bent over the glass barrier, and offered her hands to the growth. The spaghetti did not hesitate. The tendrils flexed and swirled, coiling tightly around her forearms, and then released their elixir. The more adventurous amongst them crawled even further up, reaching her shoulders and the neck. By the time half a dozen tiny eyes peeked inside her mouth, she was already in a deep trance.

Elian, hazy and surrounded by a halo, outstretched his arms. "Mommy! Hug!"

Her hands seemed tied behind her back. "I can't, sweetie. Come, give Mom a kiss."

The little boy approached. She kneeled. The boy wrapped his arms around her. "Mommy, where are you?" He sobbed. "Mommy!"

"Don't cry, Eli."

"I want you, Mommy! Come back to me! Please!"

She felt the tears of her little one smudging on her skin. If she could only hug him, offer him shelter from the void she had left, but the only tool at her disposal was her voice.

"Don't cry, sweetie, Mommy's here." She bent her neck and drew his scent into her nostrils.

"I know." The boy leaned back. It was Ayumu now. His face drifted closer. She could see the tiny pores on his nose. He gently tugged her, and they kissed quietly. His palms skimmed her cheeks. His fingers combed her hair. Then he stepped back and looked her in the eyes.

"You are not real, Ayumu," she whispered.

"Certainly. But I still love you."

"Good to know. Hug me, please. Where did Eli go?"

"Back inside you."

"Inside me? What do you mean?"

"You are his mom."

"Ah, you don't mean—" She bent her neck. Her tummy was large! She was pregnant!

Ayumu sank and kissed her belly, then returned.

"Are my hands bound?" Mirielle asked.

Ayumu peeked and nodded. "Mmm."

She gasped with a shy smile, her heart pounding. "Oh! And what are you going to do with me now?"

He brushed her hair off her face and touched her forehead with his lips. His finger trekked down her nose and came to a halt over her mouth. He smiled. "Whatever you wish."

"The game is about surprise as much as it is about trust, is it not?" She tried to grab the finger with her jaws.

"Bad girl!" Ayumu chuckled and spun her around.

Was she floating? She looked down. Yes! Her feet were not on the ground! There was no ground! Ayumu arrested the spin. Something slick and cold creeped inside her bum. She squinted, breathing through her teeth. Her groin was smoldering; now her rear had also been lit.

Ayumu flipped her, face up. Mirielle felt hands pulling her, then fingers parting her petals and the tip of a tongue threading in. It fluttered, fanning the emergent fire. "Agh . . ." Mirielle gasped and wrapped her legs around the intruder's neck. The toy oscillated, triggering a shy moan. The ripples made her squirm, exalted, dizzy, and craving so much more. She didn't want just measly sparks. She wanted the fire of ecstasy to consume her, not just keep her warm. *Ayumu!*

A familiar face floated into view, golden hair, beads, fringe, skittish blue eyes. Mirielle smiled. The girls brushed lips.

"Stelly . . . where are you?"

"In your dreams, baby. I am in your dreams. And your heart. I love you. Wanna tit?"

Mirielle traced her lips. Stella shifted nearer. Mirielle greedily drew the nipple into her mouth, while somebody pulled one of hers. Yellow man perhaps. No, her little star! She had levitated too, floating upside down . . . Mirielle exhaled a moan as Stella's cupped hands warmed her breast and her tongue wagged and rolled.

Then Ayumu made a move. His penis glided in; she quivered as the labia split to let it. The visual of Stella dispersed, then reemerged and straddled Mirielle, bringing her blossom invitingly close. Mirielle wiggled, her lips touching the mound, then she folded her legs as a pair of strong arms grabbed her hips. Flesh and bone slammed into her posterior. Ayumu for sure! His penis dived deep into her, then bowed out. Then burst in again. The rhythm of the dance sped up. Her eyes shut closed; her mouth went ajar. Teardrops congregated at the corners of her eyes. She let her voice loose. Dizzying, yet still short of her need. Just an appetizer, a light rain. Where was the deluge? She squirmed, Ayumu swayed. *Faster! Please!*

"Faster!" She issued a battle cry. She was so hungry! Her entire frame shook at each thrust. Through tears and flashes of delight, she caught a smudged silhouette casting shadow over her. "Ahh!" She dispatched a loud moan, as Ayumu behind her began pouring his juice. A steady stream of light appeared from nowhere and revealed a face. Her father! What was her old man doing here? And why was he young and naked? The blood was already in her face, as she kept blinking, hypnotized by the stare. Her lips trembled. She tried to spread her arms and launch herself into his embrace, be a child again and snuggle up.

The man turned and walked away, the silhouette disintegrating into streaks of dull paint. *Dad!* she called. Only her lips moved. *Dad!* She emptied her lungs, but no sound came out, not even a wheeze. Yet there was that screechy voice, cycling her name, "Mirielle! Mirielle!"

Then gravity returned and squashed her with its mighty hand. The voice was now familiar. "Mii'ee!"

"I'm fine!" She huffed. "I need rest."

Her dad . . . was he angry seeing her like that? It was embarrassing. Or was it? She was doing nothing wrong. He partook in the behavior, and he also never judged. And it was not real anyway. Him, Elian, Stella, Ayumu . . .

Not real? What if they were actually connected across realms? What if it was a shared dream? What if it was a call from home?

"Mii'ee!"

She growled. "I'm good. Shut up!"

"Mii'ee, you, no, good."

"Go away." She expended a breath. Her eyelids were so heavy. Had her flesh turned into lead? Her muscles disobeyed as she tried to roll on her side. Even her tongue—it was slow and very stiff. Breathing was a chore.

*
**

There were no nightmares this time. No grotesque faces, no foaming mouths. Only quiet darkness. Inside and out, then just inside. Mirielle tried her eyelids. The shutters struggled, revealing a sliver of daylight, then dropped closed.

"Ugh . . ." She grunted and moved her fingers. Were they stuck in clay? Where was her vigor? A snot bubble popped, and saliva drooled from her open mouth. She must be disgusting in her current state. But so what? Who cared? Her loved ones were so far away. Ah, damn, Imii'i, he must be around.

"Imii'i?"

"Yes?"

"I-I'm sorry. I . . . mean . . . no disrespect."

"Rest."

"Thanks."

"You, here, two, days. You, sleep, no, stop."

"Huh? Ah . . . yeah . . ."

Mirielle clenched her teeth, flipped on her stomach, and staggered up grunting and managing no further than all fours.

"Damn. Ugh."

Imii'i offered a hand. Mirielle grabbed it, wobbled to her feet, and leaned on him. "Thanks. What . . . happened?"

"I, wait, you, tell, I. You, scream, I, pull, you, scream. Your, eyes, blue."

"My eyes are blue?" She tried to arch her brows.

"Yes, blue, rings."

"I don't understand."

He traced a circle around his eye. "You, thin, too. Weight, less."

Mirielle looked at her arms. They appeared skinnier indeed. And her boobs. The fatty tissue seemed substantially reduced. Not that she possessed much to start with.

"Let's go." She took a step. Her knees quivered as she proceeded with an unsteady, tired gait. Leaning on her furry roommate, holding his arm, provided her with some comfort. She squeezed her lips. She had again failed to travel all the way to the end. She was a wreck, yet hungry, unsatisfied, ready to turn and go back, gather bundles of one-eyed stems in her arms and let them soak her life force in exchange for love, for a sweet moment in her world. Why did she always dream of sex? Was that so important? She just longed for home.

Mirielle tangled her legs and tumbled on the ground. Imii'i dragged her up and screeched something, but her device was off. She reached for the handle and turned it on.

"I, told, grandparent."

"You told grandparent?" Ah, did he mean Gran? "You told what?"

"You, and, worms."

Mirielle cursed in her mind. "Why?"

"I, worry. You, sick. You, sad. You, no, listen, me. You, friend. I, love, you."

"You love me? You call me ugly all the time."

"It, matter, not. You, friend. I, love, friend. I, love, Mirielle."

"And this is not because I rub your ears?"

Imii'i threw her a shy glance then lowered his gaze. "It, not."

TRAPPED

Mirielle sensed the attention and pivoted. Gran had filled the door-frame with his hulking physique, eyes and ears pinned on her. The large individual lifted his hand and activated his device. "May I come in?"

The young woman raised her eyebrows. The tablet spoke so well. "Yes."

"I upgraded translator. Much better now. Here, for you." Gran unfolded his arm.

"Thank you!"

"No need. You like my child. You miss your species, but you not lonely, you have us."

"I am aware that I am like your child. You never started not treating me like one."

The device was incapable of rendering the sarcasm, so the answer was: "I am glad."

Gran took a breath and screeched, "Please do not go to worms, Mirielle. I beg you. You may or may not die, that I do not know; however, worms gain power over you, over your mind. They lure you with euphoria, with images you want to see, with emotions you crave, with experiences you desire. This is how they hunt their prey in other world."

"Then why do they exist here?"

"Because we remember them. And here they cannot get us, but you, you are different, and you will be scared if you could see yourself now."

"Why, what's wrong?"

"You are skin on bones. No meat, no fat. Big purple rings around your eyes. Your face . . ." Gran sucked his cheeks in. "Like that. Like starving person. You know you not need food, so, can you explain?"

Mirielle dropped her head. Gran was right. She knew that she'd lost weight, and she had become chronically fatigued. But . . .

"I-I want to go home." Her eyes went moist. "How? How can I do that?"

"How did you come?"

Mirielle twitched and her eyes flicked around. Indeed, she had never told the story, that she leaped into the abyss. Her heart started pounding, and some color returned to her face.

"I leaped from a cliff. I can't fly like the others; I drop. I wanted to find out what would happen to me. I was certain that I wouldn't die. Like, hit me!"

Gran's ears folded, and his eyes grew somewhat larger. "Hit you? Why?"

"Just do it. With full force! You will see."

"Can you not simply tell?"

Mirielle scoffed. "OK. I cannot be harmed."

"I disagree. The worms are doing that."

"Hit me!"

Gran drew his stare, then pinned his ears and swung his long arm. The smack sent Mirielle tumbling across the large room. Gran threw the tablet and rushed after her. Mirielle struggled to get up, dizzy, her ears ringing.

Gran helped her stand and reached for the device. "Why you made me hit you? What you want to show?"

Mirielle mumbled, still holding her spinning head. "I thought . . . that I could not be harmed. Ayumu, he tried . . . and Walid . . ."

"You speak of others? Machine did not translate."

"Yes, Ayumu, Walid, my friends."

"Ayumu, Wa'ee." Gran spoke without the device. "I like these names."

"Yes." The ringing in Mirielle's ears subsided. "They couldn't land a punch. Their hands went right through me. Perhaps it is different here. Every world has its own rules."

"Perhaps. You understand now? No worms, I beg you. I can lock this room, but . . . in other world only those who wanted broke free from worms. Locks held body, no desire. Desire led body back to worms. You understand."

Gran raised his hand and caressed Mirielle's hair, then, trembling, he touched the bare skin of her cheeks.

"Let me show you." The creature took Mirielle's hands and pressed his palms against hers. "May not work for you. This is how we show affection. We hold hands. And we . . . kiss with tongue. But you not like, I guess, not your way."

"Try me." Mirielle crossed gazes with Gran and smiled.

"No!"

The disgust that accompanied the refusal struck Mirielle hard. Her eyes watered instantly. She clenched her teeth, walked to the large window, and set her gaze loose, her heart pounding. Could she break the glass and seek solace in the embrace of the pavers down there on the street? Maybe the fabric of space would tear again and let her cross back home.

"I am sorry." The device translated the quiet sequence of chirps.

"No worries, I understand."

Gran's palm rested on her shoulder. Mirielle shrugged it off, biting her lips.

"I am sorry."

"I get it, OK!" The young woman turned and walked past the imposing frame toward the door, then through the exit and down the ramp. The worms, those supposedly nasty creatures, were at least sincere in their desire to feast on her. Gran was wearing a mask; they all were! Except perhaps the youngster. Ugly, he called her. Yeah, right!

She looked around. This town was so sterile! Nothing to tear to pieces, no loose objects to kick! Mirielle squinted and burst into a building. Nothing there either. Nothing to sink one's teeth in and emit a muffled scream.

The door in front of her hissed open. On the other side she saw the worms, swaying as if beckoning her, begging her to join. She took a step back and let the door slide shut. Not now. Perhaps not ever again. She wanted to jump right in the middle of the spaghetti field, but what if she died indeed?

The rooftop garden was awash with shimmering shadows cast by hundreds of playful blueish leaves. The air was fresh and fragrant, swayed around by a warm, gentle breeze. Numerous slim lianas connected the surface with the crowns, some adorned with round yellow blossoms near the tops. Small, lizard-like animals made occasional dashes up or down these links.

Mirielle slowly sampled the surroundings then untied the cinch and let the gown pool at her feet. She spread her arms and swirled with her eyes closed. The breeze ruffled her hair. She traced her lips. Her nipples firmed. She grabbed a nearby liana and spun around it, then rose on her toes. She dreamed of music—a slow, soothing piece. The piano keys in her vision moved on their own. She finally broke a cautious smile. Playing music made her happy. Just like her mom.

And touching herself. She hugged the vine tight and flipped her eyes open. Across the street, Gran was gesticulating vividly at her roommate. Was the old guy berating him? About her? Perhaps. She pinched two fingers, licked them, and then split her labia just enough to feel a gleeful tickle. It would be much better with Ayumu or Stella around, but she had only herself. And she needed a distraction and to quench her carnal thirst. Carnal. Heh, whatever. She rubbed and gasped. Then she kneeled on the grass, her legs apart, her hand between them, her fingers unashamedly seeking her sweet spot. She imagined Stella; the two kissed. It was not her hand anymore doing the deed, it was Stella's. Mirielle let go of the vine and rolled her nipples hard with her palm. Her palm belonged to Stella too. Or Ayumu. It mattered not. Her mouth went ajar. Home. It was far, in another universe perhaps. She traced her lips again and rolled her pinched fingers inside her, then rubbed hard. The sparks in her groin became noticeably brighter. She pictured riding Ayumu, his face turning comically angry just before the volley of delight. *Not yet, friend, I am far from done.*

Mirielle rolled on her back in the springy grass. What if it was Gran between her legs? She shut her eyes tightly, her mouth stretching in a grin, and pictured Gran with his long, thick, hard tongue probing, kissing. The way the locals did when they consumed their food. Was she sweet? She squeezed her breast and emptied her mind, letting only the fuzzy image linger. The ambers in her groin grew brighter as she pushed and swirled. Her nipples, they craved to be drawn into somebody's mouth. Her entire body wanted so much to be caressed! She pushed harder, seeking the excitement of the climax. She moaned, her forehead wrinkled, her mouth twisted, her body twitched. Then the flowery shower inundated her. Then evaporated. Her hand withdrew and settled quietly between her legs; her index finger waved a shy "Goodbye."

Mirielle looked at the sky, popped her cheeks, and blew the air out. Self-gratification was like the appetizer, priming her for the main course. But here, it left her craving. The flowers had withered. She flipped face down, raking her fingers through the grass. Should she go for a steaming plate of spaghetti? But it also left her hungry, starving even, yet badly burned.

She kneeled, then wobbled up. The world around her spun. She seized the liana with both hands. Her stomach threw a fit and expelled its contents—clear, odorless liquid, which dissipated soon. As if it could be otherwise in this world.

Home! She had to get home! She tottered down the ramp, pausing at any door along the way, sticking her head inside the rooms, hoping for space to bend and reveal the lovely yellow sun, pummeling with her fists and delivering the occasional kick when the mechanism failed to operate.

The last door before the exit was slow to open. Coughing, Mirielle thrusted her fists forward, and the punches landed into something elastic and furry. Mirielle looked up and her eyes grew larger. She took a step back, tripped on her own foot, and her gaunt rear kissed the floor. She scrambled away, ignoring the pain, her gaze still fixated on the broad face.

The local dude did not react. He stood tall, silent, and motionless. The young woman squinted, rose up slowly, and brushed off her bum, eyes inseparable from the large head. Why was the creature not moving? The eyes—the eyes were glazed! The creature was dead! Mirielle was ready to scream but swallowed the shriek and ran her hand down the hairy chest instead. Then pinched the arm. It felt so natural. Was this thing a life-size doll? Or a trick of the realm—someone frozen in time? Perhaps time had stopped for her?

Mirielle squeezed herself past the lifeless figure into the large room. The reddish light streamed through the wall of glass. As usual, there were no curtains or blinds; the opacity of the glass was voice-regulated. This afterlife was more technologically advanced. One could not only vary the opacity of the slab but also select patterns, make them move, even turn the window into a giant stereoscopic viewscreen. There were many other wonders she could marvel at and explore. But her throat was tight. For so many days now.

She approached the food island, climbed on one of the straddle chairs, stretched, and activated the water fountain in the middle. The stream splashed into the bowl.

She drank, then waved her hand again to make the water stop and let her gaze explore. Tapestries hung from the tall ceiling, depicting stylized faces, plants, and animals. Stools featured rich woodwork. A paired bucket lift served a loft, and there was a hallway to the right. At the bottom of the hallway stood another of the local creatures, its back against the wall. It appeared more feminine—smaller, with a long, brightly colored mane, a golden nose hoop, a wide chainmail collar draped on its shoulders, an elaborately embroidered loincloth wrapped around its waist, and gemstone-encrusted anklets. Mirielle marched to it and stuck her fingers into the creature's abdomen. Same natural feeling. She recalled the dolls in the adult toy shop. Were these two sex dolls?

She caressed the motionless arm, then stood on her toes and gently guided the eyelids closed, wondering how these machines were brought to life. A button on the neck? A voice command? She'd left her tablet in her room. Ah, damn, she had forgotten her dress on the roof. The garment had some value; she made it herself, killing time and showing what some humans wore.

The door failed to open as she inserted herself between it and the life-size doll. Mirielle waved. "Hello!" Then she placed her palms on the darker square in the middle of the leaf. The door remained shut. Cursing, she launched both hands against the slab, inadvertently propelling herself backward. The sheer mass of the still creature behind her tried to arrest her fall but succumbed to the momentum, and the large frame crashed to the floor. Mirielle's head bounced off the crotch of the doll, then returned to a rest.

"Damn!" she cursed again, then squeezed the creature's thighs. She felt the muscles and ligaments under the skin. What were these things? She gathered herself together, kneeled, and drew her glance over the body of the local. The shiny fur looked so real. This guy wore a sleeveless jacket and what passed around here for pants.

Mirielle parked her gaze on the front flap of the creature. What was it hiding? She blushed as she bit her lip, reached, and peeled it open with some effort. Then peeked underneath and giggled. She could have asked her hosts for a lesson on their anatomy or could have procured the knowledge in some other manner, but this way was much more satisfying.

She rose and walked to the other motionless figure in the hallway, pulled its loincloth up, shamelessly peeled its flap, stared for a while, and then wrinkled her nose. Not what she was expecting. Whatever.

Mirielle returned to the large room and pushed her palms against the glass pane. The sunset was in full swing, adding a strong burning tint to the view outside. She counted four floors. This is where she lived with her hosts. Were they worried, looking for her right now? Why would they be? She'd stormed out only a short while ago.

And that door, what was wrong with it? Doors also had voice controls, but she never paid attention to the screech. The young woman yawned and went to the food island, climbed on a chair, rested her head on her crossed hands, and closed her eyes. A loud sigh broke the silence of the room. Home. How to get there? Open the damn door, that was step one. But not now. She sat upright and lifted her hands. They were trembling. And they were so heavy. Why? Mirielle buried the unsteady fingers in her hair, squeezed her lips, then sighed again. Home. She had to regain her strength. Sleeping, that seemed to be the trick. The thick, soft mattress along the far wall was so inviting. She set her feet on the floor, dragged them across the room, and crashed on the mattress face down. Her hands gathered a throw pillow underneath her head, just like the sofa in their loft. The one she often took a nap on when she was a young girl. What was Elian doing now? Was he missing her? Surely! She missed him too. This morning the day count stood at 892. Almost two and a half years. Her child had grown up. And Stella. The others should still be the same, though—Dad, Beatrice, Steve, the stretched eyes of Ayumu . . . *I-I-love . . . you . . .*

RESURRECTIONS

Mirielle almost sank her teeth into her father's flesh as he drew her into his embrace. Her heart drummed triumphantly; she itched to detach her feet from the ground and climb up his frame until she could wrap her legs around his waist, hug his head, and be his little child again. Then she found herself riding on his shoulders, and she was strangely small, her hands barely converging on his chin. And his hair was long and red.

She looked down and saw a face. Stella was smiling at her, the lush blonde hair floating over the eyes. Where did her dad go? And why did he possess cascading ginger locks? Like Beatrice. She hugged Stella and they exchanged a kiss. Were they levitating? She looked over her friend's shoulder. She was in a room, a large one, with walls painted saturated yellow and with an ugly maroon carpet on the floor. She was on an elevated platform or a stage. People had congregated in groups of three or four. Friends, she knew, but she could not discern their faces. They were all looking away. Or . . . her heart sank! They were reflections! She turned around. Stella was gone and so was her dad. There was a field, bright blue sky, bright green grass, with a large wardrobe in the distance. A bout of nostalgia squeezed her heart. She wanted to be back there, in this field, where she was so happy. But why? Where was this field? Somebody pulled her; she turned her head. Ayumu? Or Walid? The face was out of focus and the features morphed. She tugged it closer by the cheeks and aimed a kiss at the lips, but there was nothing. Just a flaking white wall and a strong sense of loss.

And something scary! Moving closer! Stairs appeared. She was in a stairwell. A low, menacing hum was approaching from below. She tried to run, but the air was so thick that she barely advanced a step. She glanced over the parapet, her eyes almost popping out of the sockets. The evil presence was getting nearer! She wanted to scream; however, she heard no other sound besides the desperate thumps of her heart.

She gathered all her strength and pushed forward. Bloody flashes erupted in her eyes. She drew a breath through her open mouth, but it failed to reach her lungs, as if the air had petrified. Mirielle squirmed like a worm caught in fast-setting amber. The horrifying presence was so close, a whisker away, and it would devour her at any moment! She squeezed her eyes shut, sobbing silently, warm liquid gushing from her crotch and running down her legs. Finally, she screamed!

The stillness of the room shrugged off the noise. Mirielle gasped for air, staring in the darkness with enlarged eyes. Just a dream. A scary one. But there was a damp spot beneath her! Light! She needed light! More than the faint glow of the curtain wall. She sat briskly on the edge and reached for her device, then retracted her hand midway. That was not . . . the place she had been calling "home."

She climbed back onto the mattress and skimmed the surface with her palms, in search of the drenched spot. Nothing, not even a trace. She needed light. The windowpane controls were usually on the left.

Mirielle slipped onto the floor, located the touchpad, and pushed the slowly blinking slider knob down. The glass surface remained unchanged. She tried again but to no avail. Was everything in this unit broken? The door, the window, the dolls?

She craved a sip of water. That discharge in her dreams—she searched for explanation in her outer memory and gasped! Had she . . . peed herself? She pushed her hand between her legs. She was dry. Maybe it happened only in the dream. Then she squinted. Was it really night?

Mirielle returned to the mattress and sat on the edge, gazing at the floor. Cold sweat ran down her temples. She picked at her nails, her eyes flipping from side to side in the dark. Fiddling with device controls was no doubt useless in this world. They were not broken. Was it her who chose this path? Hiding from the alien world? But why? She was alone anyway, a stranger amongst a bunch of local ghosts. She crashed onto the mattress, bashed it with her fists, and greeted the dark ceiling with a blank stare.

How to get out? *Think outside the box, girl.* Emotions! The ghosts were empaths. Imii'i was a strong one; he must be worried! So, there was a way! But her own senses drew blank. No waves of worry, as she would have hoped. She pulled her hair. Perhaps it was nighttime indeed. She had been away before, so no reason yet for them to be concerned. She'd try to send a call for help in the morning. That was a plan! She bounced backward like a child until she reached the center of the mattress, then rolled on her side and emptied her mind. In a short while, the quietness of the room was disturbed only by her faint breaths.

The pink sun peeked into the room and frowned, finding someone still sleeping, but it was unable to immediately dispatch a bundle of rays to wake up the offender. By the time the shadows had retreated inward enough, Mirielle had sat up, raked her hair, and focused her gaze on the street outside. It was deserted as usual, yet inexplicably alive. She slipped to the floor, walked to the window, pushed her cheek against the cold surface, and looked up, trying to catch a glimpse of the Barbie star. Barbie . . . that skinny doll from her world. Someone gifted her one when she was a kid. She kept it on her toy shelf for a while out of politeness until one day the doll disappeared. Probably because nobody gave it any thought. She was not at all interested in weird-looking, inanimate, anthropomorphic objects. And she disliked pink. Perhaps one more reason she never found comfort in this world.

Mirielle squinted hard as soon as she accomplished her pointless goal and turned her attention to the front door. It remained closed as she approached. She slapped the sensor in the middle, wondering why there was no mechanical control—a handle or a knob. Then she stepped back, almost tripping over the motionless figure on the floor, and dragged her gaze around the frame, looking for a hidden release of some sort. Nothing.

Mirielle picked at her nail, spat the shavings, closed her eyes and appealed to her hosts. Then flipped them open and sighed. Not a tiny speck of emotion tickled her mind. Were they away? Perhaps; it was almost noon, so they were certainly engaged in performing the educational theatrics for their child. Just like her own ghosts did once. Just as she would readily do for her Elian.

Elian . . . she begged for some tears to wash some of the sadness away; however, she had run dry after all this time. He should be six now. Ripe for school. She would have been the teacher, and her ghosts would have been the other kids. He would learn to read and write in a flash as he already had the knowledge inherited from her. Would he recognize any kanji, kana, or just the Latin alphabet? Would he play a clavier? Or the guitar? Was he good at drawing like his dad? And restlessly inquisitive? Mirielle rolled her hands into fists, her breath quickening. She had to find a way out! She pivoted resolutely, looked up, and shrieked!

The large creature towered over her, its eyes focused on her face, ears cast close to the head. It hurriedly stepped backward, squatted, and flipped its hands palms up. A friendly gesture. She caught her breath and flickered her eyelids, then swallowed hard. How did it come to life? When? Why so silently? Mirielle slowly rested her hands in the open palms, her body still twitching occasionally. The creature was warm now!

"A'eiy." The being whistled softly. "Aw yamp'ei."

Hi, I am Yamp'ei. That much she understood. "Mirielle, aw Mirielle." She withdrew her hands and bowed. When she looked up again, the ears were pinned on her, and the eyes of the creature were somewhat enlarged. Then it bowed awkwardly.

Mirielle laughed. The giant tried to mimic her apparently. It was cute. The locals somehow succeeded in never looking intimidating despite their large size. But was this thing a true local? It was playing dead just a moment ago. Now it had locked its gaze on her, perhaps wondering what the sound she emitted meant.

And the other? What about the one in the hallway? The young woman crossed gazes with the gentle giant, inhaled deeply, and pointed. "Ia uup." That should mean "There's another," she hoped.

The creature glanced over its shoulder, then turned back at her and sounded, "O'ya?"

Her accent was too thick, apparently. She pouted, blew some air through her nostrils, and walked to the hallway. The other creature stood there, dead, a pair of glazed eyes staring nowhere. Sensing the motion behind her, she stepped aside and raised her gaze. Yamp'ei advanced quickly past her, screeching something. He—for Mirielle had assumed the giant was male—touched the cheeks of the other, then rubbed the ears. That gesture was affectionate. Were the two creatures close? Yamp'ei's screeching took a softer tone. He slowly glided his palms down the other creature's arms until they reached and took possession of the wrists.

Mirielle gasped when he suddenly dropped on his knees, bowed his head, and tried to cover it with the pair of stiff and cold hands. She could not be mistaken; those two once shared a bond. She heard the high-pitched whistle voicing grief.

Yamp'ei rose briskly to his feet, grabbed the other's head with both hands, and stuck his tongue in its mouth. A kiss!

Mirielle scratched her thigh, her mouth ajar. Should she step aside and let the giant mourn in peace or try to provide him with some comfort? She lacked the guidance of prior observations and put her trust in her instinct. She marched forward and reached for the ears, only then realizing that she was way too short. Yamp'ei let go of his mate and turned abruptly. The back of his large hand delivered a smack and plastered her on the wall. Her head bounced off the sur-face, and she collapsed to the floor.

"O'e! O'e! Iiyaa'i!" the giant screeched loudly and kneeled beside her. He reached hesitantly. "Iiyaa'i."

Mirielle staggered up, sat on her calves, and rubbed the burning cheek.

The creature crawled back and prostrated at her knees. "Iiyaa'i! Pe a iaam!"

He was sorry. She knew that, but the right chirp for the occasion was eluding her. Instead, now that the earlobes were within reach, she leaned, held them between her fingers and her thumbs, and started rubbing gently. The creature understood. Yamp'ei remained still and eventually purred. Then, when she stopped, he rose slowly and of-fered his hands. Mirielle fanned her fingers and pushed her palms against his. Her gaze crawled up until it crossed paths with his. She saw the tip of his tongue hesitantly flicking out and in. Did he want to kiss?

She traced her lips while bouncing guesses in her mind, then parted them slightly, tilted her head back, and drew her eyelids closed. The kiss Imii'i once delivered was not unpleasant, she recalled, and she had not been kissed for so long. In a few heartbeats, the tip of the giant's tongue briefly probed her mouth, then left. Fresh and mildly sweet. She squeezed his hands. *Try again!*

When she opened her eyes, the giant had sat upright, his earlobes vibrating and his large eyes trained on her. Mirielle smiled and pro-truded her tongue. The creature's ears steadied and pointed sideways; her signal was clear. He bent forward and his face came very close. His eyelids moved downward, and their tongues met again. Her heart raced, and her breath became louder. She shut her eyes and tried to picture one of her own—Ayumu, Walid, Stella—but all she could see was the broad face with large eyes adorned with extravagant eye-lashes, and she realized that she did not mind him being so starkly different, that she was perfectly content. The innate desire of her kind to embrace and be embraced took the better of her. She pulled the creature's arms around her waist and squirmed in delight as the soft, dense fur caressed her skin.

Then she came to her senses, let go of his hands, and spread her arms. Their faces moved apart, her guilty gaze hesitantly probing his expression then quickly shying away.

"Sorry . . . I'iyaa'i," she murmured, squeezed her eyes shut, and braced herself for waves of disgust to flood her receptors any moment now.

Nothing. Absolutely nothing. Mirielle popped her eyes open and cast her gaze on the giant's face. The creature was looking at her calmly, if not mildly amused or surprised. It was hard to tell. But why? Where had all emotions gone? She closed her eyes again and tried to read Yamp'ei's mood. Nothing. As if he were not there.

She looked at him, and her heart raced anew. Maybe she was still asleep, dreaming! Yes! That made sense! There were two inanimate bodies in the unit when she arrived as far as she was concerned. A pair of life-size models of the local ghosts.

Mirielle pinched her arm. "Wake up!"

The being screeched something.

"Wake up, damn it!" She pinched herself again, then stood up, walked to the window, and banged her forehead in the glass. The pain felt as real as everything else—the room, the creature quietly following her movement with his eyes, the street outside, even . . . was it not Gran? She caught a motion with the corner of her eye and turned her head fast. But whatever it was, it was now gone.

Mirielle sighed, pivoted, and slowly dragged her gaze across the room until it settled on the being that called itself Yamp'ei. "I am hallucinating, am I not?"

"Apii'am'e."

"Of course, you don't understand. But if you are a product of my mind, you should, right?"

"Perhaps."

Mirielle stood perfectly still and with wide-open eyes.

AUTOMATA

Mirielle delivered a sleepy glance at the figure casting a shadow over her. The loincloth . . . the collar . . . the white coat . . . She took a deep breath and sat up.

"Good morning!" the creature greeted.

"Ugh. So be it." Her mind was hazy. This being came to life yesterday and spoke her tongue! Mirielle had resigned herself to the fact and sought no explanation. It was *way* too hard. She was even happy seeing how Yamp'ei leaped, grabbed, and squeezed the other creature's hands and the two exchanged a lengthy kiss. At some point, she saw both large frames shivering. Then they remembered her.

"I am Yamma'i and this is my mate." A delicate finger pointed at Yamp'ei.

"Mirielle. I am Mirielle. How does it come you speak my language? Nobody else here does."

"I don't know."

Awkward silence ruled for a while and then the creature said, "Mirielle, what are you? I have no recollection of your species or race."

"My race?"

"Yes, there are three races as you perhaps know, and you do not look like any of them. No bone ridges, no horns, no hooves, that bald skin, the sparse fur. You . . ." Yamma'i hesitated.

"Yes? Go ahead."

"You . . . you look like a mp'eeei'mp. Sorry! No offense."

"None taken." Mirielle leaned against the windowpane behind her, suddenly in need of support. "I don't even know what a mp'eeei'mp is."

Yamp'ei screeched something. Yamma'i screeched back then turned to the young woman again. "It is . . . well . . . an animal."

"Can you show me?"

Yamma'i spoke quickly to the window then punched the dials. The view remained unchanged. "The viewer is not responding."

The eyes of the creature rolled around, before it said something to its mate.

The giant twitched his head to the right. "E."

"We must find an info center or a portable," Yamma'i said.

"Sure, but can't you just explain?"

Yamma'i huffed. "OK. The mp'eeei'mp . . . it also walks upright on two legs. Its body shape and size are almost the same as yours. It has no hair, not even on its head. It secretes slime from glands under-neath its skin. Kind of like you now."

Mirielle looked at her arms. She was drenched in sweat. She tried to wipe it off her skin with her palms. "And your kind finds it repul-sive." She volunteered a guess.

"Er, I am afraid so. It rolls in feces and feeds on garbage and dead animals. And it stinks and carries diseases. Sorry, but visually you . . . you resemble one."

"Thank you, now I am disgusted too."

"Hey, no need to be." Yamma'i quickly reduced the space between Mirielle and itself and laid hands on her shoulders as they slumped. "Please! Resemblance is coincidental; you are not a mp'eeei'mp—"

"How do you know?" Mirielle spoke coldly. "Mp'eeei'mps may have evolved."

"Oh!" Yamma'i pulled abruptly back, then folded its ears, low-ered its gaze, and resolutely hugged Mirielle. "Sorry, I am so inconsiderate!"

Mirielle scrunched her eyelids, trying not to move. She needed a hug so badly that she wanted to respond—wrap her arms around the creature's waist and bury her face in the hairy chest—but she was afraid that the strong emotion Gran failed to conceal would bring her hurt again.

"I am not a Mp'eeei'mp. I came from another world. Similar to this one—an afterlife." She politely freed herself as she spoke. "I was born in it; I am not a ghost."

"Ah, er, not a ghost? What do you mean?"

Mirielle ignored the question and looked at her hands. They were shaking. She tried to hold them still. The sweat was rolling down and dripping from her chin. The weakness returned as she could barely stand. She hesitated, wondering whether to try reaching the mattress or just slump to the floor.

"Ex . . ."—she lurched forward—"cuse me. I'm . . ." She staggered past the creature and crashed on the thick pad. The worms, she had to caress the worms and look them in the eye. In the eyes. There were many worms. Worms—what an ugly word. Who called them that? Gran perhaps. Mirielle curled up. Now her entire body was shaking, and the sweat began congregating in a soggy patch. She closed her eyes, teeth chattering. What was going on? The worms. She needed them. But she was too weak and holed up. She felt somebody's hands raking through her hair. *These new guys . . . must be them.* She sank into a restless sleep.

"How are you feeling now?" Yamma'i sat on the edge. "We . . . you became ill and we didn't know what to do. Sorry." The creature looked down.

"I feel fine. I don't know what happened."

The golden giant approached with a conical glass containing thick green liquid and offered it to the young woman.

Mirielle shook her head. "E. Er, thanks, aoayaa."

"Ah, but this is good, refreshing."

"And probably as salty as the Dead Sea."

"I don't . . . we don't understand."

"What your kind eats and drinks—the flavors are way too strong for me. And there's something about it. Even when diluted, these drinks, they make me want to puke." Mirielle checked her toes and glanced away. "I haven't eaten anything in ages. I don't need food to survive, obviously, but eating is a pleasure. Anyway . . ." She rolled and jumped to the floor. "I will have some water, though. Can you open that door?"

"You mean it is locked?"

"What I mean is that I can't. And I want to get out." The worms were waiting!

Yamma'i screeched in the direction of her mate. The larger individual retracted his tongue from the glass he had decided to empty after Mirielle declined and walked to the front door. It stayed shut.

"You see?" Mirielle climbed onto the food island, splashed water on her face, then crawled back, sat on the edge, and dangled her legs.

The two pairs of raindrop-shaped eyes stared questioningly into each other. Then Yamp'ei approached the door, placed his palms near the frame, and tried to force it open. The palms kept sliding off the smooth surface, the minuscule suction cups the locals had, did not help.

"Is there no manual override mechanism?" Mirielle inquired then turned her head and looked outside.

"Not that I—"

"Wait!" Mirielle jumped to the floor, ran to the window, and began banging. "Imii'i! Gran!"

Imii'i stopped gesticulating and looked around.

"Here! Damn it, here!" Mirielle pounded even louder, then stepped back, lifted her leg and furiously struck the windowpane with her heel.

Her roommate made a full circle, said something, and leveled his ears. Gran combed his mane with a concerned expression. The big guy's eyes retraced the space, then he also uttered some words.

Mirielle shut her eyes with force and shouted in her mind, *Here! Just across the street!* Then she shot them open and delivered another blow with her fists. "Here! Why can't you see me?" Mirielle turned to the couple in the room. "Do something! Break the damn glass!" She ran to the food island, grabbed a chair, and dragged it toward the window. It was heavy. "Please! Mmoya!"

Yamma'i rushed forward and wrapped Mirielle in her arms.

"Let me free!" Mirielle wriggled. "Break the damn glass! Please!" She was crying now.

The creature's embrace became tighter. "Calm down, sweetie."

"Let me go!"

"Calm down, please! This is an internal unit. This is not a window; it is a viewscreen."

"Bullshit! Er . . . what?" Mirielle felt her heart dropping to her stomach. "You mean . . . Oh, crap! Crap!" She tilted her head backward and wailed. "Oh, crap!" Then she added with a glimmer of hope, "But they sensed me. They looked around! And they were worried too!"

She buried her face in the soft, fragrant fur and sobbed.

"They certainly did, but they can't see you. I am sorry. But we will find a way to get you out!"

The creature. It was hugging her! Why was it not disgusted? Ah, whatever. This is what she longed for—someone's warm arms around her, the comfort of another being's embrace. She closed her eyes, took a deep breath, and tried to relax and make the moment linger. And the worms . . . they were her friends, they loved her.

"Am I not a Mp'eeei'mp?" Mirielle mumbled.

"No." Yamma'i slackened her grip, ready to let Mirielle go.

"Please! Hold me for a while! I know that your species dislike it, but since you . . . well, it gives me some comfort."

"Sure." The creature drew her closer. "Sure. Seems you are a child."

Mirielle remained silent, her fingers slowly raking through the soft white fur. Right now, she wanted to be one—optimistic, happy, and carefree. As opposed to a miserable adult. At least she was no longer feeling lonely. The two large beings in the room were somehow different from all others. They made her feel welcome and cozy. They were not sending her bad vibes. They were silent. Wait! Mirielle briskly freed herself and pierced Yamma'i with her gaze.

"Tell me," she started slowly, "what are you?"

Yamma'i pinned her ears on the young woman's face and said calmly, "We are yamms, domestic automata. Servants, if you will."

Mirielle's eyes grew larger. "You are machines? But . . ."

"You appear surprised. Have you not seen yamms?"

"Er, like you? No."

"Maybe this is why I can speak your language." Yamma'i became visibly excited. "The organics, they will not be able to pronounce the words."

"But you look so real. You feel alive!"

"We *are* alive," Yamma'i replied somewhat defensively.

"Still . . . what are you doing here? Why did you suddenly become active? How did you learn my language? Ah, forget it, I know how these worlds work. They never let their secrets out." Mirielle waved her hand, walked to the food island, and climbed backward into a straddle chair. Machines, that was why she could not detect emotions. They had none. Yet, the way the golden one treated the other . . .

"Do you love Yamp'ei? Automaton Five, this is what his name means, right?"

"Love?" Yamma'i lingered. "I think that I do. I am happy when she is around; I want her to be with me."

Mirielle raised her brows. "She?"

"Yes, Yamp'ei is a replica of a female."

"And you?"

"I am a replica of a male from the oyemm'ya race."

Mirielle dropped her shoulders. All this time she'd had it wrong. She had assumed the larger, less accessorized individuals were male. Yet there were so many examples of species in her world, in her ghost's old world rather, where that was not the case. Curiosity tickled her mind.

"Hey! Tell me! Tell me more about the, er, the organics and yourselves."

BIFURCATED

Scowling, Mirielle centered the furry white face into her crosshairs. Would he not stop yapping? He'd been working out his mouth for hours. Perhaps . . . what was he even talking about? Shouldn't he concentrate on getting her out of this damn hole? Well, they tried indeed, but the door was unyielding. Still, not enough! She had to get out! The lake's shore was calling! Why should she care that the locals switched sexes once or twice throughout their lives. She could do it at will.

"Will you shut up!"

Yamma'i did exactly that. He sealed his lips, and his ears pointed squarely at her. Well done! Do as you're told!

Mirielle rolled and slipped to the floor. She went to the front door, squinted, and launched her foot against the panel. "Do something, will ya! Do something!" She kicked the door again.

"We tried, didn't we?" Yamma'i replied calmly. "Yamp'ei is working upstairs, trying to access the controller via the—"

"What if there was a fire? How would people escape?"

"The doors are designed to retract automatically."

Mirielle approached the viewscreen and rested her forehead on the glass. Under different circumstances she would have been amazed by the technology, the seamless three-dimensional projection, but now her priorities were different. Shivering, she crossed hands at her chest. She was freezing yet perspiring heavily. What could it mean? She had never experienced that before. Mirielle adjusted the sheet over her shoulders and pinched the gap shut. If only she could caress the . . . the wrigglers, if they could coil around her, enclose her into a cocoon.

"Can you tell me more about your anatomy? I can see that you are not well. You collapsed again yesterday, but I don't know what to do."

Mirielle turned her eyes into lasers, squarely aimed at Yamma'i. "How would I know? I was born into the afterlife. I am one of only two that I know of. Well, maybe three." She remembered Imii'i.

"OK." Yamma'i's ears swayed in opposite directions.

Mirielle suddenly slammed her forehead in the viewscreen and collapsed wailing to the floor. "I wanna go home."

Yamma'i rushed and kneeled beside her. His slim, sensitive fingers combed tenderly through the moist, disheveled hair.

"Leave me alone!" Mirielle quipped, stood up, and climbed onto the large mattress. She threw the sheet and began jumping on her knees. "Wanna go home! Wanna go home!" Then she slammed her fists into the soft surface. "And I want a good fuck! And some fries! And ice cream!" The young woman collapsed face down. "Fuck! A good one. And ice cream." Then she rose, sat upright, and looked tearfully at Yamma'i. "Sorry, man, not like me. I am going crazy."

Yamma'i folded his ears and screeched a few words to his mate. Yamp'ei twitched her head and climbed in the bucket of the lift.

Male, female. Mirielle switched shapes. He had forgotten what it was like to be male. Scoffing, the young man rubbed his dick. It had not been touched for ages and rose swiftly. Mirielle kneeled and rolled it between his palms. A tickle of pleasure greeted his brain. He nudged his mouth in a faint smile and repeated. Ersatz sex for the lack of a partner. Self-gratification, it was called.

Mirielle closed his eyes and pictured Stella, naked, except for a cowboy hat on her head and the red bandana around her neck and holding Mirielle's penis in her hands. He traced his lips and sighed. Imagination was all he had now that the wrigglers on the shore were out of reach. It was amazing how they made the illusion feel beyond real.

Mirielle focused on the wavering painting in his mind. Stella smiled, lifted her hand, and guided him to lie down. Mirielle complied. The blonde girl straddled the young man and held the excited appendage again; her hand moved.

Mirielle walked his sight from the pair of blue eyes smiling at her, down to the inviting breasts with nipples standing to attention, lingering at the juicy red lips. He craved the taste of the ripe strawberry. He wanted to lay his hands on the breasts and draw a nipple in his mouth. Their hands moved in sync, eliciting excitement from the soldier they both held.

Stella licked her lip, moved forward, and let the soldier slip in. Mirielle squeezed it with his hand and charged his lungs to capacity. Stella leaned, found support, and swayed her hips. The end of the bandana tickled Mirielle's chest. Stella's breasts were within reach, but his hand was busy making his manhood smile. Then the penis began giggling, as the imaginary girlfriend swayed faster.

Then came the guffaw—loud, powerful, and wet. Mirielle quivered, his eyes still shut, his mouth ajar. The warm squirt landed on his abdomen. His unsteady hand spread it, then he flipped his eyelids. Why was his hand shaking? He brought the other one into view and fanned the fingers. It, too, was trembling. And his mouth was very, very dry.

He sat up and looked around. The automata were observing silently, eyes and ears pinned on him.

"What?" Mirielle scratched his beard. "Ah . . ." He reverted to a woman.

The furry pair twitched.

"You can change your shape?"

"Did you not just witness that?" Mirielle snapped.

"Yes. Forgive me for asking such a silly question."

"Whatever." She scoffed. "Any luck?"

"Luck?"

"Are you dumb? The door! Any luck with it?"

"We were unable to open it. Normally all devices can be controlled via the home kit, but—"

"I don't care! I must get out!" Mirielle jumped to the floor. Her knees buckled and she slumped down. "Crap!"

The furry creatures sprang into action, each leaping forward and grabbing an arm.

"Ouch! Let go! What the . . ." Mirielle violently twisted her body. "Stay away!"

"B-but," Yamma'i stuttered.

"You must be broken. Both of you!"

"Why?"

"Your hands," Mirielle hissed while struggling to keep her balance despite being on all fours. "They burn!"

Yamma'i looked at his hands. He spread his fingers and flipped the palms. "No, they are not," he said calmly and outstretched his arm.

"Don't! Don't touch!"

The furry limb retreated; the ears pointed sideways. He said quietly, "E am aao'y awa."

Mirielle shivered anew, and her teeth started chattering. The air became thick, almost impossible to breathe. Her heart was beating violently, as if trying to break free from the confines of her chest. Cold sweat accumulated at the tip of her nose as she attempted to get up, then embarked on the short trip to the floor, making room for more.

"You are unwell. We are only trying to help. It is unreasonable to decline."

The young woman opened her mouth to deliver a rebuke but reconsidered and hung her head instead. Indeed, she was the broken one.

"Sorry. OK, help me up, please."

She clenched her teeth. The sunrays slashed her eyes; she shut them tightly with a frown. A pair of scorching hands pulled her slowly up, then another pair lifted her and carried her to a room somewhere in the depths of the large residential unit. She wondered why she never ventured past the living space. She used to pester her hosts to take her to places, show her their world. She was homesick yet excited. But now she couldn't care less. What was wrong with her? Why was she so angry and rude? What caused all this pain?

"Y-you are right; I am sick. F-forgive me," the young woman succeeded in stuttering, before passing out.

⁑

Mirielle rushed forward, dropped to her knees, and caressed the tender stalks. The many tiny eyes turned toward her. She bent, arched her spine, and carefully maneuvered her arms between the stems as they greeted her with a wavy dance. The glass barrier was gone now, and she craved to roll into the growth; however, her friends could not take her weight.

But why was the sky pitch black, yet there was light? As if there were no atmosphere. As if she were on the Moon.

Of course, she was dreaming. But the wrigglers—she wanted them! Even in a dream! She wanted them so much. Nobody would get hurt.

Mirielle found herself lying flat on her stomach as the dream came to an abrupt end. The darkness would have been total if not for the faux window delivering a faint glow. Two large figures, on their knees and facing each other with intertwined hands, stood motionless not far from her.

Are they dead? Mirielle rolled and sat, feeling her heartbeat in her throat. The soft sheet she was covered with tangled around her.

The hands separated and the heads turned in unison.

"Mirielle?"

"Phew, you scared me!"

"How? We were quiet, weren't we?"

"Yeah, I thought that you . . . ah, forget it!" Mirielle shook her head.

"Please, let us know what is on your mind. We are trying to understand you so we can take better care of you."

"Do you understand where you are?"

"We are in our residential unit with you—a member of a sentient species we are not familiar with, self-identifying as alien to this world."

"Describe this world, please." Mirielle stood up, wrapped herself in the sheet, and wobbled toward the food island in the big room. The light was just enough. She was afraid to ask for more, still apprehensive of the pain.

The creatures followed her.

"I cannot be very technical; I don't know what units will make sense to you. This world is the fourth planet in a red giant star system, located about two-thirds from the galaxy center—"

"No, it is not. It is the afterlife of the world you described."

"The afterlife? You keep saying that."

"Yes." Mirielle climbed on a straddle chair, activated the fountain, and drank from it. Then slumped back and listened to Yamma'i relating the information to his large brown mate.

"Can't you communicate without sound?"

Yamma'i shut up instantly.

Mirielle scoffed. "No, talk, I was just curious."

"It is not working now. We are broken, as you said."

"And so am I." She sighed. "And I want to go home." The soft features of her face morphed into a weathered rock. Tears wished to make their presence known, but she blinked them away.

"How did you come here?"

"I-I jumped. It is a long story."

"Do we have anything to do? Also, can I hug you?"

Mirielle raised her eyebrows. "You hate it, so why do you want to do it?"

"Come." Yamma'i offered his hand. "We do not. Perhaps some organics do, but we don't. You seem to like it, so why not?"

Mirielle promptly landed on the floor, dropped the sheet, and snuggled up, her skin exalted by the gentle greeting of the creature's cuddly fur.

"You are like a child sometimes. Are you sure that you are not one?" Yamma'i said softly.

"Perhaps . . ." Mirielle wrapped her arms around the creature's waist and sampled his fresh scent as her cheek rubbed into his broad chest, then outstretched her hand without looking. "Yamp'ei."

DESCENT

How many days? How many days had her confinement taken? Twenty? Thirty? She never bothered to count. Was even the coming and going of daylight a reliable indicator?

"How many days?"

"Excuse me?" Yamma'i asked softly while combing her hair.

"How many days since we met?"

"Thirty-four."

"Damn!"

"We will find a way out."

"How? Nothing has worked so far." Mirielle leaned forward and crossed her arms in her lap. "And I . . . what is happening to me? Why do I get so angry? Why do I hate?"

"Hard to tell, Mirielle. Maybe it is the air. Or your separation from your world."

"Yeah, and here, now, I am even more separated. I am locked up!" she snarled.

"Sorry, I have no explanation."

"I am aware!" Mirielle sprang to her feet and turned. "You dumb automaton, what do you know?" She furrowed her brows, then pivoted abruptly and climbed to the loft.

"Move! Ma'aaie!" she barked at the puzzled Yamp'ei, who had sat in front of the large info-center screen, absorbing the displayed information.

The large automaton folded its ears but seemed to reconsider whatever was on its mind, then rose from the chair and rode the lift down.

Mirielle looked at the screen, then reached and swiped her hand. The screen turned blank. She wanted to forget! No booze here, no weed! She could watch videos perhaps. Her hand moved quickly and operated the controls. The info-center screen was now her window to this world. Those morons—they couldn't even manage to restore the basic functions of the windowpane. It operated on its own accord— showing the outdoors during the day, then switching to a milky glow as night came.

But what would entertain her now? The wrigglers, only them, but they were out of reach. Out of reach! She was holed up! She grabbed the tablet lying in front of her and hurled it at the screen. The handle split open when the device crashed on the desk. A dark spot appeared and spread a web of tiny cracks where the viewscreen received the hit.

She climbed onto the desk, arched her spine, and started rubbing her rear on the rustic round post in the middle, while huffing angrily. She wanted to be pleasured; she wanted a climax! That was all that she had left. Nothing else!

She wailed and rubbed harder, then reached between her legs with her hand. She was getting tired doing it herself, and her skinny fingers were no match for a dick. Or a proper toy. Could these fools get her something like that? How did they copulate?

Mirielle stopped rubbing and returned to the seat. Her hand flew over the desk, revealing selections on the screen. She read them slowly, then drew air through her teeth. The script was hard to learn. Just like kanji, thousands upon thousands of glyphs. She had no clue what most characters meant. With kanji, she already spoke the language, and she could associate the logograms with meanings and sounds. But here . . .

She recognized the characters for "picture" and "motion" next to each other on the row and pointed. The screen redrew, displaying a new set. Her eyes absorbed the logograms, but her brain refused to digest the feed. Mirielle cursed. So much for watching local porn. She stepped into the bucket and kept jumping up and down while it descended the short distance to the main floor. From there she leaped and threw herself face down on the mattress.

"Mirielle—"

"Shut up!"

*
**

Day sixty-eight according to Yamma'i. Rolling on the floor and picking at her nails was her pastime of late. Her roommate and his folks were searching for her. She could sense and see. They would go back and forth along the street, drawing gazes over the façades, then dropping out of sight, but leaving a trail of disquiet that lingered for days.

Mirielle lurched between hope and desperation. Her strong emotions had reached the beings, but her thoughts had remained with her. No way to guide the rescue party.

She climbed on the food island, stretched on her back, and displayed her yang. Nothing else to do between the bouts of anger and melancholy, so she entertained herself by switching shapes. Recently, she had found a groomer and tried it on herself. It worked well. After getting rid of all hair, she oiled her body with cooking grease to the horror of the automata, or so she thought. They looked terrified with their ears fluttering, then folding back. But they kept mum.

"You like that, don't you?"

Mirielle targeted his eyeballs. Yamma'i's hand had rested on his crotch, pressing lightly.

"Yeah." Why would he lie? It had been a while since it had not been his hand. And his penis had already told the truth.

"Hm." Yamma'i fingers tickled the glans, sending playful ripples throughout. His hand moved slowly along the shaft.

"Thanks." Mirielle rested his head and closed his eyes. He had no need to paint pictures in his mind this time. He was aroused. He moaned as the hand squeezed more fuel in the fledging fire in his groin. His ring contracted when the sensation spread. Mirielle's breath gained pace led by the friendly hand. It pushed down, baring the glans, then pulled and lingered at the rim. Again, and again. Mirielle's heart melted. His body twitched; his fingers raked the polished stone. His forehead wrinkled as he swayed his hips. His mind was tranquil; the weight on his chest was gone. His body celebrated.

Mirielle pushed on his elbows and fired. The charge in his groin transformed into a storm of carnal glee. The young man relaxed, leveled his breathing, then sobbed.

Yamma'i unfurled his hand without hurry. "Did you like it?"

"Yeah. A lot! How did you know?"

"Well, we rub ears."

"Like a Ferengi?"

"What is that?"

*
**

Mirielle had sat on her heels on the floor, staring blankly at the wall. Her mind was caught between the jaws of a large vise. She yearned to go home, be with her child, her yellow man, and her petite star. The wrigglers, they could trick her, send her soaring for a while, but they were out of reach. An invisible hand kept turning the tightening screw. She targeted her eyeballs at her trembling hands, then bashed her forehead against the wall. The skin cracked; the blood gushed. She slumped, leaving a red trail. Why did she do this? It hurt! Whatever. Somebody transferred her to a bed.

"Ouch!" she screamed and turned her head when the wound began burning. Her elbows dug into the mattress, and she wriggled; however, two strong hands had pinned her down.

"Relax, Mirielle, I want to clean the split."

She huffed. "That is unnecessary."

The smell was familiar. Was the automaton cleaning the wound with some sort of booze?

"Why?"

"It will heal on its own. Soon. This is how things are around here."

"Oh! I didn't know."

"Now you do. Just watch."

Yamp'ei released her and she sat. "And what were you disinfecting me with? It smells like alcohol," Mirielle said.

"It *is* alcohol."

"Gimme the container." Mirielle outstretched her hand.

Yamma'i placed the cone in her open palm. Mirielle brought the neck to her mouth, squeezed, and drank. The liquid burned her tongue and throat. Her face contorted for a moment. Awful! But mixed with some water, it would do.

"Hey, you are not supposed to drink that!" The automaton grabbed the cone.

"Why? It is booze. It will make me forget."

"Forget what?"

"My predicament, you moron! That I am trapped here. With you two!"

Yamma'i remained silent, then stood up and walked toward the food island.

"Sorry. I was bad again." Mirielle cowered and dropped her head. "The thing is . . . I am trapped. In this world. In this room. And I want to forget. And I do, when you two, er, well, fondle me, but . . ." She sighed. "I want to hug the worms."

"Hug the worms?" The automaton pivoted and pinned its ears on her mouth. "What worms?"

"Well, not worms really. Some local life form, looks like a plant—"

"Mmp'oyaw stems?"

"Perhaps. I don't know. Gran did not use this word. Pinkish, semi-translucent, with an eye on top, about this thick." Mirielle pinched her fingers. "It lives in wet areas. Like the lakeshore."

"P'aaaawey Lake?"

"How the hell would I know? Very few of your screeches are comprehensible to me."

"These things are dangerous to organics. They produce a substance that attracts and enchants their prey. The substance is addictive. Organics use an engineered derivative, which—"

"Ah, spare me the speech, please. I am tired, and my mind is temporarily at peace. And my wound has healed, right?"

"Right."

"I told you so." Mirielle crashed onto the mattress, rolled to her side, covered her head with a pillow, and dozed off.

✳

Mirielle growled and hurled the serving cone at the window, followed by several pairs of tweezers and a bowl. "Do something! Useless twats!"

Yamma'i bent and collected the items, then looked the young woman in the eyes and said sharply, "No!"

"Agh! Damn robot!"

She threw another utensil across the room and hit the viewscreen. The automaton calmly picked it up from the floor, then walked to the pantry and deposited the lot on the respective shelves. When Yamma'i turned, Mirielle caught the motion with the corner of her eye while retching, bent over the drinking fountain sink. She was wrong, so wrong!

"Er, Yamma'i, fuck, man, I must . . ." She hiccupped and spat in the sink. "I screwed up again. Sorry!"

She slid backward on the straddle chair, dropped her arms between her legs, and let her shoulders slump.

"These are classic withdrawal symptoms from the stems. It will get worse before improving. Alien you may be, but it seems you are not immune."

"I guess so. Do you think that I locked myself up here?"

Yamma'i fluttered his ears before answering. "I have no way of knowing. But when you are not mad, you are very reasonable; therefore, I will not rule it out."

Mirielle suddenly slumped to the floor, devoid of all her strength and her stomach twisted into a convoluted knot. The pair of furry arms promptly crawled underneath and gently moved her to the large seater she often slept on. Her temples turned ice-cold, and her lips trembled. What if she completely lost control?

"How . . . many . . . days?"

"One hundred and two."

The young woman wanted to wail loudly but gurgled instead.

Mirielle quenched her thirst, climbed back onto the seater, and nestled again between the legs of the brown giant. Folded as it was, the large automaton was comfy, like a soft and warm armchair. Yamma'i had used the break to recount the end of the story in the local tongue and now followed her movements with a pensive expression on his face.

Mirielle stretched and crossed her legs, then caught a movement with the corner of her eye and catapulted toward the viewscreen. "Imii'i! Gran!" Her fists met the glass, then her arms hung. No point in pounding. She glued her nose to the smooth surface and followed her hosts, head still, only her eyeballs rolling in their sockets.

Imii'i was gesticulating, pointing—left, then right. He stopped for a moment and slowly drew his gaze around, his ears pointed forward as if emotions could be heard. Then he hung them as his lips moved and his fingers intertwined. Gran held a tablet. The large individual took some notes.

Mirielle wailed in her mind. She could sense her young roommate too, the anguish, the worry. They were missing her! A few tears rolled down her cheeks. *Imii'i, Gran . . . the pest is locked up here.*

Imii'i spoke inaudibly again. Gran's head twitched. Then the couple exited the field of view.

Mirielle turned and bumped into the white one. "Hey!" She looked up, then cast her gaze to the side. "Damn, how to tell them that we are here? Now I can't even jump. The loft won't make it."

Yamp'ei chirped something.

"What did she say?"

"Balloon."

"Huh?"

"Balloon, you can jump from a balloon. You said that this afterlife had no machines that fly. But what about a hot-air balloon? We can build one once we find a way out of here. Then you fly over the lake, and you leap."

Mirielle heard only a garbled sound. Her heart performed a drumroll, pulling all air from her lungs. Her chest felt as if it was about to collapse. She wanted to be free! Her face twisted. She pierced the automaton with her bloodied glare. Damn thing! Annoying, useless chatterbot! Her fist flew up, aimed at the nasty creature's chin.

Yamma'i grabbed the wrist. "Mirielle!"

The other fist took aim and launched, its flight cut short by a second intercept. "Mirielle, please! You can never beat me in a fistfight, and I am not going to let you vent your frustration in this way."

"Let me go, you monster! Let me go!" Mirielle pulled violently. "Let me go!"

The automaton obeyed and released his hold. The young woman looked up squinting, her breathing rasp, her hands still rolled into tight fists, nails digging into the flesh. She stared for a while, then snorted loudly, moved her jaw, and spat straight into the worried, furry face.

She dashed past the puzzled automaton, leaped, and threw herself against the jammed door. The loud ringing in her ears concealed the thud. She slumped to the floor, her eyes tightly shut, her molars showing. Her shoulders started shaking as the physical pain merged with the hatred and desperation that were consuming her. She wanted to put an end to it somehow, anyhow! If the wrigglers were around, she would let them soak every bit of her life force, knowing that she would leave her prison exalted.

That awful noise—was there no end? She looked around, drooling. A menacing figure was approaching. Mirielle gathered all her strength and launched herself against it. "Aaaaaaagh!"

The hairy monster closed his arms around her as she slammed into his chest. She popped her head, looked up—her face twisted—and tried to wriggle out of the tight grip. The creature's lips were moving, but the ringing in her ears stood in the way. She tried to scratch, then twisted her neck and sank her teeth into the monster's arm. The cold waves returned. Did she hear a scream? Streams of sweat and angry tears merged and smeared everything in sight.

"Let . . . me . . . go!" she growled and kneed her furry captor, but he did not relent. She squirmed and groaned, seeking to pull her arms free. Her heart was pounding fast and loud, and the air, the air was like powdered chalk. "Leh . . . goh . . ."

The images her eyes were sending to her brain were no longer coherent, just shapeless streaks of light. Mirielle wailed, kicking wildly. Her lungs drew in more chalk dust, and her lips turned blue. Then the ringing noise subsided, and the flashes dimmed, leaving just shadows of indistinct dark shapes, until they were gone as well. Her limbs hung exhausted. Her heart slowed down to a long beep. Her breathing leveled off and stopped. Her mind finally found rest.

ON THE OTHER SIDE

The muffled chirps and screeches reached Mirielle through layers of thick black fog. She drew her eyes open, frowned and let the shutters fall again, taking her time. The voices cut through the fog, making her wonder what they were communicating. She commanded her eyelids open again, squinted and sat on the edge. Her joints needed greasing and her back felt like the busy meeting grounds of an ant colony, buzzing with itch.

Mirielle smirked and stepped onto the floor. Her legs wobbled, prompting her hands to clutch the mattress with urgency. Millions of microscopic needles pricked her calves. She pressed her inward rolled lips together and hitched a breath. When the tingling subsided, she looked down, wiggled her toes, then eyed the wall and took a few jerky steps toward it. She pivoted and dragged her back against the sandy surface. Much better! Now, if she could get a good massage . . .

Mirielle tottered toward the door. Her inorganic friends were uncharacteristically chatty. Still squinting, she crossed into the hallway. A motionless life-sized doll, clad in a wide chainmail collar and an intricately embroidered loincloth, stared into nothingness.

"Yamma'i!" Mirielle gasped, then lurched toward the corner and stuck her head into the big room. Another doll, larger than the first, with golden-brown fur had fallen backward to the floor. The front door was no longer shut.

Imii'i and Gran turned and moved toward her, ears flapping.

"Mii'ee!" Imii'i embraced her without a trace of hesitation. He then lifted her into the air. "Mii'ee!"

Once back on the floor, Mirielle pushed him away and scurried to the doll lying on the floor. "Yamp'ei!" She grabbed the hands and shook them. "Yamp'ei!" She looked up, her eyebrows raised. "What happened to them?" Then, without waiting for the answer, she ran back to the hallway. "Yamma'i! Wake up!"

"Machines. They do not function here."

The announcement came in her own voice. She turned back to trace the source.

Gran was holding a tablet in his hand. "You woke up. Good."

Mirielle glanced at the doll. "But . . . they were working. This is Yamma'i. He can speak my tongue." Her voice trembled as she forced her bubbling tears back.

"Not possible, dear. Machines are controlled remotely. They have no brains on their own. In this world there is no connection to the controller. They cannot function here. They cannot talk like you. They are just memories of those who had them." Gran's expression changed. His restless ears came to a halt and his facial muscles visibly relaxed. "Mirielle, I am so relieved that we found you and that you woke up."

The large individual was relieved, that was true. Mirielle dragged her gaze around and almost shouted, "They were alive! They told me their names! They spoke to me!"

"Perhaps."

"What do you mean?"

"You disappeared a long time ago, over twelve octets. We found you yesterday. You were not conscious; you did not wake up. You were . . ." The translator skipped the unrecognized chirp, then continued, "I cannot rule out . . . you dreaming."

"But—" Mirielle sensed their annoyance and hung her head. She would have drawn the same conclusion.

"Can we at least put her up?" She pointed at the brown giant. Her lips turned into a thin line as Gran and Imii'i grabbed the doll and steadied it on its feet. She recalled the hatred that burned inside her and the adoration of the two beings. Now the inexplicable intense dislike had evaporated, leaving only its counterpart. She missed them. She had no idea why she had been so hostile at times. The separation from the worms? The automata caressed her, had let her hug them and snuggle up. And more, they were friendly; they were not repulsed. She had treated them badly and she wanted to apologize. The young woman sighed, then looked at Gran.

The giant caught her glance and spoke in the microphone. "Come, let's go. We did not want to move you. I had no idea what to do, but now you are awake, and you can walk. And you tell us what happened."

Imii'i grabbed her hand and fluttered his ears. He sent a burst of impatience and unadulterated joy her way. She tried to gleam back, but her eyes were fixed on the lifeless stare of the brown machine.

"Wait!" Mirielle pulled her hand and trotted back into the hallway. Her legs had become obedient again. She brushed the white fur of the other big doll, then checked the left forearm, her heart pounding. The bite mark was there, deep and relatively fresh. Mirielle stretched her mouth into a smug smile, looked up, and silently moved her lips. "Sorry!" Her palms stroked the cold limb, then she turned, straightened her face, and stepped into the big room. She concealed a wave of her hand from Imii'i and Gran as she walked past her other large friend.

⋆⋆

Mirielle didn't mind Imii'i holding her hand, but frowned when Gran did the same, as if he was trying to prevent a rowdy kid from running away. What was next, put her on a leash? The large individual, towering over her, pulling her arm, made her feel small indeed. But adding up all the days of her existence would amount to over twenty-five rounds of old Earth around its yellow sun. She was no kid. She had a kid. Who she used to put on a leash . . . Did he even remember her?

She yanked her hand free from Gran's grip, eliciting a startled glance, then a mumble: "Sorry." Gran produced a whistling sound and continued, "You so small, when I absentminded, I forget you are grown-up."

"Why are you absentminded?"

"You . . . we did search the unit we found you in before. You were not there. The machines yes, you no."

"And?" Mirielle prompted Gran to continue when the pause stretched for too long.

"This world is confusing. This existence . . . you said that you were locked inside all this time. You said the machines worked. We do not see the same things. You, what are you? And we, what are we?" Gran halted abruptly and asked sharply, "Do you want to go to the worms?"

Mirielle lowered her gaze, thinking. "Mm, no, not anymore. I want to go home for real."

The entry door retreated into its slot, and they climbed the ramp in silence. In the home, Imii'i let go of her hand and disappeared into their room. A moment later he returned and outstretched his arms. Mirielle squinted at the object he was holding, then nodded. "Thanks!" It was the dress she forgot that day on the roof, her lousy attempt at couture. "I can do without it if you stop pulling my butt cheeks apart. I use it for protection, do you know that?"

"He was doing what?" Gran pinned his ears on her.

"This." Mirielle turned to demonstrate. "Butt . . . cheeks . . . pull." Then she donned the garment.

Gran produced a screech Mirielle was familiar with—a laugh—and his ears fluttered. "Like peeling a rear flap!"

Mirielle thought of her own actions with the automata and blushed. She acted exactly like her immature roommate. She approached the window, climbed on the wide windowsill, and glued her forehead to the glass. She was no longer confined, yet unable to rejoice. Why? Why did she want to go back to the machines? She looked up at the sky and traced her lips. Behind her the stare of the large individual was warming her neck. He was also talking, but she had tuned him out. Another speech about the danger from the worms, perhaps. Or who knew what else.

"Mii'ee!"

"Ah! What?" She twisted her neck, then let the rest of her body follow and sat on the windowsill.

"I am glad that you are good! Please, no worms! I beg you!"

"OK." She gazed to the side; she'd heard that plea way too many times. Then she graced him with a stare. Unperturbed, Gran turned the tablet off, screeched something at her roommate, attached the leash to his domesticated octopod, and left the unit with the dignity of a polished brass teapot.

Mirielle chuckled and tilted her head, thinking what her exact feelings toward this guy were. Gran was certainly caring yet irritatingly patronizing in his presentation. And the disgust he let out that one time, it still burned her, even as a memory.

She glanced at the floor and said quickly, "Imii'i, can you show me a . . . the animal that looks like me?"

"What animal?"

"The one I resemble. Biped, no fur, eats trash . . ." Mirielle searched her memory for the name. Her sight rested on her roommate. The youngster was certainly doing the same, scanning the records in his head, his ears pointing sideways. "On second thought, forget it."

"Aoo'o?"

"Because I was dumb." Indeed, why risk shattering his affection. He said that she was ugly, but he liked her, despite her appearance. But she was never short of curiosity, except for perhaps the period of confinement. It was hard to keep her mouth shut!

"I'm going to take a stroll."

"I will come too," Imii'i chirped in the microphone.

"I prefer to be alone."

Imii'i drew his glance. "You not going to the worms?"

"No."

"I will come."

"I want to be alone!"

"Ee'mimii said I must be with you, not let you touch worms."

Mirielle raised her eyebrows, then scoffed. Gran had issued a decree.

"I am not going to. Besides, who is Ee'mimii to me to tell me what I shall and shall not do?"

"Ee'mimii likes you—"

"Bullshit!" Mirielle cracked. "He is repulsed, can't you feel? He is barely containing his disgust!"

"No!"

The translation was scarcely audible, drowned by the indignant shriek, and unnecessary, as she knew well what "E" meant.

"Yes!" Mirielle stormed past her roommate.

He grabbed her arm and pulled her back. "E!"

Blood rose to her face. "Let go!" she growled. "Pu'uyi!"

"E!"

She took a step back and pivoted, her eyebrows furrowed. "Pu'uyi!"

A pair of enlarged, worried eyes were trained silently on her. He was confused, afraid. Mirielle relaxed her brows and nudged her lips sideways. "OK, come."

The guy did sincerely care and was much stronger. She had no choice but to relent.

✱✱

"What did Gran tell you?" Mirielle asked as they were climbing the ramp toward the roof.

"To keep you away from worms."

"By not letting me go anywhere by myself?"

"Yes."

"Forever?"

"Ee'mimii did not say."

Mirielle glanced over her shoulder, frowning. The worms were bad for her, that she already had agreed with. They gave her a shot of ecstasy, a momentary relief, but so incomplete and at a price, indeed.

She angrily clapped her hands and gasped noisily. She had to find a way home. What if she just scaled the railing and threw herself onto the street all those floors below? She veered toward the guardrail, her heart pounding. Should she do it now?

A hand grabbed her forearm. Mirielle froze, then turned slowly, ready to pounce. The long, dense eyelashes flickered as Imii'i blinked, his mouth shaped into a ring and his ears pulled back.

Mirielle let out a laugh instead. "You look so afraid. Relax. What spooked you?"

Imii'i withdrew his hand and rubbed his palms, looking at the floor. "You want to die."

There was no way that he had read her thoughts! He was just an empath!

"Sometimes . . ." she said quietly.

"Why?"

"Because I am alone."

"You are not alone! We are all here! So many of us!"

Mirielle resumed the rooftop stroll.

"Your kind is very different. Your appearance, your biology, your customs, your food . . . I can't stand it! I mean, your delicacies, they are overdone and stink! Sorry. And the sounds you make, the way you speak . . . it is like listening to the constant swaying of a bundle of rusty old door hinges." She glanced at her friend. "This is who you people are; I can't fault you. I'm not taking revenge on you for calling me ugly."

She paused, waiting for a response, but her friend continued to tiptoe next to her in silence.

"You see, you must tiptoe, because I walk too slowly. And I depend on you entirely. Without you being around I am blind."

He finally spoke. "How? What do you mean?"

Mirielle pushed her tongue into her cheek while choosing the answer. Were people still seeing each other when she was asleep? Yeah, they were. She waved her hand. "Seems you have forgotten that you make people see others. You make everybody see me. And you are *my* eyes when other people are involved. This is what I mean."

"But you saw the machines."

"Did I? Everybody can see inanimate objects. Somebody said that this world was a shared memory, hence why. Anyway, let's go and see if they are still there."

Mirielle increased her stride, bringing some relief to her tiptoeing friend.

⁎⁎

The door slid open instantly. The automata were still there, still dysfunctional. Had she hallucinated indeed? Her throat tightened. She missed the sound of Yamma'i's voice; listening to her own broken speech had become maddening, adding to her woes. She wanted to experience the warmth and softness of the shiny coat with her skin. She needed the friendly hands. The bite mark, though, how did she make it?

Mirielle tried to lift the white doll's arm, huffing. It barely moved. She tilted her head, then attempted squeezing herself between the automaton and the wall.

"What are you doing?" Imii'i finally converted his curiosity into sound.

Mirielle stopped and measured him head to toe.

"Come." She beckoned him. "Look at this."

Her roommate's eyes and ears converged on the same point, then moved to her.

"I bit him," she said, blushing. "But as he stands now, it is impossible to leave this mark."

"You moved his arm."

"You try it."

Imii'i took hold of the doll's arm and pulled, leisurely at first, then with force. The whole frame shook.

"Understand. But how do you know that you left mark?"

"Do you want me to show you?" Mirielle menacingly bared her teeth.

"Yes."

She grabbed his arm, ready to sink her incisors into it.

Imii'i reacted fast, ripping his limb free from her grip. "Not on me!"

"I wasn't going to. I was kidding."

The sound Imii'i made was perhaps the equivalent of "Oh!" They never programmed interjections in the translators.

"You see? My people would have understood that it was a joke." Mirielle raked her hair, looking away. The automata—she would have snuggled up to them, and they would have gathered her in their arms and let her stroke their fur backward. She liked doing that for some reason.

Imii'i tiptoed in one place, his ears fluttering. Then he stepped forward and clamped her in a tight embrace.

"You like this. I do not want you sad."

Mirielle just nodded and clasped her hands behind him. He had grown bigger. Yeah, she'd been here for over a thousand days. He was a nice guy, not burdened by prejudices and fear, ready to adapt and share.

"You are so sweet, Imii'i. I kind of love you, but you are not enough, sorry."

"I understand. And you not very ugly. I love you too."

Mirielle chuckled. "Thanks!"

*
**

The window stayed clear when the night came, and the stars littered the sky. Normally it would have switched to a drawn drape, as Imii'i did not fancy early light. He was a night owl, like Mirielle. They would go on long walks through town and beyond just as she did back at home, just as her parents had done to their delight in their shared days. She remembered them kissing, making love in parks under the indignant stares of the alley lights. And her challenging her male friends. And Stella dancing naked. She did that too. It was enchanting. They would shed the covers and accessorize themselves with flowers—in their hair, on their arms and wrists and on their ankles. And entwine their bodies under the pale moonlight and kiss and caress until their own skin began to glow. Then they would levitate . . .

Mirielle shoved the memory aside and turned into bed. What if her automata only pretended to be dead, unwilling to reveal their presence in the afterlife for some reason? They were servants, so perhaps they had had enough from their masters. Or maybe it was her needs that this realm had met through them.

She flipped on her back and listened intently. Her roommate seemed fast asleep, his breathing barely audible. She rolled and stepped onto the floor, then remained still, all ears. She installed a sleepy expression on her face and purged all emotions, then quietly traversed the short distance to the door.

The touch plate changed color to a dim shade of red. The sensor triggered the mechanism, and it retracted the slab into the slot with a hiss. Mirielle froze. Silence dominated the space. Three-dimensional projections of aquatic life made occasional appearances in the window, then faded in the darkness of the deep. She advanced cautiously. Evolutionary pressures had provided the locals with considerably better hearing than her own.

The entry door opened with a ding. Mirielle cursed through her clenched teeth and dashed out. On the roof she squatted behind a large, leafy bush and caught her breath. No one seemed to be in pursuit. She sighed. Why did she always expect to be chased? Something was messing with her head.

Mirielle stepped onto the footpath, crossed the sky bridge, and found her way to the ramp between the vines hanging from the trees. On her way down, she glanced occasionally at the luminescent glyphs on each door. Random combinations of words, perhaps chosen for their sounds. When she reached her target, she read the glyphs and shrugged: "aromatic," "silver," "tree."

A step closer and the door hissed and revealed the interior she knew so well. The viewscreen was displaying drenching rain. Mirielle hesitated. She was alone and the door might malfunction again. Her arm rose and invaded the space of the unit, then her palm moved. The motion sensor heeded her request and turned the lights on. The young woman inserted her head, her eyes reduced to slits.

The large golden-brown doll did not react. Its lifeless gaze was firmly set on the opposing wall. Mirielle bit her lip, surveyed the room and stepped inside. The door closed behind her. Her heart jumped. She turned and slammed the sensor plate. The door obeyed her command. She emitted a loud gasp and approached the automaton.

"Yamp'ei!" She grabbed the furry upper limbs and shook them slightly. "Yamp'ei! Wake up! Uuei'e!"

The four-fingered hands were cold and stiff. The doll remained still. Mirielle gulped and headed for the hallway at the bottom of the room. Yamma'i looked like he was cast in amber—motionless yet alive. Mirielle came closer, looked up, and tried to cross gazes with the doll. Then she threw herself forward, embraced the machine, and squeezed her eyelids closed, seeking to contain the tears.

"Yamma'i . . . I miss you two so much." A tear escaped and rolled down her cheek. She cursed and let its peers free. "I miss you two so much, dumb machines. I don't know why. Perhaps because you have no emotions that I can sense, and you don't speak with my voice . . . I don't know." Mirielle slowly shook her head. "I was hoping that if I came alone, you would reanimate. Silly me."

The young woman sobbed once more, then sniffed loudly, stepped back, and twisted her lips in a semblance of a smile. She pivoted on her toes and marched toward the exit, determined to rein in her emotions, yet her tears kept emerging from the depths of her soul and finding their way out in the open, leaving salty residue on her cheeks before plunging to the floor.

She snorted and braked in the middle of the large room. Her gaze almost carved a trail into the walls as she dragged it slowly, wondering whether to etch the scene in her mind or purge it instead.

She didn't want to be here anymore, now that her automata showed no sign of life. She didn't want to go back across the street. The wrigglers by the lakeshore weren't calling loudly enough.

Mirielle climbed into a straddle chair and banged her head against the cold surface of the food island. This was not her world! She had to leap again! Not necessarily in the lake. She had not a shred of patience left. None! But what if she landed in yet another alien realm? Or ended up embedded in a rock? Or both? She dove into a gorge pool and emerged inside a lake.

And the horror . . . the horror of the fall! What was she thinking back then? Her body quivered. Her heart skipped a beat and then hurried up. She traced her lips, eyes enlarged, fixated on the fountain head. She peeled a flake of skin with her teeth from her lower lip and licked the blood. She needed a cigarette or a joint. The worms were useless; they'd only make her forget her troubles for a while. She had to be composed and calm.

She looked at her hands. They were shaking. Mirielle banged her head again, then squirmed and angrily spread her hair as if trying to find shelter from her emotions underneath it, but it wasn't long enough. She peeled off another flake of skin and nibbled on it, drumming with her fingers. Gran, she had to talk to Gran. Interesting, Gran was very large, yet a "he", unless the device had made a mistake. Anyway, he may find a way to lift her in the air above the damn lake. Mirielle pictured a large balloon with her sitting on a chair suspended underneath. She looked down and saw a glazed dark surface. She leaped.

The young woman straightened her spine and rolled her fists. Yes! She may be able to do it! She would be able to jump! A smile stretched her lips. The air entered her lungs with ease. She slid to the floor, pushed the chair, and approached the front door. It somewhat reluctantly retreated into its slot. She stood at the threshold, looking in. Then she turned abruptly and stretched her stride on her way up to the roof. Making a balloon or whatever else would take some time, and she'd have plenty of opportunity to wave goodbye.

The stars were still shimmering in the sky but were now competing with the early rays of the local sun. Dawn would soon arrive. Mirielle crossed the bridge, lingering midway through, leaning over the guardrail and sending her gaze down to the barely discernible cobblestones below. Weird. Now she was afraid! The experienced climber had developed a fear of heights!

Mirielle looked around, crossed her hands on the handrail, rested her chin on them, and spat. She was not a stranger to the sentiment.

When she fell from the tower, for a while she was terrified to even cast her gaze down. And ashamed. Ayumu knew nothing of the continuity of life in death, yet he scaled sky-high cliffs. She leaped and she was still around.

Mirielle pushed herself away from the handrail, walked to the end of the rooftop bridge, and climbed onto the stone balustrade. She spread her arms and sent her gaze to the horizon to meet the dawn. Her dad practiced this in his youth, walking on the parapets of bridges. He wanted to impress the girls with his bravery. She wondered if he'd succeeded in his quest. Her mom grew very angry when he pulled that stunt in front of her, and she was also scared.

Mirielle advanced cautiously along the narrow surface, waving hands and humming a tune. She was not afraid! Well, she was, but kept the fear under wraps. A gust of warm wind caressed her hair and fondled her bare breasts. Her nipples stiffened at once. She chuckled and, having reached the corner, performed a pirouette.

The wind now embraced her from behind and blew between her legs. Mirielle giggled. She'd never considered the wind to be such a beautifully shameless lover. Mirielle wanted it to touch her breasts again. She flexed her knees and pivoted on her toes like a ballerina, her arms flying high in the early morning breeze.

What would men experience in her place? Would they feel so liberated? Her mom wondered if they could comfortably ride a horse while in the nude. But Elise could not shape-shift to old age, let alone perform a sex change. Mirielle pouted and embraced her alter shape. His now larger feet exceeded the allotted space on the narrow balustrade. His right foot slipped, and he lurched toward the void of the street below. Mirielle reverted instantly, twisted her body, and spread her arms, but it was too late. All she could do was clench her teeth as she plunged toward the ground.

"Mii'ee!" She heard a shriek, followed by the crack of a giant whip accompanied by a blinding flash. Strands of hair swirled before her wide-open eyes. Then she briefly saw a girl in a black school uniform preparing to cross a street. Mirielle grazed her shoulder as she flew past her, and the girl dissolved away. Another bright flash sent her mind into a spin. Somebody grabbed her ankle. A loud screech pierced her ears. "Mii'ee!"

Then the commotion faded, and she found herself sitting on the pavement of a narrow, shady street, drooling, and with a taste of metal in her mouth. She took a deep breath and wiped her lips with the back of her hand. The crowns of the trees were alive with the flutter of the leaves. Pigeons and sparrows were pecking invisible crumbs. A cat walked past the birds without expressing any interest, squatted on the curb, and began to groom its paw.

"Mii'ee."

"Shut up!" Mirielle growled as her stare swung slowly, weighing every object that it met. Then she parked eyes on Imii'i and said, "I think that I am home. And what the hell are you doing here?"

"Oii'mm eoo p'e."

"Ah, great!" Mirielle rolled her eyes, then scrambled to her feet. She wrapped her arms around the head of her friend, shuffled his mane with her chin, and repeated pensively, "Great."